Dostoevskiĭ
Gambler

DISCARD

DATE DUE

DATE DUE		
NOV 13 2001		
JUN 0 7 2002		
JUN 1 7 2003		
OCT 0 7 2003		
MAY 2 4 2004		
SEP 2 7 2006		
NOV 1 4 2006		
APR 2 1 2008		
OCT 2 8 2010		
MAR 0 6 2013		
GAYLORD		PRINTED IN U.S.A.

APR 6   1973

The
Gambler

Edited by Edward Wasiolek

Fyodor
Dostoevsky

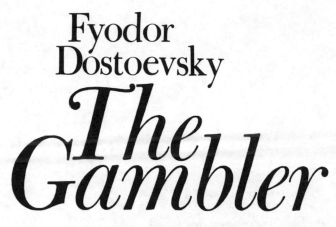

*The
Gambler*

with Polina Suslova's Diary

Translated by Victor Terras

THE UNIVERSITY OF CHICAGO PRESS
Chicago and London

The University of Chicago Press, Chicago 60637
The University of Chicago Press, Ltd., London

International Standard Book Number: 0–226–15970–1
Library of Congress Catalog Card Number: 72–80227

Contents

Introduction

Dostoevsky never wanted to write *The Gambler*. He was forced to write it by the threat of financial ruin, and he wrote, or dictated, it in less than a month to a young stenographer who was in a matter of months to become his second wife. We have to thank Stellovsky, an unscrupulous editor, for these two happy events. Dostoevsky had, with characteristic carelessness, signed a contract in 1865 with Stellovsky with the condition that he deliver a new novel to him by 1 November 1866. If the novel was not in Stellovsky's hands by that time, Stellovsky would have the right for nine years to publish anything Dostoevsky had written without paying Dostoevsky anything. Stellovsky had taken advantage of Dostoevsky's straitened circumstances and imprudent temperament, and he refused Dostoevsky's subsequent attempts to annul the contract by paying a fine.[1] Dostoevsky was in no condition to undertake another major work. In 1866 he was busy publishing and finishing *Crime and Punishment,* and he put off doing anything about the novel promised to Stellovsky as long as possible. By 1 October 1866 he

1. See (in this volume) letter 9, to A. V. Korvin-Krukovskaia, and letter 10, to Polina Suslova, in which are contained Dostoevsky's description of the financial straits that led him to conclude the contract with Stellovsky and the difficulties the contract entailed.

vii

had not written a line and in desperation hired a young student from a school of stenography. From 4 October to 29 October Dostoevsky accomplished the impossible by dictating and completing *The Gambler*. In the process he fell in love with the young stenographer, Anna Grigorievna Snitkina.

Anna was destined to bring order and efficiency to Dostoevsky's practical affairs, and to judge from the reminiscences she left us,[2] she had already begun to do so during the dictation of the novel. Dostoevsky was prone to ramble about matters unconnected with the novel, and it was the timid and awed young stenographer who would bring him back repeatedly to the task at hand. It was her practical sense also that saved Dostoevsky from the final stratagem of Stellovsky's. The novel was ready for transmittal to Stellovsky on 30 October, but the wily publisher absented himself from the city and made it impossible for them to deliver the novel to him. Anna suggested that they register the manuscript at a police station and in that way the conditions of the contract were successfully met.

Although Dostoevsky had not written a line of *The Gambler* by the beginning of 1 October 1866, he had sketched a plan for it in a letter to Strakhov in 1863 (included in this volume),[3] and if we are to believe Leonid Grossman, he was thinking of writing a novel about gambling as early as 1859.[4] It was understandable that Dos-

2. *Dostoevsky Portrayed by His Wife,* trans. and ed. S. S. Koteliansky (New York: Dutton, 1926).

3. See letter 4, to N. N. Strakhov.

4. L. Grossman is a distinguished Russian critic of Dostoevsky's works and the spare reference in his 1962 biography of Dostoevsky probably refers to an account of the gambling halls of Europe that Dostoevsky must have read about in the April issue of *Russkoe slovo* (Russian Word), 1859, in an article by F. Dershau entitled "From the Notes of a Gambler." The author gives a vivid account of the atmosphere of the halls and of the habits of the characters who flocked to Homburg, a popular gambling spa. Many of the details seem to find some reflection in

toevsky did nothing about implementing his plan from 1863 to 1866. These years were among the most creative and the most turbulent of his career. It was during this time that he burst from literary respectability to literary genius: after a ten-year hiatus in his literary career because of imprisonment and exile, Dostoevsky's literary career between 1859 and 1863 had been repeating itself. His output was respectable but there was little in it to indicate the volcanic creative energy that was to erupt with the publication of *Notes from the Underground* in 1864 and the publication of *Crime and Punishment* in 1866. It is especially remarkable that his creative energies incandesced during a period when his personal life was almost unbelievably difficult and complicated. The journal *Time,* which he edited with his brother Michael, was closed down in 1863 by a government censor because of a misunderstood article on the Polish revolution of 1863; his unloving, wrathful, and consumptive first wife died in 1864; and his beloved brother Michael died also in 1864, leaving a desperate widow and five children to be cared for by a generous but overburdened Dostoevsky. It was in 1862 during his first trip to Europe he began to gamble, a passion that was to serve his destructive instincts for almost a decade; and it was about the same time that he fell in love with a student half his age, Polina Suslova, who was to repeat the havoc and suffering he had experi-

---

Dostoevsky's descriptions. Perhaps more significant than this general influence is the specific case, which is detailed, of a young man, a barber, who wins an enormous sum of money the first time he gambles, as did Aleksei in *The Gambler* and who leaves the gambling resort presumably to enjoy his sudden fortune. Several years later, however, the narrator meets the barber in Berne, Switzerland, where he is again practicing his trade. From him he learns the melancholy details of how the barber had returned to the gambling table, convinced that if he had won once he could do so again, and proceeded to lose everything he had won except his passion to try again and again.

enced with his first wife. By 1866 his turbulent and destructive affair with Polina Suslova had run its course, but he was exhausted by work, poor health, and financial worries.[5] His strength and emotions had been drained by the preceding three years and there seemed little of either left over for *The Gambler*. Yet there was enough for him to record in the novel, as he did nowhere else, the workings of the passions of gambling and love.

The Gambler is more directly autobiographical than many of Dostoevsky's works. The press of the circumstances in which it was written drove him, it seems to impressions and events that were present in his immediate memory and imagination. The use of recently lived events is what makes it less of a novel artistically than *Crime and Punishment* and the three great novels that were to follow, but it is also what makes it somewhat unusual among his works. Except for *The House of the Dead* nowhere else is his own life brought in as directly, and nowhere else are the passions of gambling and love used with so little artistic distance. Indeed it is astounding, considering how much his gambling cost him in shame and misery, that the roulette table appears so seldom in his works. And nowhere else do we get with any directness a reflection of the three women he loved in his life.

The diary of Polina Suslova, which is published here in English for the first time, is a priceless window on the character and temperament of a woman Dostoevsky loved during the most destructive and creative period of his life. The portrait we have of her in the novel, the diary, and the short story she wrote, "The Stranger and Her

5. In April 1865 he wrote to Polina's sister, Nadezhda Prokofievna, that he still loved Polina, although he was frank about her faults (letter 5 in this volume). In August 1865 he felt still close enough to Polina to ask her for money. But his letter of 5 May 1867 (about five months after marrying Anna) is matter-of-fact and informative, although he obliquely invites more letters from her (letter 10).

Lover" (a fictional account of Dostoevsky's love for her and published here in English for the first time), adds up to considerable material from which to gain some sense of her character and temperament. Somewhere in the triple reflection from these three sources the truth of Dostoevsky's relationship with Polina and something about his emotional needs in regard to women are to be found. By way of introduction one can say that Dostoevsky was far more generous about his relationship with her than was Polina about hers with him. Her accounts are self-serving and insensitive to any part of Dostoevsky's character and actions that do not bear directly on her own feelings and needs. Dostoevsky's Polina in *The Gambler* is far more attractive and complex than is the living prototype, and he uses his relationship with her in the novel as a premise on which to explore relationships between gambling and love that go far beyond the immediate and literary experience.

Slonim wrote a whole book about Dostoevsky's three loves,[6] but the enigma of Dostoevsky's loving remains. The three women were different morally but similar in intelligence and sensitivity. All three were limited women. They bear in that sense very little relationship to the complex and enigmatic women he imagined and brought to life in his novels. Maria, the first wife, and Polina may share some of the destructive instincts of Nastasya Fillipovna, Lise, Katerina Ivanovna, and others, but they share none of their multidimensional response to life. We know the least about the first wife, the most about the third love and the second wife, Anna. Anna kept a diary and recorded reminiscences, and Dostoevsky wrote her many letters, which she dutifully preserved. Anna is the good woman in his life: faithful, loyal, sac-

6. Mark Slonim, *Tri liubvi Dostoevskogo* (New York: Chekhov, 1953), English trans., *Three Loves of Dostoevsky* (New York: Rinehart, 1955).

rificing, the devoted servant in life and, after his death, the tireless worker dedicated to protecting his name and fame.

Maria Dmitricvna Isaeva was, as far as we can tell, the very opposite of Anna. Dostoevsky's daughter, Aimée, has only the vilest things to say about her:[7] she was calculating, unloving, and unfaithful. According to Aimée, Maria slept with her lover on the eve of her marriage to Dostoevsky, and after marriage she inflicted upon him the cruelty of disclosing all the vile things she had done in secret. Aimée is grossly inaccurate about many elementary facts and her account must be taken as part fancy and part bile. Yet some of what she says must be true. There is enough in the letters Dostoevsky wrote to Baron Vrangel about Maria in 1856 to indicate that she had been playing with his emotions and inflicting needless suffering on him. Dostoevsky met her in Semipalatinsk after he was released from prison at Omsk in 1854 and fell in love with her while she was still married to a civil servant, with whom Dostoevsky got along very well. In May 1855 Maria's husband got a job in Kuznevtsk and died shortly afterward. From about March of 1856 to December 1856 Dostoevsky wrote letter after letter to Maria filled with all the torments of love and passion. He wrote to Vrangel, "I can't think of anything else. If I could only see her, hear her. I am unhappy and half-crazy with love." He told Vrangel in almost every letter that he was out of his mind with love, that he could not possibly live without her, and that he would commit suicide if he lost her.

He must have been writing the same thing to Maria, and she seems to have made the most of his passions and his willingness to suffer. She asked his advice about what to say and do if a certain middle-aged man proposed to

7. Aimée Dostoevsky, *Fyodor Dostoevsky, a Study* (London, 1921).

her, knowing full well what the effect of such a mock-naïve request would have on him. Dostoevsky recorded the effect in a letter to Vrangel on 23 March 1856: "I was struck as if by lightning, swayed, fell into a faint, and cried all night." His nights were filled with wild dreams, cries, spasms, and torrents of tears. Though she made up the matter of the middle-aged suitor, she did not make up the love for a young schoolteacher, the details of which she communicated to the hapless Dostoevsky. Dostoevsky forgave her everything and did not waver in his belief that she was an angel. He was convinced that she had been cruelly abandoned to poverty, misery, and the responsibility of a young son because of the death of her husband. She was the embodiment for him of charm, intelligence, and purity. He even forgave her her lover and her intention to marry, and busied himself in pleading with Vrangel to use his influence to get her fiancé a better job so that his beloved Maria would not have to suffer. Maria saw finally that her security lay with Dostoevsky and her passion with her lover, Vergunov. She reconciled both by marrying Dostoevsky and keeping her lover, and then repaid Dostoevsky's generosity with open contempt and distaste.

The affair with Polina, which began before his wife was dead, is something of a repetition of his love for his first wife. Dostoevsky's love for Maria was one of violent compassion and pity. Maria was not as helpless as Dostoevsky imagined, since she pursued her interests cleverly and ruthlessly. Polina was not in an especially difficult position when Dostoevsky met her: she was young, high-spirited, and firm of will, and apparently well-off enough to pursue with some comfort her studies and her travels abroad. But she was young, an aspirant to a literary career, and Dostoevsky must have been flattered and moved by a compassion for youth and the difficulties of literary ambition. He conceived of himself as the protector of Maria while he was courting her (he even compared himself in one letter with Makar Devushkin of his first novel, *Poor Folk*, a middle-aged bureaucrat who protects a young maiden Varvara, abandoned to the trials of misery and assaults on her virtue), and he must have conceived of himself also as the protector of the young Polina, who came to him with admiration, and a manuscript to be submitted to his journal *Time*. Whether she introduced herself to him by writing him the love letter Aimeé Dostoevsky claimed she did will probably never be known, since it has come down to us only in Aimeé's book and probably through her imagination. The affair was at its height in the first half-year of 1863, when Dostoevsky suggested to Polina that they spend the summer abroad together. Polina agreed and went off to Paris in the early summer, where Dostoevsky was to meet her as soon as he was able to get away. He was, however, delayed by the closing of his journal in May 1863 and the complications arising from its closing. It was not until the middle of August that he was able to get away. Despite the delays and presumably his impatience to get to his mistress, Dostoevsky interrupted his passionate journey to stop off at Wiesbaden and Baden-Baden for gambling. At Wiesbaden he won 10,400 francs and had the prudence to send half of the sum back to St. Petersburg to relatives for his dying wife. But a few days later he lost what remained at Baden-Baden and wrote his wife asking for part of the sum back. The passions of gambling and love are interlinked in Dostoevsky's life at this point, as they are in more complex fashion in the novel itself.

When he reached Paris in late August, he did not find his young mistress impatiently waiting for him. Fresh from the humiliations of his gambling losses, he now faced the humiliation of having lost his mistress. During her wait for him in Paris she had fallen in love with a young South American, who had taken her and then abandoned her. We have Polina's version of the meeting with Dostoevsky, not once but twice: in her diary and in her short story "The Stranger and Her Lover." In the first pages of the diary Polina tells us that she had written a letter to him asking him not to come to her, but the letter had been written too late, and it is with these words that she greets him when he appears at her apartment. The scene of their meeting, which Polina records in detail, speaks volumes about their relationship, and about Dostoevsky's reactions to losing at love:

I saw him through the window, but waited until the message came that he was there, and even then it was a long time before I could make myself go out to meet him. "How are you?" I said, in a trembling voice. He asked me what was the matter with me, which only intensified my agitation, along with his own uneasiness, which was also growing. "I thought that you were not going to come," I said, "because I wrote you a letter."

"What letter?"

"So you wouldn't come."

"Why not?"

"Because it is too late."

He hung his head.

"I must know everything, let's go somewhere, and tell me, or I'll die."

I suggested that we go to his room. We were silent all the way. *I did not look at him.* Once in a while he would yell "Vite, vite" to the cabman, in a desperate and impatient voice, so that the man would turn around and give us a puzzled look. I tried not to look at F[yodor] M[ikhailovich]. He was not looking at me either, but kept holding my hand all the way, pressing it hard from time to time and making some sort of convulsive movements. "Calm down, I am with you," I said.

When we got to his room, he fell at my feet, and, putting his arms around my knees, clasping them, and sobbing, he exclaimed between sobs: "I have lost you, I knew it!" Then, having regained his composure, he began to ask me about the other man. "Perhaps he is handsome, young, and glib. But you will never find a heart such as mine."

For a long time I did not have the heart to answer him.

"Have you given yourself to him completely?"

"Don't ask, it is not right," I said.

"Polia, I don't know what is right and what is wrong. Who is he, a Russian, a Frenchman, not my doctor? That one?" [An illegible word.]

"No, no."

I told him that I loved the man very much.

"Are you happy?"

"No."

"How can that be? You love and you are not happy, why, is this possible?"

"He does not love me."

"He does not love you!" he exclaimed, clutching his head in despair. "But you don't love him like a slave, do you? Tell me, I must know! Isn't it true that you would follow him to the end of the world?"

"No, I . . . I'll be going to the country," I said, bursting into tears.

"Oh, Polia, why must you be so unhappy! It had to happen that you would fall in love with another man. I knew it. Why, you fell in love with me by mistake, because yours is a generous heart, you waited until you were 23, you are the only woman who does not demand of a man that he obligate himself in any way, but at what price: a man and a woman are not one and the same. He takes, she gives."

The situation has its analogies with the love for Maria. What Dostoevsky cherished was given to a person of no particular distinction or character. Maria mocked his love with her affair with the insignificant and half-illiterate Vergunov, and Polina mocked it with a trivial and insensitive medical student. Just as Maria treated Dostoevsky to the details of her love for another man, so too Polina treats him with all the details of her love for Salvador. Dostoevsky had willingly and eagerly accepted the torments of Maria's confessions, and he implores Polina to regale him with all the details of another humiliation in love. In both cases, too, he adopts the role of the protector and consoler. Polina will be his sister and he her brother, and he succeeds in persuading her to continue their trip to Italy under that improbable arrangement. When Polina realized that neither the delights of resuming the affair with Salvador nor the satisfaction of vengeance upon him was possible, she accepted Dostoevsky's proposal, knowing undoubtedly that she would be able to purge her humiliation by passing it on to Dostoevsky. This she did with great liberality, provoking Dostoevsky's passion so as to frustrate it. Dostoevsky's generous offer that they travel through Italy as brother and sister was disingenuous, since it became rapidly clear from Polina's diary that he hoped to resume his liaison with her; and it became even clearer that Polina was determined that this would not happen: "While we were on route here he told me that he had some hope, though he had earlier insisted that he had none. I did not say anything to this, but I knew that it was not going to happen." But what was going to happen and what Polina manipulated with determined and unrelenting cunningness was the arousal of Dostoevsky's passions and the spectacle of his suffering. She was proud of this and naïve enough to record it in her diary. In the entry of 6 September at Baden-Baden, she wrote the following:

We had tea around 10 o'clock. Having finished it, I felt very tired and went to bed, asking F[yodor] M[ikhailovich] to sit close to me. I felt good. I took his hand and for a long time held it in mine. He said that he felt good sitting like that.

I told him that I had been unfair and unkind to him in Paris, that it may have seemed as though I had been thinking only of myself, yet I had been thinking of him, too, but did not want to say it, so as not to hurt him. Suddenly he got up and started to leave, but then stumbled over my shoe which was lying by the bed, and just as quickly turned around and sat down again.

"You wanted to go somewhere, didn't you?" I asked.

"I wanted to shut the window."

"Shut it then, if you want to."

"No it isn't necessary. You don't know what just happened to me!" he said, with a strange expression.

"What do you mean?" I looked at his face; it showed great agitation.

"I was just going to kiss your foot."

"Ah, why that?" I said, greatly embarrassed, almost frightened, and tucked my legs under me.

"I just got the urge, and decided that I'd kiss it."

Then he asked me if I wanted to sleep, but I told him no, I would like to sit with him some more. Thinking of getting undressed and going to sleep, I asked him whether the maid was going to clear the tea table. He assured me that she wasn't. Then he looked at me in a way that made me feel embarrassed, and I told him so.

"I feel embarrassed, too," he said, with a strange smile.

I hid my face in my pillow. Then I asked him again whether the maid would be coming, and he assured me again that she wouldn't.

"All right then, go back to your room, I want to sleep," I said.

"Right away," he said, but stayed for some time. Then he kissed me very ardently and, finally, started to light a candle for himself. My candle was burning low.

"You won't have any light," he said.

"Not so, I have a whole candle there."

"But this is mine."

"I have another one."

"There will always be an answer," he said, smiling, and

left. He did not close his door and soon came back to my room, under the pretext that he wanted to shut my window. He came up to me and suggested that I get undressed.

"I'll get undressed," I said showing him by my attitude that I was only waiting for him to go away.

He left once more, and came back still another time, under some pretext, after which he left again and closed his door. Today he mentioned yesterday to me and said that he had been drunk. Then he said that I must probably find it most unpleasant, the way he was annoying me. I answered that I didn't mind, and refused to be drawn into a discussion of the subject, so that he could neither cherish hope nor be quite without it. He said that he had noticed I had a very sly smile, that, most probably, he appeared foolish to me, that he was well aware of his own foolishness, but that it was something unconscious.

Polina made her program quite explicit with the words "so that he could neither cherish hope nor be quite without it." When his interest flagged she provoked it by suggestive gestures: "I feel once more a tenderness toward F[yodor] M[ikhailovich]. It happened that I was upbraiding him, and later I felt that I had been wrong, so I wanted to make up for it, and I got tender with him. He responded with such joy that I was moved by it, and I became twice as tender. When I was sitting next to him, looking at him caressingly, he said: 'There is that familiar look, it's a long time since I saw it last! I let my head fall on his chest and began to cry.' " When Dostoevsky attempted to liberate himself from her game, by one of his own, she saw his attempt to overcome his humiliation as a means of spiting her:

When he woke up he became unusually free and easy, cheerful, and importunate. It was as though he wanted in this fashion to conquer his own inner hurt and sadness, and spite me.

I watched these strange antics with bewilderment. It was

as though he were trying to turn everything into a joke, so as to hurt me, but I only looked at him with astonishment.

"I don't like you that way," I said simply at last.

"Why? What have I done?"

"Just so, in Pari[s] and in Turin I liked you much better. Why are you so cheerful?"

"It is a cheerfulness born of disappointment," he said and left, but he returned soon.

She conquers his cheerfulness by embracing him "with ardor" and his ardor by distance and taunting: "F[yodor] Mikhailovich again turned everything into a joke, and said, as he was leaving my room, that it was humiliating for him to leave me in this fashion (it was 1 o'clock at night, and I was lying in bed, undressed): 'For the Russians never did retreat.' "

Polina repeated the essential outlines of these scenes in the story "The Stranger and Her Lover." Though the facts as recorded in the diary and as they appear in the fictional variant are basically the same, they are suffused with a romantic and self-flattering coloring. The fictional Polina, Anna Pavlovna, is elevated into a purity and majesty that is far beyond realism and probability. Anna Pavlovna is the epitome of all virtues. Anxiety and suffering as well as "unconquerable strength and passion" are apparent in "her gentle and kind features." She is beautiful, complex, gentle, pensive, and trustful, chaste, modest, considerate, and on more than one occasion she is compared to the Madonna and the Christian martyrs. Losnitsky, on the other hand, the fictional surrogate of Dostoevsky, is petty, boastful, and vulgar; his only redeeming features consist in his appreciation of her majestic character and beauty, in his astonishment at having possessed her, and in his contrition at having lost her. As in the diary, they travel together, though the locale is changed, and during the course of the traveling he basely becomes importunate and Anna remains pure and suffering before his insensitive demands. Anna expires by drowning herself in a river. Her motive for doing so is not clear, but it is strongly implied that her spirit was too sensitive and pure to persevere in the presence of the coarseness of Losnitsky's character and in the state of the world about her.

One wonders whether this story and the manner of Anna's death were in Dostoevsky's mind when he satirized such romantic suicides in *The Brothers Karamazov*. In commenting on the mystery as to why Adelaida Ivanovna Miusov had consented to marry someone as repulsive as Fyodor Karamazov, he speculates on the possibility of some romantic madness, and he recalls the case of a romantic lady who threw herself off a high bank into a river (rather than marry a gentleman she was in love with) from the motive apparently of trying to be like Shakespeare's Ophelia. He adds that if the spot over the river had not been so picturesque, it is likely that the suicide would not have taken place.

The portrait we get of Polina in the story testifies to the power and tenacity of her fantasies about herself, and the portrait we get of her in the diary—though not inconsistent with the fictional portrait—is probably more realistic. The constraints of real life and real people, as well as the practical exigencies of everyday life, compel her to record facts about herself and the world about her that are less influenced by her tendency to idealize her character and motives. The intimate and less public form also permitted her to express more directly her disappointments and despairs.

II

If the story "The Stranger and Her Lover" bears almost no relationship to the public and historical image of

Polina that has come down to us, neither does the image that emerges in the diary correspond with the public image. She has come down to us in history as fitful, tempestuous, destructive, vengeful, cruel. She has been seen, with some justification, as the prototype of Dostoevsky's "electric" and punishing women. Aimée Dostoevsky saw Polina as the prototype of Aglaya, Grushenka, and Liza, as well as of Polina of *The Gambler*. The list is not wholly fanciful, but we have to remind ourselves that the destructive and contradictory female had already appeared in Dostoevsky's imagination long before he met Polina Suslova—Katerina of *The Landlady* is an example—and that Polina was more a confirmation than a provocation. The image, too, may be a little too much of one piece. It is based on Dostoevsky's evaluation of her in his letter to her sister,[8] Rozanov's bitter comments,[9] and selected portions of her diary. However true Rozanov's estimate of her may be, we must keep in mind that he was talking of a woman in her forties and not the girl in her twenties that Dostoevsky fell in love with.

Polina's character seems much smaller and less sinister when we read the entire diary. The femme fatale who tortured Dostoevsky for more than half a decade and then resurfaced to make the life of one of his devotees, Rozanov, miserable for several decades is not recognizable in the diary. There is the tenacity with which she holds on

8. Letter 5, to Nadezhda Prokofievna Suslova. He says of Polina: "I feel sorry for her, because I can foresee that she will always be unhappy. Nowhere will she find either friend or happiness. Whoever demands everything from others, while not feeling any obligation on his part, will never find happiness."

9. V. V. Rozanov (1856–1919), important prose writer, something of a miniaturist in his philosophical reflections and the author of a distinguished critical assessment of Dostoevsky's works. He married Suslova in 1880 and separated from her in 1886. She refused to give him a divorce and he had to live with the woman he loved outside of marriage. Rozanov compared Suslova to Catherine de Medici and believed that she would have light-heartedly committed a crime.

to her desire to avenge herself on her South American lover, but even this tenacity appears in a less than lurid light. Though she fantasizes killing him or killing herself, all she actually does is pester him with somewhat silly letters. What the diary shows us more than anything else is a young woman at sea, rootless, and in search of something she thinks she is. She is drawn to the cosmopolitan life she lives, but is consciously repelled by it. She is moved by an aimless desire to be loved, to be useful, to be intelligent. She finds none of these and consoles and excuses herself with criticism of the life of the cosmopolitan; instead of finding love she drifts apparently from one trivial love affair to another. The diary is studded with a procession of Russian emigrants, some distinguished in character, who in one way or another had participated in the liberal and radical disturbances of the early sixties and who had emigrated to Europe. To judge from the references to rather well-known liberals and revolutionaries and the snatches of conversation that are recorded, Polina lived among people who were intellectually alive and socially conscious and who answered to her own vaguely radical sentiments. Yet what she learned of these people and what significance they held for her are invariably casual and unimportant. What she perceives and records of the environment about her is banal and listless. Neither the enthusiasm of agreement nor the passion of dissent is felt in her account. She seemed to occupy a political and social stance without understanding that stance or having been sufficiently interested to reflect on it.

The Soviets have a higher opinion of her than the facts of the diary justify. They have seized on her liberal pronouncements, her desire to be of use, and her admiration of the people. But these liberal sentiments are diffuse and casual, the product of idle conversations in French pen-

sions. She flares up at one point in conversation with two
men about the uselessness of conventional views of love
and answers in the best tradition of midcentury liberal
thought, and in words remarkably similar to those of the
radical critic Pisarev:[10] "I said that I had found these
ideas medieval, that love and pride may be there, but that
it was ridiculous to cultivate them, at a time when there
is so much to be done, so much that is urgent; that there
was not time for such luxury when there was a shortage
of bread, when people were starving to death, or if they
had enough to eat, had to defend that privilege with millions of soldiers, gendarmes, and so on." But the facts of
the matter are that she never did anything, to our knowledge, of particular note or usefulness. Upon her return
to Russia she made one attempt to open a school for
young ladies, which was promptly closed down by the
authorities. Her sister, on the other hand, with whom
Dostoevsky corresponded and whom he respected, was
apparently a very talented young lady and became one
of the first female doctors in Russia. Polina Suslova is in
a minor way an example of that migration to Europe of
Russians who felt alienated from the conditions of their
native land, some of whom found their causes abroad in
dreams of a better Russia, and some of whom found an
outlet for their energy and talent in political action
abroad against the repressive regime at home.

Polina is more in the tradition of the high-minded and
useless liberals who peopled the works of Turgenev, Gon-
charov, and Dostoevsky, among others. She talks of freedom, nationalism, England's place in international affairs, and even of Hegel. But the conversations are
fragmentary, never very clear, always banal. They tell us

---

10. Dmitri Ivanovich Pisarev (1840–68), radical critic and social activist who believed that Russia's social ills and their alleviation should take
precedence over such idle pursuits as art.

of a mind that yearns for depths but can only skim on surfaces. She reads books, attends lectures, engages in intellectual conversations, writes stories, seeks out important people, but the activity and energy find no sustained pattern and the words reflect no clear intellectual interest or sustained belief. What she talks about more than anything else and what interests her most of all are men and love. The intellectual skirmishes and the flirtations with ideas are lost in an almost uninterrupted series of flirtations, significant glances, squeezings of hands, and, as best as one can tell from the guarded references, a number of trivial affairs.

Yet for all her intellectual deficiencies she is the embodiment of a distinct feminine type, almost indeed the incarnation of the verbal polemics that heated the journals of Russia at this time with the "woman question." She could have come out of Chernyshevsky's novel *What Is To Be Done*,[11] with, of course, less resolution and intelligence than his feminine heroines. What is most consistent about her is her determination to be a new kind of woman: free in her feelings and her acts. She attended the University of St. Petersburg, participated in demonstrations, traveled openly with a married man. She wanted to be more than the conventional woman, but she wasn't sure how to be it, and she wasn't all of one piece. She desired an image of herself that she could not sustain, either emotionally or intellectually: She doesn't want to have children, because she doesn't know how to bring them up, but she cries after saying that. The following self-estimate tells us something about her understanding of herself and something about the limitations of that understanding: "Only here I came to appreciate

11. Nikolay Gavrilovich Chernyshevsky (1828–89), radical critic, aesthetician, political activist, and revolutionary. His novel *What Is To Be Done* (1863) exercised considerable influence on revolutionary thought.

the true value of the friendship and respect of people who go beyond common standards, and in the security of this friendship I found courage and self-respect. Will my pride ever desert me? No, this couldn't be. I'd rather die. Better die of grief, but free, independent of things external, true to one's convictions, and return one's soul to God as pure as it was, rather than make concessions, even for a moment allow oneself to be touched by base and unworthy things, but I find life so coarse and so sad that I bear it with difficulty. My God, is it always going to be this way! Was it worthwhile to have been born!"

What she wants more than anything else, and what she fails at, both because of her temperament and because of the limitations of her own understanding of herself, is a certain kind of independence. Apart from a determined flouting of conventions and a certain boldness in her actions, she is not really very free and has very little idea of what form that freedom should take, in positive content, if she could achieve it. She is slavishly tied to the lover who has spurned her and seems incapable of either pride or independence in coming to terms with her situation. She wants freedom for herself but does not hesitate to subject others, like Dostoevsky, to her whims and pleasures. Most of all the image she pursues of herself, even when mildly or partially achieved, brings her no contentment. She cries a great deal and churns restlessly in a mire of repetitious thoughts and actions. There is something pathetic about her as she valiantly tries to wrest some significance from the banalities of her life and those of her character. One is not even sure how sincere her expressions of despair are, for so much of the diary is posture. She must have read *Madame Bovary* and thought of herself as something of a Russian counterpart of poor Emma, because in one diary entry she tells us of a visit to a local priest, as Emma had gone to the village curé, for solace to her soul; but where she finds, as did Emma, only irrelevancies and indifference. She writes, too, but as the story that is included in this volume shows, she was entirely without talent. She wanted to be a George Sand and worked doggedly at her literary ambitions and liberal sentiments, but she was unfortunately without literary talent or intellectual distinction. No wonder then that her life passed so quickly into disillusion and bile.

Apart from the opening scene, in which she tells him of his loss and her loss of Salvador, and the bedroom scenes in Italy, which she apparently relished enough to describe in more detail than anything else, she interested herself very little in Dostoevsky's character or their relationship. When she bothers to refer to him it is to consider the effect that he has had on her feelings. One is dismayed to find that it is only our interest that lifts the image of Dostoevsky in her diary from the mesh of her prosaisms. Dostoevsky disappears from the pages of her diary for long periods, and the pages are filled with such inconsequential details as her efforts to get the maid to clean her shoes, about the width of Italian streets and the style of Italian clothes, how a sympathetic shopkeeper gave her two sheets of paper for nothing, conversations that are about nothing, and, of course, the minute recording of every significant glance and attention that numberless men pay her. But her casual remarks about Dostoevsky show a consistency in her attitude toward him. Though she may think of him with fondness and tenderness at times, she is more likely to think of him with anger and contempt. She repeats more than once that he used her, that she came to him fresh with new love, and that he had in his insensitivity failed to appreciate her and her love. When in one of her many fantasies she thinks of how best she could revenge herself on Salvador and asks herself what she wants from him, she an-

swers that "he should confess his guilt, be remorseful,
that is, that he be a Fyodor Mikhailovich." In another
entry she says: "I hear about F[yodor] M[ikhailovich]. I
simply hate him. He made me suffer so much, when it
was possible not to suffer." And in yet another entry: "As
I remember what had happened two years ago, I begin to
hate D[ostoevsky]. He was the first to kill my faith." Even
after we make allowances for her need to find a scapegoat
for the converging failures and banalities of her life, her
anger at Dostoevsky and her interpretation of their relationship may have some truth in them. And the justification for considering that Dostoevsky could be insensitive and even cruel toward the women he loved comes,
remarkably enough, from the diary and reminiscences of
another young lady in Dostoevsky's life, his wife Anna.

Anna has left us some intimate reminiscences of the
first months of her marriage, dealing mostly with Dostoevsky's gambling, and they give us some insight into his
treatment of her and possibly some basis for Polina's
criticism. With due allowance for the stress he was under
in gambling and his inevitable losses, one is still appalled
by the insensitivity he shows to the costs his young bride
must bear on his account. There is no reason to doubt
the veracity of the reminiscences, since Anna never wa-
vered in her respect and admiration for, and especially
her justification of, her husband. The pattern Anna records with monotonous regularity from March to August
1867 is the systematic depredation by Dostoevsky of their
meager resources. Dostoevsky would go to the gaming
table with 5 or 10 louis d'or, return crestfallen and
ashamed, and after an outburst of penitence and self-
abuse would implore Anna to give him a few more louis
d'or, and then return again to the gaming table and then
to her with the money lost, again to breast beating and
to an appeal for a few more coins from the meager and

dwindling household fund. Anna would beg him to desist at least to the next day; Dostoevsky would become furious and insist on the money, and Anna would in the end relent and give him what he asked. There were infrequent variations: when Dostoevsky would return and pour out his winnings to Anna. But shortly afterward the raiding of the fund would begin all over again. After the money was gone, Dostoevsky would go the round of pawnshops, getting what he could for coats, boots, wedding rings. Anna's saintlike and unreal forbearance would be rent from time to time in the diary with half-permitted complaints to herself, but not to him, about his disregard of her feelings.

The picture is not pretty. Dostoevsky shows no regard for the feelings of his young wife; he is so absorbed in his conviction that fortune can be wrested from the gaming table that Anna exists for him only as an object to absorb his wrath, his self-contempt, and his penitence. He did not hesitate to pawn her winter coat, her boots, and even her wedding dress; he left her to face loneliness, worry, and the wrath of the landlord, as he took their last gulden to the gaming table. If Polina asserts with some consistency that he took her love without appreciating what she gave him, there are traits in Dostoevsky's character which would support such an assertion. He had an enormous appetite for suffering, but he also had a capacity to inflict suffering on others. He may have even inflicted the suffering so that he could suffer in return. The Anna we find in her diary and reminiscences bears little resemblance to the Polina we find in her diary. Anna is good, patient, unbelievably self-sacrificial; Polina is fretful, selfish, engrossed in her feelings and the harm others are doing to her. Polina is concerned almost entirely with herself, and Anna almost entirely with Dostoevsky's welfare. But the opposites meet, perhaps, in Dostoevsky's needs. One is almost appalled at the superhuman role of self-sacrifice that Anna imposed on herself, and astonished at her lack of sensitivity in recognizing the burden that her self-burdening placed on Dostoevsky. There is little doubt that at times Dostoevsky seemed to multiply his irritations, bickerings, and cruelty so as to provoke some reaction in Anna. He seemed to be asking for rejection, and Anna gave him patience and shame. It is hard to believe that Dostoevsky was not aware of the toll Anna exacted from him, but it was a toll that he seemed only too eager to accept. It is quite possible that in the beginning Polina suffered from Dostoevsky's insensitivities, but if that is true—as she repeatedly asserts—she learned quickly to pay him back fivefold. One is hard put to determine whether the deliberate and cruel sufferings of taunting and frustration that Polina delighted in visiting upon him were harder to bear than the undeliberate suffering that Anna's virtue imposed on him. What seems clear, though, is that Dostoevsky needed one or the other. Both women gave him money to feed his passion for gambling, Anna reluctantly, Polina more eagerly.

Polina complied with Dostoevsky's request for money with seeming generosity and promptitude, as several entries in her diary prove. Given the hate and contempt she expresses for Dostoevsky and the ungenerous side of her character that is clearly in evidence in her diary, it is difficult to understand her motives. She knew Dostoevsky well enough to know that the money she sent would find its way immediately to the roulette table, and one can only conclude that she enjoyed feeding, when she could, the sources of Dostoevsky's self-abasement and self-contempt, even at some cost to herself.

The complex interconnections between Dostoevsky's gambling and his loving are not easy to grasp from the biographical events themselves. Dostoevsky himself seemed determined to grasp them, and he attempted to do so in writing *The Gambler*. According to Anna, Dostoevsky had the insane idea that he would become rich by gambling. Dostoevsky voiced the same sentiment, but his whole life warred against this explanation. Though he complained about lack of money almost more than any writer I know, he had no passion for money, let alone for hoarding it. The recklessness with which he divested himself of whatever money he made suggests that he enjoyed being without money more than having it. He expressed frequently a contempt for money, especially for money accumulated in any systematic way, a practice he identified especially with the German mentality. At the roulette table, no matter how large the temporary winnings, he would play until he lost everything he had. He seemed at peace with himself only when there was nothing left and no possibility of getting more.

He was possessed with an irrational belief that he could win, no matter how many times he lost. All one had to do was to follow a "system," which seemed to consist of remaining calm, deliberate, and rational, and not permitting oneself to be carried away. He was, of course, carried away each time. He told himself and Anna that he could not remain calm and deliberate because others prevented his remaining so: people jostled him, or they put on airs as they played for small stakes, or they had too strong a scent on their persons. There is evidence that it was Dostoevsky who did the jostling or picked the quarrels; at least Anna was sufficiently persuaded of this to worry that he would get a reputation at the casinos for being quarrelsome and rude. If the "system" was as much a rationalization as the possession of a large sum of money, it is hard to understand what it was that left him in a trance at the gaming table and looking like a drunk

with bloodshot eyes when he left it.[12] He surely sought
the humiliation, guilt, and suffering that followed each
orgy of gambling; the breast-beating and penitence he
sought from his wife are evidence of that, as well as the
pattern of his habits in other things. It was humiliation
that he seemed to look for when he insisted on accompanying Polina on the trip to Italy, and it was humiliation
in surfeit that Polina gave to him. The biographical evidence does not take us beyond these motives but if he
wrote *The Gambler,* as I am convinced he did in part, to
discover something about his compulsive gambling, then
other explanations come into prominence.

III

Most of the characters in *The Gambler,* all in fact except
for Aleksei and Polina, are so fixed in their identities as
to teeter on caricature. The General is the pathetic Russian cosmopolitan, prey to all the evils Dostoevsky imag-
ines come with rootlessness; de Grieux is the prototypal
Frenchman, smooth, well-mannered, and unprincipled;
Mr. Astley is the quintessential Englishman, laconic,
honest, unperturbed on the surface; Mlle Blanche is the
beautiful, predatory, superficial French seductress. Even
the grandmother, no matter how likable, is the stock outspoken and shocking headstrong old woman. The stock
types would make poor literature, except for the fact that
Dostoevsky wanted them stereotyped so as to set off the
enigma and complexities of Aleksei's character and the
understandings and misunderstandings of Aleksei in
comprehending those enigmas and complexities.

Aleksei is a person without social consequence, dis-
dained by all; yet he comes to terrify those who disdain

12. Anna describes Dostoevsky in the following way, as he left a gambling hall: "It was terrible to look at him: he was all flushed, with red
eyes as though drunk." *Dostoevsky Portrayed by His Wife,* p. 122.

him and to dominate those who are his social superiors.
He is a buffoon, social maladroit, and lackey, but he
chooses his roles and as such is superior to them. He looks
back to the Underground Man, who displays and glorifies
his insignificance and knows that multiple identities and
denials give him an advantage over those who define, fix,
and cling to their identities. Aleksei pays no tribute to
appearances because he has no appearances to protect,
but he learns quickly enough that almost everyone about
him has something to protect. This is the bond between
him and the grandmother, who in her age and wisdom
cares nothing for appearances and terrifies everyone
about her by her non-caring. A good part of the dramatic
interest in the novel has to do with the manner in which
Aleksei translates his insignificance into significance, so
that progressively he gains power over the General, de
Grieux, and finally and most important, over Polina. All
of them, in one way or another, insult and humiliate him,
but before he is through with them, they come to implore
his aid. The motive he gives himself, and Dostoevsky
gives us, for his doing so is to penetrate the mysteries that
envelop the General's household, especially de Grieux's
hold over Polina. The movement of events is structured
on clarifications that Aleksei seeks, but the mysteries are
somewhat artificial and manipulated. It is perfectly clear
to the reader almost from the beginning that the General
is waiting for the grandmother to die and for the receipt
of his inheritance, that he is in debt to de Grieux, and
that both de Grieux and Blanche hope to profit from his
hapless wit and his wealthy inheritance. De Grieux's hold
over Polina is a bit more complex, but only because
Polina herself and her motives make it complex. What is
not elucidated for us until the very end, and perhaps
never to Aleksei, is the hold that Polina has over him and
the feelings he has for her.

Aleksei comes to understand everything but what moves him, and what moves him are his feelings for Polina and his passion for gambling. He had confessed and professed his love for her again and again, but on the night she comes to his room to offer herself to him, he must first rush off to the gaming table, where he is phenomenally successful. He returns to his room, where Polina has been waiting for him, with his pockets bulging with gold and gulden. There he proceeds, as if it is a drama necessary before the act of love, to pour out the money on the table and floor. Aleksei believes he is paying tribute to his love, and by such tribute permitting Polina to regain her honor before de Grieux. Yet Polina sees something more than the impulse of the lover in his act. Aleksei narrates at this critical juncture: " 'I wonder if I should put it in my suitcase until tomorrow,' I said, turning toward Polina, as if I had suddenly remembered her. She was still sitting there without stirring, yet watching me intently. It was a strange expression she wore on her face; I did not like that expression! I would not be wrong if I said that there was hatred in it." Loathing there is in Polina toward him, but also love. Polina gives herself to him between love and hate, and the next morning she pays him back for giving herself to him with hate, flinging the fifty thousand francs he had offered her to avenge herself on de Grieux in his face.

Aleksei asks the question the reader wants answered: "But what could have been the cause of that condition, and, above all, of this last performance of hers?" He gives us not one answer but several: "Was it wounded pride? Was it despair at having brought herself to come to me? Had I perhaps suggested to her, by my behavior, that I was exultant over the happiness she had granted me, and that, like de Grieux, I was about to get rid of her by giving her fifty thousand francs? But it was simply not true, that much I can say in good conscience. I think that to some extent it was her own vanity that was at fault: her vanity prompted her to distrust and to insult me, even though, most likely, she had no clear conception of her own motives. At any rate, I absorbed de Grieux's punishment and became guilty without doing too much on my own. To be sure, it all happened in a delirious state, and I knew it all too well, and . . . yet I refused to take that fact into consideration." His explanations explain something, but not everything. What he fails to notice is that his passion for gambling eclipses his passion for Polina, that when she comes to offer him love, he offers her money, no matter how noble his motives. She perceives something about him that he had not perceived about himself, and what this is becomes clear after she rushes out of his room and by the decisions that Aleksei later makes.

He turns unexpectedly and unaccountably from Polina to Blanche. The act confounds us and seems unprepared for in any way. Given the pressured manner in which the novel was written, one is tempted to think that this is the desperate stratagem of a writer attempting to dispose of his hero. But the technique is not uncharacteristic of Dostoevsky: he uses often the sudden and paradoxical gesture or act to confound our sense of probability and proportion, and in that way jostles us into rethinking what may have been settled in our minds. There is surely no reason to believe that Aleksei would turn at a critical moment in his life to Blanche, especially since he had hardly noticed or spoken to her throughout the novel. He does not go off with her because he has contracted some passion for her, nor does he turn from Polina because she has rejected him. Polina had insulted him repeatedly before, but he had only redoubled his efforts to prove his love for her. But when she flings the

fifty thousand francs in his face and finds refuge with Mr.
Astley, he shows no perseverance in explaining or seeking explanation, making only the most perfunctory inquiries about her. It is only hours after possessing the
love he had pursued throughout the novel that he is off
to Paris with a professional courtesan, one would say
almost with relief. He goes from a difficult love to an easy
love. Polina demands his love; Blanche demands only his
money. His flight from one to the other must be some
unspoken recognition that the one hundred thousand
gulden he thought were destined for the love of his life
were in reality destined for something dirtier. Blanche
is a convenient way of getting rid of the money and getting rid of the love. He seeks throughout the novel for
social position, money, and love, and when he has all
three, he is frantic to give them up. Aleksei is remarkably
at peace with himself during the weeks he spends as
Blanche's pet; neither the torments of lost love nor the
anxieties of lost money afflict him. He seems to understand something of what he really wants when he says to
himself about the money Blanche spends: "The faster it
goes, the better I like it."

After a little more than three idiotic weeks with
Blanche, he is packed off with a few thousand francs to
pursue the life of the obsessed and compulsive gambler.
Before the climactic scene with Polina and the vegetative
weeks with Blanche, he had pursued love and power over
others; he had intrigued, competed, had opinions, felt
insults, and given insults. He was alive with plans, goals,
and the feelings of accomplishment. Now he seems like a
man drained of the goals and motives that had driven
him: only the passion for gambling remains. We can conclude merely that what had driven him before, he now
recognizes as illusion. Love, social importance, and even
money hold no importance for him. He becomes a

flunkey again when his money runs out, and confesses to himself that he gambles not for money, because he would squander whatever he might win on another Blanche. What is it then that drives him to gamble? He explains it to himself in this way: "That night, the only thing I wanted was that the next day all these Hinzes, all these Ober-Kellners, all these elegant Baden ladies, that they should all be talking about me, that they should all be telling my story, that they should all wonder at me, admire me, and worship my renewed success." But he had had all that when he won two hundred thousand francs at Roulettenburg and he had thrown it away. Mr. Astley gives us a better explanation when he says to him: " 'You've become completely stale; not only have you renounced life, all your interests, private as well as public, your duties as a citizen and as a human being, your friends (yes, you had some friends), not only have you renounced having any goal at all, except winning at roulette, but you have even renounced your memories.' "

The daring to risk the last gulden on the irrational turn of the wheel gives him what the fixities of position, money, and love do not: the feeling of being open to the irrationalities of the turning wheel, and one suspects for Dostoevsky, the irrationalities of human life. Dostoevsky knew and said many times that the deepest urge in human beings is the revolt against definition and the fixities of life; the violation of reason, which sanctified definition and fixity, had, as he was well aware, its destructive side and it may be that side that he was celebrating in the portrait of Aleksei. Aleksei's passion for Polina seemed to have no bounds, at least no rhetorical bounds, when it was fed by frustration, scorn, willfulness, humiliation, and the vagaries of Polina's character. But when the love is offered to him as a goal attained, he rushes to divest himself of the love and the money he has won. For it was

not the love of Polina that he had thirsted for, but the
quest for that love. When that quest is done, he turns to
the irrationalities of the table as a substitute for the irrationalities of her character. Dostoevsky, too, had rushed
off to the gaming tables of Baden-Baden and Wiesbaden,
while he was rushing to a love he felt to be secure and
fixed. When he found in Paris a love lost and to be won
again, he faced the situation with calm and even relief.
A whole vista of new emotions, complexities, difficulties
opened up to him when Polina announced that he had
come too late. It is clear from Polina's diary that he had
drunk in the details of his humiliation, and then planned
as recompense a trip with her through Italy which he
knew would bring, given her character, a further and
more excruciating round of insults, frustrations, and humiliations. He had won in St. Petersburg and lost in
Paris, and the loss and the possibility of winning again
was better than the winning that was solid and immov-
able. It is true, of course, that Dostoevsky gave up the
gambling and gave up Polina—or she him—and settled
into what one must acknowledge to have been a healthy
love for Anna. But not without a struggle. Anna's diary
is eloquent testimony to the fact that Dostoevsky attempted to replay with variation something of the same
drama of hurt and humiliation that he had provoked and
enjoyed with Polina. Anna refused to play the game, and
this both infuriated and pleased him, for despite the fact
that he knew that man must churn spiritually and psy-
chologically in order to live, he knew also that some of
the churnings were sterile traps. His destructive tenden-
cies came to be deflected more and more, and with magnificent results, into his works, and the gallery of tormented characters of the great novels that followed *The
Gambler* is testimony to that. *The Gambler* itself, among
its significances, is a wrenching of biography into fiction

and a purification by creation. Dostoevsky had been for a time what Aleksei had been, but he was able to give some of the destruction and doom to Aleksei. The life and work of no other writer shows so eloquently that art is a salvatory force.

Editorial Note

The Gambler has been translated from the fourth volume of *F. M. Dostoevsky, Sobranie sochinenii,* edited by L. P. Grossman et al. (Moscow, 1956); Polina Suslova's diary, short story, and letters to Dostoevsky from *A. P. Suslova, Gody blizosti s Dostoevskim,* edited with an introduction by A. S. Dolinin (Moscow, 1928); Dostoevsky's letters from *Pis'ma,* edited by A. S. Dolinin, vols. 1 and 2 (Moscow, 1928 and 1930). Victor Terras has done the translation; I have written the Introduction, made the selection of materials included in the volume, and compiled the footnotes. I am indebted in part to Dolinin's excellent notes in his edition of the Suslova materials.

E. W.

The Gambler

Fyodor Dostoevsky

One

I have returned, finally, from my two weeks' absence. My friends have been here, in Roulettenburg, for three days already. I thought that they would be expecting me God knows how eagerly, but I was wrong. The General had an extremely unconcerned air, talked to me condescendingly for a few minutes, then sent me off to his sister. Clearly, they had managed to borrow some money along the way. It even appeared to me that the General looked somewhat embarrassed. Maria Filippovna seemed to be extremely busy and barely exchanged a few words with me. She took the money, however, counted it, and listened to my whole report. They were expecting Mezentsov for dinner, also the little Frenchman and an Englishman. As usual, the moment there was some money in the house, there had to be a dinner party. That's Moscow style for you. Polina Aleksandrovna, upon seeing me, asked why I had been away so long, and, without giving me a chance to answer, went off somewhere. Of course, she did that on purpose. We ought to have a heart-to-heart talk, though. There is a lot of talk about.

I was assigned a tiny room on the fourth floor of the hotel. They know here that I belong to the General's suite. It all shows that they have managed to impress people. Everybody here takes the General for a fabulously

wealthy Russian magnate. Even before dinner he managed to let me, among other errands, change two thousand-franc bills for him. I changed them at the hotel office.
Now, at least for a whole week, we'll be looked upon as
millionaires. I was about to take Misha and Nadia for a
walk, but when I was on the stairs, the General called me
back. He felt it necessary to ask where I was taking them.
This man positively can't look me straight in the eye. He
would like to very much, but every time he tries it, I respond with such an intent, or rather, disrespectful gaze
that he seems embarrassed. In very pompous language,
piling one sentence on another and getting hopelessly entangled in the end, he let me know that I was to take the
children for their walk somewhere away from the casino,
in the park. Finally, he became quite angry and added
sternly: "Or else you might, perhaps, take them to the
casino, to the roulette tables. You must excuse me," he
added, "but I know you are still young and lack proper
judgment, and you might, perhaps, be inclined to take up
gambling. In any case, though I am not your mentor, nor
do I want to play that role, at least I have the right to express my wish that you should not, so to speak, compromise me . . ."

"But I haven't got any money," I answered calmly,
"and in order to lose some money, you must have some in
the first place."

"You shall have it at once," the General answered,
flushing a little. Having rummaged through his bureau,
he checked his notebook, and it turned out that he owed
me about a hundred and twenty rubles.

"How are we to settle?" he went on to say; "we'd have
to convert it into thalers. Here, why don't you take a hundred thalers, for a round figure, and we'll settle the balance later."

I took the money without a word.

"Please, don't feel offended by my words; you are so touchy . . . If I gave you a hint, it was only, so to speak, by way of warning you, and I have, of course, a certain right to do so . . ."

As I was returning home with the children before dinner, I ran into a whole cavalcade. Our party had been out for a drive to some ruins. Two magnificent carriages, beautiful horses! In one carriage, Mademoiselle Blanche, Maria Filippovna, and Polina; the little Frenchman, the Englishman, and our General on horseback. Passersby stopped and stared: the effect was there. However, it would have to end badly for the General. I figured that with the four thousand francs which I had brought, added to what they had evidently managed to borrow in the meantime, they had now seven or eight thousand francs, which was not nearly enough for Mlle Blanche.

Mlle Blanche and her mother are also staying at our hotel, and our little Frenchman isn't very far away either. The servants call him Monsieur le Comte; Mlle Blanche's mother is called Mme la Comtesse. Well, who knows, maybe they are really *comte* and *comtesse*.

I knew beforehand that Monsieur le Comte would not recognize me when we met at dinner. The General, of course, would not have thought of introducing us or even mentioning me to him, and as for Monsieur Comte, he had been to Russia himself; he knows that there a tutor[1] is very small fry indeed. However, he knows me very well. But I must confess that I showed up at dinner uninvited. Apparently the General had forgotten to make arrangements for me, or else he would certainly have sent me to have my dinner at the table d'hôte.[2] So I came of my own accord, and the General looked at me with displeasure.

1. Dostoevsky uses the French transliteration of the Russian word for "tutor"—*outchitel*—here and throughout.
2. Used here in the archaic sense of "common table."

Kindhearted Maria Filippovna immediately made a place for me, but it was my having met Mr. Astley that saved the situation for me; because of this, I could not help seeming to belong to the party.

I first met this strange Englishman in Prussia on a train, where we were seated facing each other. This was when I was on my way to join the family. Later, I ran into him on my way to France and, finally, in Switzerland. Twice then, during those past two weeks, and now there he was again, in Roulettenburg. I never met a man so shy in my life. He is shy to the point of being stupid, and he knows it very well, of course, because he is by no means stupid. Yet he is a very sweet and gentle person. I made him talk when we first met in Prussia. He told me that he had been at North Cape earlier in the summer, and that he was very anxious to visit the fair at Nizhni Novgorod. I do not know how he became acquainted with the General. It seems to me that he is hopelessly in love with Polina. When she entered he flushed crimson. He was very glad that I sat next to him at the table, and apparently he already considers me his bosom friend.

At dinner the little Frenchman set the tone of the conversation in quite singular fashion. He is nonchalant and condescending with everybody. In Moscow too, as I remember, he used to be full of hot air. He talked a great deal about finance and about Russian politics. The General would sometimes venture to contradict, but discreetly, just enough so as not to lose his dignity altogether.

I was in a strange mood. Of course, before the dinner was half over I was asking myself that invariable and familiar question: "Why do I hang around with this General, and why didn't I leave this crowd long ago?" From time to time I glanced at Polina Aleksandrovna. She took no notice of me whatever. Finally I got mad and decided to be rude.

It all started when I suddenly in a loud voice, and for no reason at all, barged into someone else's conversation. Most of all, I wanted to pick a quarrel with the little Frenchman. I turned around to the General and, quite loudly and distinctly interrupting him, observed that this summer it was virtually impossible for a Russian to dine at a hotel table d'hôte. The General stared at me in disbelief.

"If you have any self-respect at all," I went on, "you'll surely wind up being abused and suffering all kinds of affronts to your dignity. In Paris and on the Rhine, and even in Switzerland, the tables d'hôte are so crowded with all sorts of little Poles, and little Frenchmen sympathizing with them, that you couldn't get a word in edgewise so long as you are a Russian."

I said this in French. The General was looking at me bewilderedly, not knowing whether he should get angry or simply be amazed at my forgetting myself to such an extent.

"So someone, somewhere, gave you a lesson in manners," said the little Frenchman, nonchalantly and contemptuously.

"In Paris I first had a fight with a Pole," I answered, "and then with a French officer who was backing the Pole. But then some of the French came over to my side, as I told them how I almost spit into a monsignor's coffee."

"Spit?" asked the General, with dignified perplexity, casting glances around the table. The little Frenchman looked at me suspiciously.

"Exactly so, sir," I answered. "Since I was convinced for two whole days that I might have to take a short trip to

Rome in connection with that business of ours, I went to the office of the Holy Father's embassy in Paris to get my visa. There I was met by a little abbé, fiftyish, all dried up and with a frosty expression on his face. After listening to me politely, though extremely coldly, he asked me to wait. Though I was in a hurry, I sat down, of course, took out my *Opinion nationale*,[3] and began reading some horribly abusive verbiage directed against Russia. Meanwhile I heard someone else being ushered into the monsignor's office through the next room, and also saw my abbé bow to that person. I addressed the same request to him once more and, again, he asked me to wait, but still more coldly this time. A little later another caller came in, but on business, an Austrian apparently. He was listened to and led upstairs without delay. Now I became very much annoyed. I got up, walked up to the abbé and told him resolutely that, since the monsignor was receiving callers, he might as well take care of me also. At once the abbé drew back, extraordinarily surprised. It was simply beyond his comprehension how a worthless Russian could put himself on an equal footing with the monsignor's guests. And, in the most insolent tone, as if it gave him pleasure to insult me, he measured me from head to foot and shouted: "Do you really expect the monsignor to leave his coffee on your account?" Then I, too, shouted, but still louder than he did: "Let me tell you that I spit on your monsignor's coffee! If you won't take care of my passport this very moment, I'll go and see him myself."

"What! When the Cardinal is there with him!" cried the little abbé, backing away from me in horror. Then he rushed to the door, spread his arms wide, and stood there like a cross, with an air of being ready to die rather than let me through.

3. French newspaper founded in 1859 with the support of Napoleon III. Policy of opposition to Russian oligarchy.

To which I responded that I was a heretic and a barbarian, "que je suis hérétique et barbare," and that I did not care a bit for all his archbishops, cardinals, monsignors, etc., etc. In short, I let him know that I wasn't giving up. The abbé gave me a look full of the deepest hatred, then snatched my passport from me and took it upstairs. A minute later I had my visa. Here, would you care to see it? And I took out my passport and showed the Roman visa.[4]

"You should, however," the General began . . .

"What saved you was that you declared yourself a barbarian and a heretic," the little Frenchman remarked, with a smile. "Cela n'était pas si bête."

"Really, why should I model myself on our Russians here? Here they are, sitting around not daring to utter a word and ready, I suppose, to deny that they are Russians. At my Paris hotel, at least, they began to treat me much more attentively after I had told them about my run-in with the abbé. A fat Polish *pan*,[5] my greatest enemy at the table d'hôte, faded away into the background. The Frenchmen even showed no resentment when I told them that two years ago I had met a man at whom, in 1812, a French *chasseur*[6] had fired simply in order to discharge his rifle. The man was then a child of ten, and his family had not managed to leave Moscow in time.

"That's impossible," the little Frenchman shouted, flying into a rage; "a French soldier wouldn't fire at a child!"

"Yet it happened," I answered. "The man who told me this story was a most respectable retired captain, and I saw the bullet scar on his cheek myself."

The Frenchman now began talking rapidly and at great length. The General made an effort to back him up,

---

4. See reference to this scene in Polina Suslova's diary, p. 214, below.
5. Polish word meaning "lord" or "mister."
6. "Rifleman" or "infantryman."

but I suggested that he read, for instance, some excerpts from the memoirs of General Perovsky,[7] who was a prisoner of the French in 1812. Finally, Maria Filippovna started talking about something else to change the subject. The General was very much displeased with me, for the Frenchman and I had almost shouted at each other. But Mr. Astley apparently enjoyed my argument with the Frenchman very much. Getting up from the table, he asked me if I would like to have a glass of wine with him. That night I duly succeeded in having a talk with Polina Aleksandrovna. It lasted for about a quarter of an hour and took place while we were all out for a walk. We went to the park by the casino. Polina sat down on a bench facing the fountain and let Nadia play with some children not far away. I, too, let Misha run off to the fountain, and we were at last alone.

Business was discussed first, naturally. Polina was simply furious when I handed her only seven hundred gulden. She had been quite sure that I was going to pawn her diamonds in Paris for at least two thousand gulden, or even more.

"I absolutely need some money," she said, "and have to get it, or else I am simply lost."

I went on to ask her about what had happened during my absence.

"Nothing but two messages from Petersburg, first that Grandmother was very ill, and two days later, that she had, apparently, died. The news came from Timofei Petrovich," Polina added, "and he is a reliable man. We are expecting a final, definitive message."

"So everybody here is full of anticipation?" I asked.

7. V. A. Perovsky (1795–1857) reports in his memoirs that the French shot prisoners who were not able to keep with the marching columns. Portions of his memoirs were published in *Russky arkhiv* (Russian Archive), 1865, no. 3, pp. 257–86, where Dostoevsky probably read them.

"Of course, each and every one; this has been every-body's only hope for the past six months."

"Are you hoping too?" I asked.

"Why, I'm no relation of hers, I'm only the General's stepdaughter. But I am positively sure that she will remember me in her will."

"I would imagine that you might get a great deal," I said affirmatively.

"Yes, she was fond of me. But what makes *you* think so?"

"Tell me," I answered with a question, "our marquis, it seems, is also initiated into all family secrets?"

"And what about you, why are you so interested in this?" asked Polina, giving me a cold and stern look.

"Of course I'm interested! If I'm not entirely wrong, the General has already managed to borrow some money from him."

"You have guessed quite correctly."

"Well, do you think that he would have given him any money if he had not known about Grandmother? Did you notice at dinner: some three times he referred to Grandmother as *babulenka:* '*la baboulinka*.'[8] What intimate and cordial relations!"

"Yes, you are right. The moment he finds out that I, too, have inherited something from her, he will immediately propose to me. Is that what you wanted to know?"

"So he will propose? I thought that he had been proposing to you for a long time."

"You know perfectly well that isn't true!" Polina said testily. "Where did you meet the Englishman?" she added after a moment's silence.

"I *knew* that you were going to ask about him!"

I told her about my previous meetings with Mr. Astley

8. Affectionate diminutive for "grandmother."

on my journey. "He is bashful and romantic, and, quite naturally, in love with you, isn't he?"

"Yes, he is in love with me," answered Polina.

"And also quite naturally, he is ten times as rich as the Frenchman. Do you think that the Frenchman really has something? Isn't that open to doubt?"

"No, it is not. He has some sort of château. Only yesterday the General mentioned it to me quite positively. Well, are you satisfied?"

"If I were you I would definitely marry the Englishman."

"Why?" asked Polina.

"The Frenchman is more handsome, but he is a lower sort. And the Englishman, besides being honest, is ten times as rich," I snapped.

"Yes, but on the other hand, the Frenchman is a marquis and more clever," she answered in the calmest manner possible.

"Are you sure?" I continued, in the same vein.

"Absolutely."

Polina didn't like my questions at all, and I could see that she was trying to make me angry by the tone and the absurdity of her answers. All of which I let her know at once.

"Well now, it really amuses me to see you getting worked up about this. You ought to pay for the mere fact that I'm allowing you to ask such questions and to make such suppositions."

"As a matter of fact, I do consider myself entitled to ask you all kinds of questions," I answered calmly, "precisely because I am ready to pay any price for them, and my life means nothing to me now."

Polina burst out laughing.

"You told me last time at the Schlangenburg that you were ready at a single word from me to throw yourself down head first, and it's a thousand-foot drop there, I think. Some day I shall say the word, just to see how you pay your debts, and you can be sure that I'll stand firm. I loathe you, precisely because I have allowed you so much, and I loathe you even more because I need you so. But for the time being I need you, and so I must spare you."

She got up. She had spoken with irritation. Of late she would invariably end up irritated and hating me after talking to me, truly hating me.

"Allow me to ask, what about Mademoiselle Blanche?" I asked, not wanting to let her go without an explanation.

"You know all about Mademoiselle Blanche yourself. Nothing has happened since. Mademoiselle Blanche is probably going to be the General's wife, that is, of course, if the rumor of Grandmother's death is confirmed, for Mademoiselle Blanche, her mother, and her third cousin the marquis, they all know very well that we are ruined financially."

"And is the General hopelessly in love?"

"That does not matter now. Listen and remember: take these seven hundred florins and go gambling. Win for me as much as you can at roulette; I need some money now, come what may."

Having said this, she called Nadia and walked away toward the casino, where she joined the rest of the party. I turned into the first path to the left, thinking and wondering. I felt as if someone had hit me over the head, after her orders to play roulette for her. Strange thing: there was plenty for me to think about, yet I lost myself in analyzing my reactions to my feelings for Polina. Actually, I felt better during those two weeks away from her than now, on the day of my return, even though I had been constantly fretting and had run about like a madman, even dreamed of her all the time. Once (that was in Switzerland) I fell asleep on the train and, it seems, started talking aloud to Polina, to the amusement of all the other passengers. And so again I asked myself the question, "Do I love her?" And again I found myself unable to answer it, or, rather, for the hundredth time I answered to myself that I hated her. Yes, she was hateful to me. There were moments (especially every time we concluded one of our conversations) when I would have gladly given half my life for the privilege of strangling her! I swear that if I had been given a chance to bury a sharp knife slowly in her breast, I probably would have reached for that knife with relish. Yet I swear by all that is sacred that if she had really told me, up there at Schlangenberg's tourist point, to throw myself down, I would have done so at once, and even relished it, too. I knew that. One way or another, this thing had to be settled. All this she understands amazingly well, and the thought that I knew, quite positively and distinctly, how utterly beyond reach she was for me, this thought, I am convinced, gave her extraordinary pleasure. Why else would she, a prudent and clever girl, be on so intimate and open terms with me? Up to now she seemed to look on me as if she were that empress of antiquity who began to undress before her slave because she did not consider him a man. Yes, many a time she has refused to look on me as a man . . .

I had her command, however, to win at roulette, come what may. I had no time to give any thought to why or how soon I had to win, or what new scheme had taken shape in that ever calculating brain of hers. Moreover, there had apparently developed, in the course of these two weeks, a multitude of new facts of which I had yet no idea. I had to figure it all out and try to get to the bottom of things as quickly as possible. But at this point there was no time for it; I had to go and play roulette.

Two

I must admit that I didn't like the idea. Though I had decided that I was going to do some gambling, I wasn't at all inclined to start it by playing for somebody else. It actually threw me off a bit, and so I entered the gambling hall with a most disagreeable feeling. From the first glance I disliked everything about it. I hate those corny feuilletons in newspapers the world over, but especially in our Russian newspapers, in which the same two stories are told over and over again each spring: first, about the extraordinary magnificence and luxury of the casinos of the gambling towns on the Rhine, and second, about piles of gold which are supposedly lying on the gaming tables. I am sure that the columnists are not even paid for this, but tell such stories simply from disinterested compliance. There is nothing magnificent at all about these shabby halls, and as for gold, not only are there no piles of it lying on the tables, but there is hardly any of it at all to be seen. Of course, once in a while, during the season, some eccentric or other will show up, either an Englishman or an Asiatic of some kind, like a Turk, as was the case this summer, and will suddenly lose or win a lot. Everybody else plays for a few paltry gulden, and on the average there is very little money lying on the tables. When I first entered the gaming hall (it was the first time in my life) I couldn't make myself play right away. Besides, it was very crowded. But even if I had been there all by myself, I think that even then I'd rather have left than started to play. I confess my heart was beating hard, and I was far from cool and composed. I knew then, as I had known a long time before, that something would happen to me in Roulettenburg, that there would be something, quite without fail, which would affect my destiny radically and definitively. So it must be and so it will be. Ridiculous though it is for me to expect so much much of the roulette wheel, the conventional opinion, held by everybody, that it is foolish and absurd to expect anything of gambling seemed even more ridiculous. Why should'gambling be worse than any other means of making money, such as business, for instance? It is true that only one out of a hundred wins. But what do I care about that?

Anyway, I decided to size things up first and not to try anything serious that night. Even if something did happen that night, it would happen as if by accident and be of little consequence, and I bet my money accordingly. Besides, I had to study the game itself, in spite of thousands of descriptions of roulette which I had read avidly over the years, I understood nothing of how it worked, until I saw it myself.

In the first place, it all struck me as so very sordid, somehow, morally rotten and sordid. I am not speaking at all about the greedy and troubled faces which by the dozens, or even by the hundreds, crowd around the gaming tables. I can see absolutely nothing sordid about a person's desire to win as quickly and as much as possible. I always felt that it was stupid, that answer of a well-fed and prosperous moralist to a man who justified himself by saying that "the game was for very small stakes": So much the worse, for then it is petty covetousness." As if there were any difference between petty covetousness and covetousness on a large scale. It is a matter of proportion. What is a paltry sum to a Rothschild is great wealth to me, and as for profit and gain, people try to take or win something from one another not only at roulette but everywhere. Whether or not profit and gain are immoral as a matter of principle is a different question. I am not going to solve it here. Since I was myself possessed by a very intense desire to win some money, all this covetousness and all this sordid greed seemed, if you like, even rather friendly and agreeable, as I entered the hall. It is so much more pleasant when people don't stand on ceremony but act candidly and informally. And, indeed, why should one deceive oneself? A most frivolous and extravagant pursuit! One thing that struck me as particularly unpleasant, at first sight, about the riffraff lining the roulette tables, was their respect for the business at hand, the seriousness and even reverence with which they all were crowding around the tables. This is why a sharp distinction is drawn here between the kind of game which is called *mauvais genre,* and the kind which a decent person might indulge in. There are two kinds of gambling: the genteel kind, and the plebeian or mercenary, such as that played by all sorts of riffraff. The distinction is sternly observed here, and how base it really is! A gentleman, for example, may bet five or ten louis d'or, rarely more, though he may bet as much as a thousand francs if he is very rich, but solely for the sake of the game as such, simply for amusement, and actually only in order to watch the process of winninw or losing. only in order to watch the process of winning or losing. winning per se. If he wins, he may, for instance, laugh aloud, he may remark something to one of the bystanders, he may even place another bet or double his stakes, but solely out of curiosity, for the sake of watching the

chances, or even calculating them, never out of a plebeian desire to win. In a word, he must look upon all these
gaming tables, roulette wheels, and trente et quarante
sets as no more than a pastime, arranged entirely for his
amusement. He must not even suspect the existence of
the mercenary motives and snares upon which the bank
is founded and built. In fact, it wouldn't be a bad idea
at all if he thought, for instance, that all this rabble, trembling over a gulden, were men of great wealth and gentlemen entirely like himself, and that they too, were
gambling solely for their diversion and entertainment.
Such total ignorance of the actual state of affairs and
such an innocent view of people would be, of course, exceedingly aristocratic. I have seen many a mother push
forward her innocent and elegant daughter, a lass of fifteen or sixteen, give her a few gold coins, and teach her
how to play. The young would win or lose, invariably
with a smile, and leave the table very well pleased. Our
General walked up to the table solidly and with dignity.
An attendant rushed to offer him a chair, but he didn't
notice him, spent a long time taking out his wallet, then
an equally long time producing from it three hundred
francs in gold, put them on black, and won. He did not
pick up his winnings, but left them on the table. Black
came out again. He let it ride again, and when it was red
the next time around he had lost twelve hundred francs
at one stroke. He walked away with a smile, keeping his
composure. I am positive that he was sick at heart, and if
the bet had been two or three times higher he would not
have remained so cool but would have betrayed his
excitement. However, I was present when a Frenchman
won, and then lost, as much as thirty thousand francs
gaily and without getting in the least excited. A true
gentleman doesn't get excited even when he loses his
entire fortune. Money must be so much below a gentle-

man's dignity as to be hardly worth bothering about. Of course it would be highly aristocratic to ignore completely the sordidness of all this motley rabble and of this entire setting. Sometimes, however, the opposite approach may be no less aristocratic: to take notice of all the rabble, that is, take an occasional look at them, or even examine them, say, through a lorgnette, though never in any manner other than to take the whole crowd and all the filth for a diversion of sorts, something like a spectacle staged for the amusement of gentlemen. One may jostle with people in the crowd, yet one must look around with the absolute conviction that one is really only an observer and certainly in no way a part of it. However, one should also make sure not to study the crowd too intently; that would again be ungentlemanly because the spectacle is, in any case, not worthy of much, or excessively close, attention. As a matter of fact, there are few spectacles which deserves a gentleman's exceedingly close attention. Meanwhile it seemed to me personally that all this was certainly worth some very close obsevation indeed, especially for one who had come not just as an observer but considered himself, sincerely and in all honesty, to be a part of the rabble. As for my innermost moral convictions, there is no place for them, of course, in my present reasoning. I'll leave it at that. I am saying this to relieve my conscience. But I would like to take notice of one thing: of late I have been finding it somehow extremely repulsive to apply any kind of moral standard to my actions and thoughts. I was guided by something quite different . . .

It is true that the rabble play very dirtily. In fact, I am inclined to believe that a great deal of the most ordinary thievery goes on at the gaming tables. The croupiers who are seated at each end of the table check the stakes and pay the winnings, which keeps them terribly busy.

What a rabble! For the most part they are French. I make these observations, however, and am taking mental notes not because I would like to describe the game of roulette, certainly not. I am trying to get the hang of it for my own purpose, and so I'll know how to work it in the future. I noticed, for example, that nothing was more common than for somebody else's hand to reach out and grab one's winnings. There would be an argument, often some shouting, and "Would you, please, kindly prove, or find witnesses, that this was really your bet!"

At first the whole thing was Greek to me. All I could guess and figure out was that you could bet your money on numbers, on odd and even, and on the colors. I decided to risk a hundred gulden of Polina Aleksandrovna's money that night. The thought that I was not going to play for myself somehow distracted me. It was an extremely unpleasant sensation, and I wanted to get rid of it as soon as possible. I kept thinking that by playing for Polina I would be spoiling my own luck. Can one even as much as touch a gaming table without becoming immediately infected with superstition? I started by taking out fifty gulden, and placing them on even. The wheel spun around and out came thirteen; I had lost. With a vaguely sick feeling, solely in order to get it over with and leave, I bet fifty more gulden on red. Out came red. I placed a hundred gulden on red, and it was red again. I put it all on red, and it was red again. Having collected four hundred gulden, I bet two hundred on the second dozen, not knowing what would come of it. I was paid three times my stake. In this way, instead of one hundred I had suddenly eight hundred gulden. I felt overcome by a strange and unusual feeling which I found so unbearable that I decided to leave. It appeared to me that I would have played quite differently if I had been playing for myself.

Nevertheless, I staked the whole eight hundred on even once more. This time four came out. Another eight hundred was poured out to me, and, having gathered up my whole pile of sixteen hundred gulden, I left to look for Polina Aleksandrovna.

They were all out for a walk somewhere in the park, and I wasn't able to see her until supper. This time the Frenchman was not around, and the General was in fine fettle. Among other things he thought fit to let me know once more that he did not wish to see me at the gaming tables. In his opinion, it would compromise him greatly if by any chance I were to lose badly. "But even if you were to win a lot, even in that case I'd be compromised," he added significantly. "Of course, I have no right to dictate your actions, but you must agree . . . " He left the phrase incomplete, as was his habit. I answered, drily, that I had very little money and that, consequently, I couldn't possibly lose too conspicuously, even if I were to play. Going upstairs to my room I managed to hand Polina her winnings and let her know that I wouldn't play for her again.

"But why not?" she asked anxiously.

"Because I want to play for myself," I answered, looking at her with surprise, "and playing for you interferes with playing for myself."

"So you are still absolutely convinced that roulette is your only solution and salvation?" she asked derisively. I answered, again very seriously, that I was. As for my being so certain that I was going to win, let it be ridiculous, I'd agree with that, "but why don't you leave me alone."

Polina Aleksandrovna insisted that I keep half of today's winnings and tried to make me accept eight hundred gulden, suggesting that I continue to play on those terms. I refused the half, resolutely and definitely, and declared that I couldn't play for other people, not because I didn't want to, but because I would surely lose.

"And yet I, too, as stupid as it may seem, see virtually my only hope in roulette," she said thoughtfully. "And this is why you must absolutely go on playing, half and half with me, and of course you will." Here she left me, without listening to my further objections.

Three

*A*ll the next day she did not say one word to me about gambling. In fact, she avoided having any word with me. The manner in which she treats me has not changed. The same absolute nonchalance on meeting me, and even something contemptuous and hostile in her mien. She doesn't bother to hide her aversion to me at all, this I can see. But she also does not conceal from me either the fact that she needs me for some purpose and that she is saving me for some future use. A kind of strange relationship has developed between us which, in many ways, I cannot fathom, considering her pride and haughtiness with everyone. She knows, for instance, that I am madly in love with her, actually allows me to speak of my passion; surely there couldn't be a better way to show her contempt for me than to permit me to speak to her of my love so freely and unrestrictedly. "That is to say," she tells me, "that your feeling mean so little to me I couldn't care less what you're telling me, or what your feelings are toward me." As for her own affairs, she had already discussed them with me before, though never with full sincerity. What is more, her disdainful treatment of my person included, for instance, the following subtleties: she would know, let's say, that I was familiar with a certain circumstance in her life, or knew of some

23

matter which was greatly worrying her; in fact, she would tell me herself something about her circumstances, whenever it was opportune to use me for her ends, like a slave, or to run errands for her; but she would tell me exactly as much as a man employed on her errands need know; and, seeing herself how worried and anxious I was about her worries and anxieties, what with the whole chain of events being obscure to me, she would not deign to reassure me of her full confidence as a friend. Though, inasmuch as she would use me often for errands which were not only troublesome but outright dangerous, more candor on her part ought to, in my opinion, have been in order. Indeed, why bother about my feelings? What of it if I was, perhaps, worried too, and feeling three times as troubled and anxious about her troubles and failures as she was herself?

I had known about her intention to play roulette as early as three weeks before. She had given me advance notice that I would have to play in her stead, since it would be improper for her to do any gambling herself. From the tone of her words I gathered, even then, that she had a serious problem rather than a simple desire to win some money. What could money as such mean to her? There must be some purpose, there must be certain circumstances, at which I can only guess, but of which I know nothing so far. Of course, the humiliation and slavery in which she keeps me could give me a chance, and often does, to ask rude and direct questions of her. Since I am only her slave and utterly insignificant in her eyes, there is no reason for her to take offense at my crude curiosity. But the fact of the matter is that while she allows me to ask questions, she doesn't answer them. Sometimes she doesn't even notice them. That's what it's like between us!

Yesterday there was a lot of talk about a telegram which

had been sent to Petersburg four days earlier and to which no reply had been received. The General is obviously upset and is doing a lot of thinking. It is, of course, connected with Grandmother. The Frenchman is upset too. Yesterday, for example, they had a long and serious conversation after dinner. The Frenchman's attitude toward all of us is exceedingly haughty and condescending. To this, the saying applies: "Seat [a pig] at the table, and he will soon put his feet on it." Even with Polina he is casual to the point of being rude. However, he most happily takes part in our family outings, on foot in the casino park or on horseback and by carriage in the nearby countryside. I have been familiar, for some time, with some of the circumstances which tie the Frenchman to the General. In Russia they made plans together to start a factory. I don't know whether this project has fallen through, or whether they are still discussing it. Besides, I am in on a part of their family secret: the Frenchman realy did bail out the General last year, giving him thirty thousand to make up a shortage in a government account on the occasion of the General's resignation from his post. It goes without saying that he has got the General in his clutches. Yet at the present moment, it is still Mlle Blanche who plays the main role in this whole business, and I am quite sure that I am not mistaken about that.

Who is this Mlle Blanche? In our circle it is assumed that she is of the French nobility, that she is traveling with her mother, and that she has a huge fortune. It is also known that she is somehow related to our marquis, though very distantly, being his second cousin or something of the sort. I gather that before my trip to Paris, the Frenchman and Mlle Blanche were on much more formal terms with each other, on a more refined and delicate footing, one might have said. But now their social relations, their mutual attitudes as friends and relatives, have acquired a rather coarse and intimate character. It may well be that our affairs look so extremely wretched to them that they don't even think it's very important to stand on ceremony or to keep up appearances before us. The day before yesterday I noticed how Mr. Astley was looking at Mlle Blanche and her mother. I had the impression that he knew them. It seemed to me that even our Frenchman has met Mr. Astley before. Mr. Astley is so shy, bashful, and taciturn, however, that one can be almost sure of him; he won't wash anybody's dirty linen in public. At any rate the Frenchman barely says hello to him and pays almost no attention to him, which means that he is not afraid of him. One can understand that, but why does Mlle Blanche pay almost no attention to him either? Especially considering the fact that the marquis let out the secret yesterday: he suddenly said, in the course of a general conversation, I forgot in what connection, that Mr. Astley is colossally rich, which he, the marquis, knew for a fact. So Mlle Blanche ought to have ample reason to pay some attention to Mr. Astley! All things considered, the General looks very worried. One can understand what a telegram announcing his aunt's death could mean to him!

Though I felt fairly certain that Polina was avoiding a conversation with me, and apparently for a purpose, I assumed a cool and indifferent air myself: I kept thinking that sooner or later she'd have to come to me. Instead, yesterday and today, I've been concentrating my attention mostly on Mlle Blanche. Poor General, he is most definitely done for! To fall in love at fifty, with such violence of passion, is of course a calamity. Add to this his widowerhood, his children, a completely ruined estate, debts, and, on top of it, the kind of woman he has had the misfortune to fall in love with. Mlle Blanche is a beautiful woman. Yet I don't know whether I'll be properly under-

stood if I say that she has one of those faces which one
might feel frightened of. At least I have always feared
such women. She must be about twenty-five. She is tall,
with broad, strong shoulders. Her neck and bosom are
magnificent. Her complexion is a swarthy yellow, her
hair raven black, and she's got a great deal of it, enough
for two coiffures. Her eyes are black with yellowish whites,
her look insolent, her teeth very white, and her lips always painted. Her perfume smells of musk. She dresses
spectacularly, expensively, and with chic, yet with much
taste. Her hands and feet are a marvel. Her voice is a
husky contralto. Sometimes she will laugh aloud, showing her teeth, but as a rule she wears an uncommuni-
cative and insolent expression on her face, at least in
the presence of Polina and Maria Filippovna. (There
is a strange rumor: Maria Filippovna is returning to
Russia.) I think that Mlle Blanche is wholly uneducated,
perhaps not even clever, but she is cunning and always on
her guard. I would imagine that her life has not been
totally uneventful. And, to tell the whole truth, it may
well be that the marquis is not her relative at all, and that
her mother is not her mother. But there is evidence that
in Berlin, where we first met them, she and her mother
had some reputable acquaintances. As for the marquis
himself, though I still doubt that he is a marquis, it
seems to be an indubitable fact that he is received in decent society, as for instance, in Moscow, and in some
places in Germany. I wonder, though, about France?
They say that he owns a château. I had thought that
much water would flow under the bridge in those two
weeks, and yet I still don't know for sure whether anything definitive has been said between Mlle Blanche and
the General. By and large, everythnig now depends on
our fortune, that is, whether or not the General will be
able to show them a lot of money. If, for instance, news

were to come that Grandmother had not died, I am positive that Mlle Blanche would disappear immediately. I
find it amazing and quite funny myself what a gossip I've
become, haven't I? Oh, how repulsive it is, all of it! With
what relish would I get rid of all of them, and all of it!
But how could I leave Polina? How could I quit my spying on her? Spying is base, of course, but what do I care!

I was quite intrigued by Mr. Astley, also, yesterday and
today. Yes, I am convinced that he is in love with Polina!
It is curious and funny to see how much the glance of a
bashful and painfully chaste man, very much in love,
may sometimes express, particularly when that man
would certainly much rather be swallowed by the earth
than betray or express anything at all, by word or glance.
We often meet Mr. Astley on our walks. He takes off his
hat and walks on, though he is dying, of course, to join
us. And, whenever invited to do so, he immediately refuses. Wherever we go to take the air, around the casino,
at the bandshell, or by the fountain, he'll be seen standing, quite without fail, not far from our bench; and no
matter where we might be, in the park, in the forest, or
on the Schlangenberg, all one has to do is raise one's
eyes and scan the landscape, and there, sure enough, on
the nearest footpath or behind a bush a piece of Mr.
Astley will pop up. I am under the impression that he is
looking for an opportunity to talk to me personally. This
morning we met and exchanged a few words. On occasion
he will speak somehow very abruptly. Having barely said
"good morning," he said straightaway:

"Ah, Mademoiselle Blanche! . . . I have seen many
women like Mademoiselle Blanche!"

He paused, giving me a significant look. I don't know
what he wanted to say by that, because when I asked him
"what do you mean by this?" he only nodded his head

with a sly smile and added: "That's the way it is. Is
Mademoiselle Pauline very fond of flowers?"

"I don't know, I don't know at all," I answered.

"What? You don't know that either!" he cried, greatly
astonished.

"I don't know, I just never noticed," I repeated, laughing.

"H'm! That gives me something very special to think
about." Here he nodded his head and walked on. He
looked very pleased, though. He and I converse in the
most dreadful French.

Four

*T*oday was a funny, grotesque, absurd day. It is now eleven o'clock at night. I am sitting in my little room, reviewing it. It all started with my having to go to the casino to play for Polina Aleksandrovna. I took all of her sixteen hundred gulden, but under two conditions: first, that we were not going to play it fifty-fifty, if I win, that is, and second, that Polina would explain to me that same night why she needed to win some money, and how much precisely. I simply cannot make myself believe that it is just the money. Apparently the money is needed, as quickly as possible, for some particular purpose. She promised to tell me, and I went. It was tremendously crowded in the gambling halls. How shameless and how greedy all these people are! I forced my way to the very middle and stood right next to the croupier. Then I began timidly trying my game, betting two or three coins at a time. Meanwhile, I was watching and I noticed a thing or two. It seemed to me that calculating your chances really means rather little, and certainly isn't as important as some gamblers make it out to be. They sit there with sheets of graph paper before them, mark every stroke, reckon, compute the odds, calculate, and finally place their bets. Then they lose, exactly as we simple mortals who play without calculating anything.

But then again, I came to one conclusion which is, I think, correct: there is in fact, though not a system, some sort of order in the sequence of fortuitous chances—which is, of course, very strange indeed. For instance, it will happen that after twelve straight numbers from the second dozen, the third dozen will finally come up; twice, let's say, it will hit there, then switch to the first dozen. Having fallen on the first dozen only once, it will then return to the second dozen with three or four straight hits, whereupon it is once more the third dozen with two straight numbers, and back to the first dozen for a single time, and again three straight hits in the middle, and so on and on in the same fashion for an hour and a half or two hours. One, three, and two; one, three, and two. This is very amusing. There will be a day, or a morning, for example, where red and black will alternate almost without any order, shifting every moment, so that red or black won't turn up more than twice or three times in succession. Next day, or next night, it will be nothing but red. It will happen that red, for instance, will come up as many as twenty-two times in a row, and that it will continue that way for some length of time, say, the whole day. I learned a great deal about these things from Mr. Astley, who spent the whole morning at the gaming tables without once placing a bet. As for myself, I lost every penny I had, and very quickly, too. I put two hundred gulden on even right off the bat, and won, bet another five and won again, and so two or three more times. I think I must have picked up about four thousand gulden in five minutes or so. This is where I should have quit, but some kind of strange sensation built up in me, a kind of challenge to fate, a kind of desire to give it a flick on the nose, or stick out my tongue at it. I placed the largest bet allowed, four thousand gulden, and lost. Then, flushed with my loss, I took out all the money I still had left, staked it on the same spot, and lost again, after which I walked away from the table, stunned. I actually couldn't comprehend that it was I to whom this had just happened, and I didn't tell Polina Aleksandrovna of my losing until a while later, shortly before dinner. In the meantime I wandered through the park aimlessly.

At dinner I was again in an excited frame of mind, just as three days earlier. The Frenchman and Mlle Blanche were dining with us again. It turned out that Mlle Blanche had been at the casino in the morning and had witnessed my exploits. Since she was talking to me this time, she seemed to be paying more attention to what I was saying. The Frenchman took a shorter way and simply asked me if I had really lost my own money. Apparently he suspects Polina. In short, there is something going on here. I lied without hesitating, saying that it was my money.

The General was extremely surprised: where did I get that kind of money? I explained that I started out with one hundred gulden, that six or seven straight wins, doubled, had brought me up to five or six thousand gulden, whereupon I had lost everything in two turns.

All this, of course, sounded plausible enough. As I was explaining it I stole a glance at Polina, but could make out nothing from her face. She let me go through with my lying, however, and did not set me right, from which I concluded that I was correct in telling my lie and that it was to remain a secret that I had played for her. In any case, I thought to myself, she owes me an explanation and promised me only this morning to reveal something to me.

I had thought that the General would reprimand me somehow, but he said nothing. However, I noticed a worried and uneasy expression on his face. Perhaps in his straitened circumstances it was simply painful to him to sit there and hear how such a respectable pile of gold had, within a quarter of an hour, come into and passed out of the hands of an improvident fool such as I.

I suspect that he had a rather hot encounter with the Frenchman last night. They were shut up together for a long time, talking heatedly about something. The Frenchman left looking irritated, and early this morning he came back to see the General again, very likely to continue yesterday's conversation.

Having listened to the story of my gambling loss, the Frenchman remarked caustically, even spitefully, that I ought to have had more sense than that. I don't know why he had to add that, though a great many Russians were gamblers, Russians were, in his opinion, lacking in talent even for gambling.

"Yet in my opinion, roulette is simply made for Russians," I said; and when the Frenchman responded to my comment with a contemptuous sneer, I observed that surely I had to be right, since by saying that Russians were gamblers I was certainly abusing them far more than praising them, so there was no reason to doubt my statement.

"And on what do you base your opinion?" asked the Frenchman.

"On the fact that the faculty of amassing capital has become, through a historical process, virtually the main point in the catechism of the virtues and qualities of civilized Western man. A Russian, on the other hand, is not only incapable of amassing any capital, but even when he squanders it, does so to no purpose and in hideously bad form. Nevertheless we Russians need money, too," I added, "and consequently are very fond of, and susceptible to, methods such as, for example, roulette, allowing one to get rich suddenly, in two hours, and without work. We find this exceedingly alluring. And since we gamble to no purpose, and also without real effort, we tend to be losers!"

"You may be right to some extent," the Frenchman remarked smugly.

"No, you are not right, and you ought to be ashamed to speak like that of your country," observed the General, sternly and with authority.

"For goodness' sake!" I answered, "really, who can tell which of the two is more repulsive, Russian shapelessness and lack of discipline, or the German method of saving money by honest work?"

"What a monstrous thought!" exclaimed the General.

"What a Russian thought!" exclaimed the Frenchman.

I laughed. I wanted very much to provoke them.

"Personally, I would much rather spend my whole life in a Kirghiz nomad's tent," I cried, "than worship the German idol."

"What idol?" cried the General, getting angry in earnest.

"The German method of accumulating wealth. I've not been here long, but yet I must tell you that what I have managed to observe and to verify makes my Tatar blood boil. So help me, I want no part of these virtues! Yesterday I took a hike of six or seven miles around the countryside. I'm telling you, it's all exactly as in those edifying German picture books. They have here, in every house, a *Vater* who is extremely virtuous and extraordinarily honest. So honest you dare not go near him. I hate honest people whom one is afraid to approach. Every such *Vater* has a family, and in the evenings they read instructive books aloud to each other. Elms and chestnut trees rustle over the little house. Sunset, a stork on the roof, and all of it so extraordinarily poetic and touching . . .

"Please, don't get angry, General, and allow me to

make it as touching as possible. I can remember how my
own father, God bless his soul, used to read from similar
books to my mother and myself, and also under the lin-
den trees in our front garden . . . So I am in a position to
judge these things. Well then, each and every one of these
families around here is in a condition of complete servi
tude and submission to their *Vater*. They all work like
mules, and they all save money like Jews. Suppose *Vater*
has already saved up so-and-so-many gulden and is counting on his eldest son to take over his shop, or his piece of
land. And so the daughter is left without a dowry, and
she becomes an old maid. Also, the younger son is hired
out to slave for someone else, or is sold for a soldier, and
the money realized is added to the family fortune. This
is really done here; I've inquired about it. And all this is
done out of honesty alone, an honesty so intense that the
younger son, who has been sold, actually believes that he
was sold from out of honesty alone. And that's really
ideal when the victim himself rejoices as he is led away
to slaughter. What else? What is more, the eldest son isn't
any better off: he has found his Amalchen, and their
hearts are united, but he can't marry her, because they
haven't saved enough gulden yet. So they wait virtuously
and, sincerely and with a smile, let themselves be led to
slaughter. Amalchen's cheeks have already grown hollow,
and she is wasting away. Finally, in some twenty years or
so, their fortune has grown: a lot of gulden have been
saved, honestly and virtuously. *Vater* gives his blessings
to his forty-year-old firstborn and his thirty-five-year-old
Amalchen, her chest dried up and her nose red . . . As he
does so, he sheds tears, reads them a moral sermon, and
dies. The eldest son now becomes himself a virtuous
Vater, and the same story starts all over again. In fifty or
seventy years, the grandson of the first *Vater* has already
realized what amounts to a considerable capital, which

he proceeds to hand down to his son who, in turn, leaves it to his son, and he to his, so that after five or six generations you've got Baron Rothschild himself, or Hoppe and Company,[9] or the devil knows whom. Well, sir, isn't this a majestic spectacle: a hundred or two hundred years of continuous toil, patience, intelligence, honesty, character, firmness, economy, a stork on the roof! What more do you want? Why, you can't possibly top that. And so, from that standpoint they then begin to judge the whole world and to punish the guilty, meaning those who are in any way unlike them. Well, sir, that's what it amounts to; I'd much rather indulge in debauchery, Russian style, or make my fortune at roulette. I don't want to be Hoppe and Company in five generations. I need my money for myself. Nor am I willing to consider my person a necessary accessory to capital. I realize that I have been talking dreadful nonsense, but that's all right. Such are my convictions."

"I don't know whether there is much truth in what you've been saying," the General said thoughtfully, "but I know for certain that you begin to swagger insufferably the moment you are allowed to forget yourself even a little . . ."

As was his habit, he failed to finish the sentence. Whenever our General would broach a subject which was even slightly more significant than ordinary small talk, he could never finish his sentences. The Frenchman was listening casually, with rather wide-open eyes. He had understood almost nothing of what I had said. Polina was just looking, with a sort of haughty indifference. She seemed not to hear what I, or anyone else, was saying at table that day.

9. Famous bank of the time, with branches in Amsterdam and London.

Five

S he seemed unusually thoughtful, but immediately after we got up from the table she ordered me to escort her for a walk. We took the children and walked to the park toward the fountain.

Since I was in a particularly excited mood, I blurted out the following question, stupidly and rudely: why was it that our Marquis de Grieux, the little Frenchman, was not only not escorting her on the present occasion, or whenever she went out, but hadn't even talked to her for days?

"Because he is a scoundrel," she answered strangely. I had never heard her speak of de Grieux in that way and, being afraid to interpret such irritability on her part, said nothing in response.

"Did you notice that he was at odds with the General today?"

"You want to know what's going on," she responded, drily and irritably. "You know that the General is completely mortgaged to him; his whole property is his, and if Grandmother doesn't die, the Frenchman will immediately claim title to everything that is mortgaged to him."

"So it is really true that everything is mortgaged? I had heard about it, but did not know that absolutely everything was involved."

"How else could it be?"

"And on top of it, good-bye Mademoiselle Blanche," I observed. "She won't be the General's wife, then! You know what, it seems to me that the General is so much in love that he may, perhaps, shoot himself if she leaves him. At his age it is dangerous to be so in love."

"I also feel that something will happen to him," Polina Aleksandrovna remarked thoughtfully.

"How very beautiful!" I exclaimed. "There isn't a cruder way to show that she was marrying him only for his money. No attempt, even, to observe the rules of propriety, totally without ceremony, the whole thing. Just marvelous! And about Grandmother, could one imagine anything more comic and sordid than to keep sending telegram after telegram, asking: is she dead, is she dead? Eh? How do you like it, Polina Aleksandrovna?"

"That's all nonsense," she said disgustedly, interrupting me. "Rather, I am surprised about your being in such a cheerful mood. What are you so happy about? Perhaps because you lost all my money?"

"Why did you give it to me to lose? I told you that I couldn't play for other people, least of all for you. I do whatever you tell me to do, but I can't answer for the result. Didn't I warn you that it would all come to nothing? Tell me, are you very unhappy about losing so much money? Why do you need so much money?"

"Why these questions?"

"Didn't you promise to explain to me? . . . Listen, I am absolutely convinced that when I start playing for myself (I've got one hundred and twenty gulden) I'm going to win. Then you can borrow from me as much as you need."

Her face assumed a contemptuous expression.

"Don't be angry at my suggestion," I continued. "I am so imbued with the feeling that I'm a cipher before you, that is, a nonentity in your eyes, that I feel you could even accept money from me. You couldn't possibly take offense at a present from me. Besides, I lost yours."

She gave me a quick look, and seeing that I was speaking irritably and with sarcasm, cut me short once more:

"There is nothing that might interest you about my circumstances. If you want to know, I'm simply in debt. I owe some money and would like to pay it back. I had the crazy and strange idea that I was definitely going to win, here, at the gaming tables. Why I had this idea I can't understand, but I had faith in it. Who knows, perhaps I believed it because of all the alternatives, this was the only one left."

"Or because you *needed* to win so badly. It is just like a drowning man clutching at a straw. You must agree that if he were not drowning he would never take a straw for a branch of a tree."

Polina was surprised.

"Really?" she asked, "and aren't you counting on the same thing? Two weeks ago you told me at great length how you were absolutely convinced that you were going to win at roulette, right here, and that I shouldn't think you were crazy; or were you joking then? But I remember that you were so serious about it that it couldn't have been a joke."

"It is true," I answered thoughtfully, "I am still convinced that I am going to win. I must really admit that you have just made me ask myself a question: why is it that my failure today, muddleheaded and utterly disgraceful though it was, has not left the trace of a doubt in my mind? I am still fully convinced that as soon as I start playing for myself I'll most certainly win."

"Why are you so positive about it?"

"If you insist, I just don't know. I only know that I *must* win, also that it is the only way out that's left for me. Well, maybe that's why it seems to me that I'll win for sure."

"Is this to say that you, too, *need* it very badly, since you are so fanatically sure?"

"You probably doubt that I am capable of feeling a serious need?"

"I don't care," Polina answered quietly and indifferently. "If you insist, yes, I doubt that anything could ever worry you seriously. You may worry and be unhappy, but not seriously. You are a confused and unstable person. What do you want money for? There was nothing serious in any of the reasons you presented that time."

"Incidentally," I interrupted, "you said that you had to repay a debt. Must be some debt! Could it be to the Frenchman?"

"What a question! You're particularly sarcastic today. You aren't drunk by any chance, are you?"

"You know that I feel free to say anything, and that sometimes I ask very blunt questions. I repeat, I am your slave, and one isn't ashamed of slaves, a slave couldn't possibly insult you."

"All this is nonsense! And I can't stand that 'slave' theory of yours."

"Please note that I refer to my condition of servitude not because I like being your slave, but simply because it is a fact which I can't do anything about."

"Tell me straight, what do you need money for?"

"And why should I tell you?"

"As you please," she replied, tossing her head proudly.

"You can't stand my 'slave' theory, yet demand that I act as a slave. 'Answer, and no arguments!' All right, so be it. Why money, you're asking me? How can you ask that? Money is everything!"

"I understand. But you won't fall into such madness just wanting it! Why, you've reached a condition of absolute frenzy, where you care for nothing anymore. You must have some special object in mind. Tell me without beating about the bush, I wish it."

She seemed to be getting angry, and I was very pleased that she was interrogating me so testily.

"Of course there's an object," I said, "but I don't know how to explain what it is, really. Nothing more except that with money I'll be a different man, even for you, and not a slave."

"What? How do you think you'll achieve that?"

"How shall I achieve that? Why, you can't even imagine how I could ever make you look at me as anything but a slave! That's precisely what I don't care for, such astonishment and incredulity."

"Didn't you say that you were enjoying your slavery? I certainly thought so myself."

"Is that what you thought!" I cried, with a strange feeling of delight. "Oh, how beautiful your naiveté is! Oh, sure, sure, I enjoy being your slave. Oh, yes, yes, there is enjoyment in extreme degradation and insignificance!" I went on raving. "What the devil! Perhaps the whip is pleasurable when it is laid on your back, tearing your flesh to pieces . . . But perhaps I would like to try, for once, some other kind of enjoyment. The other day, at dinner and in your presence, the General gave me a lecture for those seven hundred rubles a year which I may not even get from him. The Marquis de Grieux keeps looking at me, eyebrows raised, yet at the same time takes no notice of me. Whereas I have perhaps a passionate desire to pull the Marquis de Grieux's nose in your presence!"

"What an immature youth! One can behave with dignity in any situation. And if it's hard, the struggle will make you grow in stature, not lower you."

"Straight from the copybook! Why won't you assume,

for a moment, that perhaps I merely don't know how to behave decently. That is, perhaps I am a decent person, but I just don't know how to behave like one. Do you understand that this may actually be the case? In fact, all Russians are like that, and you know why? Because Russians are too richly and many-sidedly endowed to find the proper form of behavior in a hurry. It's a matter of form. For the most part, we Russians are so richly endowed that, to know how to behave we need genius. Well, and much more often than not there simply isn't any genius available, since it's a very rare commodity. It is only among the French, and perhaps some other Europeans, that certain forms of behavior have been developed to such perfection that a man may very well have an air of the utmost dignity and yet be a quite worthless character. That's why good form means so much to them. A Frenchman will put up with an insult, a real, deep insult, without batting an eyelid, yet he won't put up with a tweak of the nose for anything, because that is a violation of their accepted forms of propriety, perpetuated by the ages. That's why our Russian ladies have such a weakness for Frenchmen—they have such good form. Though, as far as I'm concerned, they really haven't any form; it's just the rooster in them, *le coq gaulois*. However, I don't pretend that I can understand it; I'm not a woman. Perhaps, roosters are just great. And finally, I'm talking nonsense, and you aren't stopping me. Shut me up more often; whenever I talk to you I feel like telling you everything, just everything. I lose all my form. Actually, I'm ready to admit that I am lacking not only in good form, but in moral qualities of any kind as well. This is to let you know. In fact, I'm not worried about my moral qualities. Everything has come to a stop within me. You know yourself why. I haven't got one human idea in my head. It's a long time since I knew what was going on in the world, in Russia or here. I've been through Dresden and I don't even remember what Dresden was like. You know yourself what I'm all wrapped up in. Since I have no hope whatsoever and since I am a nonentity in your eyes, I'm telling you right out: I see nothing but you everywhere, and I don't care about the rest. I don't know why or how I love you. You know, perhaps you aren't beautiful at all? Imagine, I even don't know whether you are beautiful or not, even your face! Your soul, I'm sure, is not beautiful, and your mind ignoble. That may very well be."

"Perhaps that's why you count on buying me with money," she said, "because you don't believe in my noble soul?"

"When did I count on buying you with money?" I cried.

"You've let your tongue run away with you, and you've lost your thread. If you aren't thinking of buying me, you certainly think that you can buy my respect with money."

"Oh no, that's not quite the way I mean it. I've told you that I have trouble making myself clear. You are too much for me. Don't be angry at my jabbering. You can't be angry with me; I'm simply mad. However, what difference does it make? Go ahead and be angry. Upstairs in my little room, all I have to do is remember and imagine the rustle of your dress, and I'm ready to chew my own hands. So why are you angry with me? Because I called myself your slave? Go ahead and use me, use me as your slave, use me! Do you know that some day I am going to kill you? Kill you, not because I'll no longer love you, or from jealousy, no, simply kill you because sometimes I have the urge to devour you. You're laughing . . ."

"I'm not laughing at all," she said, enraged. "I order you to stop talking."

She stopped, almost breathless with anger. I swear it, I don't know if she was beautiful, but I always liked to look at her when she stood before me like that. That's why I liked often to provoke her anger. Perhaps she had noticed this, and so got angry on purpose. I went on to tell her all of this.

"What filth!" she exclaimed in disgust.

"I don't care," I continued. "You know, there's another thing; it is really dangerous for us to walk together: I'm often overcome by an irresistible urge to beat you up, to disfigure you, to strangle you. And don't be so sure it will never come to that. You are driving me mad. Do you think that I'd be afraid of the scandal? Your anger? What is your anger to me? I love you without any hope, and I know that after a thing like that, I'd love you a thousand times more. If I ever kill you, I shall have to kill myself also. Oh well, I'll put off killing myself as long as possible, so that I can feel the insufferable pain of being without you. I'll tell you something incredible: I love you *more* every day, even though that is almost impossible. After all this, how can I help being a fatalist? Remember, the day before yesterday, on the Schlangenberg, I whispered, provoked by you: 'Say the word, and I'll jump down into the abyss.' If you had said the word, I'd have jumped. Don't you believe that I would have jumped?"

"What stupid jabber!" she cried.

"I don't care if it is stupid or clever," I cried. "I know that in your presence I must talk, talk, talk, and so I talk. I lose all my self-respect when I'm with you, nor do I care if I do."

"Why should I make you jump off the Schlangenberg?" she said drily and in a peculiarly insulting manner. "That would be absolutely useless to me."

"Magnificent!" I cried. "You said your magnificent 'useless' on purpose, so as to crush me. I see through you. Useless, you say? Yet pleasure is always useful, and savage, unlimited power, if only over a fly, is also a kind of pleasure. Man is a despot by nature, and loves to be a tormentor. You love it, awfully."

I can remember she was looking at me with a sort of particularly fixed attention. It must be that my face was expressing all of my confused and absurd sensations. I remember now that our conversation that time went almost word for word as I have described it here. My eyes were bloodshot. I was beginning to foam at the mouth. And as for the Schlangenberg, I swear it, even today: if she had told me that day to fling myself down, I'd have flung myself down! If she had said it only in jest, in contempt, with a scoff, I'd still have jumped!

"Oh no, sure, I believe you," she uttered, but in a manner only she can sometimes say things, with such contempt and venom, with such arrogance that, by God, I could have killed her that very moment. She was taking a risk. I wasn't lying about that either.

"You are not a coward?" she asked me suddenly.

"I don't know, perhaps I am a coward. I don't know . . . I haven't thought of that in a long time."

"If I said to you, 'Kill this man,' would you kill him?"

"Whom?"

"Whomever I might choose."

"The Frenchman?"

"Don't ask questions, answer me. Whomever I point out to you. I want to know if you were speaking seriously right now." She was anticipating my answer so seriously and so impatiently that I suddenly felt very strange.

"Will you tell me, finally, what is going on here!" I cried. "Are you afraid of me, or something? I can see the whole mess myself. You are the stepdaughter of that mad and ruined man afflicted with a passion for that devil, Blanche. Then there is this Frenchman and his mysterious influence on you, and now you are asking me, in dead earnest, such a question. At least let me know, or else I'll go out of my mind and do something. Or are you ashamed to deign to draw me into your confidence? You couldn't possibly be ashamed of me!"

"That's not what I was talking about. I asked you a question, and I'm waiting for an answer."

"Of course I will kill," I cried, "anyone you tell me to, but could you possibly . . . could you actually tell me to do it?"

"What do you think? That I'd feel sorry for you? I'll just tell you to, and look on. Would you stand the test? Of course not, how could you? Perhaps you would actually kill, if I told you to, but then you would come back and kill me for having dared to make you do it."

I felt as though her words had gone to my head and stunned me. Naturally, even then I took her question for half-facetious, a challenge, perhaps. And yet she had said it too seriously. Nevertheless, I was quite struck by the frankness with which she had asserted her right over me, and her willingness to take such power over me, and the way she simply said, "Go and perish, while I look on." There was something so cynically outspoken about these words that I felt she had gone too far. So then, what did she really think of me? What she had said really went beyond slavery and insignificance. If you look at a man like that, you lift him up to your own level. And, absurd and implausible though our entire conversation had been, I felt a sudden throb in my heart.

Suddenly she burst out laughing. We were sitting on a bench, with the children playing before us, across from the place where carriages stopped to let off passengers headed for the parkway to the casino.

"Can you see that fat baroness?" she cried. "That is Baroness von Wurmerhelm. She arrived here three days ago. Do you see her husband, that tall, lean Prussian carrying a cane? Remember how he was looking at us the day before yesterday? Get up immediately, approach the Baroness, take off your hat, and say something to her in French."

"Why?"

"You swore that you would jump off the Schlangenberg. You swear that you are ready to kill a man, if I tell you. Instead of all these murders and tragedies, I just want a good laugh. I want no excuses, just go. I want to see how the Baron will thrash you with his cane."

"You are provoking me. Do you think that I won't do it?"

"Yes, I'm provoking you. Go, I want you to!"

"All right, I'm going, though this is a crazy idea. Only one thing: couldn't this make trouble for the General, and through him for you, too? I swear it, I'm not worried about myself, but about you, and, well, about the General. What an idea to go and insult a woman!"

"No, I can see that you're nothing but a windbag," she said contemptuously. "Your eyes were bloodshot a while ago, that's all. Though, perhaps only because you had too much wine at dinner. Do you think that I don't know that this is silly, and vulgar, and that the General will be angry? I simply want a good laugh. I want it, and that's all there is to it! And why should you insult a woman? And be thrashed with a cane, most probably."

I turned around and, without a word, went to carry out her orders. Of course, it was stupid and of course I was doing it only because I hadn't found a way out of it. But as I approached the Baroness, I remember how suddenly something within myself egged me on to go through with it, schoolboyish mischief, perhaps. Well, and besides I was terribly overwrought, as though I were drunk.

Six

*T*wo days have already passed since that stupid day. And how much fuss, noise, talk, and uproar there has been! And how confused, messy, stupid, and vulgar it was, and I the cause of it all. Yet at times it looks funny, to me at least. I can't really tell myself what has happened to me, whether I am really in a state of frenzy, or whether I've simply become unhinged and will continue in this way until they tie me up. Sometimes I have the feeling that I am going out of my mind. And then again, it seems to me that I haven't really outgrown my childhood, that there is a lot of the schoolboy in me, and that I am simply playing crude schoolboy pranks on people.

It is Polina, it is all Polina's fault! Perhaps there wouldn't have been any schoolboy pranks if it hadn't been for her. Who knows, maybe it is all from despair (how stupid of me, though, to reason that way). And I don't understand, I simply don't understand what I find in her. All right, she is beautiful, that she is; or it seems that she is. She drives other men out of their minds, too. She is tall and slender, though very slim. It seems as if one could tie her in a knot or bend her double. Her foot is long and narrow: tormenting. Exactly so: tormenting. Her hair has a reddish tint. Her eyes are regular cat's eyes, but how proudly and disdainfully she can look with them. About four months ago, when I had just started on my job, she had a long and heated conversation with de Grieux in the drawing room one night. And she was giving him that look . . . later, when I was going to bed, I imagined that she had slapped his face, slapped him that very moment, and that she was standing there and giving him that look . . . That night I fell in love with her.

However, back to business.

I walked down the path to the parkway and stood there, right in the middle, awaiting the Baroness and the Baron. When they were five paces from me, I lifted my hat and bowed.

I remember the Baroness was wearing a huge light gray dress, with ruffles and a crinoline and train. She is short and exceptionally stout, with an ugly, fat double chin, so that you can't see her neck at all. Her face is crimson. Her eyes small, malicious, and insolent. She walks as though she were doing everybody an honor by her presence. The Baron is tall and lean. His face, in the usual German manner, is taut and covered with thousands of fine wrinkles. He wears glasses. He is about forty-five. His legs start almost from his chest: that is "race" for you. Proud as a peacock. A little awkward. A certain sheepishness in the expression on his face, passing, in its own way, for profundity.

All this flashed across my eyes in three seconds.

My bow and the hat in my hand barely caught their attention at first. Only the Baron frowned slightly. The Baroness kept floating straight at me.

"Madame la Baronne," I said loudly and distinctly, rapping out each word, "j'ai l'honneur d'être votre esclave."[10]

Then I bowed, put on my hat, and walked past the

10. "I have the honor of being your slave."

Baron, politely turning my face toward him, and smiling.

Polina had told me to take off my hat, but the bow and the schoolboy behavior were of my own invention. The devil only knows what made me do it. I felt as though I had just jumped off a cliff.

"Hein!" cried, or rather croaked, the Baron, turning toward me in angry surprise.

I turned around and stopped in respectful expectation, continuing to look at him and smile. He was evidently puzzled by it all and had raised his eyebrows to a point *ne plus ultra*. His face grew more somber every moment. The Baroness also had turned in my direction and was staring at me in angry surprise. Some passersby were beginning to look. A few stopped.

"Hein!" the Baron croaked again, the guttural sound of his voice and his wrath redoubled.

"Ja wohl," I drawled, still looking him straight in the eye.

"Sind sie rasend?"[11] he cried, waving his cane and beginning, apparently, to feel a little scared. Perhaps my external appearance puzzled him. I was dressed very decently, even elegantly, like a man belonging to the best society.

"Ja wo-o-ohl!" I shouted suddenly at the top of my voice, drawling my *o* like the Berliners, who use the expression *ja wohl* all the time and drawl the letter *o* more or less, to convey various nuances of thought as well as of feeling.

The Baron and Baroness turned quickly and almost ran away in fright. Some of the spectators began to talk, others just stared at me in amazement. I don't remember it very well, though.

I turned and walked back to Polina Aleksandrovna

11. "Are you mad?"

with my ordinary stride. But as I came within a hundred paces of her bench I saw her get up and walk with the children in the direction of our hotel.

I caught up with her at the front entrance.

"I've performed . . . the foolishness," I said, as I reached her.

"Well, so what? Now see how you'll get out of it," she answered, without even giving me a look, and went upstairs.

I spent all that evening walking in the park. As I walked through the park and then through a forest, I actually crossed over into a different principality. I had some scrambled eggs and wine at a cottage. They charged me a whole thaler and a half for this idyllic repast.

It was eleven o'clock when I got back. I was immediately sent for by the General.

Our party occupied two suites at the hotel, four rooms altogether. The first is a large one, a salon with a piano in it. There is another large room next to it, which is the General's study. He was awaiting me there, standing in the middle of the room in an exceedingly majestic attitude. De Grieux was there, too, lolling on a sofa.

"My dear sir, allow me to inquire what you have been up to," the General began, addressing me.

"I'd very much like to get straight to the point, General," said I. "You apparently want to discuss my encounter with a certain German which took place today."

"A certain German?! That German is Baron Wurmerhelm, and a very important person, sir! You have been rude to him and the Baroness."

"Not in the least."

"You frightened them, dear sir!" cried the General.

"But no, not at all! It is just that, ever since we were in Berlin, that *ja wohl* of theirs, continually repeated in every sentence and drawled in such disgusting fashion, has been ringing in my ears. When I met this man in the park, this *ja wohl* suddenly came to my mind, I really don't know why, but it had an irritating effect on me . . . And besides, the Baroness, whom I have met three times so far, has the habit of walking straight at me, as if I were a worm to be trampled underfoot. You must admit that I, too, am entitled to some self-respect. I took off my hat and politely (let me assure you, politely) said: 'Madame, j'ai l'honneur d'être votre esclave.' When the Baron turned around and shouted, 'Hein!' I suddenly felt an impulse to shout back, 'Ja wohl!' That's what I did, twice: the first time in my ordinary voice, the second time as loud as I could. That is all."

I must confess I was terribly pleased with this exceedingly schoolboyish statement. I was driven by an amazingly strong desire to work this story to the hilt, giving it the most absurd twist I could think of.

And as I went on, I was really getting the taste of it.

"Are you making fun of me?" cried the General. He turned to the Frenchman and explained to him in French that I was positively going out of my way to provoke a scandal. De Grieux laughed contemptuously and shrugged his shoulders.

"Oh, please do not think so, far be it from me!" I cried, addressing the General. "Mine was of course a reprehensible act, which I am most sincerely willing to admit. It may be even called a foolish and improper schoolboy prank, but—nothing more. And you know, General, I regret it very much indeed. However, there is one circumstance which, at least in my own eyes, almost saves me even from the remorse which I should otherwise feel. Of late, for the past two or even three weeks, I have not been feeling well. I have been feeling ill, nervous, irritable, subject to strange fancies, and at times I have lost control of myself. Frankly, there have been moments when I had a terrible urge to address myself suddenly to the Marquis de Grieux and . . . However, I shall not complete this sentence, for he may perhaps feel offended. In short, these are signs of an illness. I do not know whether Baroness Wurmerhelm will take this fact into consideration when I beg her to forgive me (for I intend to beg her forgiveness). I suppose that she won't, especially since, as far as I know, this particular fact has been rather abused lately by the legal profession: counsels for the defense in criminal trials have taken to absolving their clients, the criminals, from any blame by arguing that they were unaware of what they were doing at the moment of their crime, since crime is a form of disease. 'He beat up so-and-so,' they say, 'but has no memory of it.' And imagine, General, medical theory actually supports them, affirming, in effect, that such a condition exists, that there is such a thing as temporary insanity, a condition in which a man may be almost totally unaware of what he is doing, or only half aware, or a quarter aware. However, the Baron and Baroness belong to the older generation and are, besides, *Junkers* and of the landed gentry. It may be assumed, therefore, that these advances in the world of jurisprudence and medicine have not as yet come to their attention, so that they may not accept my explanation. What do you think, General?"

"Enough, sir!" pronounced the General, sharply and barely restraining his indignation. "Enough! I will try once and for all to rid myself of your schoolboyish tricks. You will not apologize to the Baron and Baroness. Any contact with you, even if it were to consist solely of your offering them your apology, would be too much of an insult to them. The Baron, having been informed that you are a member of my household, has already had a talk with me at the casino, and let me tell you, it was touch and go for a moment whether or not he would ask me to give him satisfaction. Do you understand what you have subjected me to, me, my dear sir! I, I was forced to ask the Baron's pardon, and to give him my word that immediately, as of this very day, you would cease to be a member of my household . . ."

"Allow me, allow me, General, so it was he who insisted that I should cease absolutely to belong to your household, as it was your pleasure to put it just now?"

"No, but I felt obliged to give him this satisfaction, and, of course, the Baron was satisfied. My dear sir, we must part now. I owe you forty gulden and three florins in local currency. Here is the money, and here is your settlement, you can check it. Good-bye. From now on we shall be strangers. I've had nothing but trouble and unpleasantness from you. I will immediately call a waiter and tell him that, beginning tomorrow, I am no longer responsible for your hotel expenses. This concludes our conversation."

I took the money and the sheet of paper on which my settlement had been written in pencil, bowed to the General, and said to him very seriously:

"General, this matter cannot be concluded like this. I regret very much that you have suffered such unpleasantness from the Baron, but, forgive me, you must blame yourself for it. Why did you take it upon yourself to answer for me to the Baron? What is the meaning of the expression that 'I am a member of your household'? I am simply a tutor in your house, that's all. I am neither your son nor your ward, and you cannot be in any way responsible for my actions. I am a legally responsible person. I am twenty-five years of age, a university graduate, a nobleman, and I am no relation or associate of yours. If it were not for my boundless respect for your personal qualities, I should demand that you give me satisfaction on the spot, as well as a further, full explanation of why you took upon yourself the right to answer for me in this matter."

The General was so thunderstruck that he threw up his hands, then suddenly turned to the Frenchman and hurriedly informed him that I had just all but challenged him to a duel. The Frenchman burst out laughing.

"However, I have no intention of letting the Baron off," I continued with perfect sangfroid, not in the least embarrassed by M. de Grieux's laughter, "and inasmuch as you, General, by consenting today to listen to the Baron's complaints and professing an interest in this matter, have made yourself, as it were, a party in the whole affair, I have the honor to advise you that no later than tomorrow I shall ask the Baron, in my own name, to give me a formal explanation of the reasons which led him to address himself, in a matter which was strictly my concern, to another person, bypassing me, as if I were unfit or unworthy to answer for myself."

What I had foreseen actually happened: the General, upon hearing this new bit of nonsense, got cold feet, and badly.

"Why, do you really mean to keep this confounded business going?" he exclaimed. "How can you do this to me, my God! Don't dare, don't dare, sir, or, I swear . . . they have authorities here, too, and I . . . I . . . in short, considering my rank . . . and the Baron's, too . . . in short, you'll be arrested and deported by the police, for creating a disturbance! Do you understand this, sir?" And though he was breathless with anger, he was also terribly scared.

"General," I answered, with a composure quite insufferable to him, "you couldn't have me arrested for creating a disturbance before there has been one. I haven't as yet begun to make my explanations to the Baron, and you are at this time entirely ignorant of my intentions regarding the procedure which I shall follow or the grounds on which I'll proceed. What I wish to clear up is the assumption, insulting to me, that I am under the guardianship of some other person who is alleged to have authority over my free will. There is absolutely no reason for you to be worried or uneasy."

"For God's sake, for God's sake, Aleksei Ivanovich, don't go through with this pointless intention!" muttered the General, suddenly changing his angry tone to a pleading one, and even clasping my hands. "Imagine what this will lead to! More unpleasantness! You will realize that I must be particularly careful here, especially now! . . . especially now! . . . Oh, you don't know all my circumstances! . . . After we leave here I'll be ready to take you back. It's just that, well, in short, you must see my reasons!" he cried in despair, "Aleksei Ivanovich, Aleksei Ivanovich!"

Retreating to the door I once more asked him emphatically not to worry, promised that everything would go well and properly and left in a hurry.

Sometimes Russians traveling abroad are entirely too apprehensive, and terribly afraid of what people will say, or how they will look at them, and whether this or that is the proper thing to do. In short, they behave as if they were all wearing corsets, especially those who have some pretensions to consequence. What they like best is some kind of ready-made, established code of behavior which they can follow slavishly—in hotels, on their walks, in assemblies, on the road . . . But the General had let slip that, in addition to all this, there were some special circumstances, that he must be "particularly careful." That must be why he suddenly was so upset and changed his tone with me. I took note of it and registered it in my mind. And, of course, he could very well be foolish enough to get in touch with some authority or other in the morning; so I really had to watch my step.

However, I had no particular desire to make the General himself angry. Rather, I felt very much like playing on Polina's nerves now. Polina had treated me so cruelly, having pushed me into this stupid situation, that I wanted very much to drive her to the point where she would have to plead with me to stop it. My schoolboyish tricks might get to where they might compromise her too. Besides, certain other feelings and desires were taking shape in my mind: for instance, if I am indeed ready to be reduced to a nonentity before her, this must not at all mean that I am a milksop before other people, and certainly not somebody whom the Baron could "thrash with his cane." I felt like having a good laugh at all of them, while looking great myself. I'll show them. Most likely she'll be afraid of a scandal and call me back. And even if she won't, she'll still see that I'm no milksop . . .

(An amazing bit of news: I have just heard from our nurse, whom I met on the stairs, that Maria Filippovna left for Karlsbad today, all by herself, by the evening train, to see her cousin. What does this mean? The nurse says that she has been intending to go for a long time. But why did no one else know about it? Though maybe I was the only one who didn't. The nurse also let out the secret that Maria Filippovna had some serious words with the General only the day before yesterday. I understand. That must be Mlle Blanche. Yes, we are approaching a critical juncture.)

Seven

*I*n the morning I rang for a waiter and told him to bill me separately as of that day. My room was not really expensive, and so there was no reason for alarm and to move out right away. I had one hundred and sixty gulden, and there . . . there, perhaps, wealth! Strange thing, I haven't won anything yet, but I act, I feel, and I think as if I were a rich man and can't imagine myself any other way.

In spite of the early hour I was getting ready to go and see Mr. Astley, who was staying at the Hôtel d'Angleterre, not very far from ours, when suddenly de Grieux entered my room. That had never happened before, and besides, that gentleman and I had of late been on the most aloof and strained terms. He had been making no effort to conceal his contempt for me or, rather, had been trying not to conceal it, and I—I had my own reasons for disliking him. To put it plainly, I hated him. His visit greatly surprised me. I understood at once that something special was brewing here.

He entered very politely and complimented me on my room. Seeing that I had my hat in my hand, he inquired whether I could be going out for a walk so early in the morning. When I told him that I intended to pay a visit to Mr. Astley on some business, he stopped to think for a moment, got the point, and then assumed an exceedingly troubled expression.

De Grieux was like all Frenchmen, that is, gay and polite whenever this might be necessary and profitable, and insufferably boring when there was no longer any need to be gay and polite. A Frenchman is rarely naturally polite. His politeness is always made to order, with an ulterior motive. For instance, if he finds it necessary to be eccentric, original, and out of the ordinary, even his silly and affected fantasy will be made up of long-accepted and trite details. But when he is natural, a Frenchman is composed of the most trivial, petty, commonplace practical sense; in short, he is the most tedious creature in the world. In my opinion, only novices, and especially young Russian ladies, are taken in by the French. A person amounting to anything at all will immediately recognize the dead conventionality of their drawing-room politeness, ease of manner, and gaiety, and find it insufferable.

"I have come to see you on business," he began, with a very unconcerned air, though politely, "and I will not conceal from you that I have come as an ambassador, or rather as a mediator, from the General. Having only a very poor knowledge of Russian, I understood almost nothing last night, but the General has explained it to me in detail, and I must confess . . ."

"But listen, Monsieur de Grieux," I interrupted, "here you have again undertaken to be a mediator in this matter. I am of course a tutor, and never pretended to the honor of being a close friend of the house or of being close to this family; so I am not familiar with its circumstances; but tell me, have you now become an actual member of this family? For you take such an interest in everything, and insist on stepping in as a mediator in every matter . . ."

He did not like my question. He could see through it too well, and he was not going to let out any secrets.

"I am connected with the General partly by business, and partly by *certain special* circumstances," he said coldly. "The General has sent me to ask you to abandon the intentions you spoke of yesterday. All the things that you were proposing to do were, of course, contrived with great ingenuity. However, the General has asked me to impress on you that you would nevertheless be utterly unsuccessful; what is more, the Baron will not receive you, and he is, in any case, well equipped to protect himself against further unpleasantness on your part. You must see as much yourself. And so, tell me, what's the use of going on with this thing? The General, meanwhile, promises quite definitely to take you back into his house at the first convenient opportunity; and until that happens, he will continue to pay your salary, *vos appointements*. Wouldn't that be very much to your advantage?"

I replied very calmly that he was slightly mistaken there; that it might very well be that I wouldn't be kicked out of the Baron's, but, on the contrary, admitted and listened to; and I asked him to admit that he had probably come precisely with the idea of finding out how I intended to go about this matter.

"Good Lord! If the General is indeed so interested, then of course he would like to know what you intend to do, and how. Isn't that natural?"

I proceeded to explain, while he listened in a lounging position with his head inclined toward me and an unconcealed ironic expression on his face. On the whole he behaved very condescendingly. I did my best to give him the impression that I took this thing very seriously indeed. I explained that by complaining about me to the

General, as if I were the General's servant, the Baron had, first, deprived me of my position, and second, had treated me as an individual whom he considered unfit to answer for himself and not worth speaking to. Of course, I said, I had a right to feel insulted. However, being aware of the difference of age, our respective positions in society, and so on and so forth (at this point I could scarcely restrain my laughter), I was not going to commit yet another indiscretion, that is, confront the Baron with a direct demand, or even a suggestion, of his giving me satisfaction. Nevertheless, I considered that I would be entirely within my rights if I offered him, and especially the Baroness, my apologies, especially since I had been feeling ill lately, overwrought, and, one might say, subject to strange whims, and so on and so forth. However, by having talked to the General rather than to me, which I took as an insult, and by insisting that the General dismiss me, the Baron had put me in such a position that I could no longer offer him and the Baroness my apologies, because if I did so, he and the Baroness and all the world would probably think that I had come to apologize out of fear, and in hope of getting back my position. From all this it had to follow, inevitably, that I was now forced to ask the Baron to apologize to me first, in the most moderate terms, by stating, for example, that he had not at all meant to insult me. Once the Baron had apologized, my hands would be untied, and I would with perfect candor and sincerity offer him my apologies, too. In short, I concluded, I was only asking the Baron to untie my hands.

"Fie, what scrupulousness and what refinement! And why should you apologize? Come on, monsieur . . . monsieur . . . admit that you are starting all this on purpose, to annoy the General . . . or could it be that you have something special in mind? . . . mon cher monsieur, pardon, j'ai oublié votre nom, monsieur Alexis? . . . N'est ce pas?"[12]

"But allow me, mon cher marquis, what business is this of yours?"

"Mais le général . . ."

"But what about the General? He said something last night about having to be particularly careful . . . and was so alarmed . . . I couldn't understand a thing, though."

"There is, there definitely is a particular circumstance," de Grieux joined in pleadingly, in a tone which sounded increasingly annoyed. "Do you know Mademoiselle de Cominges?"

"That is, Mademoiselle Blanche?"

"Well, yes, Mademoiselle Blanche de Cominges . . . et madame sa mère . . . you know yourself, the General . . . in short, the General is in love and in fact . . . in fact, the nuptials may be performed here. Now, imagine if there were a scandal, an affair . . ."

"I can see no scandal, or affair, connected with these nuptials."

"But le baron est si irascible, un caractère prussien, vous savez, enfin il fera une querelle d'Allemand.[13]

"With me, to be sure, and not with you, since I am no longer a member of your household . . ." (I was trying to act as muddleheaded as possible). "But, allow me, it is settled, then, that Mademoiselle Blanche is to marry the General? What are they waiting for? Or rather, why keep it a secret, at least from us members of the household?"

"I cannot . . . however, it is not as yet entirely . . . though . . . you know, they are expecting news from Russia; the General must settle his affairs . . ."

---

12. "My dear sir, excuse me, I've forgotten your name, Mr. Alexis? . . . Isn't it?"

13. "The baron is so irascible, the Prussian character you know, he will finally provoke a quarrel in the German fashion."

"Aha! Grandmother!"

De Grieux looked at me with hatred.

"In short," he interrupted, "I fully rely on your innate courtesy, your intelligence, your tact . . . of course you will do this for the family which received you like one of them, loving and respecting you . . ."

"Come now, they threw me out! You assure me now that for the sake of appearances only, but you must admit that if somebody were to tell you: 'Look here, I don't want to pull your ears, of course, but let me pull your ears anyway, for the sake of appearances . . .' Isn't that pretty much the same thing?"

"Well, if this is what you want, if no request will prevail on you," he began sternly and disdainfully, then allow me to assure you that the proper measures will be taken. There are authorities here; you'll be deported this very day—que diable! un blanc-bec comme vous[14] wants to challenge a personage like the Baron to a duel! And you think that you will get away with this? Believe me, nobody here is afraid of you! When I made my request to you, it was rather of my own accord, so you wouldn't disturb the General. And do you really believe that the Baron won't simply have you turned out by a servant?"

"But I am not going there myself," I replied, with the utmost composure. "That's where you are wrong, Monsieur de Grieux; all this will proceed much more decorously than you think. This very moment I am about to get in touch with Mr. Astley and ask him to be my intermediary, or in other words, mon second. The man has a liking for me and surely will not refuse. He will go to the Baron, and the Baron will receive him. Even if I am myself a tutor and might appear to be *subalterne* and, well, defenseless, Mr. Astley is a nephew of a lord, a real lord,

14. "What the devil! A nobody like you . . ."

a fact known to all, Lord Peabroke, who is present here. Believe me, the Baron will be courteous to Mr. Astley and will hear him out. And if he won't, Mr. Astley will look upon it as a personal insult (you know how persistent Englishmen are), and will send a friend of his to call on the Baron. And his friends are men of quality. Considering all this, don't you agree that things may not turn out the way you think they will?"

Now the Frenchman was decidedly becoming worried. All that I'd been saying sounded as if it could be true, and so there was a real chance that I might indeed stir up a scandal.

"But I'm begging you," he started, in an undisguisedly pleading voice, "drop this whole thing! You seem to relish the notion that there will be a scandal! What you want is not satisfaction, but a scandal! As I said earlier, it will all turn out to be most amusing and even witty, which may be what you are really after, but, in short," he concluded, seeing me reach for my hat, "I've come to hand you this brief note from a certain person; read it, since I was asked to wait for your answer."

Having said this, he produced from his pocket a little note, folded and sealed with a wafer, and gave it to me.

It was in Polina's handwriting:

"I am under the impression that you may intend to go on with this affair. You are angry and you are beginning to act silly. However, there are some special circumstances which I will tell you of later, perhaps. Meanwhile, please stop it and restrain yourself. It is all so stupid! I need you, and you promised yourself to obey me. Remember Schlangenberg. I beg you to be obedient, and, if necessary, I am ordering you. Your P.

"P.S. If you are angry with me for what happened yesterday, please forgive me."

I felt suddenly giddy having read these lines. My lips

turned white, and I began to tremble. The accursed Frenchman was standing there looking pointedly discreet, with his eyes turned away as if trying not to perceive my confusion. I'd have felt better had he laughed at me outright.

"Very well," I answered, "tell mademoiselle not to worry. Allow me, however, to inquire," I added sharply, "why you waited so long to give me this letter? Instead of chattering about all kinds of trifles, you ought to have started by handing it to me . . . as long as you came here entrusted with it."

"Oh, I wanted . . . All of this is so strange that you must forgive my natural impatience. I was eager to find out for myself, and from you personally, what your intentions were. Besides, not being familiar with the contents of this note, I thought that there was no hurry about conveying it to you."

"I understand. To put it more simply, you were told to give me the note only in the last resort, and if you could settle it orally, not to give it to me at all. Right? Tell me right out, Monsieur de Grieux!"

"Peut-être," said he, assuming an air of peculiar reserve and giving me a rather peculiar look.

I took my hat. He gave me a nod and left. I thought I noticed a sarcastic smile on his lips. And how could it be otherwise?

"I'll get even with you yet, Frenchman, we'll see who wins!" I muttered as I walked down the stairs. I was still in a daze, as if I had been struck a blow on my head. The fresh air revived me a little.

A mere two minutes later, as soon as my head had cleared up sufficiently, two thoughts stood out vividly before me: the *first,* that from such trifles, from a few schoolboyish and quite implausible threats, uttered casually by a green youth, there had arisen such a *general* state of alarm! And the *second* thought: what kind of influence could it be that this Frenchman has over Polina? A word from him, and she does everything he wants, writes a note, and actually *begs* me. Of course, their relations had been a mystery to me from the very beginning, ever since I got to know them. Yet during the last few days I had observed in her a positive revulsion and even contempt for him, while he did not even pay any attention to her and, in fact, was just plain rude to her. I had noticed this. Polina herself had told me about her aversion; of late she had let out some extremely significant secrets . . . So he simply had her in his power; she was tied to him by certain bonds . . .

Eight

*O*n the promenade, as they call it here, that is, on the walk under the chestnut trees, I met my Englishman.

"Oh, oh!" he began as he caught sight of me, "I'm on my way to see you, and you are on your way to me. So you have already left your people?"

"Tell me, first of all, how do you know all this?" I asked, quite surprised; "is it possible that everybody knows about it?"

"Oh, no, nobody knows. And why should everybody know? Nobody is saying a thing."

"Well, then, how do you know about it?"

"I know it, that is, it so happened that I learned about it. Now, where are you going after leaving here? I like you and this is why I was coming to see you."

"You are a nice person, Mr. Astley," I said (I was, however, terribly surprised; how did he find out?), "and since I haven't had my morning coffee yet, and you can surely stand another cup, let's go to the café in the casino. We'll sit there a while, smoke a cigarette, and I'll tell you everything . . . and you'll tell me something, too."

The café was only a hundred steps away. We ordered coffee, I lighted my cigarette, Mr. Astley did not light one, but, fixing me with his eyes, got ready to listen.

"I'm not going anywhere, I'm staying here," I started.

"I was sure you were going to stay," Mr. Astley observed, approvingly.

On my way to see Mr. Astley I hadn't had the slightest
intention of telling him anything about my love for
Polina; in fact, I had expressly told myself not to say a
thing about it. During all those days I had hardly said a
word to him that might have hinted at it. Besides, he
was himself very bashful. I noticed, from their very first
meeting, that Polina had made a great impression on
him; yet he never as much as mentioned her by name. But
strangely enough, now suddenly, no sooner had he sat
down and fixed me with his intent, metallic gaze, I felt,
I don't know why, a desire to tell him everything, that is,
all about my love, and with all its nuances. I spoke for a
whole half-hour, finding it to be a most agreeable experience, since it was the first time I had ever told anybody
about it! Noticing that at certain particular ardent junc-
tures he became embarrassed, I purposely increased the
ardor of my narrative. Only one thing I regret: I said,
perhaps, more than I should about the Frenchman . . .

Mr. Astley listened, sitting there facing me, motionless,
without uttering a word or a sound and looking me
straight in the eye. But when I mentioned the Frenchman, he suddenly cut me short and asked me sternly if I
had a right to bring up this circumstance, which was none
of my concern. Mr. Astley always formulated his questions very strangely.

"You are right. I am afraid not," I answered.

"You can say nothing about Miss Polina and this marquis, except for your own speculations; am I right?"

I was again taken aback by so categorical a question
coming from the otherwise so bashful Mr. Astley.

"No, nothing definite," I answered, "nothing, of
course."

"If so, you have done wrong not only by bringing it up

before me, but even by thinking of it in your own mind."

"All right, all right! I admit it, but that is not the point now," I interrupted, wondering to myself. Here I told him all about yesterday, the whole story with all the details: Polina's prank, my encounter with the Baron, my dismissal, the General's exceedingly cowardly behavior, and finally, I described in detail de Grieux's visit earlier that morning, giving all the nuances. Finally I showed him the note.

"What do you make of all this?" I asked. "I have come expressly to find out what you think of it. As for myself, I could have killed that miserable Frenchman, and maybe I shall do it yet."

"I share your feelings," said Mr. Astley, "but in regard to Miss Polina, then . . . you know that one may enter into relations even with people whom one detests if one is compelled by necessity. There may exist here certain relations of which you have no knowledge, and which depend on extraneous circumstances. I believe that you may set your mind at rest—partly, of course. As for her action yesterday, it was strange, of course—not because she decided to get rid of you by exposing you to the Baron's walking stick (which, for reasons beyond my understanding, he failed to make use of, though he had it in his hand), but because such a prank is for such . . . for such a wonderful young lady . . . improper. Of course, she couldn't foresee that you would carry out her wish uttered in jest, so literally . . ."

"You know what?" I cried suddenly, looking closely at Mr. Astley. "It seems to me that you have already heard about all this, and do you know from whom? From Miss Polina herself!"

Mr. Astley looked at me with surprise.

"You have a twinkle in your eyes and I can read your suspicion in them," he said, quickly regaining his former composure, "yet you haven't the slightest right to express your suspicions. I cannot allow you this right and absolutely refuse to answer your question."

"Well, enough of it! Nor do you have to!" I cried, getting strangely excited and not knowing why this thought had suddenly occurred to me. And really, when, where, and how could Mr. Astley have been chosen by Polina to be her confidant? Though, of late, I had to some extent lost sight of Mr. Astley, and Polina had always been an enigma to me, so much so that now, for instance, having launched into an account of the story of my love to Mr. Astley, I was suddenly struck, even as I was telling my story, by the fact that I could say hardly anything precise or positive about my relations with her. Quite on the contrary, everything about them was fantastic, strange, unlikely; in short, I had myself never seen anything quite like it.

"All right, all right. I am utterly confused by it all, and right now there is a great deal that I just can't understand," I answered, breathlessly. "However, I can see that you mean well. Now, there is another matter, and I am asking, not your advice, but your opinion."

I stopped for a moment, then continued:

"Why do you think the General got so scared? Why did they all get so wrought up about my silly antics? So wrought up that even de Grieux himself deemed it necessary to intervene (and he will intervene only on the most important occasions), paid me a visit (imagine!), begged me, pleaded with me—he, de Grieux, pleaded with me! Finally, note that he came at nine o'clock, rather before nine, and Miss Polina's letter was already in his hands. If this is so, one can't help asking: when was it written? Could it be that they waked Miss Polina to get it? (Apart from the fact that Miss Polina is

obviously his slave for she even begs my forgiveness!),
quite apart from that, how is she involved in all this,
she personally? What is her interest in this? Why are they
frightened by some Baron? And what of it, if the General is marrying Mademoiselle Blanche de Cominges?
They say that they must be *particularly careful* on account of that circumstance, but isn't this a little too
particular, wouldn't you agree? What do you think? I
can tell by your eyes that in this matter, too, you know
more than I do."

Mr. Astley laughed and nodded.

"You are right, it seems that I know in fact a great deal
more than you," he said. "The whole thing has to do with
no one but Mademoiselle Blanche, and I am quite sure
that this is the truth of it."

"Well, what about Mademoiselle Blanche?" I exclaimed impatiently (I suddenly had a hope that now I'd
hear something about Mlle Polina's secrets).

"It appears to me that Mademoiselle Blanche has at the
moment a very special reason for avoiding any encounter
with the Baron and Baroness, even more an unpleasant
encounter, and worse still a scandalous one."

"Well, well!"

"Two years ago Mademoiselle Blanche was here during the season. I was then in Roulettenburg also. Mademoiselle Blanche was not called Mademoiselle de Cominges then, and her mother, Madame veuve Cominges
was nonexistent then, at least there was never any mention of her. As for de Grieux, there was no de Grieux
either. I am most deeply convinced that they are not only
unrelated but also have only very recently made each
other's acquaintance. Likewise, de Grieux has become a
marquis only very recently—I am sure of that in view of a
special circumstance. It can be assumed, in fact, that he

began to call himself de Grieux only recently. I know a man here who has met him before under a different name."

"But he really has a most respectable circle of acquaintances."

"Oh, that may be. This may be true even of Mademoiselle Blanche. But two years ago Mademoiselle Blanche, following a complaint by this same Baroness, was asked by the police to leave town, and did so."

"How did this happen?"

"She showed up here first with an Italian, a prince of some sort, with a historic name, Barberini[15] or something. A man all bedecked with rings and with diamonds, and not false ones either. They drove around in a magnificent carriage. Mademoiselle Blanche played trente et quarante, winning at first; but then her luck changed, as I remember. As I recall, one night she lost a very large sum. But worst of all, *un beau matin* her prince disappeared, and also the horses and the carriage; everything disappeared. A huge bill at the hotel. Mademoiselle Selmà (no longer a Barberini, she suddenly had become Mademoiselle Selmà) was in the utmost despair. She wailed and shrieked all over the hotel, and rent her dress in a fit of fury. There was a Polish count staying at the same hotel (all Polish travelers are counts), and Mademoiselle Selmà, rending her garments and scratching her face like a cat with her lovely, perfumed hands, made an impression on him. They talked things over, and by dinner time she had overcome her grief. That night he showed up at the casino with her on his arm. Mademoiselle Selmà was laughing again, and as usual rather loudly. Her manner was somewhat more free and easy than be-

15. Distinguished Roman name.

fore. She now definitely joined the ranks of those ladies at
the casino who, as they approach the roulette table, give a
shove to another player to clear a space for themselves.
This is considered particularly chic among such ladies.
You must have observed them, of course?"

"Oh, yes."

"Really not worth it. To the annoyance of the decent
public there are always many such women here, those
who can change thousand-franc bills at the table every
day. The moment they cease doing that, however, they
are asked to leave. Mademoiselle Selmà still continued to
change hers, but her luck was even worse than before.
You will note that these ladies are often quite lucky in
their play; they have marvellous self-control. However,
this is where my story ends. One day, just as the prince
had done before him, the count disappeared. That night
Mademoiselle Selmà showed up at the casino alone, and
this time no one offered her his arm. In two days she had
lost everything. Having staked her last louis d'or and lost
it, she glanced around and saw standing next to her Baron
Wurmerhelm, who was scrutinizing her intently and
with deep indignation. But Mademoiselle Selmà failed
to notice the Baron's indignation and accosted him with
that familiar smile, asking him to put ten louis d'or on
red for her. Thereupon, following a complaint from the
Baroness, she was asked that same night not to show herself at the casino again. If you are wondering how I
could be familiar with all these trivial and entirely improper details, it is because I heard them, finally, from
Mr. Feeder, a relative of mine, who that very night carried off Mademoiselle Selmà in his carriage, going with
her from Roulettenburg to Spa. Now, you must understand this: Mademoiselle Blanche would like to become
the General's wife so that in the future she will no longer

receive invitations such as she had from the police at the casino two years ago. She no longer does any gambling, but this is because there is reason to believe that she now has capital of her own which she lends out at interest to gamblers here. Much better business, this. I even suspect that the unfortunate General owes her money, too. Perhaps also de Grieux. Though maybe de Grieux is her associate. You will agree that, at least until the wedding, she would prefer not to attract the attention of the Baron and Baroness in any circumstances. In a word, the last thing she needs in her present position is a scandal. Now, you are connected with their party, and your actions could very easily lead to a scandal, especially as she is seen every day walking arm in arm with either the General or Miss Polina. Now do you understand?"

"No, I don't understand!" I cried, banging my fist on the table so hard that the *garçon* came running in alarm.

"Tell me, Mr. Astley," I repeated frantically, "if you knew this whole story and, consequently, read Mademoiselle Blanche de Cominges like an open book, why didn't you at least warn me, or the General himself, or, most of all, Miss Polina, who has been showing herself here at the casino, in public, arm in arm with Mademoiselle Blanche?"

"I had no reason to warn you, because you couldn't have done a thing," Mr. Astley answered calmly. "Besides, warn of what? It is quite possible that the General knows as much about Mademoiselle Blanche as I do, or even more, and still keeps walking around with her and Miss Polina. The General is a most unfortunate man. I saw Mademoiselle Blanche yesterday, galloping along on a beautiful horse with Monsieur de Grieux and that little Russian prince, and the General galloping after them on a chestnut. In the morning he told me that his legs ached, but he rode his horse well. And there, that very moment, the thought occurred to me that this was an utterly ruined man. Besides, all this is no business of mine, and it is only lately that I have had the honor of making Miss Polina's acquaintance. And moreover," Mr. Astley suddenly recalled, "I have already told you that I do not recognize your right to ask certain questions, even though I have a sincere liking for you . . ."

"Enough," I said, getting up, "it is clear as daylight to me now that Miss Polina, too, knows everything about Mademoiselle Blanche, but that she cannot give up that Frenchman, and so brings herself to taking walks with Mademoiselle Blanche. Believe me, no other influence in the world could have made her walk around with Mademoiselle Blanche and beg me in a note not to touch the Baron. There must definitely be that influence, to which everybody yields! And yet, it was she herself who egged me on to get at the Baron! The devil take it all, I can't figure it out!"

"First, you are forgetting that this Mademoiselle de Cominges is the General's fiancée, and second, that Miss Polina, the General's stepdaughter, has a little brother and sister, the General's own children, whom this crazy man has already utterly abandoned and, it seems, robbed as well."

"Yes, yes! That must be it! To leave would mean to abandon the children altogether, to stay means to protect their interests and, perhaps, to save some fragments of their property. Yes, yes, all this is true! But still, but still! Ah, now I understand why they are all so concerned about Granny!"

"About whom?" asked Mr. Astley.

"That old witch in Moscow who won't die, and about whom they are expecting a telegram saying that she is dead."

"Well, yes, of course, that is the only thing that matters

now. It's the inheritance that courts! If the inheritance comes through the General will marry; Miss Polina will be set free also, and de Grieux . . ."

"Well, what about de Grieux?"

"De Grieux will get his money; that's all he is waiting for."

"But is it all? Do you really think this is all he wants?"

"I know of nothing else," said Mr. Astley and lapsed into an obstinate silence.

"But I do, I do!" I repeated, flying into a rage. "He is waiting for the inheritance too, because Polina will get a dowry, and as soon as she has got the money she will throw herself on his neck. All women are like that! And it's precisely the very proudest among them who later turn out to be the most commonplace slaves! Polina is capable only of loving with passion, and nothing else! That is my opinion of her! Look at her, especially when she sits there alone, lost in thought: there is something foreordained, fated, damned about her! She is capable of all the horrors of life and passion . . . she . . . she . . . but who is calling me?" I suddenly exclaimed. "Who is shouting? I heard someone shout in Russian: 'Aleksei Ivanovich!' A woman's voice, listen, listen!"

By this time we were approaching our hotel. We had left the café a long time ago, almost without noticing it.

"I heard a woman calling, but I didn't know who was being called; it was in Russian; now I can see where the shouting comes from," Mr. Astley was pointing in a direction; "it is that woman sitting in a large armchair who has just been carried inside by a crowd of attendants. They are carrying her suitcases after her; it must be that the train has just arrived."

"But why is she calling me? She is shouting again; look, she is waving to us."

"I can see that," said Mr. Astley.

"Aleksei Ivanovich! Aleksei Ivanovich! Good Lord, what a dolt he is!" I heard someone shout desperately from the hotel entrance.

We almost ran to the doorway. I took the few steps, reached the landing, and . . . stood there in amazement, my feet rooted to the ground, feeling very weak inside.

Nine

*O*n the top landing of the broad front
entrance of the hotel, having been
carried up the steps in her armchair,
surrounded by servants, maids, and the many members of
the hotel staff, all eager to give satisfaction, and headed by
the Ober-Kellner himself, who had come out to welcome
the exalted guest who had arrived with such fanfare and
éclat, with her own servants and with all kinds of portmanteaus and trunks, there was seated—*Grandmother!*
Yes, it was she herself, redoubtable and rich, seventy-five-
year-old Antonida Vasilievna Tarasevicheva, landowner
and grand lady of Moscow, "la baboulinka," about whom
telegrams had been sent and received, who had been dying but had refused to die and who, like a bolt from the
blue, had suddenly appeared before us in person. Though
an invalid and carried in her chair, she had arrived as
always for the last five years, alert, perky, and sure of
herself as ever before, sitting upright in her chair, shouting in a loud and imperious voice, scolding every one—
in short, she was exactly the same as she had been on the
two or three occasions on which I had had the honor of
seeing her since I became a tutor at the General's house.
Naturally I just stood there, speechless with amazement.
But she had detected me a hundred paces away, with her
lynxlike eyes, as she was being carried inside, and called

me by my name and patronymic—which she had remembered, as she invariably did. "And this is the woman they expected to see in her coffin, buried, and leaving them her fortune," flashed through my mind; "why, she will outlive us all, and everyone in this hotel! But, my God, what will become of our family now, what will the General do? She will turn the whole hotel upside down!"

"Well, sir, why do you just stand there, staring at me?" she went on shouting at me; "don't you know how to make a bow and wish a person good morning? Or have you grown too proud to do so? Or, perhaps, you don't recognize me. Do you hear that, Potapych," she turned to a white-haired old man wearing a dress coat and white tie and with a pink bald pate, her butler, who accompanyed her on her journey; "do you hear that, he won't acknowledge me! They've buried me! They send one telegram after another: 'Is she dead, or isn't she dead?' As you can see, I know all about it! And as you can see for yourself, I am very much alive."

"For heaven's sake, Antonida Vasilievna, why should I wish you any harm?" I answered cheerfully once I had recovered my senses; "I was merely surprised . . . And how could I help being surprised, so unexpected . . ."

"What's so surprising about it? I just took a train and came here. Had a smooth, comfortable ride. You've been out for a walk, haven't you?"

"Yes, I took a walk to the casino."

"It is pleasant here," said Grandmother, looking around; "it's warm, and they've got fine trees here. I like that! Are our folks at home? The General?"

"Oh! Yes, I think so; around this time they ought to be in."

"So they have fixed hours here, and all kinds of formalities. Giving themselves airs. I hear that they keep a carriage, les seigneurs russes! They've blown everything back home, so they go abroad! And is Praskovia with them?"

"Yes, Polina Aleksandrovna, too."

"What about the Frenchman? Oh, well, I'll see them all myself. Aleksei Ivanovich, show me the way, straight to him. Do you like it here?"

"It's all right, Antonida Vasielievna."

"And you, Potapych, tell that dolt, the Kellner, that I want a comfortable suite, a nice one, not too high, and take my things there at once. And why are they all so anxious to carry me? Who asked them? Flunkies! Who is that with you?" she asked, addressing me again.

"This is Mr. Astley," I answered.

"What Mr. Astley?"

"A tourist, a good friend of mine. He also knows the General."

"An Englishman. There you see, he is staring at me, without unclenching his teeth. I like Englishmen, though. Well, carry me upstairs then, straight to their rooms. Where are they?"

They carried her upstairs, with me leading the way up the broad stairway of the hotel. Our procession was a most spectacular one. Everyone we met stopped and stared. Our hotel was considered the best, the most expensive, and the most aristocratic of the resort. On the stairways and in the halls one could always meet magnificently dressed ladies and distinguished looking Englishmen. Many people were asking the Ober-Kellner downstairs about her and he was greatly impressed himself. Of course he told everybody who asked that this was a distinguished foreign lady—une russe, une comtesse, grande dame—and that she was going to occupy the same suite in which la grande duchesse de N. had been staying the week before. Grandmother's imperious and authoritative appearance as she was carried up in her chair was mainly responsible for the sensation that she created. Every time she met someone new she would measure that person curiously from head to foot, and question me about everybody in a loud voice. Grandmother was a woman of substantial build, and though she did not get up from her chair, one could see that she was quite tall. She kept her back straight as a board and never leaned back in her chair. Her large gray head with its massive and bold features was held erect. Her face wore a positively haughty and defiant expression, and one could see that her attitude and gestures were perfectly natural. In spite of her seventy-five years her complexion was still quite fresh, and even her teeth were still rather good. She was wearing a black silk dress and a white cap.

"I find her very interesting," Mr. Astley whispered to me as he walked up with me.

"She knows about the telegrams," I thought. "She is also familiar with de Grieux, but I imagine that she doesn't know much about Mlle Blanche as yet." I immediately communicated this observation to Mr. Astley.

After the first surprise was over, I was looking forward with immense and evil glee to the thunderbolt which was about to strike the General. I felt as if something were egging me on to it, and I led the way with great alacrity.

Our family was staying on the third floor. I did not announce her arrival or even knock on the door, but simply flung it wide open, and Grandmother was carried in, in triumph. As luck would have it, they were all there, assembled in the General's study. It was twelve o'clock and apparently they were planning some excursion. Some were to go by carriage, others on horseback, the whole crowd; also, some acquaintances had been invited to join the party. Besides the General, Polina and the children, and the nurse, there were present in the study: de Grieux, Mlle Blanche, again wearing her riding habit, her mother Mme. veuve Cominges, the little prince, and another learned tourist, a German, whom I had not seen with them before. Grandmother's chair was set down in the middle of the room, right in front of the General. Good Lord! I shall never forget this scene! When we entered the room the General was telling the others something, and de Grieux was making a correction in his narrative. It must be mentioned that Mlle Blanche and de Grieux, during the last two or three days, had for some reason been particularly attentive to the little prince, *à la barbe du pauvre général.*[16] The atmosphere, though perhaps artificial, was cheerful and congenial. Upon seeing Grandmother, the General just stood there dumbfounded, his mouth wide open, unable to finish the word he was going to say. He stared at her, his eyes bulging, as though spellbound by a basilisk. Grandmother stared at him in silence also, without moving, but what a triumphant, provocative, and mocking look it was! They gazed at each other for a full ten seconds in the midst of complete silence on the part of everybody present. De Grieux seemed petrified at first, but soon an expression of extraordinary uneasiness appeared on his face. Mlle Blanche raised her eyebrows, opened her mouth, and stared wildly at Grandmother. The prince and the scholar were watching the whole scene, deeply puzzled. Polina's expression revealed extreme surprise and bewilderment, but then, suddenly, she turned white as a sheet. A moment later the blood rushed rapidly to her face, flushing her cheeks. Yes, this meant disaster for everybody! I could do nothing but keep turning my eyes from Grandmother to the people around her, and back. Mr. Astley stood on one side, calm and sedate as usual.

"Well, here I am! Instead of a telegram!" Grand-

16. "To the General's face."

mother finally broke the silence, in her loud voice; "you didn't expect me, did you?"

"Antonida Vasilievna . . . auntie . . . but how on earth . . ." muttered the unfortunate General. If Grandmother had remained silent for a few more seconds, he might have had a stroke.

"How on earth what? I just took a train and came here. What else is the railway for? And you all thought that I had turned up my toes and left you my fortune? I know very well how you kept sending telegrams from here. You must have spent quite a bit of money on them, too. Must be quite a bit, all the way from here. Well, and I decided to go for a trip, and here I am! Is this the Frenchman? Monsieur de Grieux, I imagine?"

"Oui, madame," de Grieux responded, "et croyez, je suis si enchanté . . . votre santé . . . c'est un miracle . . . vous voir ici, une surprise charmante . . ."[17]

"Charmante, I dare say. I know you, mountebank that you are. I don't believe you this much!" and she showed him her little finger. "Who is this?" she asked, pointing at Mlle Blanche. The spectacular Frenchwoman, in a riding habit, crop in hand, evidently impressed her. "Is she from these parts?"

"This is Mademoiselle Blanche de Cominges, and this is her mother, Madame de Cominges; they are staying in this hotel," I reported.

"Is the daughter married?" asked Grandmother, unceremoniously.

"Mademoiselle de Cominges is a maiden lady," I answered, as respectfully as possible and purposely in a low voice.

"Lively?"

I pretended not to understand the question.

17. "Yes, madame and be assured that I am so delighted . . . your health . . . it's a miracle . . . to see you here, a charming surprise."

"Fun to have around? Does she understand Russian? De Grieux here, he picked up some Russian in Moscow, had a smattering of it."

I explained that Mlle de Cominges had never been to Russia.

"Bonjour!" said Grandmother, suddenly turning abruptly to Mlle Blanche.

"Bonjour, madame," Mlle Blanche curtsied ceremoniously and elegantly, making haste to express, under the cover of extraordinary modesty and politeness, yet with her whole face and figure, her extreme astonishment at such a strange question and manner of address.

"Oh, she's casting down her eyes; she is putting on airs and graces. Shows what kind of creature she is, some actress, probably. I am staying downstairs here at the hotel," she suddenly turned to the General; "I'll be your neighbor, are you glad or aren't you?"

"Oh, auntie! Believe that I feel sincerely . . . pleased," the General joined in. He had by now recovered himself to some extent, and as he could, on occasion, express himself aptly, with gravity, and even with some pretension to eloquence, he promptly began to display his gifts now. "We were so alarmed and upset by the news of your illness . . . We received such despairing telegrams, and all of a sudden . . ."

"Come on, stop this nonsense!" Grandmother interrupted at once.

"But how could you," the General, in his turn, quickly interrupted her, raising his voice and trying not to notice the "nonsense," "how could you bring yourself to undertake such a long journey? You must admit, at your age and considering your health . . . in any case, it is all so unexpected that our astonishment is understandable. But I am so very glad . . . and we all [here he began to smile officiously and rapturously] will try our utmost to make your stay here during this season a most pleasurable one . . ."

"Come, enough of that; so much idle chatter; you're talking rubbish as usual; I can take care of myself without your help. However, I don't mind your being around, I don't bear a grudge. You're asking me how I got here. What's so surprising about it? Very simple. And why is everybody so surprised? How are you, Praskovia? What are you doing here?"

"How do you do, Grandmother," said Polina, approaching her, "how long did it take you to get here?"

"Well, she's the only one to ask a sensible question, everybody else says nothing but oh! and ah! Well, you see, I lay in bed and got all kinds of treatments for a long time, until I finally decided to get rid of all my doctors and sent for the sexton from St. Nicholas. He had cured a peasant woman of that same disease by means of hay dust. Well, and he helped me, too. On the third day I worked up a good sweat and was able to get up. Then my Germans gathered around me again, put on their glasses, and began to argue: 'If you'd go abroad now,' they said, 'to a watering place, and take a course of treatment, your obstruction may disappear altogether.' And why not, I thought to myself. Then the fools started moaning and groaning: 'How could you possibly make it there?' Well, so here I am. It took me just one day to get packed, and last Friday I took a maid, and Potapych, and a footman, Fyodor, but I sent Fyodor back home, from Berlin, because I saw that I didn't need him at all. In fact, I could have got here all by myself . . . I took a private compartment and there are porters at every station. For twenty kopecks they'll carry you wherever you like. See! What a suite you have taken!" she said in conclusion, looking around. "Where did you get the money for it, my dear man? Why, everything you've got is mortgaged. What a pile of money you owe to the Frenchman here alone! I know all about it, every bit of it!"

"I say, auntie . . ." said the General, very much embarrassed, "I am surprised, auntie . . . I think I can, without anyone checking on me . . . and besides, my expenses here do not exceed my means, and we are here . . ."

"They don't, eh? Is that what you said? Then you must have robbed your children of the last penny! Trustee!"

"After this, after such words . . ." started the General, indignantly. "I really don't know . . ."

"There you are, you don't know! I bet you hang around the roulette table here all the time? Have you blown everything yet?"

The General was so startled he almost choked on a surge of excited emotion.

"Roulette! I? In my position . . . I? You can't mean that, auntie; you must still be ill . . ."

"Come, don't lie to me. I bet they couldn't drag you away from it. It's all lies! You know what, I'm going to see for myself what this roulette is like, this very day. You, Praskovia, tell me, what are the sights here, and let Aleksei Ivanovich point them out to me, and you, Potapych, write down all the places we'll have to see. What sights have they got here?" she suddenly turned to Polina again.

"Not far from here are the ruins of a castle; then there is the Schlangenberg."

"What's the Schlangenberg? A forest, or what?"

"No, it's not a forest, it's a mountain; it's got a point . . ."

"What point?"

"The very highest point on the mountain; they've got an enclosed platform there. The view from there is magnificent."

"So they'd have to lug my chair up a mountain? Do you think they could do it?"

"Oh, we could find porters," I answered.

At this moment, Fedosia, the nurse, came in to greet Grandmother, bringing along the General's children.

"Come, they don't have to kiss me! I don't like to kiss children; their noses are always dirty. Well, how are you doing here, Fedosia?"

"It's very, very nice here, Antonida Vasilievna, madam," answered Fedosia. "And how have you been, madam? We've been fretting about you something terrible."

"I know, you are a good soul. Say, do you always have your rooms full of guests?" turning again to Polina. "Who is this mousy little man wearing spectacles?"

"Prince Nilsky, Grandmother," Polina whispered.

"Ah, a Russian? And I thought he wouldn't understand what I said! Maybe he didn't hear it. I've already met Mr. Astley. Ah, here he is again," said Grandmother, catching sight of him; "how do you do?" she suddenly turned to him.

Mr. Astley bowed to her, without saying a word.

"Well, what's the good word from you? Tell me something! Translate that to him, Polina!"

Polina did so.

"That I am greatly delighted to be in your presence, and that I am glad that you are in good health," Mr. Astley answered seriously, but without a moment's hesitation. It was translated to Grandmother, and it evidently pleased her.

"What nice answers an Englishman will always give you," she remarked. "For some reason I've always liked the English, no comparison between them and those Frenchmen! Come and see me some time," she said, addressing Mr. Astley again. "I'll try not to bother you too much. Translate that to him, and tell him that I'm staying right here, downstairs, downstairs, do you hear?" she repeated for Mr. Astley, pointing downward.

Mr. Astley was extremely pleased with this invitation.

Grandmother measured Polina from head to foot with an attentive and satisfied look.

"I could be fond of you, Praskovia," she said suddenly, "you are a fine wench, the best of the lot, but what a temper—wow! Well, I've got a temper myself. Turn around a bit. You're not wearing a wig, are you?"

"No, Grandmother, it's my own."

"That's better. I don't care for today's silly fashions. You are very pretty. I'd fall in love with you if I were a young gentleman. Why aren't you married? But it is time for me to go. I want to get some fresh air, I've been on the train long enough . . . Well, are you still angry with me?" she turned to the General.

"Oh, heavens, no, auntie, how could I!" the General recovered himself, delighted; "I understand, at your age . . ."

"Cette vieille est tombée en enfance,"[18] de Grieux whispered to me.

"Look, I want to see everything here. Will you let me have Aleksei Ivanovich for some time?" Grandmother went on to the General.

"Oh, for as long as you please, but I will myself . . . and Polina, and Monsieur de Grieux . . . we'll all take pleasure in accompanying you . . ."

"Mais, madame, cela sera un plaisir," de Grieux chimed in, with his most charming smile.

"Plaisir, to be sure. I find you funny, my dear sir. I'm not going to give you any money, though," she added suddenly, addressing herself to the General. "Well, and now to my room: I must look it over, and then we'll go and see all the sights. Come, lift me up."

Grandmother was lifted up again and everybody flocked downstairs, following her chair. The General was

18. "This old woman has become childish."

walking along as though stunned by a blow on the head. De Grieux was obviously thinking very hard. Mlle Blanche at first was going to stay behind but then changed her mind and joined the rest of us. The prince followed her at once, and there was no one left in the General's suite but the German and Madame veuve Cominges.

Ten

*A*t watering places and, I believe, all over Europe, hotel managers and Ober-Kellners, in assigning rooms to their guests, are guided not so much by the demands and wishes of the guests as by their own personal opinion of them. It ought to be added that they are rarely mistaken. They had assigned to Grandmother, for reasons obscure to me, so sumptuous a suite that it actually overshot the mark somewhat: four splendidly furnished rooms, with a bath, quarters for the servants, a special room for her personal maid, and so on and so forth. A grand duchess had actually stayed there the week before, a fact which the new occupant was informed of immediately in order to enhance the value of the suite. Grandmother was carried, or rather wheeled, through all her rooms, and she looked them over attentively and sternly. The Ober-Kellner, bald and advanced in years, accompanied her respectfully on this first inspection.

I don't know whom they all took Grandmother to be, but they apparently assumed she was an extremely important and, above all, wealthy person. They immediately put down in the book, "Madame la générale princesse de Tarassevitcheva," though Grandmother had never been a princess. The servants, a special compartment on the train, that mass of superfluous portmanteaus, suitcases, and even chests which had arrived with her, probably laid the foundation of her prestige; and her chair, the abrupt tone of her voice, her eccentric questions, asked in the most natural manner and without permitting any contradiction, in short, Grandmother's whole appearance, erect, vigorous, imperious, did the rest to create the awe in which she was held by all. During the inspection Grandmother would time and again tell them to stop her chair, point to some piece of furniture, and address some unexpected question to the Ober-Kellner, who was still smiling respectfully, though he was obviously beginning to get scared. Grandmother asked her questions in French, which she spoke rather badly; so I translated for her most of the time. The Ober-Kellner's answers for the most part did not please her and left her unsatisfied. Then, too, she seemed to be asking questions that were quite beside the point, heaven knows about what. For instance, she suddenly stopped in front of a picture, a rather mediocre copy of some well-known original depicting a mythological scene.

"Whose portrait is that?"

The Ober-Kellner explained that it was most probably some countess.

"How is it you don't know? You're living here and don't know who it is. Why does it hang here? Why is she squinting?"

The Ober-Kellner was unable to give satisfactory answers to all these questions and became quite flustered.

"There's a blockhead for you!" commented Grandmother, in Russian.

They carried her further. The same thing happened with a Dresden figurine, which Grandmother looked at for a long time and then ordered it removed for some unknown reason. Finally, she began to pester the Ober-Kellner about the bedroom carpets: what did they cost, and where had they been woven? The Ober-Kellner promised to make inquiries.

"What asses!" Grandmother grumbled, concentrating her whole attention on the bed.

"What a fancy canopy! Open it up."

They opened the bed.

"More, more, roll it all up. Take off the pillows, the pillowcases, lift up the feather bed."

They turned everything around. Grandmother examined it carefully.

"A good thing they haven't got any bedbugs. Take off all the linen! Make it up with my own linen and my pillows. But all this is too fancy. An old woman like me won't need this kind of place: I'll be bored all alone. Aleksei Ivanovich, you must come and see me often, whenever you are through teaching the children."

"I left the General's service yesterday," I answered, "and I'm living at the hotel strictly on my own."

"Why is this?"

"Some days ago an important German Baron with his wife, the Baroness, arrived here from Berlin. Yesterday, in the park, I said something to him in German, without keeping to the Berlin accent."

"Well, so what?"

"He thought it an impertinence and complained to the General, and the General dismissed me on the spot."

"Well, did you call the Baron names, or something? (Though if you did, so what!)"

"Oh, no. On the contrary, the Baron raised his stick to hit me."

"And you, sniveler, allowed your tutor to be treated that way!" she suddenly turned to the General, "and fired him in the bargain! Milksops! You're all milksops, as I can see."

"Don't you worrie, auntie," answered the General,

with a touch of condescending familiarity; "I can manage my own affairs. Besides, Aleksei Ivanovich has not given you quite an accurate account of the matter."

"And you put up with it just like that?" she turned to me again.

"I was going to challenge the Baron to a duel," I answered as modestly and calmly as I could, "but the General was against it."

"And why were you against it?" Grandmother turned to the General again. "(And you can go now, my good man; I'll call you when I need you," she now turned to the Ober-Kellner, "no need to hang around gaping; I can't stand these Nuremberg faces!)" The man bowed and left, of course without understanding Grandmother's compliment.

"For heaven's sake, auntie, you can't fight duels these days!" the General replied, with an ironic smile.

"Why not? All men like to strut and swagger, so let them fight, too. Milksops, that's what you all are, as I can see, can't stand up for your country. Come, pick me up! Potapych, see that two porters are always ready, hire them, and make all arrangements. I don't need more than two. They have to carry me only up and down stairs; where it is level, in the street, they can wheel me. Explain that to them. And pay them beforehand, that'll make them more respectful. But you yourself, always stay near me, and you, Aleksei Ivanovich, show me that Baron when we take our walk: so I know what this 'Von' Baron looks like, at least. Well, where is the roulette?"

I explained that the roulette tables were located at the casino, in several halls. Then she asked more questions: were there many of them? were there many people playing? did they play all day long? how were they set up? I finally said that it would be best if she saw it all with her own eyes, and that it was rather difficult to describe it.

"Well, then, take me straight there! Lead the way, Aleksei Ivanovich!"

"Why, auntie, aren't you at least going to take a rest after your journey?" the General asked solicitously. He was beginning to look a little worried; in fact, they all seemed a bit flurried and were exchanging significant glances. Probably they felt somewhat uneasy, or even embarrassed, about accompanying Grandmother straight to the casino, where she was naturally likely to commit some of her eccentricities, but this time in public; nevertheless, they all offered to accompany her.

"And why should I take a rest? I'm not tired, I've been sitting still for five days anyway. And then, later, we'll go and see what springs and medicinal waters they have here, and where they are. And then . . . what did you call it, Praskovia, the 'point,' or what?"

"That's right, Grandmother, point."

"Well, point, if that's what you call it. And what else have you got here?"

"There are many objects of interest here, Grandmother," said Polina, hesitating a little.

"Well, you don't know yourself! Marfa, you'll come with me, too," she said addressing her maid.

"But why should she come with us, auntie?" the General said, getting flustered, "and in fact it's impossible, and I also doubt whether Potapych will be admitted into the casino."

"Well, that's nonsense! So she is a servant, so I have to leave her behind! She is a human being, too, isn't she? Here we are, on the road for a whole week, so she'd like to see a few things, too. How could she go anywhere, except with me? She wouldn't dare show her nose in the street by herself."

"But, Grandmother . . ."

"So you're ashamed to be with me, is that so? Then

stay home, I didn't ask you to come. Look, what a general he is! I'm a general's widow myself. And why should the whole crowd of you drag behind me? I can look at it all just with Aleksei Ivanovich . . ."

However, de Grieux insisted categorically that we should all accompany her, and entered upon the most polite phrases about what a pleasure it was to accompany her, et cetera. We all started.

"Elle est tombée en enfance," de Grieux repeated to the General, "seule elle fera des bêtises . . ."[19] I could not hear what he said then, but he evidently had his plans, and, perhaps, he was cherishing some hope again.

It was about a third of a mile to the casino. The way led along a park lane lined with chestnut trees and then to a square. The General felt somewhat reassured now, for our procession, though rather eccentric, was, nevertheless, seemly and decorous. There was after all nothing surprising about the fact that an ailing and disabled person, an invalid, had come here to take the waters. However, quite obviously, the General was afraid of the casino: why should a sick person, an invalid, and an elderly lady at that, go to the roulette tables? Polina and Mlle Blanche walked on each side of the chair as it was wheeled along. Mlle Blanche was laughing in a modestly cheerful way and telling Grandmother polite pleasantries, so very well that the latter finally said something approving of her. Polina, on the other side, had to answer Grandmother's incessant and innumerable questions, such as: "Who was that? who was that woman driving by? how large a city is this? how large is this garden? what are those trees? what are those mountains? have they got eagles here? what is that funny looking roof?" Mr. Astley who was walking beside me whispered that he expected a great

19. "Alone she will do some stupid things."

deal from that morning. Potapych and Marfa walked behind, close to the chair; Potapych had on a dress coat and white tie and a visored cap; Marfa, a fortyish, red-cheeked woman with graying hair, wore a cap, a cotton dress, and creaking goatskin shoes. Grandmother turned back to talk to them quite often. De Grieux and the General trailed behind by a few steps, discussing something very heatedly. The General looked very crestfallen, while de Grieux talked with an air of determination. Maybe he was trying to reassure the General; evidently he was giving him some sort of advice. Yet Grandmother had already pronounced, a while ago, the fateful words: "I'm not going to give you any money." Perhaps to de Grieux this announcement seemed incredible, but the General knew his aunt. I noticed that de Grieux and Mlle Blanche kept winking at each other. As for the prince and the German tourist, I could see them at the farther end of the parkway; they had fallen behind and were now walking away from us.

We entered the casino in triumph. The doorman and attendants displayed the same respectfulness as the people at the hotel. However, they looked at us with some curiosity. Grandmother at first asked to be shown all the various rooms, some of which she approved of, remaining indifferent to others. She had questions about them all, though. Finally they got to the gambling halls. The attendant who was standing at the closed door like a sentinel, suddenly flung it wide open, looking thunderstruck.

Grandmother's appearance at the roulette tables made a deep impression on the public. There was a crowd of a hundred and fifty or two hundred players, several rows deep around the roulette tables and at the other end of the hall, where there was a table for trente et quarante. Those who had succeeded in pushing their way through the crowd right up to the table would usually stand firm and give up their place only when they had lost everything; for those who are only spectators are not allowed to occupy a place at the gaming tables. Though there are chairs set around each table, few gamblers ever use them, especially when there is a large crowd, because one can pack them more tightly when they are standing, and so save some space, and besides, it's more convenient to place one's bets standing up. The second and third rows were crowding around the first, waiting and watching for their turn; but sometimes an impatient gambler would push a hand through the front row and place a bet. In this way some players managed to squeeze a bet through even from the third row. As a result of this practice ten or even five minutes rarely passed without some "incident" over disputed stakes at one end of the table or the other. The casino police are fairly efficient, though. There is no escaping these crowded conditions, of course, since large numbers of people are naturally welcome on account of the profits. But eight croupiers seated around each table keep a close eye on the stakes; they also keep score of all winnings, and whenever there is an argument they are ready to settle it. In extreme cases the police are called, and the incident is all over in a minute. The police officers wear plain clothes and mingle with the crowd of spectators so that they cannot be recognized. They are especially on the lookout for thieves and other shady operators who are particularly numerous at the roulette tables because of the extraordinary ease with which they can ply their trade there. Indeed, in any other place a thief must pick pockets or break locks, which, if something goes wrong, may cause him a great deal of trouble. But here, all a thief has to do is to walk up to the roulette table, start playing, and suddenly, openly and publicly, pick up someone else's winnings and put them in his pocket. If there is an argument, the crook insists, loudly and emphatically, that the money is his. If the whole thing is done cleverly and the witnesses are hesitant, the thief very often walks off with the money, if it is not a very large sum of course. If it *is* a large sum, either the croupiers or one of the other players is virtually certain to have taken note of it beforehand. But if it is not too large a sum, the real owner may sometimes simply give in, shrinking from a scandal, and walk away. But whenever a thief is exposed, he is at once ignominiously ejected from the casino.

Grandmother was watching all these goings-on from a distance, with wide-eyed curiosity. She very much approved of a thief's being turned out of the casino. She showed little interest in trente et quarante; she liked roulette much better, what with the little rolling ball. She declared finally that she would like to have a closer look at the game. I don't know how it happened, but the attendants and a few other officious agents (mostly little Poles who, having themselves lost, were now foisting their services on more fortunate players and foreigners of all sorts) at once, and in spite of the crowd, found and cleared a place for Grandmother near the very middle of the table, next to the chief croupier, and wheeled the chair to it. Many visitors who were not playing but just watching the play (mostly Englishmen with their families) immediately crowded around that table to watch Grandmother from behind the players. Numerous lorgnettes were turned upon her. The croupiers perked up: such an eccentric player certainly seemed to promise something quite special. Naturally, an old lady of seventy, an invalid, yet wanting to gamble, was not a sight to be seen every day. I jostled my way up to the table also and took my stand at Grandmother's side. Potapych and Marfa were left somewhere far behind, among the crowd.

The General, Polina, de Grieux, and Mlle Blanche also stood aside among the spectators.

Grandmother started by looking over the players. In a half whisper she asked me curt, abrupt questions: who is this man? who is this woman? She took a particular fancy to a very young man at the end of the table who was playing for very high stakes, putting down thousands at a time. The rumor was that he had already won as much as forty thousand francs, and piles of gold and bank notes lay in front of him. He was pale. His eyes were flashing and his hands were trembling. He was already making his bets quite aimlessly, just putting down what he could grab with his hand, yet he kept on winning and winning, raking in more and more money. The attendants were busying themselves around him, moving up a chair for him, clearing a place around him so that he would be more comfortable, making sure that the other players would not crowd in on him—all in expectation of a big tip. Some players who have won a lot tip the croupiers without counting the money and from sheer joy just give them a handful. At the young man's side a little Pole had already established himself. He was trying very hard to make himself useful, whispering in his ear solicitously and uninterruptedly, probably telling him how to play, giving advice, and directing the game—of course, he, too, expected a gratuity later. The gambler scarcely looked at him, but kept betting at random and raking in the money. He obviously no longer knew what he was doing.

Grandmother watched him for several minutes.

"Tell him," she suddenly got very excited and nudged me, "tell him to quit, tell him to take his money quickly and go away. He will lose it all, he'll lose it all if he doesn't quit right away!" she was so concerned that she almost lost her breath from excitement. "Where is Potapych? Send Potapych over to him! Come, tell him, tell him," she kept nudging me; "where, indeed, is Potapych! Sortez, sortez!" she began herself shouting to the young man. I leaned over to her and whispered, very resolutely, that one wasn't allowed to shout like that here, that even talking just a bit loud was forbidden, because it interfered with people making their calculations, and that they would throw us out directly.

"What a shame! The man is lost. Well, it's his own doing . . . I can't look at him, it makes me sick. What a dolt!" And Grandmother quickly looked the other way.

There, on the left, on the other side of our table, a young lady, accompanied by a dwarf of some sort, caught her attention. I don't know who this dwarf was, whether some relative of hers or just brought along to make an impression. I had noticed the lady before; she showed up at the gaming tables every day, at one o'clock in the afternoon, and left exactly at two, playing one hour every day. They already knew her at the casino, and a chair was set for her at once. She would then take out some gold, a few thousand-franc bills, and proceed to place her bets quietly, coolly, and calculatingly, taking notes with a pencil on a sheet of paper of the numbers that were coming up and trying to find the pattern according to which the chances fell at a given moment. She bet considerable sums. Every day she would win a thousand, two thousand, or at the most three thousand francs—not more, and having won this much, she would immediately walk away. Grandmother observed her for a long time.

"Well, that one won't lose! That one won't lose for sure! What sort is she? You don't know? Who is she?"

"She must be a Frenchwoman of some kind," I whispered.

"Ah, one can tell a bird by its flight. This one has a sharp claw, you can see that. Tell me now what every turn of the wheel means and how you place your bets."

"I explained as best as I could the many different combinations in which the bets could be placed: *rouge et noir, pair et impair, manque et passe,* and, finally, the various subtleties in the system of numbers. Grandmother listened attentively, remembered, asked questions, and was learning the game. Since examples for each system of play were readily available all the time, a lot of it could be learned and remembered very quickly and easily. Grandmother was quite pleased.

"But what is *zéro?* Look, that croupier, the curly-haired one, the head man, shouted *zéro* just now? And why is he raking in everything that's on the table? Look at the pile he has grabbed, all for himself. What's going on?"

"*Zéro* means that the bank wins, Grandmother. Whenever the little ball stops at *zéro,* everything that's on the table goes to the bank. It is true, you get another chance to recover your loss, but at any rate the bank cannot lose."

"Is that so! And so I get nothing at all?"

"No, Grandmother, if you had put your money on *zéro,* and *zéro* came up, you'd have been paid thirty-five times the amount you had put down."

"What? thirty-five times, and does it come up often? Why don't they put their money on it, the fools?"

"The odds are thirty-six to one against it, Grandmother!"

"What nonsense! Potapych! Potapych! Wait, I've got some money myself, there!" She pulled out her tightly packed purse and took out ten gulden. "There you are, place it on *zéro* at once."

"Grandmother, *zéro* has only just been up," I said, "which means that it will be a long time before it turns up again. You'll lose a great deal; wait a little, anyway."

"Stop talking nonsense and put it down!"

"As you please, but it may take all night before it

comes up again; you may lose a thousand; it has happened."

"Come on, nonsense, nonsense! If you're afraid of the wolf, stay out of the forest. What? I lost? Bet again!"

Ten more gulden were lost, and ten more bet. Grandmother could hardly sit still in her seat. Her eyes were eagerly fixed on the little ball dancing along the notches of the turning wheel. The third ten gulden were also lost. Grandmother was quite beside herself; she couldn't sit still at all, and she even banged her fist on the table when the croupier announced *trente six* instead of the expected *zéro*.

"There, look at it!" Grandmother said angrily; "how long will I have to wait until that miserable little *zéro* comes up? For the life of me, I'm not going to leave here before *zéro* comes up! It's all that cursed curly-headed little croupier's fault; he will never let it come! Aleksei Ivanovich, put down two gold pieces at once! At this rate, even if *zéro* comes up finally, you won't get much."

"Grandmother!"

"Put it down, I told you! It's not your money."

I bet twenty gulden. The ball whirled around the wheel for a long time, then at last began to bounce around the notches. Grandmother froze in anticipation and squeezed my hand, and suddenly: bang!

"*Zéro*," announced the croupier.

"You see, you see!" Grandmother turned to me quickly, all beaming and pleased. "Didn't I tell you! The Lord himself put it into my head to stake two gold pieces. Well, how much do I get now? Why aren't they paying up? Potapych, Marfa, where are they now? Where is everybody? Potapych, Potapych!"

"Later, Grandmother," I whispered, "Potapych is at the door, they won't let him in here. Look, Grandmother, they are giving you the money, take it!" A heavy roll of

gold pieces, worth five hundred gulden and sealed in
blue paper was tossed to Grandmother, and two hundred
extra gulden were counted out to her. I scooped it all together with a little shovel and pushed it toward Grandmother.

"Faites le jeu, messieurs! Faites le jeu, messieurs! Rien
ne va plus?[20] called the croupier, inviting the players to
place their bets and getting ready to turn the wheel.

"Oh, my God! we're late! he'll start turning it! put it
down, put it down!" Grandmother urged me, excitedly;
"don't dally, quick"; she was quite beside herself and
kept nudging me with all her might.

"Where do you want me to put it, Grandmother?"

"On *zéro*, on *zéro*! On *zéro* again! Bet as much as you
can! How much have we got altogether? Seven hundred
gulden? No need to worry about them, put down two
hundred gulden at once."

"Think what you are doing, Grandmother! It may not
come up two hundred times running! I assure you, you'll
lose your whole capital."

"Oh, nonsense, nonsense! put it down! And stop wag-
ging your tongue! I know what I am doing," Grandmother was actually beginning to shake with excitement.

"According to the rules you can't place more than one
hundred and twenty gulden on *zéro*, Grandmother; here,
I've done that."

"Why can't I? Aren't you lying to me? Monsieur! Monsieur!" she started nudging the croupier who was sitting
to her left and was just getting ready to spin the wheel,
"combien *zéro*? cent vingt? cent vingt?"[21]

I quickly explained the question in French.

20. "Place your bets, gentlemen! Place your bets, gentlemen! No more
bets?"
21. "How much [on] zero? one hundred and twenty? one hundred and
twenty?"

"Oui, madame," the croupier confirmed politely. "Just so that no single stake shall exceed four thousand florins, according to regulations," he added in explanation.

"Well, too bad, put down a hundred and twenty, then."

"Le jeu est fait!" said the croupier. The wheel began to turn, and thirteen came out. We had lost!

"Once more! once more! put it down once more!" cried Grandmother. I no longer argued with her, but, shrugging my shoulders, placed another hundred and twenty. The wheel spun around for a long time. Grandmother was positively shaking as she watched the wheel. "Does she really think that *zéro* is going to win again?" I thought, looking at her with wonder. Her face beamed with a secure conviction of her winning, a certain expectation that in another moment they would shout *zéro!* The ball jumped into a slot.

"*Zéro!*" the croupier announced.

"Wow!!!" Grandmother turned to me in a frenzy of triumph.

I was myself a gambler; I felt it that very moment. My limbs were trembling, and I felt dazed. Of course, this was a rare occurrence, *zéro* coming up three times in some ten turns of the wheel; yet there was nothing particularly amazing about it. I had myself witnessed, two days earlier, how *zéro* came up three times in a row, and a player who had been keeping track of the winning numbers observed aloud that only the day before that same *zéro* had turned up only once during a twenty-four-hour period.

Since Grandmother had won a most significant sum, her winnings were counted out to her with particular care and attention. She was to receive exactly forty-two-hundred gulden. They gave her the two hundred in gold, and the four thousand in bank notes.

This time Grandmother no longer called for Potapych. She had other things on her mind. She no longer nudged anybody, or shook outwardly. She was, if one may say so, shaking inwardly. Her whole mind was concentrated on only one thing, as if she were aiming directly at something:

"Aleksei Ivanovich! didn't he say that you can bet only four thousand florins at a time? There, take it, put the whole four thousand down on red," Grandmother said firmly.

There was no sense contradicting her. The wheel began to turn.

"Rouge!" the croupier proclaimed.

Again she had won four thousand florins, that is, eight thousand in all. "Let me have these four, and put the other four on red," Grandmother commanded.

I bet another four thousand.

"Rouge!" the croupier announced again.

"Makes twelve thousand! let me have it all. Pour the gold here into my purse, and put away the bank notes."

"Enough! Home! Wheel my chair out!"

Eleven

*T*he chair was wheeled to the door at the other end of the hall. Grandmother was beaming. Our whole group at once thronged around her with congratulations. Eccentric though Grandmother's behavior had been, her triumph made amends for a great deal of it, and the General was no longer afraid of being compromised in public by his relationship with so strange a woman. With a condescending and cheerfully familiar smile, as though he were humoring a child, he congratulated Grandmother. He was, however, visibly impressed, as were all the other spectators. All over the place people were talking and pointing at Grandmother. Many passed by to get a closer view of her. At one side Mr. Astley was talking about her with two of his English friends. Several majestic ladies were examining her with awed amazement, as though she were a marvel of some kind. De Grieux, all smiles, profusely congratulated her.

"Quelle victoire!" he said.

"Mais, madame, c'était du feu!"[22] Mlle Blanche added, with an ingratiating smile.

"Yes, I just went and won twelve thousand. Twelve, indeed, but what about the gold? Together with the gold

22. "But, madame, it was terrific!"

it will be almost thirteen; how much is that in our money? Must be about six thousand, right?"

I reported that it made more than seven, and that, at the present rate of exchange it might go as high as eight thousand.

"Really? eight thousand! And you milksops just sit around here, doing nothing! Potapych, Marfa, did you see it?"

"Madam, how did you do it? Eight thousand rubles!" cried Marfa admiringly.

"Here you are, I'm giving you five gold pieces, take them!"

Potapych and Marfa rushed to kiss their mistress's hand.

"And let the porters have ten gulden each, also. Give each of them a piece of gold, Aleksei Ivanovich. What about that flunkey bowing, and the other one, too? Congratulating me? Give each of them ten gulden, too."

"Madame la princesse . . . un pauvre expatrié . . . malheur continuel . . . les princes russes sont si généreux," a mustachioed character in a shabby jacket and gay colored waistcoat came around fawning, holding his cap in his outstretched hand and wearing a servile smile . . .

"Give him ten gulden, too. No, give him twenty. Well, that's enough, or there will be no end with them. Pick me up and carry me! Praskovia," she turned to Polina Aleksandrovna, "I'll buy you some material for a dress tomorrow, and I'll buy mademoiselle . . . what's her name, Mademoiselle Blanche, isn't it? I'll buy her some, too. Translate that for her, Praskovia!"

"Merci, madame," Mlle Blanche curtsied sweetly, twisting her lips in an ironic smile, which she exchanged with de Grieux and the General. The General was rather embarrassed and was very glad when we had reached the parkway.

"Fedosia, well, won't Fedosia be surprised," said Grandmother, remembering the General's nurse, whom she knew. "I must buy her a dress also. Hey, Aleksei Ivanovich, Aleksei Ivanovich, give something to this beggar!"

A ragged looking character was passing by, his back bent, and looking at us.

"But, Grandmother, maybe he isn't even a beggar, but some sort of crook, or something."

"Give it to him, I tell you! Give him a gulden!"

I went up to the man and gave him a gulden. He looked at me in wide-eyed amazement, but took it without saying a word. He smelled of liquor.

"And you, Aleksei Ivanovich, have you tried your luck yet?"

"No, Grandmother."

"But your eyes were burning, I saw it."

"I'll try it yet, Grandmother, I surely will, later."

"And bet on *zéro* right away! You'll see! How much money have you got?"

"Only two hundred gulden, Grandmother."

"That isn't much. I can loan you five hundred, if you want. Here, take this roll, but as for you, my dear man, don't you expect anything, for I won't give you anything!" she suddenly turned to the General.

It nearly doubled him over, but he said nothing. De Grieux frowned.

"Que diable, c'est une terrible vieille!"[23] he muttered to the General through clenched teeth.

"A beggar, a beggar, another beggar!" shouted Grandmother. "Aleksei Ivanovich, give him a gulden, too."

This time it happened to be a white-haired old man with a wooden leg, wearing a long blue frock coat and carrying a long cane in his hand. He looked like an old

23. "The devil take it, she's a terrible old woman!"

soldier. But when I held out my gulden to him, he took a step back and gave me a menacing look.

"Was ist's der Teufel!" he shouted, adding a dozen other oaths.

"Well, he's a fool!" cried Grandmother, giving up on him. "Let's get going! I'm hungry! Now we'll have dinner directly, then I'll have some rest, and then we'll go back there."

"You want to gamble again, Grandmother?" I exclaimed.

"And what did you think? If you keep sitting around here and moping, must I watch you all the time?"

"Mais, madame," de Grieux approached her, "les chances peuvent tourner, une seule mauvaise chance et vous perdrez tout . . . surtout avec votre jeu . . . c'était terrible!"[24]

"Vous perdrez absolument," chirped Mlle Blanche.

"What business is that of yours, all of you? It won't be your money, but my own! But where is that Mr. Astley?" she asked me.

"He stayed at the casino, Grandmother."

"Too bad. Now that's a nice man for you."

On returning home, Grandmother met the Ober-Kellner on the stairs, stopped him, and bragged to him about her winnings; she then sent for Fedosia, gave her thirty gulden, and ordered dinner to be served. Fedosia and Marfa showered her with compliments at dinner.

"I was watching you, madam," Marfa twittered, "and I told Potapych: 'What is it our lady intends to do?' And there's money on the table, money, good gracious! All my life I haven't seen so much money, and it's all gentlefolk standing there, nothing but gentlefolk sitting there. 'And where,' said I, 'do all these gentlefolk come from, Pota-

---

24. "But, madame . . . your luck can change, one bad bet and you will lose everything . . . especially the way you're playing . . . it was terrible!"

pych?' So I thought to myself: 'May Our Lady herself help her.' And there I was, praying for you, madam, and my heart sinking, simply sinking, and myself trembling all over, just trembling. 'Lord help her,' I thought, and there's where the Lord gave it to you. I am still trembling, madam, still trembling all over."

"Aleksei Ivanovich, after dinner, around four o'clock, get ready and we'll go. And now let's say good-bye for a while, and don't forget to get me a doctor. After all, I'm here for the waters, too. Go now, and don't forget it."

I left Grandmother in a sort of stupor. I was trying to imagine what would happen to all our people and what turn things might take now. I saw clearly that they (and the General in particular) had not yet recovered from the first shock, not from the very first impression, even. Grandmother's appearance, instead of a telegram announcing her death (meaning, of course, the inheritance of her fortune), had so completely shattered all their previous plans and decisions that their reaction to Grandmother's further exploits at the roulette table was evidently one of bewilderment and a sort of shock. Meanwhile this second fact was almost more important than the first, for even though Grandmother had said twice that she was not going to give the General any money, yet, who could know—there was no need to give up hope altogether. Certainly de Grieux, involved as he was in all the General's affairs, was not losing hope. I am convinced that Mlle Blanche, also very much involved (and with ample reason: becoming a General's wife, plus a substantial inheritance!), could not have given up hope either, but would use every bit of her beguiling coquetry on Grandmother—in contrast to the stubborn and proud Polina, who was incapable of currying anybody's favor. But now, now that Grandmother had scored such a triumph at roulette, now that her personality had shown itself so clearly and tangibly (an obstinate, domineering old woman, *et tombée en enfance*), now, it would seem, all was lost. Why, she had been pleased as a child to have tried it, and of course she would lose her last penny eventually. Lord! I thought (and, God forgive me, with a most malignant laugh), why, every ten-gulden piece Grandmother bet just now must have touched an open sore in the General's heart, must have infuriated de Grieux, and driven Mlle de Cominges to a frenzy, as she saw the prize slipping from her grasp. And there was another fact: even after she had won and was so overjoyed that she handed out money to everybody and took every passerby for a beggar, even then Grandmother had felt compelled to say to the General: "I'm not going to give anything to you, though!" That means that she had been thinking about it for a long time, that she was going to stick to it, and that her mind was set about it—dangerous, very dangerous!

All these considerations were going around in my head as I walked up the front stairs from Grandmother's suite to my own little room on the top floor. I was greatly intrigued by it all. To be sure, I had been able, even earlier, to make some conjectures regarding the most important and the strongest threads that might be linking the actors before me; yet I still had no definite knowledge of all the factors and secrets of the play. Polina had never been entirely open with me. Though on occasion she would, indeed, sort of inadvertently open her heart to me, yet I noticed that often, in fact almost every time, after such confidences she would turn everything into a joke, or would try to confuse things so that I might get a wrong slant on everything. Oh, yes, she was hiding a great deal! At any rate, I had the feeling that the finale of this mysterious and tense situation was approaching. Another stroke, and everything would come to an end and be revealed. I felt almost no concern about my own fortunes, though I was involved in it all, too. What a strange mood: there I was, with two hundred gulden in my pocket, far away from home in a foreign land, without a job or means of support, without hope, without plans, and—not in the least worried! If Polina hadn't been so much on my mind, I would have simply abandoned myself to the pure comic interest of the impending denouement and laughed my head off. But Polina worried me. I could feel her fate being decided; but I must confess it was not at all her fate that was troubling me. I wanted to get to the bottom of what she was hiding. I wanted her to come to me and say, "Don't you know that I love you." And if not, if this was just senseless madness, then . . . what was I to wish for? Do I even know what I want? I'm as if in a trance myself. All I want is to be with her, to be in the light of her halo, to be irradiated by her radiance, forever, all my life. I know nothing beyond that! And how could I leave her?

On the third floor, as I was passing through the corridor by the General's suite, I felt as if something stopped me. I turned around and saw, some twenty paces from me, Polina coming out of a door. It seemed as if she had been waiting and watching for me. She beckoned me to her.

"Polina Aleksandrovna . . ."

"Quiet!" she warned me.

"Imagine," I whispered, "I just felt as if something nudged me in the side; I look around, and it's you! It's as though you were emitting electric signals!"

"Take this letter," Polina said with a frown, and in a worried tone, probably not hearing what I had just said, "and deliver it to Mr. Astley in person. As fast as you can, I beg you. There is no need of an answer. He will himself . . ."

She did not finish her sentence. "To Mr. Astley?" I made sure I had it right, in surprise.

But Polina had already disappeared behind the door.

"Aha, so they are in correspondence!" Of course I immediately went to look for Mr. Astley, first at his hotel, where I failed to find him, then at the casino, where I ran through all the halls without seeing him, and, finally, as I was returning home quite frustrated and almost desperate, I met him by accident in a cavalcade of some English men and women on horseback. I waved to him, stopped him, and handed him the letter. We had no time even to exchange glances. But I suspect that Mr. Astley purposely spurred his horse on.

Was I tormented by jealousy? Certainly I was in a most depressed state of mind. I did not even care to find out what their correspondence was about. And so he was her confidant! "A friend is a friend," I thought, "so much is clear (though when did he manage to become her friend?); was there any love involved here? Of course not," my common sense whispered to me. But in cases such as this, common sense alone just won't do. At any rate, this matter, too, had to be cleared up. The whole thing was growing unpleasantly complicated.

No sooner was I back at the hotel than the doorman and the Ober-Kellner, who came out of his room let me know that I had been wanted, looked for, and asked for three times; I had been asked to come as quickly as possible to the General's suite. I was in a singularly bad mood. In the General's study I found, besides the General himself, de Grieux and Mlle Blanche, alone, without her mother. The mother was decidedly an *ad hoc* person, used strictly for the sake of appearances; when it came to real *business* Mlle Blanche acted for herself. Besides, the mother probably knew very little about her so-called daughter's affairs.

The three of them were in the middle of a heated discussion, and the door of the study was actually locked, which had never happened before. As I approached the door, I could make out three loud voices: the insolent and caustic tone of de Grieux, Blanche's impudent abuse and furious screams, and the plaintive voice of the General, who was apparently trying to defend himself about something. As I entered the room they all made an effort to pull themselves together and assume a more proper pose. De Grieux smoothed his hair and changed his angry face into a smiling one, with that wretched, formally polite French smile which I hated so much. The General, crushed and confused, assumed somehow a mechanical air of dignity. Only Mlle Blanche hardly changed expression of her face, which was blazing with rage, but merely fell silent, fixing her eyes on me in impatient anticipation. Let me note that she had so far treated me without any regard whatsoever, had even refused to respond to my polite bows—she had simply refused to take notice of me.

"Aleksei Ivanovich," the General began in a tone of delicate reproach, "let me tell you that I find it strange, very strange indeed . . . in short, your actions in relation to my family and myself . . . in short, very strange indeed . . ."

"Eh, ce n'est pas ça," de Grieux interrupted him, angrily and contemptuously. (Obviously he was in charge!) "Mon cher monsieur, notre cher général se trompe,[25] to use this tone" (I give the rest of his speech in Russian), "but he wanted to tell you . . . that is, warn you, or, rather, to beg you most earnestly that you should not ruin him—well, yes, that you should not ruin him! I use this term on purpose . . ."

"But how, how?" I interrupted.

25. "My dear sir, our dear general is mistaken."

"Heavens, you undertake to act as the guide (or how should I call it?) of this old woman, cette pauvre terrible vieille," even de Grieux was beginning to get confused, "but she will lose everything; she will lose everything to the last penny! You saw it yourself, you were a witness of the way she gambles! Once she starts losing she'll never quit, from obstinacy, from anger, but keep on playing just keep on playing; and in such cases luck never turns, and then . . . then . . ."

"And then," the General joined in, "then you will have ruined the whole family! My family and I, we are her heirs, she has no nearer relations. I tell you frankly: my affairs are in a bad way, in an extremely bad way. You are yourself partly aware of it . . . If she loses a considerable sum or worse, her whole fortune (my Lord!)—what will become of them, of my children!" (The General stole a glance at de Grieux.) "Of me!" (He looked at Mlle Blanche, who turned away from him with contempt.) "Aleksei Ivanovich, save us, save us! . . ."

"But tell me, General, how can I . . . What have I to say in this matter?"

"Refuse to go with her, just refuse, leave her alone! . . ."

"Then someone else will turn up!" I exclaimed.

"Ce n'est pas ça, ce n'est pas ça," de Grieux interrupted again, "que diable! No, don't leave her alone, but at least try to talk some sense into her, dissuade her, try to divert her attention . . . Well, and if nothing else, don't let her lose too much; divert her in some way."

"But how am I supposed to do it? Why won't you undertake this task yourself, Monsieur de Grieux?" I added, as naïvely as possible.

Here I intercepted a quick, fiery, questioning glance from Mlle Blanche at de Grieux. And in de Grieux's own face there was a flicker of something peculiar, something like sincerity, something he could not help expressing.

"That's exactly the point, she won't receive me now!" he exclaimed, with a wave of his hand. "If only she would! ...later..."

De Grieux gave Mlle Blanche a quick and meaningful look.

"O mon cher Monsieur Alexis, soyez si bon," Mlle Blanche herself, *in person,* took a step toward me and, with a seductive smile on her lips, seized both of my hands and pressed them firmly. Damn it all! That devilish face of hers could change in a second. At that instance she suddenly had such an imploring, sweet face, such a child-like and even mischievous smile. As she finished speaking, she gave me a roguish wink, to me alone and for no one else to see; did she mean to wrap it up right there? It was really very well done; but it was terribly coarse.

Then the General leaped up, too, and I mean "leaped up."

"Aleksei Ivanovich, forgive me for talking to you as I did, a moment ago, I really did not mean it that way . . . I beg you, I implore you, I bow down before you, Russian style, you alone, you alone can save us! Mademoiselle de Cominges and I, we both implore you—you must understand, you do understand, don't you?" he pleaded, indicating Mlle Blanche with his eyes. He was very pathetic.

At that instant there were three subdued and respectful knocks at the door. We opened; it was a bellboy and behind him, a few steps away, Potapych. They had been dispatched by Grandmother. They had been ordered to locate and deliver me at once. "Madam is angry," reported Potapych.

"But it is only half past three!"

"Madam couldn't fall asleep, kept tossing about, then suddenly got up, told me to get her chair, and you. Madam is at the front entrance now, sir . . ."

"Quelle mégère!"[26] exclaimed de Grieux.

And in fact I found Grandmother already sitting at the front entrance, having lost all her patience because I wasn't there. She could not wait until four o'clock.

"Well, pick me up!" she cried, and we were on our way back to the casino.

26. "What a shrew!"

Twelve

Grandmother was in an impatient and irritable mood; one could see that she was deeply preoccupied with roulette. She paid little attention to anything else and seemed generally distracted. Thus, for instance, she did not ask any questions along the way as she had before. When she saw a truly splendid carriage whirl by, she perfunctorily raised her hand and asked, "What is that? Whose is it?" But I believe that she did not even hear my answer. She was sunk deep in thought and awoke now and then to gesture fitfully and impatiently. As we were approaching the casino I pointed out to her, at a distance, Baron and Baroness Wurmerhelm. She took an absent-minded look and said, with complete indifference: "Ah!" Then, turning around quickly to Potapych and Marfa, who were walking behind her, she snapped out to them:

"Why must you drag along? I can't take you with me every time! Go back home! All I need is you," she added, addressing me, as the other two hurriedly made their bows and walked back home.

They were already expecting Grandmother at the casino. They immediately vacated the very same place for her, right next to the croupier. The croupiers, who were always so well-mannered and who seemed to be just ordinary officials almost ordinarily indifferent to whether the bank won or lost, were in reality very much concerned about the bank's losses. And most certainly they are given instructions regarding how to attract players and how to protect the interests of the establishment, for which they no doubt receive prizes and bonuses. At least they were already eyeing Grandmother as their sure prey. Then, what my friends had anticipated actually happened.

This is how it went.

Grandmother pounced at once on *zéro* and immediately ordered me to stake one hundred and twenty gulden at a time. We bet once, twice, a third time—*zéro* never came up. "Put it down, put it down!" Grandmother nudged me impatiently. I did as she said.

"How many times have we played it now?" she finally asked, gnashing her teeth with impatience.

"That was already the twelfth time, Grandmother. We have lost fourteen hundred and forty. I tell you, Grandmother, maybe it won't come up until tonight . . ."

"Quiet!" Grandmother interrupted. "Put it down on *zéro,* and also lay a thousand gulden on red. Here, take the bank note."

Red came up, while *zéro* lost again. We had won back a thousand gulden.

"You see, you see!" Grandmother whispered, "we've won back almost everything we lost. Put it down on *zéro* again. We'll play it ten more times or so and then give it up."

But after the fifth time Grandmother was already quite tired of it.

"Let this wretched *zéro* go to the devil. Here, put all four thousand gulden down on red," she ordered.

"Grandmother! Won't this be too much? What if red

doesn't turn up?" I pleaded, but Grandmother almost hit me. (By the way, she kept nudging me so hard it felt as if she were hitting me.) So there was nothing to be done, and I placed the whole four thousand gulden, which we had won earlier, on red. The wheel turned. Grandmother sat there, calmly and proudly erect, fully confident that she would win.

"*Zéro,*" the croupier announced.

At first Grandmother failed to realize it, but when she saw that the croupier was raking in her four thousand gulden, along with everything else on the table, and learned that *zéro,* which hadn't turned up for so long and on which we had staked and lost nearly two thousand, had turned up the very moment she had sent it to the devil, she gasped and flung up her hands in view of the whole hall. A few snickers were actually heard around us.

"For heaven's sake! That's where the cursed thing had to turn up!" Grandmother wailed, "the accursed, miserable thing! It's your fault! It's all your fault!" she fell upon me furiously, pushing me. "You told me not to play it."

"Grandmother, I was just telling you a fact; how can I answer for all the chances?"

"I'll give you a chance!" she whispered threateningly; "go away, leave me alone."

"Good-bye, Grandmother," I turned to leave.

"Aleksei Ivanovich, Aleksei Ivanovich, stay here! Where are you going? Come on, what's the matter with you? Are you mad at me? Fool! Come on, stay a while. Come, don't be angry, I'm a fool myself! Well, tell me, what shall I do now?"

"Grandmother, I'm not going to tell you anything, because you'll blame me if you lose. Play for yourself; just tell me and I'll place the bets."

"Well, come on then! Put down another four thousand

gulden on red! Here, take my pocketbook." She took it out of her pocket and handed it to me. "Come, take it quickly, here's twenty thousand rubles in cash."

"Grandmother," I whispered, "such a large sum . . ."

"As sure as I'm alive, I'm going to win it back. Put it down!" I did, and we lost.

"Put it down, the whole eight thousand, put it down!"

"You can't, Grandmother, the highest stake is four thousand! . . ."

"All right, put down four!"

This time we won. Grandmother took heart. "You see, you see!" she started nudging me again, "put down another four thousand!"

We staked it and lost; then we lost again and again.

"Grandmother, the whole twelve thousand are gone," I announced.

"I see they're gone," she said with the calm of fury, if this is a correct expression; "I see, my dear man, I see," she muttered, with a fixed stare and as if trying to make up her mind; "eh! as sure as I'm alive, put down another four thousand guldens!"

"But there's no money left, Grandmother. Here in your pocketbook you've got some Russian 5 percent bonds, and some money orders, but no cash."

"What about my purse?"

"There's some small change, Grandmother."

"Have they any money changers here? I was told that one could change any of our notes here," Grandmother inquired resolutely.

"Oh, as much as you like! But what you'll lose on the exchange, well . . . it would make a person's hair stand on end!"

"Nonsense! I'll win it all back! Take me there. Call those blockheads!"

I wheeled the chair away, the porters came, and we left

the casino. "Faster, faster, faster!" Grandmother commanded. "Lead the way, Aleksei Ivanovich, take the shortest way . . . is it very far?"

"Just a few steps, Grandmother."

But as we were turning from the square into the parkway we were met by our whole party: the General, de Grieux, Mlle Blanche with her mother. Polina Aleksandrovna was not with them, nor was Mr. Astley.

"Come on, come on, don't stop!" Grandmother cried; "come, what do you want? I have no time for you now!"

I was walking behind. De Grieux came running up to me.

"She lost everything she won earlier, plus twelve thousand gulden of her own money. We are on our way to cash some 5 percent bonds," I whispered to him quickly.

De Grieux stamped his foot and ran to tell the General. We kept rolling along.

"Stop her, stop her!" the General whispered to me frantically.

"Well, why don't you try to stop her?" I whispered back.

"Auntie!" said the General, approaching her, "auntie . . . right now we . . . right now we . . ." his voice was trembling and failing him, "we're going to hire some horses and drive out into the country . . . a magnificent view . . . the point . . . we were on our way to invite you to join us."

"Leave me alone, you and your point!" Grandmother waved him off petulantly.

"There's a village there . . . we're going to have tea . . ." the General continued, utterly desperate.

"Nous boirons du lait, sur l'herbe fraîche,"[27] added de Grieux, who was seething with fury.

"Du lait, de l'herbe fraîche," that is the Parisian bour-

---

27. "We'll drink milk out on the fresh grass."

geois's whole conception of the perfect idyll; that, in substance, is his view of "la nature et la vérité"!

"Oh, go away with your milk! Guzzle it yourself, it
gives me a bellyache. And why do you pester me?" Grandmother shouted angrily, "I tell you, I haven't got time for
you!"

"Here we are, Grandmother!" I cried, "right here!"

We had reached the building where the bank was. I
went in to cash the securities, leaving Grandmother waiting at the entrance. De Grieux, the General, and Blanche
stood to one side, not knowing what to do. Grandmother
gave them a wrathful look, and they walked away in the
direction of the casino.

The exchange rate offered me was so ruinous that I
hesitated to accept it but went back to Grandmother for
instructions.

"Ah, but that's highway robbery!" she cried, flinging
up her hands. "Well, never mind, change it anyway!" she
went on, resolutely; "wait, call the banker out to me!"

"Maybe one of the clerks will do, Grandmother?"

"Well, a clerk, what's the difference. Ah, highway
robbers!"

The clerk consented to come out when he learned that
he was being asked by an aged, invalid countess who
couldn't walk. Grandmother spent a long time reproaching him in a loud and angry voice for trying to swindle
her, and wrangled with him in a mixture of Russian,
French, and German, with the help of my interpreting.
The clerk, a serious faced man, kept looking at the two
of us and shaking his head, without saying anything. In
fact, he was staring at Grandmother with such intent
curiosity that it bordered on disrespect; at last he broke
into a smile.

"Well, be off!" Grandmother cried, "I hope you'll
choke on my money! Change it with him, Aleksei Iva-

novich, there's no time, otherwise we'd go elsewhere . . ."

"The clerk says that the other banks will give you even less."

I don't remember the exact figures, but they were exorbitant. I received close to twelve thousand florins in gold and bank notes, got my receipt, and carried it out to Grandmother.

"Well, let's go! Come on! No time to count it," she said, waving her hands, "faster, faster, faster!"

"I'll never bet again on that accursed *zéro,* nor on the red either," she said, as we arrived at the casino.

This time I tried my best to impress on her that she should keep her stakes low, assuring her that with a change of luck she would always be able to raise them. But she was so impatient that, even though she agreed with this at first, there was no way to stop her once she had started to play. No sooner had she won a few bets at a hundred or a hundred and twenty gulden than she started pushing me: "There, you see! There, you see! I won, didn't I? If we had put down four thousand, instead of a hundred, we'd have won four thousand, and what have we got now? It's all your fault, your fault!"

And so, though I felt exasperated by the way she was playing, I finally decided to keep quiet and to give no more advice to her.

Suddenly de Grieux leaped into action. All three of them had been standing nearby. I noticed that Mlle Blanche was standing to one side with her mother, flirting with the little prince. The General was obviously out of favor, almost in the doghouse. Blanche would not even look at him, though he was trying to ingratiate himself as best he could. Poor General! He alternately flushed and grew pale, he was shaking all over, and he had even given up watching Grandmother play. Blanche and the little prince finally left the hall, and the General ran after them.

"Madame, madame," de Grieux whispered to Grandmother in a honeyed voice, bending all the way down to her ear. "Madame, such a bet is impossible . . . no, no, it is impossible . . ." he said in broken Russian, "no!"

"How, then? Well, teach me!" said Grandmother, turning to him. De Grieux suddenly started babbling something very rapidly in French. He gave her his advice, fussed about, and told her that she must bide her time; he then began to make some sort of calculation, jotting down various figures . . . Grandmother did not understand a word of it. He kept turning to me, asking me to translate; he poked his finger at the table, pointing at something; finally, he grabbed a pencil and started figuring something on a sheet of paper. At last Grandmother lost her patience.

"Well, be off, get going! you're talking a lot of nonsense! 'Madame, madame!' He doesn't know a thing about it himself; be off!"

"Mais, madame," de Grieux kept up his chatter, continuing to poke at the table and showing her something. The whole thing had really got to him.

"All right, then place a bet once the way he says," Grandmother ordered, "let us see: maybe it will work out that way."

All de Grieux wanted was to stop her from betting large sums. He suggested that we lay bets on numbers, individually, and as groups. Following his instructions, I put a ten-gulden piece each on the series of odd numbers in the first twelve, and a fifty-gulden piece each on the groups of numbers from twelve to eighteen, and from eighteen to twenty-four, a hundred and sixty in all.

The wheel turned. "*Zéro*," said the croupier. We had lost it all.

"What a blockhead!" shouted Grandmother, addressing de Grieux. "Why, you miserable little Frenchman! That's the kind of advice you get from him, the monster! Be off, be off! Doesn't know a thing, and comes butting in!"

De Grieux, terribly offended, shrugged his shoulders, gave Grandmother one contemptuous look, and walked away. He was himself feeling embarrassed that he had got into this. He just hadn't been able to restrain himself.

An hour later, try everything as we did, we had lost it all.

"Home!" Grandmother shouted.

She did not say a word until we had reached the parkway. There, as we were approaching the hotel, she finally broke down, exclaiming:

"What a fool! What a silly fool! Oh, you old, old fool, you!"

The first thing when we were back at her suite: "I'll have some tea!" And then, "Start packing right away! we're leaving!"

"Where, madam, where are we going?" Marfa tried to ask.

"What business is it of yours? Mind your own business! Potapych, get everything ready, all the baggage. We are going back to Moscow! I've just *verspielt* fifteen thousand rubles!"

"Fifteen thousand, madam! My God!" Potapych cried, flinging up his hands pathetically, probably meaning to humor her.

"Come, come, you fool! No use whimpering! Quiet! Get packed! Let me have the bill, quick, quick!"

"The next train goes at half past nine, Grandmother," I inserted, to stop her frenzy.

"And how late is it now?"

"Half past seven."

"What a nuisance! Well, all right! Aleksei Ivanovich, I haven't a penny left. Here are two more notes. Run over and change these for me, too. Or I'll have nothing for the journey."

I set off. When I returned to the hotel half an hour later, I found our whole party at Grandmother's. Having learned that Grandmother was returning to Moscow, they were apparently more upset about that fact than even by her gambling losses. Granted her departure would save her fortune, but then, what was going to become of the General now? Who was going to pay de Grieux? Mlle Blanche, of course, would not wait until Grandmother died, but would most certainly take off with the little prince or with somebody else. They were all standing before her, consoling her and trying to persuade her not to take it to heart. Polina was still not there. Grandmother was shouting at them furiously.

"Leave me alone, you devils! What business is it of yours? Why does that goat's beard come and poke his nose into my affairs?" she was screaming at de Grieux, "and you, my fine bird, what do you want of me?" she turned to Mlle Blanche; "what are you fussing about?"

"Diantre!"[28] whispered Mlle Blanche, with an angry flash of her eyes, but then suddenly she burst into loud laughter and left the room.

"Elle vivra cent ans!"[29] she shouted to the General, as she was leaving.

"Aha, so you are counting on me to die?" Grandmother screamed at the General. "Out with you! Turn them all out, Aleksei Ivanovich! What do you care? I've blown my own money, not yours!"

The General shrugged his shoulders, bowed, and walked out. De Grieux followed him.

28. "Damn it!"
29. "She'll live a hundred years."

"Call Praskovia," Grandmother told Marfa.

Five minutes later Marfa returned with Polina. All this time Polina had been sitting in her room with the children, and apparently had not been out all day on purpose. Her face was serious, sad, and preoccupied.

"Praskovia," began Grandmother, "is it true, as I learned recently by accident, that this fool, your stepfather, wants to marry that silly featherhead of a Frenchwoman—an actress, or worse than that? Tell me, is this the truth?"

"I don't know anything about it for certain, Grandmother," answered Polina, "but I gather from the words of Mademoiselle Blanche herself, who does not bother to conceal anything, that . . ."

"Enough!" Grandmother interrupted her energetically, "I understand everything! I always reckoned that he would do such a thing, and I've always considered him a most worthless and frivolous person. He is full of swagger about being a general (they promoted him from colonel on his retirement), and thinks he is terribly important. My dear girl, I know everything about how telegram after telegram was sent to Moscow, asking: 'Will old granny turn up her toes soon, will she?' Waiting for their inheritance. Without money that vile hussy, what's her name, de Cominges or whatever, won't take him for her flunkey, false teeth and all. She's got a lot of money herself, they say, she lends it out at interest, and I won't ask how she made it. Praskovia, I'm not blaming you. You weren't the one who sent those telegrams, and let bygones be bygones. I know that you have a bad temper—stings like a wasp. And your sting hurts. But I feel sorry for you, because I was fond of your mother, the late Katerina. Well, what about it? Leave everything here and come with me. You have no place to go, you know. Nor is it fitting for you to stay with them now. Wait!" Grandmother stopped Polina, who was about to reply, from interrupting her, "I'm not through yet. I'm not asking anything of you. As you well know, my Moscow home is really a mansion. You can have a whole floor to yourself, and you need not come down and see me for weeks at a time, if you can't stand my temper. Well, what about it?"

"Allow me to ask you first: do you really mean to leave right away?"

"Do you think I'm joking, my dear? I said so, and this is it. Today I squandered fifteen thousand rubles playing that accursed roulette of yours. Five years ago I promised that I would rebuild that wooden church on my estate near Moscow in stone, and now I've blown my money here instead. Now, my dear, I'm going home to build my church."

"But what about the waters? Didn't you come here for the waters, Grandmother?"

"You and your waters! Don't make me angry, Praskovia. Are you doing it on purpose? Tell me, are you coming or aren't you?"

"I thank you very, very much, Grandmother," Polina began, with feeling. "I thank you for the refuge which you are offering me. In a way you've guessed right what position I am in. I am so very grateful to you, and, believe me, I'll come to you, and maybe even soon. But right now there are reasons . . . important ones . . . and I can't make a decision now, not at this very moment. If you'd stay only for two weeks . . ."

"This means you don't want to come?"

"This means that I can't. Besides, at any rate, I can't leave my brother and sister here, and since . . . since . . . since it actually could happen that they'd be abandoned, in that case . . . if you'd take me together with the little ones, Grandmother, in that case I'd come to you of course, and, believe me, I'd earn it!" she added emphatically, "but without the children I couldn't, Grandmother."

"All right, don't whimper!" (Polina had no intention of whimpering, in fact, she never cried.) "We'll find a place for the chicks, too, the chicken coop is big enough. Besides, it's time for them to start going to school. So you are not coming now? Well, Praskovia, watch out! I wish you well, but I know why you aren't coming. I know everything, Praskovia! That Frenchman will bring you no good."

Polina blushed. I positively started. (Everybody knows all about it! I must be the only who knows nothing!)

"All right, all right, don't frown. I'm not going to make a big thing of it. Just keep out of harm's way, understand? You are a clever girl; I'd feel sorry for you. Well, enough, I wish I'd never seen any of you! Go! Good-bye!"

"But I'll see you off, Grandmother," said Polina.

"You don't have to; don't get in my way; I'm sick and tired of you all."

Polina kissed Grandmother's hand, but she pulled her hand away and kissed Polina on the cheek.

As she was passing me, Polina gave me a quick glance, then looked the other way.

"Well, good-bye to you, too, Aleksei Ivanovich! It's just an hour until train time. I must have tired you out, I think. Here, take these fifty pieces of gold."

"No, thank you, Grandmother, I'm ashamed . . ."

"Come, come!" cried Grandmother, but so energetically and menacingly that I dared say no more and took the money.

"If you should find yourself in Moscow, running around without a job, come to see me. I'll recommend you to someone. Now, leave me!"

I went to my room and lay down on my bed. I think

that I lay there for half an hour, flat on my back, with my
hands clasped behind my head. Disaster had struck, and
there was a lot to think about. I decided that I would talk
to Polina seriously the next day. Ah! That miserable
Frenchman? So it was true then! But what was at the bottom of it all? Polina and de Grieux! My God, what a
match!

It was all simply unbelievable. I suddenly jumped up,
quite beside myself, intending to look up Mr. Astley and
at all costs make him speak out. Why, of course, even in
this matter he knew more than I did. Mr. Astley? There
I had another mystery facing me!

But suddenly there was a knock at my door. I looked,
and there was Potapych.

"Aleksei Ivanovich, sir; madam wants you, sir!"

"What is it? She isn't leaving, is she? It's twenty minutes until train time."

"Madam is nervous, sir, so that she can barely sit still.
'Quick, quick!' she says, meaning you, sir. For the sake
of Christ, sir, come quickly."

I immediately ran downstairs. Grandmother was already waiting in the corridor. She had her pocketbook in
her hand.

"Aleksei Ivanovich, lead the way, let's go! . . ."

"Where, Grandmother?"

"As sure as I'm alive, I'll win it back! Come, let's go,
and no questions asked! You can play there until midnight, can't you?"

I was stunned for a moment, but thought it over
quickly, and made my decision right there.

"Do as you please, Antonida Vasilievna, but I'm not
coming."

"Why not? What now? Are you all out of your heads,
or what?"

"Do as you please: I would blame myself afterward. I

just won't. I don't want to see it, I don't want any part of it. Forgive me, Antonida Vasilievna. Here are your fifty pieces of gold. Good-bye!" And, after having put the fifty pieces on the little table near Grandmother's chair, I bowed and walked away.

"What nonsense!" Grandmother shouted after me; "so don't come if you don't want to; I'll find my own way! Potapych, come with me! Come, lift me up, let's go."

Mr. Astley was not in, and I returned home. Late that night, going on one o'clock, I learned from Potapych how the day had ended for Grandmother. She lost everything that I had converted into cash for her that evening, that is, another ten thousand rubles in our money. That same little Pole, to whom she had given twenty gulden earlier in the day, attached himself to her and directed her game all night. At first, before the Pole came around, Grandmother had tried to use Potapych and made him place the bets for her, but she got rid of him soon, and that's when the little Pole jumped in. As luck would have it, he understood some Russian and even babbled away, after a fashion, mixing three languages, so that they understood each other, more or less. Grandmother abused him mercilessly all along, and though he was incessantly "laying himself at the lady's feet," yet of course, "there was no comparing him with you, Aleksei Ivanovich," Potapych was telling me. "She treated you *exactly like a gentleman,* while that man—well, sir, I saw it with my own eyes, so help me God—stole her money right off the table. She caught him at it herself, once or twice, and did she give it to him, sir, did she give it to him, calling him all sorts of names, even pulled his hair once, upon my word, I'm not lying, so everybody around was laughing, sir. She lost it all, sir, every bit of it, everything you had cashed for her. We brought her back here, the dear, and she only asked for some water to drink, crossed herself, and went to bed. She must have been worn out, to be sure, for she fell asleep at once. May the Lord send her heavenly dreams! Oh, damn these foreign countries!" Potapych concluded his account, "I said that it would lead to no good. If we could only go back to Moscow as soon as possible! What is it that we don't have back home in Moscow? A garden, flowers of the kind they haven't even got here, sweet air, the apples getting ripe, lots of space—no, we had to go abroad! Oh, oh, oh! . . ."

Thirteen

*A*lmost a whole month has passed
since I last touched these notes of
mine, which were begun under the
influence of impressions that, though quite disorganized,
were nevertheless intense. The catastrophe which I then
felt to be approaching actually came, but a hundred
times more suddenly and unexpectedly than I had ever
thought. It was all very strange, hideous, and even tragic,
at least as far as I was concerned. A few things happened
to me that bordered on the miraculous; or, at least, this
is how I see them at this very moment, while from another point of view, and especially considering that I was
then in the middle of a whirl of events, the same things
would have appeared as no more than slightly unusual.
But what amazes me most is my own attitude to all these
events. To this day I cannot understand myself! And all
this has passed like a dream, even my passion, and it was
a powerful and sincere one, but . . . where is it now? To
be truthful, it just isn't there, and at times the thought
flits through my brain, "Could it be that I was out of my
mind then, and spent all that time in an insane asylum,
and perhaps I'm in one right now—so that the whole
thing took place only in my *imagination,* and I am still
imagining it to have been true? . . ."

I have put my notes together and read them over.
(Who knows, perhaps simply to make sure that I did not

write them in an insane asylum?) Now I am all by myself. It is fall, and the leaves are turning yellow. I'm stuck
in this dismal little town (oh, how dismal little German
towns can be!), and instead of giving thought to what I
should do next, I continue to live under the influence of
those recent sensations, under the influence of my fresh
memories, under the influence of that whirl of events
which caught me in its vortex only to spew me out again,
leaving me high and dry. At times it seems to me that I
am still caught up in that whirlwind, and that any moment the storm will be back and carry me off on its wings,
that I will again lose all sense of order and proportion,
and, again, go whirling, whirling, whirling around . . .

However, I may perhaps settle down and quit whirling
around, if I give myself a clear account, as best I can, of
what has happened to me during this past month. I feel
like writing again. Besides, there is absolutely nothing
to do in the evenings. Strangely enough, just to do anything at all, I even take from the wretched local lending
library the novels of Paul de Kock (in German translation!), which I can't stand, and read them, wondering at
myself—as if I were afraid of breaking the spell of what
has just happened by a serious book or any serious occu-
pation. Is it really true that this grotesque dream and all
the impressions it has left in my mind are so dear to me
that I'm actually afraid to touch it with something new,
lest it go up in smoke? It must be very dear to me still,
all of it, it seems? Why, of course, it is dear to me. Perhaps
I'll remember it even forty years from now . . .

And so I am taking up my notes again. However, I can
give a brief and partial account of it all now: the actual
impressions were altogether different . . .

First of all, let me finish with Grandmother. The following day she really lost everything. It was quite inevitable: any time a person such as she gets started on that

road, it's like sliding down a snow-covered hill on a sled; you pick up speed, going faster and faster. She gambled all day, until eight o'clock at night. I was not present and know what happened only from what I heard from other people.

Potapych was in constant attendance on her at the casino all day. Several little Poles took turns guiding Grandmother's play during the day. She started by getting rid of the little Pole of the day before, the one whose hair she had pulled, and hired another, who turned out rather worse than the first. She fired that one and rehired the first, who had refused to leave but during the whole period of his disgrace had kept breathing down her neck, poking his head in from behind her chair continually. They were positively driving her to despair. The second little Pole, having been fired, also refused to budge, and so one of them stationed himself to her right and the other to her left. They argued and abused each other over every bet that was placed, calling each other *lajdak*[30] and other such compliments in Polish, then making up again and throwing money around without rhyme or reason. When they quarreled, each would place bets on his side; one of them would play red, the other black. In the end they had Grandmother so bewildered and confused that she finally, almost in tears, appealed to the croupier, a man of advanced age, to, please, help her get rid of the pair. They were, in fact, immediately turned out, in spite of all their screams and protests. They were both yelling at once, claiming that Grandmother owed them money, that she had deceived them about something, and that she had treated them dishonorably, bascly. Poor Potapych told me all this with tears that very night, after she had lost all. He complained that they had stuffed their pockets with money, that he had seen how

---

30. Polish word meaning "scoundrel."

they shamelessly stole her money, slipping quantities of it into their pockets all the time. For instance, one of them would beg her to give him fifty gulden for his efforts and would promptly put down the money right next to Grandmother's bet. Grandmother would win, but he would scream that his money had won and that hers had lost. As they were being ejected from the casino, Potapych came forward and reported that they had their pockets full of gold. Grandmother immediately asked the croupier to look into this matter, and in spite of the outcries of the two little Poles (they cackled like two trapped roosters), the police appeared on the scene and their pockets were immediately emptied and the money returned to Grandmother. Until she lost everything, Grandmother had enjoyed obvious prestige with the croupiers and the whole casino staff the whole day long. Her fame had gradually spread all over town. Visitors of every nationality who had gathered at the watering place, ordinary ones as well as the most prominent, all thronged to have a look at "une vieille comtesse russe, tombée en enfance," who had already lost "several millions."

But Grandmother profited very, very little from being rescued from the two little Poles. They were replaced immediately by a third Pole, one who spoke perfectly pure Russian and was dressed like a gentleman, even though he still had a touch of the lackey, with huge moustaches and "a sense of honor." He, too, kissed "the lady's footsteps" and "laid himself at the lady's feet," but to those around them, he behaved haughtily, took charge of things despotically—in short, he immediately established himself not as Grandmother's servant but as her master. He continually and at every bet addressed her, swearing with terrible oaths that he was himself an "honorable *pan*," and that he wasn't going to take a single kopeck of Grandmother's money. He repeated his oaths so many times that Grandmother was completely intimidated. But since this *pan* actually seemed to improve her game and in fact almost started winning, there simply was no way for Grandmother to rid herself of him, even on her own account. An hour later the two little Poles of before, who had been ejected from the casino, turned up behind Grandmother's chair again, offering their services once more, if only to run errands for her. Potapych swore that the "honorable *pan*" winked at them and actually slipped something to them. Since Grandmother had gone without dinner and had hardly left her chair all day, one of the two Poles, in fact, made himself useful: he ran once to the casino dining room to get her a cup of bouillon, and later brought her some tea. But toward the end of the day, when it was clear to everybody that she was about to lose her last bank note, as many as six little Poles were standing behind her chair, having appeared from nowhere. But when Grandmother was at the point of losing her last coins, they all not only ceased to obey her, but barely took notice of her anymore; they reached over her head to the table, snatched up the money themselves, made their own decisions and placed the bets as they pleased, quarreled among themselves, shouted, talked things over with the "honorable *pan*" with whom they were now on the most familiar terms, while the "honorable *pan*" himself seemed by then almost oblivious to Grandmother's existence. Even after Grandmother had definitely lost everything and was returning to the hotel at eight o'clock, three or four little Poles still refused to leave her alone, but kept running after her, on both sides of her chair, shouting at the top of their voices and claiming, in an incessant patter, that Grandmother had cheated them out of something and was supposed to give them something. They followed her right up to the hotel, whence they were finally kicked out by the staff.

According to Potapych's reckoning Grandmother had

lost on that day close to ninety thousand rubles in all, not counting her losses of the day before. She had converted, one after another, all of her securities: the 5 percent bonds, the government bonds, all of the stocks and bonds which she had with her. I expressed my wonder at how she could endure sitting there in her chair for seven or eight hours, scarcely leaving the table at all, but Potapych told me that she had actually had about three significant winning streaks, so that, carried away by new hope, she was quite incapable of tearing herself away. But any gambler will tell you that a man may spend as much as twenty-four hours at cards, glued to his seat and without ever taking his eyes off the game.

Meanwhile, at our hotel very critical things were also happening all day. That morning, before eleven o'clock, when Grandmother was still at home, the family, that is the General and de Grieux, decided to take one final step. Having learned that Grandmother had no intention of leaving but, on the contrary, was getting ready to go back to the casino, they went to see her in full conclave (excepting Polina) to have one final and even *open* talk with her. The General, trembling and with a sinking heart in view of the frightful consequences it might have for him, actually overdid it: after having pleaded and begged for half an hour, and even having made a clean breast of everything, including all his debts and his passion for Mlle Blanche too (he had quite lost his head), the General suddenly assumed a menacing tone; in fact, he began shouting and stamping his feet at Grandmother; he yelled that she was disgracing their name, that she had become a scandal to the whole town, and finally . . . finally: "You are bringing shame upon the name of Russia, madam!" cried the General, "and there's still the police for such cases!" Grandmother finally drove him out with her stick (a real stick). The General and de Grieux got together another time or two that morning, consulting this possibility: would it perhaps be possible, after all, to bring in the police under some pretext? Say, that there was that unfortunate but venerable old lady, evidently senile, who was losing her last savings, and so on. In short, would it be possible to have her put under some sort of guardianship or restraint? . . . But de Grieux only shrugged his shoulders and openly laughed at the General, who was by now talking complete nonsense as he ran back and forth in his study. Finally, de Grieux gave up and walked out. In the evening it was learned that he had moved out of the hotel altogether, after a most earnest and highly secret consultation with Mlle Blanche. As for Mlle Blanche, she had taken decisive measures early in the morning: she cast off the General quite definitely and would no longer admit him to her presence. And when the General ran after her to the casino and met her there, arm-in-arm with the little prince, neither she nor Mme veuve Cominges deigned to recognize him. The little prince did not greet him either. All that day Mlle Blanche kept sounding out the prince and needling him so that he would finally declare his intentions. But alas! She was cruelly deceived in her hopes regarding the prince! This little catastrophe took place in the evening, when it suddenly became clear that the prince was as poor as a church mouse and, what is more, had been himself counting on borrowing some money from her on a promissory note to try his luck at roulette. Blanche turned him out with indignation and locked herself up in her room.

In the morning of the same day I went to see Mr. Astley, or rather, I went looking for Mr. Astley but could find him nowhere. He was not at home, or in the casino, or in the park. He was not dining at his hotel that day. It was going on five o'clock when I suddenly saw him walk-

ing from the railway station straight toward the Hôtel
d'Angleterre. He was obviously in a hurry and seemed
preoccupied, though it is always hard to detect any mark
of anxiety or any other perturbation in his face. He held
out his hand to me cordially, and uttered his habitual
exclamation, "Ah!" But he did not stop and walked on
with a rather rapid step. I joined him, but he managed
to answer me in such a way that I ended up not even asking him about anything. Besides, I found it terribly embarrassing, for some reason, to bring up Polina in our
conversation, and he did not ask a thing about her. I told
him about Grandmother. He listened attentively and
earnestly and shrugged his shoulders.

"She'll lose everything," I observed.

"Oh, yes," he answered, "didn't she start playing the
other day, when I was about to leave? That's why I knew
for sure that she would lose everything. If I get the time,
I'll walk over to the casino and have a look, because I find
it interesting . . ."

"Where have you been?" I exclaimed, surprised at myself for not having asked that question earlier.

"I've been to Frankfort."

"On business?"

"Yes, on business."

Well, what else could I ask him? However, I kept walking along with him, until he suddenly turned into the
Hôtel des Quatre Saisons, which was on our way, nodded
to me and disappeared. On my way home I realized, little
by little, that even if I had kept talking to him for two
hours, I still wouldn't have learned anything at all, because . . . there was nothing that I could have asked him!
Yes, of course! There simply was no way to formulate my
question.

All that day Polina was either out, walking in the park
with the children and their nurse, or she just sat at home.

She had been avoiding the General for some time and hardly spoke to him, about anything serious at any rate. I had noticed that a long time ago. But knowing what condition the General was in that day, I thought that he could hardly have avoided her, that is, there ought to have been some sort of heart-to-heart family talk between them. However, as I was returning to our hotel after my conversation with Mr. Astley, I met Polina and the children, and her face expressed nothing but the most serene calm, as if she alone had remained quite untouched by the recent family tempests. I bowed to her, and she responded with a nod of her head. I got home in an ugly mood.

I had, of course, avoided talking to her and had not met her face to face ever since the incident with the Wurmerhelms. There was some pose and affectation in this, to be sure; but as time went on, there was more and more genuine indignation smoldering in my heart. Even if she had no fondness for me at all, it would still seem to be wrong to trample on my feelings in this fashion and to receive my avowals with such disdain. Didn't she know that I really loved her? Didn't she herself allow me to speak to her as if I did? To be sure, our relationship had had a strange beginning. Some time ago, in fact, quite some time ago, maybe two months back, I had noticed that she was trying to make me her friend, her confidant, and that she was actually sounding me out. For some reason it did not work out at the time, and instead, there remained this present, strange relationship of ours; this is why I had begun to speak to her as I did. But if she found my love offensive, why didn't she simply forbid me to mention it?

I was not forbidden; in fact, there had been times when she had herself provoked me to talk, and . . . of course, she did it just for fun. I know certainly; I had noted it all too well: she liked to listen to me and work me up to a point where I was so excited it actually hurt, then suddenly send me reeling by a display of utter contempt and disregard. And yet she knows that I can't live without her. It is now three days since that incident with the Baron, and already I can't endure our *separation* any longer. When I met her near the casino just now, my heart started beating so hard that I turned pale. But isn't it true that she couldn't get on without me, either? She needs me, and—could it really be true that she needs me only the way Anna the Empress needed Balakirev, her court jester?

She was guarding a secret—that was clear! Her exchange of words with Grandmother had really given me a stab in the heart. Hadn't I begged her a thousand times to be sincere with me, and didn't she know that I was truly ready to give my life for her? But she always kept me at a distance with her almost contemptuous treatment of me and, instead of the sacrifice of my life which I offered her, she demanded that I commit some silly prank, such as the one with the Baron! Wasn't that outrageous? Could it really be true that this Frenchman meant everything in the world to her? And what about Mr. Astley? But at that point the whole thing became utterly incomprehensible, yet in the meantime—my God, how I suffered!

Back in my hotel room, in a fit of fury, I snatched up my pen and scribbled the following note to her:

"Polina Aleksandrovna, I see clearly that the denouement is at hand which is bound to affect you also. I repeat for the last time: do you or don't you need my life? If you need me in *any way whatever,* dispose of me as you wish, and I shall stay meanwhile in my room, at least most of the time, and I most certainly shall not leave town. If you need me, write or send for me."

I sealed this note and sent it off by a bellboy, telling him to deliver it to her in person. I did not expect a reply, but three minutes later the bellboy returned with the message that "the lady extended her greetings."

It was past six o-clock when the General sent for me.

He was in his study, dressed as though he were ready to go out. His hat and cane were lying on the sofa. It looked to me as I entered the room as if he had been standing in the middle of the room with his legs wide apart, his head hanging, talking aloud to himself. But as soon as he saw me he rushed to meet me almost crying out, so that I involuntarily backed up a step and was ready to turn around and run. But he seized me by both hands and dragged me to the sofa. He then sat down on the sofa himself and offered me a seat in an armchair facing him. Then, without releasing my hands, his lips trembling, and with tears in his eyes, he addressed me in an imploring voice:

"Aleksei Ivanovich, save me, save me, don't let me down!"

For some time I could not understand a thing he was saying. He kept talking, talking, talking, and repeating: "Don't let me down, don't let me down!" Finally I realized that he expected something in the way of advice from me; or, rather, abandoned by all, in his anguish and anxiety, he remembered me and had sent for me simply to talk and talk and talk to me.

He was incoherent, or at least utterly confused. He clasped his hands and was on the point of falling on his knees before me, to implore me (what do you think?) to go at once to Mlle Blanche and to prevail upon her, by appealing to her conscience, to return to him and marry him.

"For heaven's sake, General," I cried, "why, Mlle

Blanche at this point scarcely knows that I exist! What could I do?"

But it was quite useless to object: he did not understand what was said to him. He fell to talking about Grandmother, too, but in a most incoherent way; he was still clinging to the idea of sending for the police.

"In Russia, in Russia," he started, suddenly boiling over with indignation, "in short, in Russia, in a well-organized state, where we have government authority, this old woman would have been put under guardianship at once! Yes, sir, yes, my dear sir," he went on, suddenly falling into the tone of a superior giving a tongue-lashing to a subordinate, jumping to his feet, and beginning to pace about the room, "you may not have been aware of this fact, my dear sir," he said, addressing some imaginary "dear sir" in the corner, "so you shall learn about it . . . yes, sir . . . in our country, such old women are brought under control by force, by force, by force, sir, yes, sir . . . oh, what the devil!"

And he flung himself on the sofa again, and, a moment later, told me, almost sobbing, gasping for breath, and rushing on, that Mlle Blanche was not going to marry him because, instead of the telegram, Grandmother had arrived, and it was clear that he would not come into the inheritance. Apparently he thought that I did not know any of these things. I brought up the subject of de Grieux, but he waved me off: "He's gone! He's got a mortgage on everything that's mine. I'm stripped of everything! That money you brought . . . that money, I don't know how much there is of it, I think there are about seven hundred francs left, enough, sir, that's all I've got, and what's to come—Idon's know, sir, that I don't know, sir! . . ."

"How, then, will you pay your hotel bill?" I cried in alarm, "and . . . what then?"

He gave me a thoughtful glance, but evidently had not understood my question, perhaps not even heard it. I made an attempt to bring up the subject of Polina Aleksandrovna and the children, but he gave me a hurried "Yes! yes!" and immediately went back to talking about the prince, about how Blanche was now going to take off with him, and then . . . and then, "What am I to do then, Aleksei Ivanovich?" he suddenly turned to me again, "I swear, by God! What am I to do? Tell me, isn't this ingratitude? Isn't this ingratitude?"

Finally he burst into a flood of tears.

What could one do with a man like that? It would have been dangerous, too, to leave him alone; really, something might have happened to him. However, I managed to take leave of him, though not without telling the nurse to keep an eye on him. I also spoke to the bellboy, a very sensible fellow. He, too, promised to stand by and keep his eyes open.

I had hardly left the General when Potapych came to summon me to Grandmother. It was eight o'clock and she had just returned from the casino after her final loss. I went down to see her. The old lady was sitting in an armchair, utterly exhausted and evidently ill. Marfa was offering her a cup of tea, almost forcing her to drink it. Grandmother's voice and tone were strikingly changed.

"How are you, my dear Aleksei Ivanovich," she said, inclining her head slowly and with dignity; "forgive me for bothering you once more, you must excuse an old woman. I left it all there, my dear, nearly a hundred thousand rubles. You were right yesterday, refusing to go with me. Now I am penniless, I haven't anything left. I don't want to wait another moment, I'll be leaving at half past nine. I've sent to that Englishman of yours, Astley is his name, I think, asking him to let me have three thousand francs for a week. So could you persuade him not to take it wrong and turn me down? I am still fairly rich, my dear. I've got three villages and two houses. And there is still some money left, I didn't take it all with me. I'm telling you this so he wouldn't have any second thoughts about it . . . Ah, here he is! One can see he is a good man."

Mr Astley had hastened to come at Grandmother's first invitation. Without hesitation or wasting any words he promptly counted out three thousand francs for a promissory note, which Grandmother signed. Having concluded this transaction, he took his leave and left without further delay.

"And now you can go, too, Aleksei Ivanovich. I have a little over an hour left. I want to lie down, my bones ache. Forgive a silly old woman. From now on I shall no longer blame young people for doing foolish things, and, yes, it would be sinful for me now to blame that hapless General of yours. I'm still not going to give him any money, as he wants me to, because, to my thinking, he's just too stupid; though I myself, old fool that I am, can't say that I'm more clever than he is. Verily, even in our old age God exacts retribution and punishes us for our pride. Well, good-bye. Marfusha, lift me up."

I wanted to see Grandmother off, however. Besides, I was in a state of suspense, expecting all the time that in another moment something would happen. So I couldn't sit still in my room. I went out into the corridor several times, even went for a short stroll along the parkway. My letter to her had been clear and resolute, and the present catastrophe was quite definitely a final one. I heard in the hotel that de Grieux had left. Finally, if she was indeed rejecting me as her friend, perhaps she would not reject me as a servant. I could be useful to her, if for nothing else, then at least to run her errands. Surely I'd be useful, what else?

At train time I ran over to the railway station and saw Grandmother off. Her whole party took their seats in a special family compartment. "Thank you, my dear, for your selfless sympathy," she said, as we parted, "and remind Praskovia of what I told her yesterday—I'll be waiting for her."

I went home. Passing by the General's suite I met the nurse and inquired about the General. "Oh, he's all right, sir," she answeᵣed dejectedly. I went in, however, but stopped in absolute amazement as I reached the door of the General's study. Mlle Blanche and the General seemed to be outdoing each other in laughing aloud about something. La veuve Cominges was sitting right there, on the sofa. The General was evidently quite beside himself with delight; he was babbling all kinds of nonsense and kept going off into prolonged fits of nervous laughter, which twisted his face into innumerable wrinkles, hiding his eyes altogether. I later found out from Blanche herself that, having kicked out the prince and heard about the General's tears, she had decided to comfort him and had dropped in at his suite for a moment. But the poor General did not know that in the meantime his fate had been decided and that Blanche was already packing, intending to catch the first train to Paris in the morning.

Having stood still in the doorway of the General's study for a moment, I changed my mind and walked away unnoticed. I walked upstairs to my room, opened the door, and suddenly noticed, in the half-dark corner by the window, a figure sitting on a chair. She remained seated as I entered. I went up quickly, looked, and my heart stood still: it was Polina!

Fourteen

I actually cried out.

"What is it? What's the matter?" she asked in a strange voice. She was pale and looked wretched.

"What's the matter, you ask? You? Here, in my room?"

"If I come, then I come with *all* of me. I've got that habit. You'll see that immediately; light a candle."

I lit a candle. She got up, stepped up to the table, and put a letter with a broken seal before me.

"Read," she commanded.

"This is de Grieux's hand!" I cried, snatching up the letter. My hands were trembling and the lines danced before my eyes. I have forgotten the exact wording of the letter, but here it is—not verbatim, but at least the gist and general drift of it.

"Mademoiselle," wrote de Grieux, "unfortunate circumstances force me to leave without delay. You must, of course, have noticed yourself that I purposely avoided a definitive explanation with you until the whole situation had cleared up. The arrival of your aged relation (*de la vieille dame*) and her absurd action have resolved all my doubts. The unsettled state of my own affairs definitely forbids me to nurture any further the delightful hopes which I had allowed myself to entertain for some time. I regret the past, but I trust that you will find

149

nothing in my behavior that might be unworthy of a gentleman and man of honor (*gentilhomme et honnête homme*). Having lost almost all my money in loans to your stepfather, I find myself compelled by necessity to take advantage of what is left me. I have already advised by Petersburg friends to make immediate arrangements toward the sale of the property mortgaged to me. Knowing, however, that your frivolous stepfather has also squandered the money that properly belonged to you, I have decided to remit to him fifty thousand francs, and I am returning him part of my claims to his property in that amount. This will put you in a position to recover all that you have lost by demanding restitution of your property by due process of law. I trust, mademoiselle, that as things stand now, my action will be very much to your advantage. I trust, also, that by this action I have fully met my obligations as a gentleman and man of honor. Rest assured that the memory of you will forever remain imprinted upon my heart."

"Well, that is all clear," I said, turning to Polina; "did you really expect anything else?" I added, with indignation.

"I expected nothing," she answered, with seeming composure, but still with a hint of a tremor in her voice; "I made up my mind a long time ago. I could read his mind and knew very well what he was thinking. He thought that I was seeking . . . that I was going to insist . . ." (She stopped without concluding her sentence, bit her lip, and fell silent.) "I purposely increased my contempt for him," she started again, "I waited to see what he would do. If a telegram had come telling of our inheritance, I would have flung him the money which that idiot (my stepfather) owed him, and kicked him out! I've loathed him for ages and ages. Oh, he used to be a different man, a thousand times different, but now, but now! . . . Oh, how gladly I would fling those fifty thousand in that foul face of his and spit at it . . . then spread the spit all over his face!"

"But the paper, I mean the mortgage which he returned, doesn't the General have it? Take it and give it back to de Grieux."

"Oh, that's not it! That's not it!"

"Yes, you're right, it isn't the same thing! Besides, what could you expect of the General now? But what about Grandmother?" I cried suddenly.

Polina gave me what seemed to me a distracted and impatient look.

"What about Grandmother?" she said with a tone of annoyance, "I can't go to her . . . Nor do I want to ask anybody's forgiveness," she added irritably.

"What's to be done?" I exclaimed, "and how, tell me, how could you have loved de Grieux? Oh, the scoundrel, the scoundrel! Well, do you want me to kill him in a duel? Where is he now?"

"He is in Frankfort now and will stay there for three days."

"A word from you and I'll leave tomorrow by the first train!" I said with a sort of stupid enthusiasm.

She began to laugh.

"Why, he'll probably say: 'Return those fifty thousand francs first.' And why should he fight a duel with you? . . . What nonsense!"

"But where, where shall we get these fifty thousand francs?" I repeated, gnashing my teeth, as though there were a chance to pick them up from the floor at once. "Listen, what about Mr. Astley?" I asked, turning to her with a strange idea beginning to dawn on me.

Her eyes flashed.

"What? Could it be that *you yourself* want me to leave you for that Englishman?" she said, looking straight at me with a piercing glance and giving me a bitter smile. It was the first time she had ever addressed me with the familiar pronoun.

I believe that she began to feel giddy with emotion that moment; she suddenly sat down on the sofa as though she were utterly exhausted.

I just stood there, as though struck by lightning, just stood there, not believing my eyes, or my ears! Why, that meant that she loved me! She came to see *me*, and not Mr. Astley! She, a young girl, had come alone to my hotel room, meaning that she had compromised herself before everybody, and I, I was just standing there, refusing to understand it!

A wild idea flashed through my mind.

"Polina! Give me just one hour! Wait here only an hour and . . . I shall return! This . . . this must be! You'll see! Stay here, stay here!"

And I ran from the room, without reacting to her amazed and questioning glance. She yelled something after me, but I did not turn back.

Yes, sometimes the wildest idea, an idea which would seem utterly impossible, will become fixed in one's mind so firmly that one finally begins to take it for something practicable . . . Even more than that: once such an idea is connected with a powerful, passionate desire, one may eventually take it for something fated, inevitable, predestined, for something that simply must be and is bound to happen! Perhaps there is even more to it, some sort of coincidence of presentiments, some kind of extraordinary exertion of the will, self-poisoning by one's own imagination, or something else yet—I don't know what, but anyway, that night (which I shall never in my life forget) something miraculous happened. It is fully backed up by laws of arithmetic, but to me it is nevertheless a miracle to this day. And why, why had that conviction taken such deep and such firm roots in my mind, and for so long a time? Oh yes, I certainly had been thinking of it, and let me repeat this, I had been thinking of it not as a chance possibility among others (that is, something that might or might not happen), but as something that was absolutely bound to happen!

It was a quarter past ten. I entered the casino with such firm confidence, yet, at the same time, in a state of such excitement as I had never experienced before. There were still plenty of people in the gambling halls, though only half as many as in the morning.

After ten o'clock only the truly desperate gamblers are left at the gaming tables, those for whom nothing else exists at a spa but roulette, those who have come there for that alone, who hardly notice what is going on around them and take no interest in anything during the entire season, but play from morning until night and would probably play all night until dawn, if it were possible. And they always leave unwillingly when the game of roulette is finally shut down at midnight. And when the chief croupier announces, at closing time, just before midnight, "Les trois derniers coups, messieurs!" they are ready to stake on those last three strokes every penny they have in their pockets—and this is precisely where they most often lose everything. I went to the very table where Grandmother had sat the other day. It was not very crowded; so I could soon take my place standing at the table. Right in front of me the word *Passe* was scribbled on the green cloth. *Passe* is the series of numbers from nineteen to thirty six, while the series from one to eighteen is called *Manque*. But what did I care for that? I was not calculating; I hadn't even heard what number had been up on the last stroke, nor did I inquire about it as I began to play—as any half-way circumspect player would have done. I pulled out all of my two hundred gulden and plunked them down on *passe,* the word in front of me.

"Vingt deux!" cried the croupier.

I had won and again staked everything: my initial bet plus what I had just won..

"Trente et un," cried the croupier. I had won again! This meant that I now had eight hundred! I moved the whole eight hundred on the twelve middle numbers (you win three to one, but so are the chances against you). The wheel turned and twenty-four came up. I was given three rolls at five hundred gulden each and ten gold coins; in all, I had now two thousand gulden.

I was virtually delirious by then, and put the whole pile of money on red—and suddenly realized what I was doing! And for the only time that night, while playing, I was seized by such cold fear that my hands and feet began to tremble. I felt the horror of the thought which came to me in a flash: what it would mean to me if I lost now; my whole life was at stake!

"Rouge!" cried the croupier, and I drew a breath, as I felt the tingle of fiery pins and needles all over my body. I was paid in bank notes. It amounted to four thousand eight hundred. (I could still keep count at that stage.)

Then, if I remember it right, I placed two thousand gulden on the twelve middle numbers again, and lost; then my gold and eight hundred gulden, and lost. I was in a frenzy: I grabbed the two thousand left me and put them on the first dozen—haphazard, at random, quite without thought! There was a moment, though, as I was waiting, which may perhaps have resembled the feeling experienced by Mme Blanchard[31] when she was hurtling to the ground from her balloon, in Paris.

"Quatre!" cried the croupier. I was back at six thou-

31. Marie Blanchard (1778–1819), wife of a pioneer of balloon flying. She died in a balloon fire.

sand, counting the money I had bet. Now I felt like a winner and was afraid of nothing, of nothing in the world, as I plunked down four thousand on black. At least nine people hastened to follow suit and also placed on black. The croupiers were exchanging glances and trading remarks. People all around were talking and waiting.

Black won. From here on I don't remember any count, nor the order of my bets. I only remember, as though it had been in a dream, that I had already won something like sixteen thousand, then lost twelve of these by three consecutive unlucky strokes, moved the last four thousand on *passe* (feeling, however, hardly anything at all as I did it; I was just waiting, mechanically, without thinking)—and won again. Then I won four times in a row. I only remember that I raked in money by the thousands. I also remember that the middle twelve came up most often, so that I stuck to them. They kept turning up with some sort of regularity, certainly three or four times in a row, then they would fail to show up twice running, and then come back for three or four times in succession. Sometimes streaks of such amazing regularity will occur, and this is precisely what throws off inveterate gamblers who with pencil in hand calculate their odds. And what terrible ironies of fate sometimes happen here!

I believe that no more than half an hour had passed since I had arrived when the croupier suddenly informed me that I had won thirty thousand gulden, and that, inasmuch as the bank had a policy of not meeting any claim higher than this at one time, the roulette game would be closed until next morning. I seized all my gold, poured it into my pockets, grabbed all the banknotes, and immediately went to the adjoining hall, where they had another roulette going. The whole crowd rushed after me. There a place was cleared for me immediately, and I went back to betting as before, haphazardly and without keeping count. I don't understand what saved me!

There were moments, though, when certain calcula-tions went through my mind briefly. I would begin to stick to certain numbers and chances, then quickly aban-don them again and go back to placing bets almost uncon-sciously. I must have been very absent-minded. I can recall that the croupiers several times corrected my game. I made gross mistakes. My temples were wet with per-spiration and my hands were trembling. Some little Poles tried to offer me their services, but I just didn't listen to anybody. My luck was holding up! Suddenly there was a lot of loud talk and laughter around me. "Bravo, bravo!" everybody shouted, and some people even clapped their hands. I had just taken thirty thousand here also, and the bank was again closed until the next day!

"Go away, go away," a voice whispered on my right. It was a Frankfort Jew who had been standing beside me all the time and, it seems, had helped me here and there in my play.

"For heaven's sake, go away," another voice whispered in my left ear. I glanced about hurriedly. It was a lady of about thirty, very modestly and properly dressed, with traces of her former, marvellous beauty still visible in spite of the sickly pallor of her tired face. At that moment I was stuffing my pockets with bank notes, which I simply crumpled up as best I could, and gathering up the gold that was left on the table. Picking up the last roll of five hundred gulden, I managed to slip it to the pale lady without anybody's noticing it. I had an over-whelming desire to do it, and I remember how her delicate, thin little fingers firmly pressed my hand to show her warm gratitude. All this happened in an instant.

Having gathered up all my winnings, I moved on to trente et quarante.

The game of trente et quarante is patronized by an aristocratic clientele. It is not roulette; it is a card game. Here the bank will meet claims of up to a hundred thousand thalers at once. The maximum stake is also four thousand gulden. I was not familiar with the game at all, and hardly knew any other way of placing my money except on the red and the black, which one could play here also. So I stuck to red and black. The whole casino was crowding around me. I don't remember whether I thought of Polina even once in all that time. I was then experiencing an overwhelmingly pleasurable feeling which I got from scooping up and raking in the bank notes which were piling up before me.

Certainly it looked as though fate were pushing me. This time, as luck would have it, a special circumstance occurred, though I must say that it was something which happens quite often in games of chance. For example, luck will stay with red for something like ten or even fifteen times in succession. I had heard, just two days earlier, that on one day of the previous week red had come up twenty-two times in succession. No one at the casino could remember having seen anything like this before, and people were talking about it with amazement. It goes without saying that everybody stays away from red, so that after the tenth time, for instance, almost no one will dare to bet on it. But no one of the seasoned players will bet on black either in a situation such as this. The seasoned player knows well what a "caprice of chance" means. For example, after red has been up sixteen times running it would seem a cinch that black will come up next. This is where novices believe they see their chance. They jump at it, whole crowds of them, doubling and trebling their stakes, and lose heavily.

But I, having noticed that red had been up seven times in succession, by some strange perversity made a point of putting my money on it. I am convinced that half of it was vanity; I wanted to impress the spectators by taking mad risks. And then—what a strange sensation!—I remember distinctly how all of a sudden a terrible craving for risk took possession of me, now quite apart from any promptings of vanity. It may be that, in passing through so many sensations, the soul does not become sated but is only stimulated by them and will ask for more and ever stronger sensations until utterly exhausted. And I am not lying as I say that if the rules of the game had allowed me to bet fifty thousand at once, I'd certainly have done so. People around were shouting that this was madness, that red had won fourteen times in succession!

"Monsieur a gagné déjà cent mille," I heard a voice near me.

I suddenly recovered my senses. What? I had won a hundred thousand gulden that night? What more did I want? I pounced on my bank notes, crumpled them up and stuffed my pockets with them, then I scooped up all my gold, all the rolls of it, and ran out of the casino. As I walked through the halls everyone around laughed as they saw my bulging pockets and my uneven gait under the weight of all that gold. It must have weighed over twenty pounds. A number of hands were held out to me; I passed it out by the handful, as much as I could hold. Two Jews stopped me at the exit.

"You are brave! You are very brave!" they told me, "but be sure to leave tomorrow morning, as early as possible, or else you will lose it all . . ."

I didn't listen to them. It was so dark in the parkway

that I could barely see my own hand. It was about a third of a mile to the hotel. I never was afraid of thieves or robbers, even when I was a small boy; I was not thinking of being robbed then. However, I don't remember what I was thinking on my way home; I had no thoughts. I was only aware of a tremendous feeling of exhilaration —success, triumph, power—I don't know how to express it. Polina's image flitted through my mind also. I remember her and knew that I was on my way to her, that in a moment I would be with her, telling her, showing her . . . Yet I could hardly remember what she had told me earlier, and why I had gone to the casino; and all the feelings that I had experienced a mere hour and a half earlier now seemed to me remote, long since changed, old-fashioned—something that would not be brought up again, because everything would begin anew now. Almost at the very end of the parkway I was suddenly gripped by fear: "What if I were murdered and robbed right now?" My fear increased with every step. I was almost running. Suddenly, there was the end of the park, and I saw our hotel in the glare of its innumerable lighted windows—thank God, I was home!

I ran up to my room and quickly opened the door. Polina was there, sitting on my sofa with her arms crossed, with a lighted candle in front of her. She looked at me with amazement, and it goes without saying that I must have presented a rather strange sight at that moment. I stood before her and began to throw all my money on the table in one large pile.

Fifteen

I remember her terribly intent gaze as she looked at my face without moving from her seat or even changing her position. "I have won two hundred thousand francs," I cried, as I threw out my last roll of gold. A huge pile of bank notes and rolls of gold filled the whole table, and I could not take my eyes off it. There were moments when I completely forgot about Polina. At one moment I was sorting my bundles, folding them up together, at the next I was arranging all the gold in a single pile; then I left it all and began to pace up and down the room with rapid steps, suddenly lost in thought; then, a moment later, I was back at the table, counting the money again. Suddenly, as though coming to, I rushed to the door and hurriedly locked it, turning they key twice. Then I stopped beside my little suitcase and stood there pondering.

"I wonder if I should put it in my suitcase until tomorrow," I said, turning toward Polina, as if I had suddenly remembered her. She was still sitting there without stirring, yet watching me intently. It was a strange expression she wore on her face; I did not like that expression! I would not be wrong if I said that there was hatred in it.

I took a quick step toward her.

160

"Polina, here are twenty-five thousand gulden—that's fifty thousand francs, or even more. Take them, throw them in his face tomorrow."

She gave me no answer.

"If you want me to, I'll take them to him myself, first thing in the morning. Shall I?"

She suddenly began to laugh. She laughed for a long time.

I looked at her with surprise and with a feeling of sadness. This laughter of hers was a lot like the sarcastic laughter I had heard so often, even recently, every time I made one of my passionate declarations to her. She finally stopped laughing and frowned, looking at me with a stern and sullen expression on her face.

"I won't take your money," she said contemptuously.

"What? What is it?" I cried, "Polina, why?"

"I won't take money for nothing."

"I offer it to you as a friend, I offer you my life."

She gave me a long, searching look, as though she wanted to see right through me.

"You are giving too much," she said, with a laugh, "de Grieux's mistress is not worth fifty thousand francs."

"Polina, how can you talk to me like that!" I cried, reproachfully; "am I de Grieux?"

"I hate you! Yes . . . yes! . . . I don't love you any more than I love de Grieux," she cried, her eyes suddenly flashing.

Here she covered her face with her hands and became hysterical. I rushed to her side.

I realized that something had happened to her in my absence. She seemed quite out of her mind.

"Buy me! Don't you want to? Don't you want to? For fifty thousand francs, just like de Grieux?" she gasped between convulsive sobs. I embraced her, kissed her hands, her feet, fell on my knees before her.

She began to get over her hysterics. She put both hands on my shoulders and looked at me intently; it seemed as if she were trying to read something in my face. She was listening to me but apparently did not hear what I said to her. A careworn and thoughtful expression appeared on her face. I was afraid for her: I very definitely had the impression that she was going out of her mind. At one moment she would begin to draw me softly to her, with a trustful smile beginning to play on her face, then, suddenly, she would push me back again, and, her face darkened once more, renew her scrutiny of me.

All of a sudden she began embracing me.

"Tell me, you do love me, don't you?" she said; "tell me, you did want to fight the Baron for me, didn't you?" And then she burst out laughing, as though something that was funny as well as sweet had suddenly come to her mind. She was crying and laughing all at once. Well, what was I to do? I was myself almost delirious. I remember that she began saying something to me, but that I could understand almost nothing of what she said. It was a sort of delirium, a sort of incoherent babble—as though she were in a great hurry to tell me something—a delirium, interrupted from time to time by the merriest laughter, which began to frighten me. "No, no, you dear, dear!" she kept repeating. "You are my faithful one!" And again she put her hands on my shoulders, again giving me that intent look and saying over and over again: "You love me . . . love me . . . will you love me?" I could not take my eyes off her. I had never seen her in anything like these fits of tenderness and love; to be sure, this was just her delirious state, but . . . after noticing the passion in my eyes, she would give me a sly smile, then, apropos of nothing, suddenly start talking about Mr. Astley.

Anyway, she kept bringing up Mr. Astley again and again (especially when she tried to tell me something particular that night), but I was unable to grasp exactly what she meant. It seemed that she was actually making fun of him; she kept repeating that he was waiting . . . and did I know that he was most probably standing under the window right now? "Yes, yes, under the window—go, open it, look, look, he's here, he's here!" She pushed me toward the window, but the moment I made a move in that direction she immediately went off into peals of laughter. I stayed close to her, and she again flung herself into my embrace.

"Are we going to leave? We're leaving tomorrow, aren't we?" she suddenly asked, growing restless, "well . . ." (here she lost herself in thought). "Well, do you think we'll catch up with Grandmother? I suppose we'll catch up with her in Berlin. What do you think, what is she going to say when we get there and she sees us coming? And what about Mr. Astley? . . . Well, he isn't the kind that will jump off the Schlangenberg, or is he, what do you think?" (She burst out laughing.) "Come, listen: do you know where he is going next summer? He wants to go to the North Pole, on a scientific expedition, and asked me to join him, ha-ha-ha! He says that we Russians know nothing and can do nothing without European help . . . But he has a good heart! Do you know that he tries to find excuses for the General? He says that Blanche . . . that passion—well, I don't know, I don't know," she repeated all of a sudden, as though her mind were wandering and she had forgotten what she was talking about. "The poor dears, how I feel sorry for them, and for Grandmother . . . Come, listen, listen, really, how would you go about killing de Grieux? And did you really think that you were going to kill him? Oh, silly! How could you think that I would let you fight de Grieux? Come, you aren't going to kill the Baron either," she added, beginning to laugh again. "Oh, how funny you were with the Baron that time. I watched the two of you from my bench. And how reluctantly you went, when I ordered you to go. How I laughed, how I laughed then," she added, laughing aloud.

And all at once she was kissing and embracing me again, pressing her face to mine passionately and tenderly. I no longer thought of anything at all and I could no longer hear anything. My head began to go around . . .

I think it was about seven o'clock in the morning when I woke up. The sun was shining into my room. Polina was sitting beside me. She was looking around in a strange way, as though she had just emerged from some darkness and was now trying to collect her thoughts. She, too, had only just awakened and was gazing intently at the table where the money was. My head was heavy and it ached. I tried to take Polina's hand; she pushed me away and jumped up from the sofa. The new day was overcast. It had been raining before dawn. She went up to the window, opened it, and leaned out, her head and chest outside, her hands on the windowsill and her elbows against the sides of the window frame. She remained in that position for about three minutes, without turning around or listening to what I was saying to her. A dread thought went through my head: what would happen now and how was this going to end? Suddenly she stepped back from the window, went up to the table, and, looking at me with infinite loathing, her lips trembling with rage, she said to me:

"Well, give me my fifty thousand francs now!"

"Polina, not again, not again!" I tried to retort.

"Or have you thought better of it? Ha-ha-ha! Maybe, you're already regretting it, too?"

There were twenty-five thousand gulden, counted off the night before, lying on the table. I picked them up and gave them to her.

"So they are mine now, aren't they mine? Aren't they?" she asked me, with hatred in her voice, holding the money in her hands.

"Why, they were always yours," I said.

"Well then, take your fifty thousand francs!"

She leaned back and flung the money at me. The bank-roll hit me painfully in the face and scattered all over the floor. Having done this, Polina ran out of my room.

I know, of course, that she was not in her right mind at that moment, though I have no explanation for such temporary insanity. It is true that she is still ill today, a month later. But what could have been the cause of that condition, and, above all, of this last performance of hers? Was it wounded pride? Was it despair at having brought herself to come to me? Had I perhaps suggested to her, by my behavior, that I was exultant over the happiness she had granted me, and that, like de Grieux, I was about to get rid of her by giving her fifty thousand francs? But it was simply not true, that much I can say in good conscience. I think that to some extent it was her own vanity that was at fault: her vanity prompted her to distrust and to insult me, even though, most likely, she had no clear conception of her own motives. At any rate, I absorbed de Grieux's punishment and became guilty without doing too much on my own. To be sure, it all happened in a delirious state, and I knew it all too well, and . . . yet I refused to take that fact into consideration. Could it be that now she won't forgive me because I didn't? Yes, but that is now. What about then? Why, she wasn't all that delirious and all that ill as to be totally oblivious of what she was doing when she came to me with de Grieux's letter, or was she? So it must be that she knew what she was doing.

I hurriedly thrust all my bank notes and gold into my bed, covered it up somehow, and left my room some ten minutes after Polina. I was convinced that she had run home and so I meant to slip quietly into their suite and ask the nurse how the young lady was that morning. But how great was my surprise when I met the nurse on the stairs and learned from her that Polina had not yet returned home, and that she, the nurse, was on her way to me to get her.

"She just left my room no more than ten minutes ago," I said; "where could she have gone?"

Nurse gave me a reproachful look.

In the meantime the thing had turned into a regular scandal and was all over the hotel in no time. In the doorman's room and at the Ober-Kellner's it was whispered that Fräulein had run out of the hotel, into the rain, at six o'clock in the morning, and that she had run off in the direction of the Hôtel d'Angleterre. From their words and hints I gathered that they all knew already that she had spent the night in my room. However, it was the General's whole family that was the subject of discussion. It had become known all over the hotel that the General, the night before, had gone mad and had been crying all over the place. It was also said that Grandmother, who had just left, was really his mother, who had come here all the way from Russia to stop her son from marrying Mlle de Cominges, and to disinherit him if he disobeyed her. And since he had in effect refused to listen to her, the Countess had purposely and under his very eyes lost all her money at roulette, just so he should get nothing. "Diese Russen!" the Ober-Kellner kept repeating, shaking his head indignantly. Others were laughing. The Ober-Kellner was making out the bill. My winning at roulette was generally known. Karl, my bellboy, was the first to congratulate me. But I had no time for any of them. I stormed to the Hôtel d'Angleterre.

It was still early in the morning, and Mr. Astley was

seeing no one. But learning that it was I, he came out into the hall to meet me. He stopped in front of me and, without saying a word, fixed his metallic eyes upon me, waiting for me to do the talking. I asked him about Polina at once.

"She is sick," answered Mr. Astley, still staring and refusing to take his eyes off me.

"Then she is really with you?"

"Oh yes, she is with me."

"But how will you . . . do you mean to let her stay with you?"

"Oh yes, I do."

"Mr. Astley, this is going to create a scandal, you just can't do it. Besides, she is quite ill. Perhaps you haven't noticed that?"

"Oh yes, I have noticed it, and I've already told you that she is ill. If she hadn't been ill she wouldn't have spent the night with you."

"So you know that, too?"

"I know it. She was on her way here yesterday, and I would have taken her to a lady relative of mine. But as she was ill, she made a mistake and went to you."

"Imagine that! Well, my congratulations, Mr. Astley. By the way, you make me think of something: weren't you standing all night under our window? Miss Polina all night long kept asking me to open the window and look for you standing there. She kept laughing very hard about it, too."

"Is that so? No, I was not standing under the window. I was waiting in the hall and walking around."

"But she needs medical care, Mr. Astley."

"Oh yes, I have already called for a doctor, and if she dies you will answer to me for her death."

I was amazed. "But Mr. Astley, for heaven's sake, what is it you want?"

"And is it true that you won two hundred thousand thalers yesterday?"

"Only a hundred thousand gulden."

"Well, you see! So why don't you leave for Paris this morning?"

"Why?"

"All Russians, when they have some money, go to Paris," Mr. Astley explained, in a tone as if he were quoting information from a book.

"What am I going to do in Paris now, in the summer? I love her, Mr. Astley! You know that yourself."

"Are you sure? I am convinced that you don't. And besides, if you are going to stay here, you will most probably lose everything and you will have nothing left to go to Paris with. But good-bye now, for I am perfectly sure that you will leave for Paris today."

"All right, good-bye then, only I'm not going to Paris. Mr. Astley, think of what's going to happen to our family now, I mean, the General . . . and now this thing must happen to Miss Polina—why, it will be all over town."

"Yes, all over town. But I believe that the General won't give much thought to that, having other things on his mind. Besides, Miss Polina has every right to stay wherever she pleases. And, speaking of that family, I think it is correct to say that the family no longer exists."

As I was walking home I laughed to myself at the Englishman's strange confidence about my going away to Paris. "He also wants to kill me in a duel," I thought, "if Mademoiselle Polina dies—there's another thing to worry about!" I swear, I felt sorry for Polina, but strangely enough, from the moment I had touched that gaming table the night before and had begun to scoop up those bundles of money, my love had somehow receded to the background. I say this now, but at the time I had yet no clear realization of it. Could it be that I am really

a gambler, could it be true that I really . . . loved Polina
in such a strange fashion? No, I still love her, God is my
witness! And when I was walking home after talking to
Mr. Astley, I genuinely suffered and blamed myself. But
. . . here a very strange and silly thing happened to me.

I was hurrying to see the General when suddenly, not
far from his suite, a door opened and someone called me.
It was Mme veuve Cominges and she was calling me, for
Mlle Blanche had told her to. I entered Mlle Blanche's
suite.

It was a small one, with only two rooms. I could hear
Mlle Blanche laugh and call out from the bedroom. She
was just getting up.

"A, c'est lui!! Viens donc, bête! Is it true, que tu as
gagné une montagne d'or et d'argent? J'aimerais mieux
l'or."[32]

"Yes, it is true," I answered, laughing.

"How much?"

"A hundred thousand gulden."

"Bibi, comme tu es bête. Come on in here, I can't hear
a thing. Nous ferons bombance, n'est ce pas?"[33]

I went in. She was relaxing under a pink satin quilt,
from which her dark, healthy, amazing shoulders were
showing—shoulders such as one only dreams about—
covered flimsily by a batiste nightgown bordered with
shining white lace, wonderfully becoming to her dark
skin.

"Mon fils, as-tu du coeur?"[34] she cried, seeing me, and
burst out laughing. Her laughter was always very gay,
and at times quite genuine.

"Tout autre . . ." I began, paraphrasing Corneille.

32. "Ah, it's he! Come here you silly thing! . . . that you have won a
mountain of gold and silver? I'd prefer gold."
33. "We'll have a good time, won't we?"
34. "My son, do you have the courage?" A quotation from Corneille's
Le Cid (1636).

"You see, vois-tu," she suddenly went into a patter, "first of all, find my stockings for me and help me put them on, and second, si tu n'es pas trop bête, je te prends à Paris. You know I'm about to leave."

"Right away?"

"In half an hour."

And, indeed, all her belongings were already packed. All her suitcases and things were standing there ready. Coffee had been served some time before.

"Eh bien! Do you want to? Tu verras Paris. Dis donc qu'est ce que c'est qu'un outchitel? Tu étais bien bête quand tu étais outchitel.[35] But where are my stockings? Come, put them on for me!"

She stuck out her positively delightful little foot, dark-skinned, tiny, not in the least disfigured, as feet that look so small in shoes almost invariably are. I laughed and began drawing her silk stocking on for her. Meanwhile Mlle Blanche just sat there, on her bed, prattling away.

"Eh bien, que feras-tu, si je te prends avec? First of all, je veux cinquante mille francs. You will give them to me in Frankfort. Nous allons à Paris. We'll be living together there et je te ferai voir des étoiles en plein jour.[36] You will see women such as you have never seen. Listen . . ."

"Wait a moment, so I'll give you fifty thousand francs, and what will be left for me?"

"Et cent cinquante mille francs, you have forgotten, and besides, I'll be willing to share an apartment with you for a month, or two, que sais-je! In those two months we'll certainly run through those one hundred and fifty thousand francs; you see, je suis bonne enfant and I tell you this beforehand, mais tu verras des étoiles."

35. "You'll see Paris. Tell me what is an *outchitel* [tutor; see note 1 above]. You were indeed silly when you were an *outchitel*."
36. "Well then, what will you do, if I take you with me? . . . I want fifty thousand francs . . . We will go to Paris . . . and I'll make you see stars in the daytime."

"What? all in two months?"

"What? Does this scare you? Ah, vil esclave! Don't you know that one month of that life is worth more than your whole existence. One month—et après, le déluge! Mais tu ne peux comprendre, va! Go away, go away, you don't deserve it! Ouch, que fais-tu?"

That very moment I was putting a stocking on her other little foot, but could not resist kissing it. She pulled it away and began kicking my face with the tip of her foot. Finally she chased me away altogether. "Eh bien, mon outchitel, je t'attends, si tu veux, I'm leaving in a quarter of an hour!" she called after me.

On returning to my room I felt as though my head were going around. Well, it wasn't my fault that Mlle Polina had thrown the whole pile of money in my face and had only yesterday preferred Mr. Astley to me. Some of the scattered bank notes were still lying all over the floor. I picked them up. At that moment the door opened and the Ober-Kellner stood there in person (before, he hadn't ever as much as looked at me). He had come to suggest that I move downstairs, into a magnificent suite which had just been vacated by a Count V.

I stood there, giving it some thought.

"My bill!" I cried suddenly, "I'm leaving in ten minutes." And I was thinking to myself: "If it must be Paris, Paris it is; must be fate, or something!"

A quarter of an hour later the three of us were actually seated in a private compartment of the train: Mlle Blanche, Mme veuve Cominges, and I. Mlle Blanche laughed gaily as she looked at me; she was almost hysterical with laughter. Mme veuve Cominges seconded her. I can't say that I felt very cheerful. My life was breaking in two, but since the previous day I had been conditioned to risking everything on one card. Perhaps, too, all that money was really too much for me and it had turned my head. Peut-être, je ne demandais pas mieux. It seemed to me that this was merely a temporary change of scenery, only temporary. "But in a month I'll be back here, and then . . . and then, watch out, Mr. Astley, we'll see who wins!" No, as I recall it now, I was terribly sad even then, even though I tried to laugh as heartily as that silly goose Blanche.

"But what do you want? How silly you are! Oh, how silly!" Blanche kept crying, interrupting my laughter and beginning to scold me in earnest. "All right, all right, we are going to run through your two hundred thousand francs, but in return, mais tu seras heureux comme un petit roi. I'll tie your tie for you myself, and I'll introduce you to Hortense. And when we've spent all our money, you'll come back here and break the bank again. What did the Jews tell you? The main thing is courage, and you've got it. You'll be back in Paris, bringing me more money, not once, but often. Quant à moi, je veux cinquante mille francs de rente et alors . . ."[37]

"And what about the General?" I asked her.

"Well, the General, as you know very well, every day at this time goes out to get a bouquet of flowers for me. This time I purposely told him to get me some very rare flowers. The poor dear will come back and find the birdie has flown away. He'll come flying after us, you'll see. Ha-ha-ha! I'll be very glad to see him. I can use him in Paris. And Mr. Astley will pay his bill here . . ."

And so that's the way I left for Paris that day.

37. "As for me, I want fifty thousand francs of income and then . . ."

Sixteen

What shall I say about Paris? Of course it was all madness, and silly. I spent a little over three weeks in Paris, and in this time a hundred thousand francs of my money were totally finished. I am speaking of one hundred thousand only, for the other hundred thousand I gave to Mlle Blanche in cash—fifty thousand in Frankfort and three days later, in Paris, another fifty thousand by check. She cashed it a week later, "et les cent mille francs qui nous restent, tu les mangeras avec moi, mon outchitel."[38] She used to call me "outchitel" all the time. It is difficult to imagine anything in the world more calculating, stingy, and niggardly than the class of creatures such as Mlle Blanche. But that was in the spending of her own money. Regarding my hundred thousand francs, she openly told me later that she needed them to establish herself in Paris. "So now I have established myself in decent style once and for all, and nobody is going to put me out, not for a long time, at least that's the way I've got it planned," she explained. I hardly saw those hundred thousand, however. She kept the money the whole time, and my wallet, into which she looked every

38. "And the hundred thousand francs that we have left, you'll devour them with me, my *outchitel*."

173

day, never contained more than a hundred francs, and usually less.

"What do you need that money for?" she would say, sometimes, in the most natural manner, and I wouldn't argue the point. But it must be said that with the money she furnished and decorated her apartment very nicely indeed, and later, when she showed me the rooms as she was about to move in, she said: "Do you see what care and good taste can do even with the scantiest means." These "scanty means," though, amounted to no more and no less than fifty thousand francs. For the remaining fifty thousand she bought a carriage and horses; also, we gave two balls, two parties, that is, which were attended by Hortense and Lisette and Cléopâtre, remarkable women in a number of ways and not at all bad looking. At those parties I was forced to play that most stupid role of host, to receive and entertain the dullest small-time business- men of recently acquired wealth, armies of incredibly ig- norant and insolent lieutenants, and a bunch of wretched minor authors and journalistic insects, who showed up wearing the most fashionable swallowtails and pale yel- low gloves and displayed a vanity and conceit of such proportions as would be unthinkable even back home, in Petersburg—and that is saying a great deal. They ac- tually took it into their heads to make fun of me, but I got drunk with champagne and passed out in a back room. I found the whole thing loathsome to the last de- gree. "C'est un outchitel," Blanche said about me, "il a gagné deux cent mille francs, and without me he wouldn't know how to spend them. And after it's all over he'll go back to teaching—does anyone know of a job for him? We must do something for him." I started to take recourse to champagne quite often, because I was very sad all the time, and terribly bored. I was living in the most bourgeois, in the most mercenary milieu, where

every sou was calculated and accounted for. Blanche disliked me heartily during the first two weeks, that much I
noticed. To be sure, she dressed me up in elegant clothes
and personally did my tie for me every day, but at heart
she genuinely despised me. I paid no attention to it whatever. Bored and downcast, I got into the habit of going
down to the Château des Fleurs,[39] where I got drunk
regularly every night and learned to dance the cancan
(which they dance disgustingly there), in the end even
acquiring a fame of sorts. Eventually Blanche gauged my
true character. Initially, she had somehow got the idea
that, during the entire period of our cohabitation, I
would be trailing her, pencil and paper in hand, to check
how much she had spent, how much she had stolen, how
much she was going to spend, and how much she was going to steal. And of course she expected that we were
going to have battles over every ten francs she spent. And
so, to every anticipated attack on my part, she had an answer ready ahead of time. Then, seeing that there was no
attack, she took to defending herself even though I had
said nothing. There were times when she would launch
into a heated explanation, but then, seeing that I wasn't
saying a thing—most of the time I'd be just lounging
around on a couch and staring at the ceiling, motionless
—she would at last stop, really puzzled. At first she
thought that I was simply stupid, "un outchitel," and
simply cut short her explanation, most probably thinking
to herself: "Why, he is stupid, so let's not give him any
ideas, as long as he hasn't caught on himself." So she
would walk away, then come back ten minutes later (this
would happen at the time she was doing her most reck-
less spending, including some expenses that were entirely
beyond our means: for instance, she had traded in our

39. A popular dance hall in Paris.

horses and had bought another pair for sixteen thousand francs).

"Well, Bibi, you aren't angry, are you?" she said, coming up to me.

"N-o-o! You're boring me!" I said, pushing her away from me. But this thing fascinated her so much that she immediately sat down beside me:

"You see, I decided to spend so much on them because they were such a bargain. I could sell them again for twenty thousand francs."

"I believe it, I believe it. Fine horses. You've really got yourself a fine equipage there. It'll come in handy. Well, enough of that."

"So you aren't angry?"

"For what? You are very smart getting yourself some of the things you need. They'll be good to have, later. I can see that you really must establish yourself in such style, or you'll never make a million. Here our hundred thousand francs are a mere beginning, a drop in the bucket."

Blanche, who had been expecting anything but reflections of this order from me (instead of outcries and reproaches!), seemed to come down from the clouds.

"So you . . . so that's the kind you are ! Mais tu as l'esprit pour comprendre! Sais-tu, mon garçon, though you are only a tutor, you should have been born a prince! So you don't mind that our money is going so quickly?"

"To hell with it, the quicker the better!"

"Mais . . . sais-tu . . . mais dis donc, you aren't rich, are you? Mais sais-tu, you're overdoing it, this despising of money. Qu'est ce que tu feras après, dis donc?"

"Après, I'll go to Homburg and win another hundred thousand francs."

"Oui, oui, c'est ça, c'est magnifique! And I know that you will win that much and bring it all here. Dis donc, why, that way some day you'll make me really love you!

Eh bien, for being like that, I'll love you the whole time you're here, and I won't be unfaithful to you once. You see, all this time, though I did not love you, parce que je croyais que tu n'étais qu'un outchitel (quelque chose comme un laquais, n'est-ce pas?), I've still been faithful to you, parce que je suis bonne fille."[40]

"Come, you're lying! Didn't I see you with Albert, that swarthy little officer, last time?"

"Oh, oh, mais tu es . . ."

"Come, you're lying, you're lying. Do you really think I'm angry? Why, I don't give a damn, il faut que la jeunesse se passe. How could you chase him away, since he was there before me, and you love him? Only don't give him any money, do you understand?"

"So you aren't angry about that either? Mais tu es un vrai philosophe, sais-tu? Un vrai philosophe!" she cried enthusiastically. "Eh bien, je t'aimerai, je t'aimerai—tu verras, tu seras content!"

And in fact from that time she actually seemed to become attached to me, perhaps even fond of me, and so our last ten days passed. I never saw the "stars" promised me, but in some respects she really did keep her word. Moreover, she introduced me to Hortense, a woman truly remarkable in her own way, whom we used to call Thérèse-philosophe[41] in our circle . . .

However, there is no need to go into that here. It all might make a separate story, of a different color, which I do not want to introduce into this story. The fact of the matter was that I hoped from the bottom of my heart that the whole affair would be finished as soon as possible. Our hundred thousand francs, as I have already men-

40. "Because I thought you were only a tutor (something like a lackey, isn't it?) . . . because I'm a good girl."

41. From an anonymous erotic book *Thérèse-philosophe; ou Mémoire pour servir à l'histoire de D. Dirray et de Melle Erodice la Haye* (1748).

tioned, lasted us nearly a month, which frankly surprised me: Blanche had spent at least eighty thousand on things which she bought herself; so there were only twenty thousand francs left for our living expenses—and we still made it. Blanche, who toward the end was almost honest with me (at least there were some things about which she didn't lie to me), declared that at least I wouldn't be responsible for the debts she had been forced to incur. "I didn't let you sign any bills or promissory notes," she told me, "because I felt sorry for you. Most any other girl would have certainly done it and got you in prison. You see, you see how I loved you, and what a kind heart I have! Think of what that damned wedding alone is going to cost me!"

There was really going to be a wedding. It took place toward the very end of that month of ours, and it may be assumed that the last remains of my hundred thousand francs were spent on it. And that's how it all ended, that is, that's how "our month" ended, as immediately thereafter I was formally dismissed.

This is how it happened. A week after we had established ourselves in Paris the General arrived. He came straight to Blanche, and from his first visit virtually lived with us. To be sure, he had a small flat of his own somewhere. Blanche received him most heartily, with happy squeals and laughter, and even rushed to embrace him. It turned out that it was she herself who insisted he stay around and follow her everywhere: on the boulevards, driving around in her carriage, to the theater, seeing friends. The General was still good for this kind of employment. He was a man of rather imposing and decorous presence: rather tall, with dyed sideburns and huge moustaches (he had served in the Cuirassiers), and a handsome though somewhat flabby face. His manners were excellent, and he wore his evening dress well. In

Paris he began wearing his decorations. To walk down
the boulevard with a man like this was not only permis-
sible, it was, if I may say so, even *commendable*. The
good-natured and muddleheaded General was terribly
pleased with all this. He had been expecting something
quite different when he first showed up at our apartment
after his arrival in Paris. He had come then, almost trembling with fear, thinking that Blanche would start yelling
at him and have him kicked out. Therefore, when things
took this turn, he was positively delighted and spent the
whole month in a state of senseless rapture. And he was
still in that state when I left him. I learned only later
that after our sudden departure from Roulettenburg he
had suffered something resembling a fit the same morning. He had collapsed, unconscious, and later had been
like a madman all week, talking incoherently. He had
been getting some medical treatment, but suddenly he
had quit everything and taken the train to Paris. Naturally, the reception Blanche gave him was the best possible cure for him. The symptoms of his ailment, however, remained long after, in spite of his cheerful and
rapturous frame of mind. He was now quite incapable
of thinking or even of conducting any kind of halfway
serious conversation. Whenever this became necessary,
he would just say "H'm!" and nod his head at every word
—which would be his whole contribution to the conversation. He used to laugh a great deal, but it was a nervous,
sickly sort of laugh, as though he were hysterical. Then
again he would just sit there for hours, gloomy as night,
knitting his bushy eyebrows. There were many things
which he didn't even remember. He had become dis-
gracefully absent-minded and had acquired a habit of
talking to himself. Only Blanche could revitalize him.
And, indeed, his fits of gloom and depression, when he
would sit in a corner moping, merely signified that he

had not seen Blanche for a long time, or that she had gone off somewhere without taking him with her, or that she had forgotten to be nice to him before leaving. Furthermore, he was not capable of telling what he wanted, or why he was gloomy and sad. After just sitting around for an hour or two (I noticed this a couple of times when Blanche was gone for the whole day, probably to be with Albert), he would suddenly begin to look around, get flustered, cast nervous glances in all directions, then seemingly remember something and start looking for it; but, seeing nobody, and not remembering, after all, the question he was going to ask, he would lapse into silence again, until Blanche suddenly appeared, gay, playful, all dressed up, and with her ringing laughter. She would run up to him, tease him, even kiss him—the latter, though, was a rare treat, granted only rarely. There was one time when the General was so glad to see her he actually began to cry—it really made we wonder.

From the very first day he appeared at our establishment, Blanche had started to plead his cause before me. She even waxed eloquent in doing so. She reminded me of the fact that she had betrayed the General for my sake, that she had been virtually engaged to him, that she had given him her word, that he had abandoned his family on her account, and, finally, that I had been in his service and ought to feel accordingly, so—why, really, wasn't I a bit ashamed . . . I kept saying nothing to all this, and she just kept prattling away. At last I began to laugh, and that's where the matter ended, or, rather, she thought, at first, that I was a fool, whereas later she came to the conclusion that I was a very nice and understanding person. In short, I had the good fortune, in the end, to gain undoubtedly the fullest favor of this excellent young woman. (Blanche, it ought to be said, was indeed a very nice, good-natured girl—in her own way, of course; I did

not appreciate her enough in the beginning.) "You are
a kind and a clever man," she used to tell me toward the
end, "and . . . and . . . it's just a pity you're such a fool!
You'll never, but never amount to anything!"

"Un vrai russe, un calmouk!"[42] Several times she sent
me to take the General for a walk, exactly the way she
would tell a servant to walk her dog. I took him to the
theater, though, and to the Bal-Mabile, and to various
restaurants. For this, Blanche would even give me money,
although the General had some of his own, and he very
much liked to take out his wallet before people. Once I
almost had to resort to force to prevent him from buying
a brooch for seven hundred francs which caught his eye
at the Palais Royal and which he definitely wanted to
give to Blanche. Really, what was she going to do with a
brooch worth seven hundred francs? Besides, the General had no more than a thousand francs in all. I never
found out where he got them. I presume it was from Mr.
Astley, especially as the latter had also paid their bill at
the hotel. Regarding the General's attitude toward me
during all this time, he didn't even seem to suspect what
my relations with Blanche were like. Though he had
heard, in a sort of vague way, that I had won a large sum
of money, he probably assumed that I was something like
a private secretary to Blanche, or perhaps even a servant.
At least he always spoke to me condescendingly, as superior to inferior, and occasionally went as far as to give me
a tongue-lashing. One morning, as we were having coffee
together, he reduced Blanche and me to fits of laughter.
He was not normally quick to take offense, but that time
he suddenly got very angry at me, and for what?—I have
no idea to this day. Of course he didn't know himself either. In short, he just kept rambling on and on, *à bâtons-*

42. From "Kalmyk," region, now Kalmyk Autonomous Soviet Socialist
Republic, on northwest shore of Caspian Sea.

rompus, shouted that I was a no-good, that he was going
to teach me a lesson . . . that he was going to show me
. . . and so on and so forth. Nobody could understand
a word of what he was saying. Blanche laughed and
laughed. At last we somehow managed to calm him down
and took him out for a walk. However, there were many
times when he became sad, when he seemed to be regretting something or feel sorry for somebody, when he appeared to be missing somebody, even though Blanche was
present at the time. On these occasions he would sometimes start talking to me of his own accord but never
managed to express clearly what was on his mind. Instead, he would reminisce about his military service,
about his late wife, about his family affairs, about his
country estate. Often he would hit upon some word and
be so pleased about it that he would repeat it a hundred
times that day, even though it did not at all express either
his feelings or his thoughts. I tried a few times to talk to
him about his children. But he would fend this off by
keeping up his rapid chatter and by quickly changing the
subject: "Yes, yes, the children, the children, you are
quite right, the children!" Only once he became sentimental about it. We were on our way to the theater
together: "Those are unhappy children!" he said suddenly, "yes, sir, yes, those are un-n-happy children!" And
then, later that night, he repeated the phrase: "unhappy
children!" a number of times. Once, when I turned the
conversation to Polina, he actually flew into a rage. "She
is an ungrateful woman," he exclaimed; "she is wicked
and ungrateful! She has disgraced the family! If they had
any laws here, I'd make her knuckle under! Yes, sir, I
would!" As for de Grieux, he could not bear even to hear
his name. "He has ruined me," he used to say; "he has
robbed me blind, he's been my undoing! He was my
nightmare for two long years! He used to haunt me in

my dreams for months! It's—it's, it's . . . Oh, don't mention him to me, ever!"

I could see that the two of them were coming to an understanding, but, as usual, I kept quiet about it. Blanche was the first to tell me. It was exactly a week before we parted. "Il a du chance," she jabbered away; "babouchka is really sick now and will certainly die. Mr. Astley has sent a telegram. You must agree, he is her heir, after all. And even if not, he won't be in the way. To begin with, he's got his pension, and second, he'll live in a back room, where he'll be perfectly happy. I shall be "madame la Générale." I'll belong to a nice social set (Blanche dreamed of that all the time), later I'll be a Russian landowner; j'aurai un château, des moujiks, et puis j'aurai toujours mon million."

"Well, but what if he becomes jealous, if he demands . . . God knows what, you understand?"

"Oh, no, non, non, non! How dare he! I've taken measures, don't you worry. I've already made him sign several promissory notes in Albert's name. Let him just try the least thing, and he'll be punished right away. Besides, he won't dare!"

"All right, then marry him . . ."

The wedding was celebrated without any great pomp, a quiet family affair. Only Albert and a few other intimate friends were invited. Hortense, Cléopâtre, and the rest were strictly excluded. The bridegroom took great interest in his position. Blanche personally tied his tie for him, pomaded his hair, and in his swallowtails and white tie he looked *très comme il faut*.

"Il est pourtant très comme il faut," Blanche herself observed to me emerging from the General's room, as though the idea that the General was "très comme il faut" were a surprise even to her. I took so little interest in all the details, participating in the whole proceedings as a mere idle spectator, that I have actually forgotten a lot of what took place there. I remember only that it turned out that Blanche wasn't "de Cominges" at all, just as her mother wasn't "veuve Cominges," but rather "du-Placet." Why they had been de Cominges up to that point, I don't know. But the General was perfectly content with this, too, and in fact he liked du-Placet even better than de Cominges. On the morning of the wedding, all dressed up for the part, he kept pacing up and down the drawing room, repeating to himself with an unusually serious and grave air: "Mademoiselle Blanche du-Placet! Blanche du-Placet! Du-Placet! Miss Blanca Dew-Plassett! . . ." And his face beamed with a certain smugness, even. In church, at the *maire*'s, and at the wedding repast at home he appeared not only cheerful and content but even proud. Something had happened to both of them. Blanche, too, was beginning to wear an air of particular dignity.

"I must behave quite differently from now on," she told me, very seriously, "mais vois-tu, I never gave any thought to one nasty detail: imagine, I still can't remember my new surname: Zagoriansky, Zagoziansky, madame la générale de Sago-Sago, ces diables des noms russes, enfin madame la générale à quatorze consonnes! comme c'est agréable, n'est-ce pas?"[43]

At last we parted, and Blanche, that silly Blanche, actually had tears in her eyes when she said good-bye to me. "Tu étais bon enfant," she said, sniveling. "Je te croyais bête es tu en avais l'air, but it suits you." And, pressing my hand just before parting, she suddenly exclaimed: "Attends!" rushed to her boudoir, and returned a minute later with two thousand-franc bills. I would have never

43. "Madame general from Sago-Sago, damn these Russian names, well then madame general with a name of fourteen consonants! pleasant, isn't it?"

believed that! "This will come in handy; maybe you are a very learned *outchitel*, but you are an awfully stupid man. I won't give you more than two thousand no matter what, because you'll gamble it away in any case. Well, good-bye! Nous serons toujours bons amis, and if you should win again, be sure to come back to me, et tu seras heureux!"

I also had five hundred francs left of my own. Besides, I've still got a beautiful watch worth a thousand francs, some diamond cufflinks, and a few other things, so that I could go on for quite some time without having much to worry about. I am staying in this little town on purpose, to get ready for my next step, and, what is more important, I am waiting for Mr. Astley. I found out for sure that he will pass through this town shortly and stay here for twenty-four hours, on business. I'll find out about everything . . . and then, straight on to Homburg. I am not going to Roulettenburg, perhaps next year. In fact, it is said that playing the same table twice in a row gives you bad luck, and, besides, Homburg really is *the* place for gambling.

Seventeen

A year and eight months have gone
by since I last looked at these notes,
and I do so now only because, in
my dejection and misery, I suddenly decided to amuse
myself by reading them over. So that's where I left off,
planning to go to Homburg. My God! How lightheart-
edly, relatively speaking, I wrote those last lines! Not
really with a light heart, that is, but with what self-confi-
dence, with what unflagging hopes! Did I have even the
slightest doubt of myself? And now more than a year and
a half has passed, and I am, to my own mind, a lot worse
than a beggar! So what if I am a beggar! Being a beggar
doesn't mean a thing. I've only ruined myself! It is virtually impossible to make any comparisons, though, and
what's the use of moralizing to oneself At a time like
this, nothing could be more absurd than speaking of
morals! Oh, these self-satisfied people: with what proud
self-satisfaction are these windbags ready to deliver their
lectures! If they knew to what extent I am myself aware
of the complete loathsomeness of my present condition,
they certainly couldn't force themselves to continue their
admonitions to me. Well, what, what can they tell me
that's new to me, that I don't know? And is this the
point? The point is that one turn of the wheel could
change everything, that these very same moralists (of this

I am convinced) would be the first to congratulate me with friendly banter. And no longer would everybody turn away from me, as is the case now. To hell with them all! What am I right now? *Zéro*. What can I be tomorrow? Tomorrow I may rise from the dead and begin a new life! I may still discover the man in me, so long as he is not lost altogether!

I actually went to Homburg that time, but . . . later I went back to Roulettenburg, and I also went to Spa. Once I was even in Baden, where I went as valet to a man named Hinze, a "councillor," a scoundrel, and my former master here. Yes, I was a flunkey for five whole months! This happened immediately after I got out of jail. (Yes, I did some time in prison in Roulettenburg for a debt I incurred there. An anonymous friend paid my debt and got me out. I wonder who it was? Mr. Astley? Polina? I don't know, but, anyway, the debt was paid, two hundred thalers in all, and I was set free.) What was I to do? So I entered the service of this Hinze. He is a young man, and of a frivolous temper, as well as lazy, and I can speak and write in three languages. At first I was to be a kind of secretary to him for thirty gulden a month. But I ended up being a regular valet: he no longer could afford to keep a secretary, so he reduced my wages. I had no place to go, and I stayed on—and so I automatically became a flunkey. I didn't have enough to eat or to drink in his service, but I did save seventy gulden in five months. One night, in Baden, I announced to him that I was quitting his service. That same night I went to the casino. Oh, how my heart was pounding! No, it wasn't the money that I wanted so much! That night, the only thing I wanted was that the next day all these Hinzes, all these Ober-Kellners, all these elegant Baden ladies, that they should all be talking about me, that they should all be telling my story, that they should all wonder at me, ad-

mire me, and worship my renewed success. All these are
but childish daydreams and anxieties, but . . . who knows:
perhaps I would meet Polina, and I'd tell her everything,
and she would see that I was above all these absurd acci-
dents of fate . . . Oh, it isn't money that's dear to me! I
am convinced that I would have thrown it away once
more to some Blanche, and for three weeks of driving
around Paris in my own carriage driven by a pair of
horses worth sixteen thousand francs. I know for sure
that I am not avaricious; I even think that I am a spend-
thrift. And yet, with what trepidation, with what palpi-
tation of my heart, I hear the croupier's cry: "Trente et
un, rouge, impaire et passe!" or, "Quatre, noir, pair et
manque!" With what avidity I stare at the gaming table
on which louis d'or, gulden, and thalers are scattered, at
those little columns of gold pieces, when the croupier's
shovel breaks them down into piles of gold that glow like
embers, or at those huge rolls of silver, over two feet long,
that lie around the wheel. Even as I approach the gambling hall, as soon as I hear, still two rooms away, the
jingle of money poured out on the table, I almost go into
convulsions.

Oh, that night I took my seventy gulden to the roulette
table, was quite remarkable, too. I started off with ten
gulden, and again from *passe*. I am prejudiced in favor
of *passe*. I lost. I had sixty gulden in silver money left. I
thought for a moment, then chose *zéro*. I began placing
five gulden at a time on *zéro*. At the third turn *zéro* came
up, all of a sudden; I almost died of joy, receiving one
hundred and seventy-five gulden. The time I won a hundred thousand gulden I wasn't nearly so glad. I immediately placed a hundred gulden on *rouge,* and won; then
the whole two hundred on *rouge,* and won; the whole
four hundred on *noir,* and won again; the whole eight
hundred on *manque*—it won also. Counting what I had

had in hand, I now had seventeen hundred gulden, and this in less than five minutes! Yes, it is at moments like this that one forgets all one's earlier failures! Why, I had got this at the risk of more than my life itself. But I had dared to risk it, and there I was once again, a man among men!

I took a room at a hotel, locked myself in, and just sat there, counting my money, until three o'clock at night. When I woke up in the morning I was no longer a flunkey. I decided to leave for Homburg that very same day: I had not been a flunkey or been in prison there. Half an hour before train time I went to the casino to try two bets, no more, and lost fifteen hundred gulden. Yet I went to Homburg all the same, and now I have been here for a whole month . . .

Of course I live in a state of continuous excitement. I play for the smallest stakes and keep waiting for something, calculating, standing around the gaming tables for whole days, and *observing* the game. I even dream of gambling. Yet at the same time I have a feeling that I have grown numb, somehow, as though I were buried in some kind of mire. I gather this from my impressions when I met Mr. Astley. We had not seen each other since that time [in Roulettenburg], and we met here by accident. This is how it happened. I was walking in the gardens, figuring that I had almost no money left, but that I still had fifty gulden and, besides that, I had paid my hotel bill in full just the other day. This meant that I had one more chance to try my luck at roulette. If I won anything at all, I'd be able to continue playing; if I lost, I'd have to get myself another job as a flunkey, unless I could find some Russians who needed a tutor. Absorbed in these thoughts, I took my daily route through the park and through the forest and to the adjoining principality. Sometimes I spent up to four hours walking like this and returned to Homburg tired and hungry. I had just entered the park, coming from the gardens, when I suddenly saw Mr. Astley sitting on a bench. He noticed me first and called my name. I sat down beside him. But detecting in him a certain reserve, I immediately restrained my delight. But I was very glad to see him.

"So you are here! I actually thought that I was going to run into you," he told me. "Don't bother to tell me your story: I know it, I know everything; I am familiar with all the details of your life during this last year and eight months."

"Oh! Look what a watch you keep on your old friends!" I answered. "It is very much to your credit that you haven't forgotten . . . Wait a moment, though, you've just given me an idea. Wasn't it you who got me out of prison in Roulettenburg, where I was being held for non-payment of a debt in the amount of two hundred gulden? Some unnamed person paid it for me."

"No, but no! I never got you out of Roulettenburg jail, where you were locked up for a debt of two hundred gulden. I knew, though, that you were in prison for a debt of two hundred gulden."

"That means, at least you know who got me out?"

"Oh, no, I can't say that I know who got you out."

"Strange. I don't know any Russians here, and, besides, our Russians here are hardly the kind who would do such a thing. Back home in Russia it might happen that an Orthodox Christian would get another Orthodox Christian out of prison. So I thought that it might have been some eccentric Englishman who did it to be different."

Mr. Astley listened to me with some surprise. Apparently he had expected to find me despondent and crushed.

"I am very glad, though, to see that you have fully

maintained your independence of spirit, and even your cheerfulness," he observed, rather unpleasantly.

"That is, deep inside you're gritting your teeth with vexation at not finding me crushed and humble," I said, laughing.

He did not immediately understand my remark, but when he did, he smiled.

"I like your observations. I recognize in these words my former, clever, enthusiastic, yet, at the same time, cynical, old friend. Only Russians can combine in themselves so many opposites at the same time. It is true, a man likes to see his best friend humbled, and much of what friendship is, is based on this fact. This is an old truth, well known to all wise men. But in the present case, let me assure you that I am sincerely pleased to see that you haven't lost heart. Tell me, don't you intend to give up gambling?"

"To hell with gambling! I'll quit immediately, as soon as . . ."

"As soon as you've won back what you lost? That's what I thought. You don't have to tell me—I know—you said that inadvertently, and, therefore, you were telling the truth. Tell me, besides gambling, is there anything else you're doing?"

"No, nothing at all . . ."

He began examining me. I knew nothing. I had hardly looked into the newspapers, and I definitely had not opened a single book during that entire time.

"You've become completely stale," he observed; "not only have you renounced life, all your interests, private as well as public, your duties as a citizen and as a human being, your friends (yes, you had some friends), not only have you renounced having any goal at all, except winning at roulette, but you have even renounced your memories. I remember you at an ardent and intense moment of your life. But I am convinced that you have forgotten all the best impressions which you had then. Your dreams, your most urgent desires, I mean those that you have now do not go beyond *pair* and *impair, rouge, noir,* the twelve middle numbers, and so on and so forth, I'm quite sure of that!"

"Enough, Mr. Astley, I beg you, I beg you not to remind me of this," I cried out, quite annoyed and almost angry; "let me tell you that I have forgotten nothing at all, but that I have temporarily cleared my mind of all these things, including even my memories— until I have effected a radical improvement in my circumstances; then . . . then you shall see me rise again from the dead!"

"You'll be here still in ten years," he said. "I bet I'll remind you of this on this very bench, if I'm alive by then."

"Well, enough," I interrupted him impatiently, "and to prove to you that I'm not quite so forgetful of the past as you think, allow me to ask: where is Miss Polina now? If it wasn't you who got me out of jail, it must have been she, for sure. I haven't had any news about her since that one day.

"No, oh no! I don't think that it was she who got you out of jail. She is now in Switzerland, and you will do me a great favor if you'll stop asking me questions about Miss Polina," he said resolutely, even angrily.

"This is to say, she hurt you quite a bit, too!" I laughed involuntarily.

"Miss Polina is the finest human being I've known and deserves the highest respect, but, let me repeat, you'll do me a great favor if you'll stop asking me questions about Miss Polina. You never knew her, and it outrages my moral sentiments to hear her name from your lips."

"Is that so! However, you are wrong there. Listen, what else is there for me to talk to you about, except that,

think for yourself? Why, that's what the shared memories of both of us amount to. Don't worry, please, I'm
not trying to find out anything that's private or secret
between you and her . . . I am only interested, so to say,
in Miss Polina's external circumstances, in her present
external condition. That's something you could tell me
in a few words."

"All right then, but under the condition that these
few words will be the end of it. Miss Polina was ill for a
long time. She is still not well today. She spent some time
with my mother and sister in the north of England. Half
a year ago her grandmother—remember, that same crazy
woman—died and left her, personally, a fortune of seven
thousand pounds. At the present time Miss Polina is traveling with the family of my sister, who was married in the
meantime. Her little brother and sister, too, are provided
for by their grandmother's will and are attending school
in London. The General, her stepfather, died in Paris of
a stroke a month ago. Mademoiselle Blanche treated him
well, but managed to transfer everything that he received
from the grandmother to her name . . . there it is, I think
this is about all."

"But what about de Grieux? Isn't he traveling in Switzerland, too?"

"No, de Grieux is not traveling in Switzerland, and I
don't know where de Grieux is. Besides, I warn you once
and for all to avoid such insinuations and dishonorable
linking of names, or else I shall certainly make you regret
it."

"What? In spite of our friendly relations in the past?"

"Yes, in spite of our friendly relations in the past."

"A thousand apologies, Mr. Astley. But allow me, nevertheless: there is nothing insulting or inappropriate
about what I said, and I am not blaming Miss Polina for
anything. Besides, a Frenchman and a young Russian

lady—that's a combination, Mr. Astley, which neither you nor I could ever hope to explain or fully understand."

"If you will not mention de Grieux's name in conjunction with that other name, I would ask you to explain to me what you mean by your expression: 'a Frenchman and a young Russian lady.' And what kind of 'combination' is this? Why, precisely, a Frenchman, and why absolutely a young Russian lady?"

"There you are, I've got you interested in it. But that's a long story, Mr. Astley. There's a lot one must know before going into it. But it is an important question, however silly it may appear at first sight. A Frenchman, Mr. Astley, is the perfection of beautiful form. You, being British, may disagree with this. I, a Russian, certainly disagree, though perhaps from envy—I'll admit that. But our young ladies may be of a different opinion. You may find Racine affected, tortuous, and perfumed. Most probably you don't even read him. I, too, find him affected, tortuous, and perfumed, even ludicrous from a certain point of view. But he is still delightful, Mr. Astley, and, what is more, he is a great poet, whether you and I like it or not. The national character of a Frenchman, that is, of a Parisian, began to be molded into an elegant form at a time when we were still bears. The Revolution continued the traditions of the aristocracy. Today the most ordinary little Frenchman may have manners, gestures, modes of expression, and even thoughts, the form of which is perfectly elegant, even though his own initiative, his own soul, his own heart have had no part whatever in the creation of this form. It has all come to him through inheritance. As individuals, they may be the shallowest of the shallow, or the vilest of the vile. Well, Mr. Astley, let me tell you that there is not a creature on earth more trustful and more candid than a kindhearted, clever, and not too sophisticated young Russian lady. A de Grieux, appearing in any given role, so long as he is wearing a mask, can conquer her heart with extraordinary ease. He's got elegance of form, Mr. Astley, and the young lady takes that form for his own soul, for the natural form of his heart and soul, and not for what it is: an external garment, which has come to him by inheritance. To your great displeasure, I must confide to you that Englishmen are for the most part angular and inelegant, and Russians are rather sensitive to beauty and are easily captivated by it. But in order to detect beauty of soul and originality of character a person will need incomparably more independence and freedom than is found in our women, let alone in our young ladies, and, needless to say, a great deal more experience. And so, Miss Polina— forgive me, what's said can't be unsaid—will need a very, very long time before she could make up her mind to prefer you to that scoundrel de Grieux. She may think very highly of you, she may become your friend, she may open all her heart to you; and yet, who will continue to reign over that heart—who but that hateful scoundrel, that despicable and petty money-lender de Grieux! If for no other reason, this will continue out of mere stubbornness and vanity, for that very same de Grieux appeared to her at one time in the guise of an elegant marquis, a disillusioned liberal, a man who had ruined himself (as though he did!) helping her family and that frivolous General. All his tricks came to light later. But what does it matter that they came to light? What she wants is still the de Grieux of old—that's what she wants! And the more she loathes the present de Grieux, the more she pines for the former one, though the former never existed except in her imagination. Are you in the sugar-refining business, Mr. Astley?"

"Yes, I am a partner in the well-known sugar refinery Lovell and Company."

"There you have it, Mr. Astley. On the one side, a man

who deals in sugar, and on the other—the Apollo Belvedere. It's all somewhat incongruous. And as for me, I even haven't got a sugar refinery; I am simply a small-time gambler at roulette; I've even been a flunkey, which I suppose Miss Polina knows very well, because she seems to have some good informants.

"You are bitter, that's why you talk all this nonsense," Mr. Astley said coolly, after giving the matter some thought. "Besides, there is nothing original about what you're saying."

"Agreed! But the terrible thing is, my high-minded friend, that all these accusations I've just made, no matter how out dated, stale, and farcical they may sound, still happen to be true! And you and I are still nowhere!"

"This is vile nonsense . . . because, because . . . you shall know it, then!" Mr. Astley proclaimed, his voice trembling and his eyes flashing. "Know then, thankless and unworthy, shallow and miserable man that you are, that I've come to Homberg expressly at her wish, to get together with you, to have a long and sincere talk with you, and to report everything to her—your feelings, your thoughts, your hopes, and . . . your memories!"

"Really! Really!" I exclaimed, as tears came gushing from my eyes. I just could not hold them back. I believe that it was the first time in my life this had happened.

"Yes, unhappy man, she loved you, and I can reveal this to you, because you are a lost man! What's worse, even if I were to tell you that she still loves you, why, you would stay here just the same! Yes, you have destroyed yourself. You had some abilities, a lively disposition, and you were not a bad man. In fact, you might have been of service to your country, which needs men so badly. But you are going to stay here, and your life is finished. I am not blaming you. It seems to me that all Russians are like that, or are disposed to be like that. If it isn't roulette, it's something else, but similar to it. The exceptions are all too rare. You are not the first who does not understand what work is (I'm not talking of your plain people). Roulette is preeminently a Russian game. So far you've remained honest and have preferred being a flunkey to stealing . . . But I dread to think what may happen in the future. Enough, good-bye! You need some money, of course? Here, take these ten louis d'or, I'm not going to give you more, for you'll gamble it away in any case. Take it, and good-bye! Come, take it!"

"No, Mr. Astley, after all the things said here today . . ."

"Ta-a-ke it!" he cried. "I am convinced that you're still an honorable man, and I'm giving you the money as a friend to a true friend. If I could only be sure that you would quit gambling immediately, leave Homburg, and go back to your country, I'd be willing to give you at once a thousand pounds so that you could start a new career. The reason why I'm not giving you a thousand pounds, but only ten louis d'or, is that there is absolutely no difference for you right now between a thousand pounds and ten louis d'or—you'll gamble away one as well as the other. Take it, and good-bye."

"I'll take it if you'll allow me to embrace you for a farewell."

"Oh, with pleasure!"

We embraced with sincere feeling, and Mr. Astley left.

No, he is wrong! If I was harsh and silly about Polina and de Grieux, then he was harsh and rash in judging Russians. I'm not saying a word about myself. However . . . however, that is not the point at all. These are words, words, nothing but words, when deeds are in order! Switzerland is the thing now! Tomorrow, first thing— if I could only leave tomorrow! To be reborn, to rise from the dead! I must show them . . . Let Polina see that I still can be a man. All I need is . . . it's too late today, though, but tomorrow . . . Oh, I have the presentiment, and how could it be otherwise? I have now fifteen louis d'or, and there were times when I started with fifteen gulden! If I'd start carefully . . . oh, really, am I really childish enough to believe this? Could it be that I still refuse to admit that I am hopelessly lost? But then, why couldn't I rise again? Yes! All it takes is to be calculating and patient just once in your lifetime—that is all! All it takes is to keep control of yourself just once, and your whole life will be changed in one hour! Control yourself, that's the main thing. Only remember what happened to me in Roulettenburg, seven months ago, just before I definitely lost everything. Oh, there was a remarkable case of determination: I had lost everything then, absolutely everything . . . As I was leaving the casino I looked, there was still one gulden in my vest pocket: "Ah, so there's money for my dinner!" I thought. But then, having walked a hundred more paces, I changed my mind and went back to the casino. I staked my gulden on *manque* (that time it was *manque*), and, believe me, there is something special about that feeling which you have, all alone, in a foreign country, far from home and from your friends, not knowing what you'll eat tomorrow, as you bet your last, your very, very last gulden! I won, and left the casino twenty minutes later, with one hundred and seventy gulden in my pocket. That is a fact, yes, sir! That's what the last gulden can sometimes mean for you! And what if I had lost heart that time, if I had not dared to take that last chance? . . .

Tomorrow, tomorrow it will be all over!

Polina
Suslova's Diary

Wednesday, 19 August [1863]

I visited with Salvador. He began asking me what I had been doing, and whether I had been thinking of him. I told him that the other day I had recalled the lines: "Show me the way to the thorny path."[1] He asked me to explain to him what kind of verses these were. I told him their meaning. He liked it. He was listless at first; I wondered if he had been working a lot. And I was right. But in spite of that, there was still something else wrong with him, even though he assured me that this was his normal condition. He told me that he was having some trouble with his brother-in-law, because of money—the brother-in-law is something like a guardian, or father, to Salvador—and that he will have to go to A[merica]. Although I had been expecting this, it still came as a shock: my feelings of fright and suffering must have expressed themselves in my face. He kissed me. I bit my lips and made an unbelievable effort not to begin to sob. He kept kissing me and said that most probably he would be gone for a short while only, but perhaps forever, he added, when I had gained control of myself and had calmed down. "But you can go with me," [he] said, and I hastened to assure him that I certainly could, that my father would allow it and let me have the funds. He asked me again when I would start learning Spanish. I have just received a letter

1. From a poem by Nikolai Alekseyevich Nekrasov, "Rytsar' na chas" (Knight for a While) (1860).

from F[yodor] M[ikhailovich]. He is due to arrive in a few days. I had wanted to see him, so I could tell him everything, but now I have decided to write him a letter.

19 August

You are coming a little too late . . . Only very recently I was dreaming of going to Italy with you, and I even began to learn Italian: everything has changed within a few days. You told me one day that I would never surrender my heart easily. I have surrendered it within a week's time, at the first call, without a struggle, without assurance, almost without hope that I' was being loved. I was right to get angry with you, when you began to sing my praises. Don't think that I am blaming you, but I want only to tell you that you did not know me, nor did I know myself. Good-bye, dear!

I would like to see you, but what would it lead to? I would like very much to talk to you about Russia.

At this moment I am very, very sad. How generous, how high-minded he is! What an intellect! What a soul! This time Salvador asked me for my portrait, and inquired whether I had been taking his medicine, and whether I was feeling better. "Bien vrai?" he asked when I said that I was better. He also asked me when I was going to Italy (that was before he told me about his own departure), as I had once told him about that when we were still only friends. I told him that I didn't know when. Perhaps I wasn't going there at all, that I had wanted to go there with a man whom I loved.

*

Sunday, 23 August

Yesterday I was with Salvador. It seemed to me that he was a little angry with me, because I did not stay with him for breakfast and because I was a little sad. I looked at the lines in the palm of his hand and told him that he would be happy in one respect (I was thinking of marriage). He kept badgering me: in what? I told him that I couldn't tell him because I didn't want to think of it without being sad. He kept pestering me something awful, but I didn't give way. Later he began to talk about himself, that he would like to stay in Paris for some four years, but then, again, he might be going to America. From all this I could see that he was not giving any thought to me. I leaned my head against his breast, as tears were welling up in my eyes. He tried to look at my face, and kept asking why I was sad, and what I was thinking about. I told him that I was thinking of him and tried to remain calm. He asked me: what was it, exactly, that I was thinking? I answered that I could not tell him. "So you have secrets from me," he said. Later he asked if I would like to have breakfast with him, and I refused. "As you wish," he said. Somebody knocked. He said that it was his friend, and again asked if I would like to have breakfast. I refused, and as the friend entered the room, I started putting on my hat. Salvador escorted me to the other room and asked me when I was going to come. "When are you free? What about Tuesday?"—"Come on Tuesday, if you can't come earlier." He asked me if I was taking the medicine, and remarked that I was not cleaning my teeth, that this was bad, and that I had fine teeth.

It appeared to me this time that he does not love me, and I felt a strong desire to make him love me. This is possible, only one must act more coolly. I know his weaknesses: he is very vain.

The last time, in his friend's presence, he asked what the title of my novel was, having never spoken of it earlier. He asked me what I was doing, and asked me to say something in Italian. Today I have been thinking a great deal, and I almost felt glad that Salvador loves me so little; it makes me freer. I feel like seeing Europe and America, going to London for some advice, and then joining the *beguny* sect.[2] The life

2. Russian text has *sektu begunov* but *sektu beginov,* "the Beguine sect," may be meant. The Beguine sect was a religious association of lay women dating from the thirteenth century.

which I had been planning for myself is not going to satisfy me. One must liver a fuller and ampler life.

What do I want? . . . Oh, how many desires I have!
How their energy needs an outlet!
So much, it seems at times that by their inner anxiety
My brain will be incinerated and my breast rent asunder.[3]

Tuesday, 24 August

Today I went to see S[alva]dor, but he was not at home. I waited for him a whole hour, but he did not come . . . There were many thoughts and feelings flitting through my head, as I was sitting in his room, but I am not going to discuss them here. I sat there, with my head between my hands, without taking my eyes off the hands of the clock, my heart throbbing. Meanwhile the tears kept welling up in my eyes, and I started at the slightest sound. I wanted to write him a very serious letter, but resisted the temptation, writing only:

> I was at the hotel G today, but you were not in. Tell me what this is to mean, and why you did not write me that you were not going to be at home. Don't you know that your absence causes me pain? I thought about you a great deal and even meant to write you several times. However, I have also been working a lot. Soon I shall be looking for a Spanish teacher. I am wondering how to go about it.
> I am waiting for your reply.
>
> A. S.

I am very sad that I did not see you, but I hope that this did not give you any pleasure. I am saddened by your absence, but I am still trying to persuade myself that you love me.

I recall how at our last meeting I said, in some connection: "Don't deceive me." "Me deceive you?" he said with

3. Quatrain from N. P. Ogarev. The first line is not quoted correctly by Suslova. Should be "What do I want . . . Oh, so many desires I have."

dignity. This is a remarkable trait. However, it seems to me that he is entirely dependent on his family.

Wednesday, 27 [August]

I have just received a letter from F[yodor] Mikh[ailovich], this time through the local mail. How glad he is that he is going to see me soon. I sent him a very short letter which I had prepared beforehand. I feel very sorry for him.

What diverse thoughts and feelings will agitate him, once the first sensation of grief has worn off! I am only afraid that, having got tired of waiting for me (my letter won't reach him very soon), he may come here today, before he ever gets my letter. I won't keep my composure if it comes to such a meeting. It is good that I warned him to write me first, or else something might happen. And Salvador still has not written me . . . I'll see much grief from that man.

Same date, evening.

That's precisely what happened. I had barely managed to write the above lines when F[yodor] M[ikhailovich] showed up. I saw him through the window, but waited until the message came that he was there, and even then it was a long time before I could make myself go out to meet him. "How are you?" I said, in a trembling voice. He asked me what was the matter with me, which only intensified my agitation, along with his own uneasiness, which was also growing. "I thought that you were not going to come," I said, "because I wrote you a letter."

"What letter?"

"So you wouldn't come."

"Why not?"

"Because it is too late."

He hung his head.

"I must know everything, let's go somewhere, and tell me, or I'll die."

I suggested that we go to his room. We were silent all the way. *I did not look at him.* Once in a while he would yell "Vite, vite" to the cabman, in a desperate and impatient voice, so that the man would turn around and give us a puzzled look. I tried not to look at F[yodor] M[ikhailovich]. He was not looking at me either, but kept holding my hand all the way, pressing it hard from time to time and making some sort of convulsive movements. "Calm down, I am with you," I said.

When we got to his room, he fell at my feet, and, putting his arms around my knees, clasping them, and sobbing, he exclaimed between sobs: "I have lost you, I knew it!" Then, having regained his composure, he began to ask me about the other man. "Perhaps he is handsome, young, and glib. But you will never find a heart such as mine."

For a long time I did not have the heart to answer him.

"Have you given yourself to him completely?"

"Don't ask, it is not right," I said.

"Polia, I don't know what is right and what is wrong. Who is he, a Russian, a Frenchman, not my doctor? That one?" [An illegible word.]

"No, no."

I told him that I loved the man very much.

"Are you happy?"

"No."

"How can that be? You love and you are not happy, why, is this possible?"

"He does not love me."

"He does not love you!" he exclaimed, clutching his head in despair. "But you don't love him like a slave, do you? Tell me, I must know! Isn't it true that you would follow him to the end of the world?"

"No, I . . . I'll be going to the country," I said, bursting into tears.

"Oh, Polia, why must you be so unhappy! It had to happen that you would fall in love with another man. I knew it. Why, you fell in love with me by mistake, because yours is a generous heart, you waited until you were 23,[4] you are the only woman who does not demand of a man that he obligate himself in any way, but at what price: a man and a woman are not one and the same. He takes, she gives."

When I told him what kind of a man the other was, he said that he experienced a feeling of disgust at that moment: that he felt better knowing that this was not a serious person, no Lermontov. We went on to talk about a lot of extraneous subjects. He told me that he was happy to have met a human being such as I was, in this world. He begged me to remain his friend, and to continue to write him, particularly whenever I was especially happy or unhappy. Then he suggested that we travel to Italy together, while remaining like brother and sister. When I told him that, most probably, he would be writing his novel, he answered: "Who do you take me for! Do you think that all this is going to pass without leaving any impression!" I promised him that I would come to see him the next day. I felt relieved after I had talked to him. He understands me.

I still haven't got a letter from Salvador, and to make sure, I am writing him this letter:

"You were not at the hotel on Tuesday, nor did you write me a word about it. Perhaps you did not get my letter. But in any case you could have written me. Or don't you know how I love you? I love you to distraction. I am beginning to think that some great calamity has befallen you, and this thought causes me great distress. I can't tell you how much I love you, and if you knew it, you would not have made me suffer what I have suffered during these last two days, waiting for word from you."

I am writing him still another letter, which I shall give him later.

"I want to tell you how much I love you, even though I know that it is beyond my powers to express it in words. I feel that you ought to know it, though. I have never been

4. This would indicate that the affair started in 1862. Polina was born in 1839.

happy. All the people who loved me made me suffer, even my father and mother. All my friends are kind people, but weak and poor in spirit; they are abundant in their words, but poor in their deeds. I haven't met a single one among them who would not be afraid of the truth, or who wouldn't have retreated before the conventions of life. They also condemn me. I cannot respect such people. I consider it a crime to talk one way and act another. As far as I am concerned, I fear only my conscience. And if it were to happen that I had sinned before it, I would admit it only to myself. I am not particularly indulgent to myself, I think, but weak and timid people are hateful to me. I avoid people who deceive themselves, without knowing it—so I won't have to depend on them. I am thinking of settling in the country, among peasants, and trying to be of some use to them, because to live without being of any use to other people I consider unworthy of a human being."

Monday, 1 September

I did not mail those last two letters to Salvador, because here is what happened: one night I came home from F[yodor] M[ikhailovich]'s rather late, went to bed, without lighting a candle, and slept poorly all night, thinking about Sal[vador]. I woke up when it was still dark, at daybreak. I began walking from room to room, and suddenly noticed a letter on my table. I did not recognize the handwriting. It was a letter from his friend. He told me that Salvador had typhus, *that he had been sick ever since the last time he saw me*, and that I could not see him now, because he was with some friends, recommended by his family, and that this gentleman would take care of him, and would become suspicious if I were to go there. I immediately wrote an answer to the letter, telling him that I considered it barbaric that I could not see Sal [vador] and begging him to write to me more often and tell me about his friend's health. That same day I wrote still another letter to Sal[vador], thinking him on the edge of the grave. I wrote to assure him that he would get well, that it would be an injustice if he didn't. I was in a state of terrible despair, having heard that the dispease was particularly dangerous to young people. F[yodor] M[ikhailovich] gave me some reassurance, for he told me that what with the air they have here, and the medical care available, it shouldn't be dangerous. I moved to Mir., and all day Saturday I waited for a letter. On Sunday, I was expecting him [Salvador's friend] in person (I had invited him, so I could ask him about Sal[vador]). At 6 o'clock on Saturday I went out for a walk in the rue de la Sorbonne and ran into Sal[vador]. I saw him at a distance, but simply could not believe that it was he. It seemed so incredible to me, until he walked up to me, smiling but very pale, and took my hand. My legs almost gave way under me, and for some time I could not say a word. I did not suspect anything as yet, but I felt hurt about his not having written me. His first words were that he had been very ill and that this was the first time he had been out for a walk. "Yes, you are very pale," I said. At that moment I raised my eyes, and looked at him. There were red spots on his cheeks.

"You weren't angry with me about my not coming on Tuesday, but hadn't you said that you were coming on Thursday?"

At these words, my head was beginning to clear, but I was suffering so much that I hadn't the strength to become indignant even. Tears gushed from my eyes.

"Where are you going?" he asked.

"Just taking a walk, and you?"

"I'm going to see a friend, in the rue de Souffle."

"Let's walk together a little. I thought that you were dying. Your friend wrote me that kind of a letter. Here it is,"—I took the letter from my handbag—"look what it says in it, read it. I wrote him twice, asking him to come and see me."

"I am very angry that he put it that way. I thought that it was typhus, but it turned out otherwise."

He looked at the letter and, apparently, saw nothing in it, or else it was known to him. He gave it back to me.

"Read it," I said, "read it later, at home."

But he opened it again, perhaps in order not to have to talk to me. Before we ever reached the rue de Souffle, he said that he had to turn left (he was feeling embarrassed with me).

"In that case, good-bye," I said, "I must walk straight on."

"But I can walk with you," [he] said. (Was he feeling pity, or was his conscience bothering him?)

We reached the rue de Souffle in silence (he was reading his friend's letter).

"That is where I have to go," he said, pointing at a house directly [across] the street from which we had come.

Once alone, I quickly understood what had happened. When I found myself alone in my room, I became hysterical. I screamed that I was going to kill him. Nobody heard it. Then I lay down and for a while thought of nothing. I felt the fever rising to my head, I thought that I was going to fall ill and was glad about it. Then I began to think about what I should do and made up my mind . . . I even wanted to write my sister a letter. I made everything ready, burned some of my notebooks and letters (those letters which could compromise me). I felt wonderfully well. I only felt sorry for my mother, and for the Hogermans, who might be placed in a difficult position because of me. I kept wondering whether there wasn't a way to keep them out of it, to say that I had never lived with them. I did not sleep all night and on the following morning, at 7 o'clock, went to see Dost[oevsky]. He was asleep. When I came, he got up, opened the door for me, and went back to bed, wrapping himself up in his blanket. He looked at me with astonishment and apprehension. I was rather calm. I told him that he should come to my place right away. I wanted to tell him everything and ask him to be my judge. I did not want to stay at his place because I was ex-jecting Salv[ador]. When F[yodor] M[ikhailovich] came to me, I met him with a piece of bread in my hand, as I was just having my breakfast. "Well, you can see that I am calm," I said laughing.

"Yes," he said, "and I am very glad about that, but who can tell anything for sure, when it comes to you?"

After a few unimportant questions, I began to tell him the

whole story of my love, and then about the encounter yesterday, not concealing anything.

F[yodor] M[ikhailovich] said that I should pay no attention to this matter, that I had, of course, sullied myself, but
that it had been only an accident, that Sal[vador], being a
young man, needed a mistress and I happened to be available, so he took advantage of me, and why shouldn't he have
done so? A pretty woman, agreeable to all tastes.

F[yodor] M[ikhailovich] was right, I understood perfectly
well, but how hard it was for me!

"I'm only afraid that you may come up with some foolishness" (I had told him about my thoughts, once, when
Salva[dor] had failed to keep an appointment).

"I would not like to kill him," I said, "but I would like to
torture him for a very long time."

"Enough," he said, "he isn't worth it, he won't understand
a thing, he's a pest that ought to be exterminated with insect
powder," and it would be foolish to ruin one's own life on
account of him.

I agreed. But I still love him very much, and I am ready
to give away half my life just to make him feel the pangs of
conscience, before he comes back to me to repent. Of course,
I can hardly expect this to happen on his part, and sometimes
I become depressed again. Right now I suddenly feel a desire
which I thought I had overcome—a desire to avenge myself,
but how? By what means? Most probably he has a mistress,
some lady who has innumerable admirers. Most likely he had
quarreled with her, and on account of that had this affair
with me. But now, it must be that they have made up again.

He did not come yesterday, and, of course, he won't come
today either, nor tomorrow, but what, then, is he going to
do? Didn't he promise to come, at a time when I still hadn't
been begging him for it? It seems to me that his vanity won't
allow him to remain a liar in my eyes. What could it have
been he was hoping for, when he made up that story about
his illness? I have made up my mind to send him the money
for . . . [one illegible word] F[yodor] M[ikhailovich] is going
to tell me that this is unnecessary. He despises him too much,

and besides, it seems that he finds I ought to suffer (renounce my vengeance) for my stupidity, yet his stupidity had a meaning.

2 September

F[yodor] M[ikhailovich] actually said that it was not necessary to send him the money, that this was just a trifle. He thought that, subconsciously, I was using this as a pretext to get in touch with Sal[vador]. F[yodor] M[ikhailovich] said that this would lead to his getting a chance to set himself right with me again and deceiving me once more. "Should one really be afraid of this, refusing to trust oneself?" said I; "if one must be afraid of being deceived, one ought not have any self-respect."

F[yodor] M[ikhailovich] definitely failed to understand me, and did not know about this letter; here it is:

"Dear Sir, on a certain occasion I received from you a service, which is usually reimbursed in money. I believe that one may accept free services only from people whom one considers one's friends and whom one respects. I am sending you this money to correct my mistake in regard to you. You have no right to interfere with this intention of mine.

"P.S. I would like to add that there is no reason for you to hide and to be afraid of me: I have no intention of pursuing you. You can meet me (perhaps this will happen) as though we had never known each other; I am even asking you to. I tell you this, assuming that you will take my money. If otherwise, I do advise you to hide yourself somewhere away from me, as far away as you can (because, in that case, I will be angry with you, which might be rather dangerous).

"This will be better for you, since I am a person of no culture (I am entirely a barbarian) and don't appreciate your affected pleasantries at all. I say this in all seriousness."

I told F[yodor] M[ikhailovich] about the content of this letter, whereupon he said that I could send it, of course, since at least it would not make me look too passive. I mailed the letter the day before yesterday, and so far I have not received a reply (and, most probably, I never will). I must admit that I did not expect that. The man is not so sophisticated as to remain silent from a sense of dignity, nor is he so shameless as to act that way from sheer insolence. He must have got cold feet. However, it may be that he will think of something to answer me, though I doubt it. Judging by his character, I presume that if he weren't afraid of me, he would have returned the money to me, even without a letter. This letter must have greatly hurt more than his vanity, for he has a sense of honor of sorts, which is not part of his nature, or even of his intellect, but it is in his memory, taken from the Catholic catechism.

Baden-Baden, 5 September

I was very sad before leaving Paris. It is not just a matter of having grown accustomed to a place, for I left Pet[ersburg] with a light heart. I left it with hope, while in Paris I lost a great deal [of hope]. It seems to me that I shall never love anybody. A thirst for revenge burned in my soul for a long time after, and I decided that, if I do not become distracted in Italy, I will return to Paris and do as I had planned . . . Along the way F[yodor] M[ikhailovich] and I got to talking about Lermontov. I recalled [one of his] characters, and all that had happened to me appeared so petty, so unworthy of any serious attention . . .

"And he wanted to bless nothing in the world."[5]

He was right. Why let oneself be carried away?

I feel sick. That would be too unjust. It seems to me that certain laws of justice exist in nature.

Baden-Baden, 6 September

The journey here with F[yodor] M[ikhailovich] was rather entertaining. As he was getting our visa, he had a row at the

5. "And he wanted to bless nothing in the world," from Lermontov's "Demon."

papal embassy;[6] he spoke in verse during the entire trip, and, finally, here, where we had some trouble finding 2 rooms with two beds, he signed the guest register as "Officier," at which we had to laugh a lot. He plays roulette all the time and is generally very carefree. While we wcrc cn route here he told me that he had some hope, though he had earlier insisted that he had none. I did not say anything to this, but I knew that it was not going to happen. He liked my having left Paris so resolutely; he had not expected it. But he should not build any hopes on this, quite the contrary. Last night these hopes were expressed by him with particular emphasis. We had tea around 10 o'clock. Having finished it, I felt very tired and went to bed, asking F[yodor] M[ikhailovich] to sit close to me. I felt good. I took his hand and for a long time held it in mine. He said that he felt good sitting like that.

I told him that I had been unfair and unkind to him in Paris, that it may have seemed as though I had been thinking only of myself, yet I had been thinking of him, too, but did not want to say it, so as not to hurt him. Suddenly he got up and started to leave, but then stumbled over my shoe which was lying by the bed, and just as quickly turned around and sat down again.

"You wanted to go somewhere, didn't you?" I asked.

"I wanted to shut the window."

"Shut it then, if you want to."

"No, it isn't necessary. You don't know what just happened to me!" he said, with a strange expression.

"What do you mean?" I looked at his face; it showed great agitation.

"I was just going to kiss your foot."

"Ah, why that?" I said, greatly embarrassed, almost frightened, and tucked my legs under me.

"I just got the urge, and decided that I'd kiss it."

Then he asked me if I wanted to sleep, but I told him no, I would like to sit with him some more. Thinking of getting undressed and going to sleep, I asked him whether the maid was going to clear the tea table. He assured me that she

6. This scene of obtaining a visa at the papal embassy appears in a fictional and expanded form in *The Gambler* itself. See p. 9.

wasn't. Then he looked at me in a way that made me feel embarrassed, and I told him so.

"I feel embarrassed, too," he said, with a strange smile.

I hid my face in my pillow. Then I asked him again whether the maid would be coming, and he assured me again that she wouldn't.

"All right then, go back to your room, I want to sleep," I said.

"Right away," he said, but stayed for some time. Then he kissed me very ardently and, finally, started to light a candle for himself. My candle was burning low.

"You won't have any light,' 'he said.

"Not so, I have a whole candle there."

"But this is mine."

"I have another one."

"There will always be an answer," he said, smiling, and left. He did not close his door and soon came back to my room, under the pretext that he wanted to shut my window. He came up to me and suggested that I get undressed.

"I'll get undressed," I said, showing him by my attitude that I was only waiting for him to go away.

He left once more, and came back still another time, under some pretext, after which he left again and closed his door. Today he mentioned yesterday to me and said that he had been drunk. Then he said that I must probably find it most unpleasant, the way he was annoying me. I answered that I didn't mind, and refused to be drawn into a discussion of the subject, so that he could neither cherish hope nor be quite without it. He said that he had noticed I had a very knowing smile, that, most probably, he appeared foolish to me, that he was well aware of his own foolishness, but that it was something unconscious.

In the evening of the same day.

I just remembered my sister; she would have censured me for my trip to Italy, but I don't feel that way myself. I have a kind of passion for traveling: to learn, to see, and isn't this legitimate? And actually, that catechism which I made up for myself, and which I was so proud to have lived by, now seems very narrow to me. It was an involvement which would lead to narrowness and dullness of spirit. Isn't this, though, a transition to an entirely new and opposite course . . . No, in that case I would have admitted it to myself. Didn't I give it mature thought? And besides, I have my peace of mind now. I notice that a revolution is taking place in my thinking.

F[yodor] M[ikhailovich] has lost some money gambling and is a bit worried about not having enough money for our journey. I feel sorry for him, sorry, to some extent, about not being able to pay him for all these troubles of his, but what is there to do—I can't. Do I really have an obligation? No, this is nonsense.

Turin, 14 September 1863

Yesterday F[yodor] M[ikhailovich] and I had dinner at the *table d'hôte* in our hotel. The people having dinner with us were all French, young men. One of them gave me most insolent looks, and even F[yodor] M[ikhailovich] noticed that the man motioned somehow suggestively in my direction, as he talked to his friend. It angered F[yodor] M[ikhailovich] and placed him in a difficult position, because it would be rather hard for him to protect me, if there were a need. We decided to have dinner at a different restaurant. After the Frenchman had motioned in my direction to his neighbor, F[yodor] M[ikhailovich] gave him such a look that he dropped his eyes and tried to say something witty, quite unsuccessfully.

Turin, 17 September 1863

I feel once more a tenderness toward F[yodor] M[ikhailovich]. It happened that I was upbraiding him, and later I felt that I had been wrong, so I wanted to make up for it, and I got tender with him. He responded with such joy that

I was moved by it, and I became twice as tender. When I was sitting next to him, looking at him caressingly, he said: "There is that familiar look, it's a long time since I saw it last!" I let my head fall on his chest and began to cry.

As we were having dinner, he said, looking at a little girl who was taking her lessons: "Well, imagine, there you have a little girl like her with an old man, and suddenly some Napoleon says, 'I want this city destroyed.' It has always been that way in this world."

Genoa, Tuesday, 22 September

What a city! The houses are as tall as bell towers, while the streets are very narrow. The houses are all decorated and of appalling design, the roofs overgrown with grass. Barechested Italians and women with white headdresses fill the streets. The headdresses are a substitute for hat and mantilla.

Yesterday, in Turin, I read something about philosophy and, contrary to my expectations, understood a thing or two. The auth[or] says that Kant stopped at the proposition: "We cannot comprehend things in themselves." Meanwhile Hegel arrived at the position that things exist only in the concept. By the word "concept" he means not any individual concept, but the concept which rests with things as such. Then, the auth[or] distinguishes between concept and cognition. Cognition is, according to him, universal, absolute, while a concept is particular, individual. Then, about concept and reality. He says that, though they are both mediate, they are still diametrical opposites: a concept pertains to a thing which is or may be, whereas reality is a thing, of which there exists, or may exist, a concept.

Livorno, on board ship, Thursday, 24 September

Yesterday we were tossed so badly I thought we were going to be lost. There is a sailor on board who speaks Russian, and a Norwegian writer who has read and translated a few things from Russian literature, a man advanced in years. Today we must stay in Livorno all day, as a new cargo is being put on board ship. The sailor who speaks Russian took me all over the ship, whenever I had to go anywhere, and kept saying "thou" to me, which I liked a great deal (it reminds me of the Russian muzhik, who never uses "you"), and, why not, since he had learned his Russian from muzhiks.

I have just met two Italians who were with us when we crossed the Mont Cenis. One of them is very young, the other about 32. Both are very serious, even stern. En route the older of the two was reading *Petit Napoleon*.[7] The younger offered me some grapes that time. I like them both. That other Italian who is on board with us, the one who keeps inquiring about my health and takes care of all the sick people, I don't like him, he is rather like a Frenchman, especially when he talks to a young girl whom he is courting rather after the French fashion.

At this moment I am sitting on the upper deck, quite close to the two Italians. A Frenchwoman who is on a pilgrimage to St. Peter's said, in passing by, that I probably would not like to waste any time. I answered that I had too much work and that I felt sorry about having to lose so much time while en route.

Rome, 29 September

Yesterday F[yodor] M[ikhailovich] was importunate again. He said that I took too serious and stern a view of things that really were not worth it. I said that I had one reason which so far I had not been forced to reveal. Later he said that my utilitarian attitude was my ruin. I said that there was no such attitude in me, though I might have some tendency toward it. He did [not] agree, saying that he had proof. Apparently he wanted to know the reason for my stubborn refusal. He tried to make a guess.

7. Reference to Victor Hugo's *Napoleon le petit,* a pamphlet he wrote in 1852 against Napoleon III's seizure of power in 1851.

"You don't know, that's not it," I answered to his various assumptions.

He had the notion that it was just a caprice, a desire to torture him.

"You know that," he said, "you can't torture a man this long, for he will eventually quit trying."

I could not help smiling and almost asked why he said that.

"There is one main reason for all of this," he began, in a tone of conviction (later I learned that he had not been sure of what he was saying), "a reason which inspires me with loathing: it's the peninsula."[8]

This unexpected reminder disturbed me very much.

"You are still hoping."

I remained silent.

"Now you are not objecting," he said, "now you are not saying that this is not it."

I remained silent.

"I feel nothing toward that man, because he is much too worthless a person."

"I entertain no hopes at all, I have no reason for hope," I said, having given it some thought.

"That does not mean a thing; you may be rejecting all expectations with your reason; that still won't prevent you."

He was expecting some objection, but none came, as I felt the truth of his words.

He suddenly got up and lay down on his bed. I started pacing up and down the room. The thought suddenly came back to me, and, indeed, some kind of hope flashed through my mind. I began hoping again, without being ashamed of it.

When he woke up he became unusually free and easy, cheerful, and importunate. It was as though he wanted in this fashion to conquer his own inner hurt and sadness, and spite me.

I watched these strange antics with bewilderment. It was as though he were trying to turn everything into a joke, so as to hurt me, but I only looked at him with astonishment.

"I don't like you that way," I said simply at last.

8. Reference to Spain and thus to Salvador, who is of Spanish origin.

"Why? What have I done?"

"Just so, in Par[is] and in Turin I liked you much better. Why are you so cheerful?"

"It is a cheerfulness born of disappointment," he said and left, but he returned soon.

"I am unhappy," he said, seriously and sadly, "I look at everything as though it were my duty, as though I were learning a lesson; I had thought that at least I would manage to distract you."

I embraced him with ardor and said that he had done a lot for me, and that I found it very pleasant.

"No," he said sadly, "you'll be going to Spain."

Any mention of S[alvador] gives me a terrifying, painful, and sweet feeling. However, what rubbish that whole thing was, everything that happened between me and Salv[ador]. What a mass of contradictions in his attitude toward me!

F[yodor] M[ikhailovich] again turned everything into a joke, and said, as he was leaving my room, that it was humiliating for him to leave me in this fashion (it was 1 o'clock at night, and I was lying in bed, undressed): "For the Russians never did retreat."

Naples, 6 October

In Rome I saw a procession in the street: they were taking two thieves somewhere; they were young men (20 and 16). A huge crowd had gathered to watch the spectacle. Ladies stopped their carriages and stood up to watch.

In Naples, the moment we stepped out into the street on our first day there, a woman thrust a yellow flower into my hand and started asking for money. I met several such women that first day, but now I don't see them anymore. Children, too, keep begging for [illegible word], and if you give one of them something, a whole crowd will gather around you. If you won't give them anything, they keep up their begging by any means: they try to make you laugh, they make faces at you, they do somersaults, they open up their rags and show their naked bodies. Any time you give a cabman an extra dime, he will rush to kiss your hands. In the streets, any time you ask a question and have trouble understanding what you've been told, a whole crowd of people will gather around you, trying to explain things to you. Yesterday I was at the Coliseum. The soldier who escorted us there told me right away that I was a Russian; he had recognized it by my face. In a restaurant next to the Coliseum I ran across a gentleman who began talking Russian to me. He started by saying that he had experienced such a sharp change in climate in just a few days (he is from Petersburg), then went on to say that Genoa was dull, that there was no intellectual life there, that he did not like it there, though he had himself been born there; his ancestors had lived there for seven hundred years, and he had an estate there.

He managed to tell me that he had a wife and 10 children in Russia, that he knew Russia and had been managing an estate there, that he was now employed here, in Naples.

On our way from Rome to Naples we were searched very often, and we had to show our passports all the time.

Paris, 22 October

I arrived here at 4 o'clock, and at 5 I was at M.['s]. As I got out of the cab I asked the cabman how much I owed him (even though I knew that the fare was 2 francs). He said 2 francs, and I gave them to him, but then he suddenly said 2½. Without a word, I gave him the balance. He carried my bag into the yard (cabmen here usually don't do that) and tried to be of some service, as though he were embarrassed. I knocked at M.'s door, and everybody was still asleep, though it was 5 o'clock. Mme R. met me with great solicitude, asked me if I wanted something to eat, and went to make my bed for me. She brought me my breakfast upstairs, and all in all she was most solicitous.

All this goodwill for an old skirt that I had given her . . . poor people! Now, coming downstairs for some ink, I met

Katherine. She asked obligingly if it was ink that I needed, offered to get me some, and I let her, as I intended to give her some cufflinks which I had bought for her in Naples. When she came back I gave them to her, and she was delighted. She asked me right away always to turn to her when I needed something.

Poor, poor people!

En route, on board ship, right in Naples we met Her[zen], with his whole family. F[yodor] M[ikhailovich] introduced me as a relative, in very vague terms. He conducted himself in their presence as though he were my brother, or even closer, which must have puzzled H[erzen] somewhat. F[yodor] M[ikhailovich] told him a great deal about me, and H[erzen] listened attentively. I also talked to young H[erzen].[9] He is a kind of desperate young man. Speaking of my impressions abroad, I said that I had found more or less the same disgusting situation everywhere, and he went on to prove that it was not "more or less" but equally disgusting everywhere. As I was conversing with him, being quite animated myself, F[yodor] M[ikhailovich] walked by, without stopping, and I asked him to join us, which made him glad. Young H[erzen] said that he was going to be in Paris in the winter and would look me up. He asked for my address, but added that he would get it from B. [illegible surname]. I told F[yodor] M[ikhailovich] about it, and he suggested that I give him my address, so as to show him more attention. As we parted (in Livorno), I gave my address to H[erzen]. F[yodor] M[ikhailovich] accompanied H[erzen] and was with them at their hotel. When he returned he told me nervously that I absolutely must write him if H[erzen] were to see me. This I promised to do. And in general, he did not discuss young H[erzen] with me at all, though when I brought up his name first, in a rather casual manner, he responded and spoke of him, not entirely in favorable terms. He also told me that at H[erzen's] he had seen my calling card, which I had given

9. Aleksandr Aleksandrovich Herzen (1839–1906), famous physiologist. He was a professor of physiology in Florence from 1877 and in Lausanne from 1881.

him with my address. On it, Alexander had written his father's phrase: "With reason alone people wouldn't have got very far."

On the day of our departure from Naples F[yodor] M[ikhailovich] and I quarreled, but on board ship, that same day, under the influence of our meeting with H[erzen], which animated us, we had a heart-to-heart talk and made up again (it was about the emancipation of women). From that day on we no longer had any arguments. I was with him almost as I had been before, and I felt sorry having to part with him.

My sister writes me that it is quite impossible to stay at the academy any longer, on account of the silly tricks played by students, and she asks me to find out if it might be possible to attend some lectures in Paris. It seems that it ought to be possible. Yes, I shall find out about that from Monsieur Émile. Monsieur Émile is turning out to be a serious young man, and yet, how I felt about him at one time . . .

Immediately after arriving home, I felt sleepy, lay down, but could not fall asleep. My thoughts were somehow confused, but little by little I got them straightened out . . . I recalled how I had left Paris . . . As I was thinking, certain hopes kept going through my head against my own will, a wish to hurt, to take revenge, or was there something else about it . . . My heart was suffering and exacting its due, persuading, flattering with hope. Oh, how it ached, how it churned inside me! I went out for a walk and found myself on St. Denis, near St. André des Artes. Poor heart, what's the use deceiving oneself? As I got home and back to my room, I immediately noticed a spot on the floor—a trace of my burning those papers the day I had last seen him.

Paris seems positively revolting to me.

27 October

Yesterday I received a letter from F[yodor] M[ikhailovich]. He had lost all his money gambling and asked me to send him some money. I did not have any money: I had just given all I had to Mme Mir. I decided to pawn my watch and chain, and asked Tum.'s advice about it. He thought that I should ask M. for the amount I would fall short, and, besides, offered some of his own money, of which he had 50 francs. Mme M. gave me the whole 300 francs, for a month. There was some trouble with sending the money. Tum. explained to me how I was to go about it, and I set off. But then I lost my way a little, came back, and met—Alkh[azov],[10] who had come to explain to me how to go about sending money. But it did not end there, for I had to go back home and start out again. I had just got there when T. arrived, also to help. As I was talking to the pos[tmaster] about that letter, there came to the post office a young man who looked to me like Baskov. He was standing behind me. I turned around and threw a quick glance at him. I am almost sure that it was he, and I started talking to Tu. He walked away and began reading the announcements on the wall. As I was leaving, I gave him a look, though not a very intent one, and I know that it was he. He saw why I had been there, and must have heard the name of the city, Hamburg.[11] He also saw that I was sending money and was taking it out of my purse, consequently it must have been my transaction, and my companion was only helping me.

Today, at table, the conversation turned to cafés. Somebody said there were no cafés in London, so that the men were at home more, which, of course, was agreeable to the ladies. A lady remarked that perhaps ladies liked it better and found it merrier without their husbands. Whereupon the maître d'hôtel replied that only dishonorable ladies would feel that way. Then he went on to defend cafés by saying that one could meet friends there and discuss pol[itics]. An En[glishman], taking his side, said: "Take, for instance, the Russians. They have no need for cafés, since they have

10. Peter Alkhazov, a Petersburg student who was arrested and imprisoned because of his part in student disturbances on 11 October 1861. He was released in December of the same year and managed to escape abroad.

11. Possibly a mistake and Homburg, the gambling spa is meant—Translator.

no political sense either. I wanted to tell him that he knew neither the Russian people nor history.

9 November

A week ago I sent the following letter to S[alvador]:

> I feel forced to write you this letter in order to ask you if you received the letter which I wrote you toward the end of August. On account of certain well-known circumstances, I am afraid that it may have got lost. I must absolutely know whether or not you have received that letter, because I don't want to remain in the position of not having sent you, or having told you, what I wanted to send and tell you. I am told that letters sent the way I sent mine usually do not get lost, but I am not sufficiently reassured by these statements, nor am I satisfied with them, but rather, I want to know if you got my letter. You know very well that this is a commercial and not a private matter. You gave me no answer to my first letter, nor to my second letter, to which I did not ask you to reply, as a matter of fact.
>
> If you do not give me an answer to this letter, I will assume that you did not get the letter which I sent you in August, and I shall send you another such letter.

Sunday, 15 November

Having received no reply whatsoever to my letter, I sent S[alvador] another letter, with the money (I had no money, and I pawned my ring). Here is that letter:

> Your silence, dear sir, proves to me that you either did not receive the letter which I sent you in August, or, at least, that you want to get another, similar letter. I have duplicated that letter, with all enclosures, as I had prom-

ised you. When I had sent you those wretched 15 francs in that letter, I wanted to reimburse you for the service which you had given me, a service which, at the time, I took for a sign of friendship. I do not want to continue being obligated to you, as it is against my principles to be obligated to people whom I do not respect. I wrote you in that letter that I have nothing against you, just as I would have nothing against a piece of debris that fell on me by accident in the street. But if you decided that you wanted to protest against my letter, I would look upon you in a different way, i.e., as upon an animate creature. However, right now I presume that I can discount that latter reservation . . . People like you are endowed with an instinct of self-preservation . . . You will have a very long and very happy life.

As I send you this letter, I am taking every precaution to protect myself against fraud, as I am foreign to these parts.

I sent this letter by messenger, telling the man to deliver it to the addressee in person and to ask for a receipt. I explained to the messenger that 2 letters which I had sent the same way before had got lost and instructed him to tell this to S[alvador].

"Brothers, let me die with you."

TRAVEL NOTES

I did not see anything of Germany. I spent forty-eight hours in Ber[lin], and then went all the way to Paris, without stopping anywhere. I had meant to see the Dresden gallery, to take a trip on the Rhine, but gave up these plans merely after having seen the Germans. These Germans positively drove me out of my mind. The dullness and narrow-mindedness of the officials and workers on the railroad are simply legendary.

This unfortunate nation, so it seems to me, has definitely been treated most unkindly by the Lord. Thanks to them I missed my train once, and another time I arrived at a place where I was not supposed to go at all, both times when changing trains.

Paris, Monday, 16 November

Yesterday I went to the messenger service through which I had sent the letter to Cor. and did not find the man there. So I left a message with the janitor, asking the man to come and see me at 6 o'clock . . . He did not come today, so I went there myself. The *commissionnaire* barely looked up at me when I walked in and asked him about my commission. He returned my letter to me and said that he had failed to find Cor. He had been told, he said, that no such gentleman was living there, or had ever lived there. This made me mad. He couldn't even lie well, Cor. Had he at least said: "He isn't in." But he must say: "Never lived here." So I sent the letter by mail.

I almost sent S[alvador] the following letter:

I would not have thought of writing you, nor would I have written you this letter, of course, if you had not decided to hide from me. You bribed that wretch of a messenger, so he would tell me that you don't exist and that you never existed. Perhaps I would even have believed that, if I hadn't written to that address before, without getting any response . . . This very awkward subterfuge of yours gives me the right to assume that you actually received all of my letters. I am asking you to tell me if this is so, or not. I really [do not want to] see it happen that somebody is accused, innocently perhaps, of having embezzled the money. If you won't give me a satisfactory reply, I will be forced to petition my embassy to find out, with the help of the French police, who stole that first letter of mine which I addressed to you. So don't try to avoid giving me a direct answer, for you'll get entangled even worse, as usually happens with you.

17 November

Today, when I returned home for dinner, Mme R. told me that a gentleman had been there asking for me, and that he would come back later. I was surprised that somebody had come to see me. In spite of myself I thought of S[alvador], and my heart began to throb.

"A young man?" I asked.

"Yes, a tall one."

"With a beard?" I asked, guessing it might have been young Her[zen].

"With a black beard."

I could not think of anybody who would fit that description. After dinner I was called out, as somebody was there to see me. It was a tall, slender young man. He told me that S[alvador] had sent him. I flushed and began to tremble. I took a candle and asked him to follow me to my room. When we got there, I offered him a chair and closed the door. Then I sat down and asked him what he wanted of me (my voice was trembling very badly). He had brought me fifteen francs and said that S[alvador] had already received the money in August and that he did not care to get any more.

I had a hunch that this was S[alvador's] brother, judging by a portrait which he had once shown me . . . What a marvellous specimen of a planter, this young man: handsome, polite, well dressed, serious. When he said that I had insulted S[alvador], his eyes flashed. He really thinks that I insulted S[alvador]. I said that I could not discuss with others things that pertained solely to Monsieur S[alvador] and myself. I spoke very poorly, I had forgotten every French word I knew; I was extremely excited. Our conversation was very brief. I got up, having remarked that there was nothing else to be said between us. He offered to give me S[alvador's] address, saying that, perhaps, I would like to write him, but I said that I had no use for it whatever. As I saw him to the door, I held a candle for him. He asked me not to bother, but I saw him to the antechamber, then went to the drawing room myself, hearing the sound of music coming from there, but then I quickly went back to my room. My heart was gripped by a deep sadness, and I began to recite aloud:

"Show me the way to the thorny path," etc.—the way one reads a prayer to ward off demons. It made me feel better.

Tuesday, 24 November

A very strange story! There is at Mir. an Englishman, with whom I have conversed a few times. He is no longer young, and very serious. Several times, when we were left alone in the drawing room after dinner, we talked with great sympathy: about the French, about trends in Russian society. It was always I who started the conversation. Later I somehow stopped talking to him, but I was still in the drawing room at the usual time, and he would be there, too.

Neither of us would say a word.

On Sunday (the 22d) he announced that he was going home in two days. At dinner that day I was very sad and ate almost nothing, so that it was noticed (by Tum. and Mme). I felt bored that day especially because I felt so lonely. Mme Mir., A. . . , Tum., et al. went to a concert, without telling me, even though I had earlier mentioned that I would like to go to a concert. "To hell with them," I thought, and after dinner I struck up a conversation with the Englishman. I asked him about John Stuart Mill. To this initiative of mine he responded with great alacrity. Then Alkhazov joined in our conversation. I started telling them about a young man in the library who had tried to strike up a conversation with me several times and who had shown me, in a book he was reading, some philosopher's treatise about love, asking for my opinion on the subject, which I found very funny.

In that essay, the author says that man is born to think, but that this is not sufficient for a full development. One should also experience passion, love, and pride.

Alkh[azov] and the Englishman laughed a great deal about that. Alkhazov remarked that this young man must have been very young. They asked me what I had answered him. I said that I had found these ideas medieval, that love and pride may be there, but that it was ridiculous to cultivate them, at a time when there is so much to be done, so much that is urgent; that there was no time for such luxury when there was a shortage of bread, when people were starving to death, or if they had enough to eat, had to defend that privilege with millions of soldiers, gendarmes, and so on. I related this with great ardor; there were many people in the room, and, among others, William,[12] who sat next to the Englishman and exchanged an occasional word with him. "This young man," said the Englishman, pointing at William, "just said that we are in sympathy."

"Maybe," I said.

"Maybe," said he, "and what about the young man (in the library)?"

"As for that," I said, in a merry mood, "I am not a monopolist."

And we laughed a great deal, since the Englishman apparently liked my saucy reply.

He returned the conversation to the young man and said that this was funny, but perhaps interesting from a personal point of view. Then he said that maybe the young man was personally interested in love and pride. I said that I did not have the right to think that. Suddenly the Englishman tells me that within a year he will give me a better explanation of his own opinion regarding love . . . and pride. I looked at him in amazement. Mme was sitting not far from us.

"That is to say, in a year's time I hope to speak better French," he said.

On the next day, when we met at breakfast, he was gruff with me. Mar. asked where he lived in London, since he was going to England in January and would look him up.

"Will you be in Paris in January?" asked Mme.

"C'est probable!" the Englishman answered coolly.

After dinner I went to the drawing room as usual, and he

12. Probably a friend of Herzen, who refers to him in a letter to his daughter of 17 August 1863.

came there too, soon after. We sat there together for some time. He was morose and said nothing .

The next morning (today, that is) Mme asked him:

"Are you leaving tomorrow, Mousieur?"

"I don't know," he said; "I can't tell you yet."

I felt a strong urge to burst out laughing, and leaned back in my chair, thus hiding my face from the Englishman's glance. Yet I was curious to see what else I would hear from him after all this, but so far there has been nothing.

And yet I still love S[alvador].

Saturday, 5 December

Yesterday I was at the café Rotond, where I met and became acquainted with a young physician,[13] a citizen of the Netherlands, who may be, however, considered a Russian: he speaks and thinks in Russian, he was born and raised in Russia, and wants to serve Russia. Today he was at my room, and we had a long talk. A strange man! When I said, in some connection, that in such a case men would have lowered themselves to the level of animals, he answered: "So you are an aristocrat!" and later tried to prove that animals are wiser than people, for they know how to conduct themselves with people and understand them, while man in the company of animals is much more of an ignoramus, that he felt that horses were saints, and that the only thing that he respected in nature were nerves, which, he said, he would never allow himself to disturb in animals without having a reason for it, also that religion is a very good remedy against scoundrels. When I mentioned my desire to go to America, he retorted that there was nothing good to be found there, that I could see snakes right at the Jardins des Plantes, which would be much more convenient, as they were in a cage there.

13. He will figure quite prominently in Polina's notes and the romantic complexities of her thoughts and actions. He will also be referred to as Benin, and it is conceivable that he is the brother of Arthur Ivanovich Benin, who figured prominently in revolutionary circles during the sixties.

I hate Paris and can't tear myself away from it. Perhaps because this city really has something that appeals to those who lack their own home and a set goal. I still feel a desire to go to America . . . In spite of the presence of new people, new activities, I am still being pursued by one idea, one image . . . And what did I find in him? . . . Could it be the narrowness of his views, the fact that he is incapable of judging certain things? No, it is simply that there are no men around, that in other men everything is so petty, so prosaic.

Saturday, 12 December

Zadler was here today.

"You know what," he said, "we plan on going to England, just so, with a small party. Would you like to join us?"

"Indeed, but how? And when?"

"Soon, there is a convenient and what's most important an inexpensive trip available if we go soon, 37 francs round trip, the ticket is good for a month, we can stay there a week, see all the sights, and come back."

"Indeed, this sounds pretty good."

"So will you join us?"

"All right, but tell me, do you know the language?"

"No, but that doesn't matter, one can always learn it."

"But how, and when?"

"Well, we'll have to hurry, get yourself a teacher, we'll work on it for a week, and that will do."

"What? only a week?"

"Well, yes, and why not? Do you think we must make a thorough study of it? 'give me, get me, allow me to ask, where is such-and-such street?'—that's all we need."

"But only one week! You must see that."

"Why waste so much thought on it? Let's start learning English tomorrow; I'll go and look for a teacher today. Look what you've got there! Why, you've got Reif's dictionary here, it will come in handy, you've got English words in here."

He opened the dictionary.

"Well, here you are, let's see what you've got here, really, I used to study English at one time."

"Well, look at what he's got here, what words: 'illuminate, sanitate . . .'—well, those we don't need. What else? 'rubescence, regeneration,' well, we don't need that either . . . 'turn,' there it is: *return . . . turn, take off*. 'Sir, allow me to ask, how can I turn into such-and-such street?' We've already got *return*, so we must look for 'allow me,' then "street,' you look for 'street.' Why, we'll be prattling away in no time, no problem! We'll take a look at the streets, the buildings, we'll go to the theater, we'll visit their parliament, we must see Palmerston, yell 'Long live!' for him, that we must do! I was in Berlin and went to their legislative chamber, yelling 'Hurrah! hurrah!' Wait a moment, how's that in English: *to see*. Why, it actually resembles German. So then, are we going?"

"All right."

"Wonderful. 37 francs for the passage, 50 for miscellaneous expenses, 10 francs a day for food, 100 francs in all. We can stay at some cheap hotel, why stand on ceremony."

Later he told me how some professors here behave toward their students.

An old gentleman of 60 will come to his class. "Well, gentlemen, I'm starting my lecture, take notes if you please. Listen you, in the back row, why are you just sitting there, and not taking notes? And why are you staring at me?"

"To hiss a professor off his podium," he says, "why, would you dare to hiss at me?"

"So-and-so was hissed off his podium only the other day," he is told.

"What? What?"

"They hissed at G. for such-and-such opinion."

"What! You don't say! Why, I am of that opinion, too. Well, come on! Hiss at me!"

"Professor, sir, I am not in the least against that opinion, on the contrary, I just told you that G. was hissed at."

"Ah, so you agree with this opinion?"

"Absolutely."

"Excellent, let me shake hands with you."

Zadler brought along a book by Thiers, [14] which he had already read. He said that as he was reading about the Holy Alliance he had to blush for mankind. He said that after having read that book he was ashamed of being a member of the human race.

Saturday, 12 December

Everything, but everything is for sale in Paris, everything is against nature and against common sense, so much so that I, in my capacity as a barbarian, will say as that famous barbarian once said of Rome: "This nation will perish!" The best European minds think so. Everything is for sale here, everything: conscience, beauty. This venality shows in everything: in the poses and well-turned phrases of Monsieur M., the wasp waists and fluffed up hair of those young women who walk the streets in pairs. One particularly senses this venality when living alone. I have become so used to getting everything for money—the warm atmosphere of my room, a cordial welcome—that, as a result, I find it strange to get anything at all without paying for it. If I [ask] anyone about something in the street, I feel ill at ease, I actually become apprehensive, involuntarily, about paying too much, as happened on one occasion . . .

I remember the grapes which I ate, free of charge, on Mont-Saint, absolutely free of charge.

Today at dinner the conversation turned to the quality of champagne wine. Monsieur M., with great ardor, tried to prove its individual character, which somebody had thought to challenge.

Wednesday, 23 December

Sometimes the stupidity of the people I meet drives me to

14. Adolphe Thiers (1797–1877), French historian and man of state,

desperation. So it was on Sunday: the maître d'hôtel was trying to prove that . . . a marriage of convenience is a very good thing, and nobody presented any serious argument against it; they just did not know how; some preposterous things were said; to refute this contention, it was stated that . . . if you marry that way, you may go wrong, hitting upon an immoral woman, but the maître d'hôtel said that one couldn't go wrong in such a case, since one could gather the most accurate information, and he was right of course. This unsettled me so much that I could no longer stand it and went out for a walk. I walked around for a long time, with my mind gone blank, forgetting where I was. I don't know how many times I simply began to cry.

I have begun to study Spanish—I find it most interesting, I even like the actual process of learning a language. I am most content when I am studying Spanish, but sometimes, in the middle of my studies, the thought of him suddenly overwhelms me, and my heart is wrung with pain.

Today two new roomers showed up, two Americans (North Americans). I like them very much, especially one of them: such an energetic and serious face. He gave me an attentive and serious look, and I met his glance. These ought to be men, thank God. But perhaps I won't be able to make friends with them?

Thursday, 31 December

Today after dinner I stayed in the dining room to read a letter which I had just received. The maître d'hôtel, his wife, the Georgian, and one more person were in the drawing room. The maître d'hôtel said something about me, his wife responded, I heard only "Cette pauvre fille" . . . Then she fell quiet (apparently somebody had told her that I was in the next room), then Tum. came in, gave me some trivial

---

known particularly for his works on the French revolution and the Napoleonic era. Tolstoy consulted him in writing *War and Peace*.

phrase, asked me what news I had received, and left again. Having read the letter, I went out to tell them the news about Chernysh[evsky],[15] then left soon after, as some gentleman arrived.

Tomorrow at breakfast I'll strike up a conversation with somebody about how *misérables* travelers look in a foreign country, and especially in Paris, and especially Russians.

7 January 1864

Recently I attended a lecture by Francis. I liked this man very much. His ideas, bold, honest, and vivid, do not go to the unfortunate extreme of justifying everything by a goal. His language is vivid, without affectation. This man perfectly personifies my ideal of a Frenchman, I even liked his external appearance: a lean old man with a lively face, piercing eyes, and a subtle irony in his face; yet at the same time he has a certain simplicity and nobility.

He is an elegant, aristocratic figure; I noticed his hands, with thin, long fingers. I observed that he knows how to flatter a crowd . . . and that he doesn't mind doing it. He made a good impression on me. For a long time I haven't heard an honest, living word.

Today I was at the library. I started going there the day before yesterday, and yesterday I met my friend for the first time, but I was sitting at a different place, for which he reproached me as he came up to me. Today, as I entered the library, he was already there. "I'm sure you'll stay at your old place today," he said, as I walked by him.

And I did. We talked a lot. He asked me for my opinion about the Polish uprising, he asked me if there were any educated women in my country, and if I attended public

15. See note 11 of Introduction. This reference may be to Chernyshevsky's trial, which took place on 2 December 1863. He spent from 1862 to 1884 in prison, where he wrote his most influential work, *What Is To Be Done?* (1863).

lectures. Then he asked me about my specialty. I also asked him about his. He studies philosophy. He asked me many questions about Russia and said that he might go there. He told me that he has a friend, a young man who knows Russian, and began asking me for the meaning of some words, which he tried to understand letter by letter. But I, with my usual frankness, told him that I could understand nothing, that he should rather show me the little note from which he was reading. He was a bit embarrassed, but showed it to me. I read the words: "My dear, my good, my sweet girl." I said that this was all nonsense. "All right, then I'll tear it up," he said. He is a dear boy, a very dear boy. The mere fact that he got to talk to me is worth something; that takes courage.

For some time now, I have been thinking of Salvador again. I would be rather calm, be doing good work, but then suddenly I would remember the insult, and a feeling of indignation would well up in me. Now I think of him particularly often, and the idea that I haven't paid him back won't leave me. I do not know how and in what way I shall pay him back, I only know that I'll do it for sure, or I'll die of anguish.

I know that as long as the house and the street in which I was insulted continue to exist and that as long as this man enjoys respect, love, happiness, I cannot find peace of mind; an inner feeling tells me that this cannot remain unpunished. I have been insulted many times by those whom I loved, or by those who loved me, and I suffered it . . . but the feeling of hurt dignity never died in me, and right now it is crying out to be expressed. Everything that I see and hear every day insults me, and, by paying him back, I'll be paying them all back. After long thought, I have arrived at the conviction that one must do everything that one finds necessary. I don't know what I will do, I only know that I'll do something. I don't want to kill him, because that is not enough. I'll poison him with a slow-working poison. I'll take away his happiness, I'll humiliate him.

Paris, 13 February

Today I bought a pair of shoes. It was the second time for me in that shop. The dealer and his wife were extraordinarily obliging to me, they tried on and showed me an immense number of shoes. I even felt embarrassed that I only purchased a pair for 3 francs, they were so helpful. In the end it turned out that they had cheated me by $\frac{1}{2}$ franc. I was amazed at that.

Paris, Sunday, 14 February

Yesterday I visited Guior.[16] I had been terribly unsettled for a number of days, and I cried on my way to see G. Yet it seemed to me that I was going to find something very good in him. Before my mind's eye there appeared the ideal of a kindly old man, steeped in love and sorrow. I got there at one o'clock. Nobody there. I stood there for a long time, not knowing where to go. Finally I heard somebody cough behind a door. I knocked. "Amen," I heard someone say in a loud voice.

"Excuse me," I said, opening the door.

I entered: A corpulent, sturdily built man was sitting there at a desk, writing something. Strangely enough, he looked to me quite different from what he had looked like to me in church.

"What can I do for you?" he said, raising his head, with a stern and impatient expression on his face.

This reception crushed me completely. Even so, my nerves were in a highly excitable state. I felt like breaking into tears and was unable to utter a single word. "Well?" he said, looking at me with puzzlement and vexation.

Here I could not restrain myself any longer and burst into tears. He began looking out of the window. At that moment

16. Approximate rendering of a French name spelled in Cyrillic letters "Ger."—Translator

somebody knocked at the door. A workman entered and discussed with him the purchase of certain things and the printing of certain announcements. F[ather] haggled like a Jew. This discussion gave me time to regain my senses. "You are Russian," he said after the other party had left.

"You must have some clergyman of yours here. Why didn't you go to Monsieur B.?" . . .

"I beg you to forgive my coming to see you. I did this from inexperience, I had heard about you."

"Oh, that's all right," said the Father condescendingly, "but I think that it would be much more proper if you went to your own clergyman."

I stood there, in silence, hanging my head.

"Could I be of any use to you?" he asked somewhat more kindly.

For a long time I could not say anything.

"Are you looking for a position? You haven't got any money, no relatives, or friends?" the Father asked me quickly, "or have you sinned against the laws of morality?" he asked, with particular severity.

I blushed and involuntarily raised my head. Seeing that I was not answering, and seeing that it was something else, he could not understand what was wanted of him, but at last, apparently having got the idea, more or less, he began to talk to me of God, but in a tone as if he were teaching a lesson—he even closed his eyes.

In conclusion, he told me that all my ideas were just plain nonsense. That, if there were crime and suffering on Earth, there had to be a law, too. And that only idlers and drunkards suffered. And Emperor Alex[ander] was an ideal monarch and man.

17 February

Once again I am thinking of vengeance. What vanity! I am alone now and I look at the world as though apart from it, and the more I keep looking at it, the more nauseated I get.

What are they doing! What are they fussing about! What are they writing about! I've got this booklet here, 6 editions of it came out in 6 months. And what's in it? Lobulo is all carried away by the fact that in America a baker can make several tens of thousands a year, that a girl can marry there without a dowry, and a 16-year-old can already support himself. These are their hopes, this is their ideal. I could tear them to pieces.

Wednesday, 3 March

Yesterday I attended a lecture by Philaret Charles and was amazed at the clowning of this gentleman. Stepping onto the speaker's platform, this gentleman closed his eyes and began to lecture, waving his arms . . . [illegible] sometimes, for a comic effect; and to the great delight of his public, he would bounce around so that he would almost lie down on the table. This is how he lectures:

I am going to give you a lecture in a way no one has ever lectured before: nobody in Europe has ever thought of using this method . . . Let me talk to you about the age of Louis XIV. You think it was a great age? Sure enough, all you have to do is read up on it. That's right, go and read up on it, just read . . . Only recently a book has come out by a certain German. I expect that you haven't read it. Why, I am convinced that none of you here has ever so much as heard the name of this German. So then, Louis XIV. You think he was a patron of the sciences, the arts, literature? Well, yes, it may be true that he liked art: Apollo Belvedere, the Medicean Venus, because there you have beauty, the Sun. But do you know what his attitude was toward the Flemish school of painting? That, he would say, is trash; they present peasants with pipes in their paintings. You know, the Dutch and the English. These are serious people, they did not paint a whole lot—no time for it, lots to do, and when they did paint, they didn't chase after beauty, they looked for truth only. They haven't

got any sun there, perhaps just a little, a drop of sunshine.
It is not always beautiful, those southerners don't like it
too well, don't like it at all, hate it. Well, so there you
have Louis XIV—he had all those executioners: the head
executioner, then an executioner somewhat below the first,
then his minor executioner, and finally, the very smallest
executioner of them all. That is how he used to take care of
literature: he would say to his head executioner: "Outlaw
literature, persecute it, burn it." Once in a while they
would still burn a man for a book he'd written . . . Against
His Majesty, you think? Against *Mme Mentenon* [*sic*]. Oh,
those were harsh times, very harsh, I am very glad that I
am not living in those times, or else, who knows, with this
temperament of mine, I might have fared badly. And
how do they write novels these days? Take a contemporary
novel: at the first word you find it entertaining, at the
second word—a little boring, then, at the third and fourth
word, you begin to get interested, at the fifth you absolutely want to find out what happened to such-and-such a
girl; that's a French novel for you. English novels are
written differently; their novels are sermons, lectures. Some
people fall asleep reading such novels, but there are some
who read them easily.

Speaking of the mutual hatred between the French and
the English:

I was brought up in England, and don't you believe that
I am an Anglomaniac: I am a pure Frenchman. Once I
went into a church, such a modest little boy I was, standing
in a corner; so they all began staring at me—they realized
that I was French, because my necktie wasn't tied the way
they tie them in England. So they stared at me "There,"
they said, "stands a monster." So help me God (there may
be Englishmen in the audience, but never mind that).
Well, now even the English agree that Molière wasn't a
fool. And we, too, read Shakespeare.

In the beginning I laughed a lot; soon I noticed that the
others were laughing also; only they were laughing for a

different reason—they were laughing and applauding. I felt annoyed by it.

Somehow my person attracts people's attention, and I am getting tired of it. It isn't that there are no women attending lectures or using the library, there are quite a few, but their faces are different from mine. These are women with flowers, with frills and flounces, with veils, accompanied by their mothers. There are some serious women, too, one in particular—she is a perfect nihilist.

The thing is that I behave, while she claps her hands, stamps her feet, and yells "bravo." She is also dressed poorly. She comes all by herself, but nobody pays any attention to her, because she is no longer young. Everybody finds it quite natural that a maiden lady, grown old while awaiting her fate, should have got tired of it all and taken to learned pursuits for want of anything better to do. But they won't leave me alone; every time they keep bothering me during breaks between lectures: "You must be a teacher of English? Are you a foreigner? Are you devoting yourself to the study of some particular subject?" I have grown tired of this, and so, during breaks, in order to stop people from asking me questions, I take a book . . . *Letters from France,* and pretend that I am absorbed in my reading.

"Is it a Polish or a Greek book that you've got there? You are a foreigner, aren't you?" they invariably ask me.

"It is neither Polish nor Greek," I respond, without raising my eyes and blushing with anger, as I don't want to reveal my nationality so as not to draw even more attention to myself.

"So what language is it in?"

Tuesday, 8 March

I am bored in the extreme. The weather is beautiful, there is a marvellous view from my fifth floor window, and I am sitting here in my room, like a wild beast in a cage. Neither English verbs, nor Spanish translations—nothing can help

me to overcome my feeling of depression. I was about to indulge in some tea, but no, it does not help any, either.

17 March

Yesterday I went to see Macht. He has an elegant flat and a
large library with Swedish, English, French, and Russian
books, living in perfect comfort. He sits in front of his fireplace and keeps scribbling away. What a banal life! And yet,
how many young men do I know who work hard to get this
kind of life for themselves. How much strength and how
many convictions are sacrificed to the acquisition of such a
library and such pictures!   .

2 April

A nagging feeling of depression won't leave me. I am in the
grip of a strange, oppressive feeling, as I look down on the
city from my balcony. The thought of being lost in that
crowd frightens me.

3 April

Yesterday I entered a shop. Nobody was there. After a few
minutes the owner came in from the street, red [two illegible
words] in a dirty shirt, with snuff sticking to his nose, and a
little tipsy.
   "I made you wait, Mlle," he said; "I hope that I had a good
watchman in you?"
   As he was selling me some paper, he decided that he would
give me two sheets *pour rien.*
   "You are very generous," I told him.
   "There can be no generosity great enough when a young
lady is involved," he answered. This conversation was conducted in the most serious tone.

A few days ago I took a walk along the rue de Médecin in the evening. On the corner of the boulevard de Sévastopole I saw several young men standing, and with them a pretty young woman, bareheaded, with a luxuriant, carefully done coiffure. "Dites donc," she was saying to one of the young men, in a capricious voice and putting her hands on his shoulders. This picture left a deep impression on me, and, I don't know why, after witnessing it, I felt some relief from my earlier sufferings, as if I were illuminated by some light. I know nothing more repulsive than these women. I have seen women with sharp gestures and impudent facial expressions, and I find them more supportable.

17 April

Recently I made the acquaintance of two personages: Evgenia Tur[17] and Mar[ko] Vovchok.[18] Evgenia Tur had heard about me from Koram., and had asked her to send me over. She charmed me completely from our very first meeting. Lively, passionate, she left a strong impression on me. And with all her intellect and learning, she has such simplicity. With her I did not experience that uneasiness and tension which I usually feel when I first meet a person, even if I am dealing with well-educated and humane people. I talked to her as though I were talking to my mother. We cried and kissed each other when she told me about the events in Poland. After our very first meeting she invited me to move in with her (she lives with her son),[19] promised to give me French and English lessons, and to speak French with me

17. Pseudonym for Elizaveta Vasilievna Salias de Turnemir (1815–92). Sister of the writer Sukhovo-Kobylin, and close friend of Turgenev. She enjoyed great popularity in the fifties, especially with the short novel *Mistake,* but in the sixties her popularity waned.

18. The pseudonym of the writer Maria Aleksandrovna Markovich (1834–1907), a Ukranian writer who had the honor of being translated by Turgenev and praised by Dobroliubov. A fictionalized biography of her is to be found in the Ukranian *Na Svitanku* (At Daybreak) by Jurij Tys (Chicago: Denysiuk, 1961).

19. Evgeny Andreevich Salias (1840–1908). Popular writer of some note. His novel *The Pagachevtsy* enjoyed wide success. He was also quite

always. Later, she invited me to visit her at her friend's summer residence, and said she was very sorry that we had not
met earlier. On the next day she came to see me with her
friends, and the 5 of us together went to the cemetery. Along
the way, Luginin,[20] who was sitting across from me (the
Countess had specially introduced him to me, and had said
to him: whenever you want to go out somewhere, take Mlle
Suslova along), was trying to entertain me, but I was listening
to the Countess, who was conversing with the other gentleman. She does not like to compromise. I was amazed at her
energy.

"If at 20 years of age," she said about a certain gentleman,
"he is willing to get reconciled, while I, having lived so much,
at 40 still have the strength to hate, what will he be doing at
30! He'll be a police spy by then."

Then the gentleman with whom she was talking told her
that conservative ideas, too, had the right to exist. "This is
precisely what I have been arguing about so much," she said,
with fervor, "certainly they have a right to exist, but not the
way it is with us. There are, for example, conservative parties
in England, in France, but there has been no precedent for a
conservative party standing in support of the whip, as is the
case in our country; on the contrary, it is sometimes more
liberal and more humane than the revolutionary parties."

She has broken off her friendship with Tur[genev] on
account of the fact that he wrote a letter to the tsar in which
he said that, out of respect for him, he had broken off all his
relations with the friends of his youth.[21]

---

active in revolutionary circles at this time and in correspondence with
Herzen and Ogarev. He is referred to later in the notes as "Vadim,"
which is the peudonym he used for one of his novels.

20. Vladimir Fyodorovich Luginin (1834–1911), well-known revolutionary who enjoyed the respect of both Turgenev and Herzen. He left
Russia in 1862 and subsequently enjoyed a successful career as a chemist.

21. This is a reference to Turgenev's letter to Alexander II explaining his relations with Herzen and his anti-government activities. Turgenev had been requested by the Third Section to return to Russia to
explain these relations, but he obtained permission to answer the questions by letter. Turgenev effectively disavowed any connection with the
"friends of his youth" and especially with the radical liberalism of
Herzen.

I went to [Mme] Markovich without any letter of recommendation. She received me cordially and simply, saying that she had heard of me and had wanted to come and see me herself, but had not had my address. For a few minutes she had me charmed. She offered me some tea, which I did not refuse because I happened to be terribly thirsty. Then, very soon, I realized that I should have declined. Her cordiality seemed to me like that of a typical Russian gentlewoman who is always ready to welcome anybody to her house and treat a guest to food and drink. Having conversed with me for a while, she asked me (God only knows why) to wait while she wrote a letter and mailed it, then asked me again to wait, but I went home instead, leaving with her. The weather was beautiful, Mme Mar[kovich] walked with me to the bus station . . . Along the way we talked about many things: about Her[zen], about what she was writing, and about what I was writing and had written before. She talked more about how much various journals paid, whether I had bought myself any summer dresses, for how much, and what kind.

And on the whole, I noticed in her a certain coldness, cautiousness; somehow, she observes people very closely. One can see that she is a calculating, sober-minded woman, who won't let herself be carried away. The Co[untess] said that this woman was subtle, but I didn't see her that way at first, at least not with me. The Co[untess] agrees with me that she is cold. In spite of myself I compared the two women. I thought that with [Mme] Markovich I wouldn't have started to cry, but it turned out different: the next day I went to see her, having been invited to come at a set hour; she had promised to prepare for me those of her works which I had not yet read. Along the way, as I was passing through a narrow alley, I met a rather young woman, dressed very poorly but neatly, who was crying. She approached me timidly. I thought that she wanted to ask me about a street. "Please give me 2 sous," she said; "I haven't eaten anything." I was struck by her decent and sadly submissive air. I gave her 1 franc, the only piece of small change I had on me. She thanked me and walked away. I was about to continue on my way, but this encounter left a strong impression on me; I wondered if I could not perhaps help that woman in some way. I turned around and caught up with her. "Listen," I told her, "maybe I can be of some use to you. It must be that you have been ill, or that some misfortune has befallen you. If you can work, perhaps I can find some work for you. Come and see me." I was going to write down my address, but could not find a pencil. She told me that she could not remember an address by heart, and suggested that we enter a shop and ask for a pencil. I wrote down the address for her and asked the shopkeeper how much I owed him for using his pencil. He said [I owed him] nothing. I thanked him and went on. I was in a great hurry. "I shall never forget you," said the poor woman with feeling, as she took leave of me. I did not find [Mme] Markovich at home.

Her mother suggested that I wait, saying that her daughter had gone to see Tur[genev], and tried to let me know that yesterday Tur[genev] had waited two full hours for her daughter, and then had to leave anyway, as she had not returned. She also told me that today the wife of the arist Yakobi[22] would come, a very pretty, very young, and what's most important, a very good woman, according to her. And sure enough, very soon a pretty young woman showed up. I guessed that this must be [Mme] Yakobi. We started talking. She gave herself liberal airs, tried to make an impression on me, most unsuccessfully. At last [Mme] Markovich arrived. "Get acquainted," she said to us, without saying our names, though. We shook hands without a word. [Mme] Markovich said that she had not prepared the books for me, then again started to talk about money. Later we looked at her portraits, with which she was greatly dissatisfied. What I found unfelicitous about these portraits was merely her pose, her draping herself in a sort of mantle which was unbecoming to her homely face.

Somehow we got to talking about [Countess] Salias.[23] I

22. Valery Ivanovich Yakobi (1834–1902), popular painter in the sixties, known especially for the compassion for the downtrodden which he expressed in his paintings.
23. See note 17, above.

happened to say that she had been at my house. They probably thought that I was name dropping. "If you are going to be at the Countess's, please tell her that she should send me my books." "Countess Salias?" I asked. She paid no attention to my question and went on talking and talking until, at last, it became clear what Count[ess] she was speaking of. "Oh, I'll be very glad to deliver your message," I said, "but could you please give me your name." "Oh, how careless I am," said [Mme] Markovich; "I introduced you, but failed to mention your surnames." "Yakobi," said the pretty young woman, and though I made a point of expressing my astonishment at hearing this name, she most probably thought that I was so ignorant as not to be familiar with it, for, looking at me with deep commiseration, she offered to write it down for me. I said I would not forget it even without that. She insisted that I write it down; so I finally told her that the name was familiar to me. I could not help smiling as this was going on (of course I am not going to tell the Countess about the books, and I'll tell the pretty young woman that I forgot). It made me terribly sad to look at these "triumphant" and "idly chattering" women. I was invited to stay for coffee, but since I had had breakfast just before coming on this visit, I declined and went home. The hostess noticed my sadness and, as she was seeing me to the door, began to ask me the reason. This made me even sadder; my nerves were in an exceedingly excitable state; I could no longer restrain myself, and tears welled up in my eyes. "Tell me, what has happened to you?" Mme Markovich asked, taking my hand with a concerned expression and leading me to the bedroom. I followed her instinctually, as the tears were streaming from my eyes whether I willed them or not; I was tormented by a feeling of helplessness and shame. I blamed it all on that scene in the street and soon went home. She told me that if I were to have any difficulties, I should turn to her.

"What difficulties could one have in a civilized state?" I said, with an ironic and sad smile.

"But you had some with your landlady," she said.

Then she said that she would come to see me the following day, repeating it several times. She arrived punctually. I saw her coming through the gate, as I was looking from my window, and went to meet her downstairs in the yard. I greeted her with all due cordiality, but without any reverence. We talked for about an hour, then I accompanied her on her way home, and we talked a great deal more. She reminded me of my promise to let her have my works; and, since I did not have them with me, made me promise that I would come and see her in a week to read my story to her.

During our walk in the cemetery, Luginin promised to give me a list of historical works that might be useful to me. Apparently, he wishes to educate me. He very naively tried to explain idealism and materialism to me, when I said that I could not very well define these concepts.

[Mme] Markovich asked what my name was. I told her. "And they told me that it was 'Nadezhda Suslova,' " she said. I have a sister whose name is Nadezhda . . .[24]

Tuesday, 3 May 1864

As I was returning from Brussels, I was asleep when we arrived in Paris. My only companion in the car woke me up when the train had stopped. I quickly got up and started gathering my things. There was almost nobody left on the train. The conductor came to my car and opened the door: "Ah, you are still here," he said, and, seeing that I was hurrying, added: "Don't hurry, there is enough time." "I am ready," I said, stepping up to the door. He stretched out his hand; I was glad to take it, and jumped down. "It's cold . . ." he started saying, but I was already running toward the station building.

24. Nadezhda Prokofievna Suslova-Erisman, Polina Suslova's sister. She studied medicine in Russia, but was forbidden to complete her studies there. She finished her work at the University of Zurich and became one of the first women in Russia to pursue this career. Dostoevsky had great respect for her. See letter 5 in this volume.

Saturday, 8 May

Yesterday I visited [Mme] Markovich. She read my story (the first)[25] and liked it. [Mme] Markovich said that this story was better than [any by Countess] Salias. I read my unpublished story to her, and she liked it, except the end, which she did not like. While I was reading, [Mme] Markovich kept saying: "This is good! Excellent!" Later, during our conversation, she said, "One ought to look at people with one's eyes wide open." I answered that I could not do that, that I felt it to be cynical.

And indeed, what fun is it to live, having to look and watch out at every step? I want no part of happiness, even, if it must be acquired by such means. That would be manufactured happiness . . . Let people deceive me, let them laugh at me, but I want to believe in people, let them deceive me. And besides, they can't do very great damage, can they?

22 May

Today I got up for the first time after having been sick for 2 weeks, during which time Countess Salias took care of me in a motherly way, so that I'm now in love with her even more than before.

Luginin and Usov[26] visited me frequently during my illness, and I talked to them a lot. Once we had a dispute about the Russian nation; it turned out that they have no respect for it. That same time, Usov said that he liked the custom of certain savages: their adult sons kill and eat their fathers. He said that it might not be a bad idea to adopt the first of these two measures.

25. Polina's first story "Pokuda" (In a While) was published in Dostoevsky's journal *Time* in 1861.
26. Peter Stepanovich Usov (1832–97), engineer and friend of Herzen; something of a middle-of-the-road liberal.

Today Countess Salias and both of these gentlemen were here. The Countess spoke of the education of her nephew, whom she is sending to school in Switzerland.

Among other things, she mentioned that there is one bad thing about a Swiss education, that it makes the children into cosmopolitans. Luginin tried to assert that this was excellent, that cosmopolitanism was a very good thing; wasn't it all the same whether it was a Russian or a Frenchman whom one wished well? He said that he would most gladly serve France or England, but that he would stay in Russia because he knew Russian customs and the Russian language, though he had nothing in common with the Russians, either the peasant or the merchant, not sharing their beliefs or respecting their principles. "I welcome the Parisian associations much more than . . ." I did not hear the whole sentence, or perhaps he did not complete it. I was furious, but said nothing. The Countess also remained silent. In the beginning, she alone defended patriotism a little, though only from the viewpoint of tradition. When the Countess said something about my doctor, I had to express certain opinions of mine which were opposed to theirs. The Countess objected heatedly. So this is what they are like! No, I won't join these people. I was born into a peasant family, I was brought up among the people until I was 15, and I shall live with the muzhiks; there is no place for me in civilized society. I'll go to the muzhiks, and I know that they are not going to hurt me in any way.

Spa, 15 June

It is good here. And here's a miracle for you: I like the Germans better than the French. The landlady, who is Dutch, stuffs me with *tartines* and plies me with beer. They eat about five times a day. The landlord is sullen, looks like a murderer, but is a kind man. Besides myself, a French couple also rent a room here. The landlady told me what conditions he worked out with her in writing (for 6 weeks), wondering about his distrustfulness. There was one condition, for instance, that there shouldn't be any fleas. How mean, and how much like a Frenchman! The cook, a German woman, is the funniest, primitive human being, a naive creature. When the weather was bad, she worried a great deal about how back home [in] Mecklenburg *les grains,* sown by her father, would perish. She even wanted to run away. How her presence would help *les grains* remains unknown. Now she sometimes comes up to me and asks: "What about it, Mlle, do you think that it will rain tomorrow?" I say, "Maybe," but then, remembering those cherished *grains,* I add that, even if it is going to rain, then only in Spa.

Spa, 16 July 1864

Letter

Dear Countess: I received your letter a few days ago and read it with particular pleasure. You are so kind . . .[27]

Spa, 21 July

More and more I am occupied with the affairs of my sister, regarding her education. My further stay in Paris also depends on that. I [have] almost [surrendered] myself to these petty things and unpleasant details. But for that, I was already beginning to return to my belief that life is meaningless . . . This is man: sometimes he finds life meaningless, then again he keeps on waiting (to gratify only) a whim.

Versailles, 30 August

Today E[vgenia] Tur and I had a discussion about Swift. She said that he was a wicked and spiteful man. I retorted: "He was an embittered man." "By what, against whom? What did he suffer? Wasn't he rich and respected?" "The

27. The unfinished letter seems to be to Countess Salias.

fact that he was personally happy even more justifies his bitterness."

"What was it that made him so bitter? That the human race is evil; where does such a vile view come from? Doesn't it prove the absence of higher strivings? A failure to understand that mankind is destined for a high purpose. I know an educated, cultured man, who was in Siberia, where he was whipped, yet he believes in mankind, and loves it. That means that his is a lofty soul."

"That means that he is a mystic," I thought.

"While Swift," she continued, "sought to obtain an archbishopric, was consumed by ambition, and for that reason repeatedly changed sides."

"Perhaps he sought that office in order to acquire some influence."

"What influence? You say that just to contradict me."

I did not argue the point. Perhaps she was right and he was stupidly ambitious, but can one really blame him for that? This is a sad fact, but are we to accuse him, without having any proof? I have a great deal of respect for people who suffer in spite of material prosperity and personal happiness; I can understand their suffering.

Once in my presence she inveighed against a girl who had refused to marry a good man, whom she did not love, but with whom she surely would have been happy. I sided with the girl, saying that one should never lower one's standards. "So in that case be an old spinster, and live with that witch, your mother." "I respect that girl ever so much more because she refused to compromise even under such adverse conditions."

She reproached me for my gloom, presenting to me the advantages which I was enjoying compared with other girls. As if my melancholy had anything to do with them.

Then she attacked Pomialov[sky][28] for a phrase of his,

28. Nikolai Gerasimovich Pomialovsky (1837–63), writer of some popularity in the sixties. Influenced by Chernyshevsky and Dobroliubov. The reference here is probably to his novel *Molotov*, which takes his hero, after travels about Russia in search of a social ideal, to middle-class duties and enjoyments.

which I love, saying that man is made not for his own pleasure, but for fulfilling his duty. Duty! What duties can a private person have before society, what can he do for it?

Paris, 15 September

Today my physician was here. He said that he had read *On the Eve,* and that he was enraptured by Insarov's happiness.[29] "Could it be true," he said, "that there are such girls?" I said that I was surprised to find in him, a medical man, such attention to an interest in belles lettres. He went on to demonstrate that not chemistry, but they (belles lettres) educate people. "I have just read it, and I have had such moments as no chemistry can give me."

"Yes, I understand that one may have those moments."

"Those moments leave a deep impression, and they account for a person's intellectual development."

Then we talked about Pek.,[30] about Stoianov,[31] about Luginin, whom he called a Russian Girondist. He told me that when he met him for the first time, Luginin was reading Proudhon's book on federalism. He had just finished it and kept claiming that patriotism and nationalism were all nonsense. "A fine fellow that Luginin, he has read Proudhon and that's it, everything's definite."

Ever since my arrival I had almost invariably kept silent at dinner. To one side, there sat some old ladies, to the other, a student with his mistress, who started coming to dinner soon after I had arrived. But after a certain time, a gentleman started sitting next to me, separating me from the old ladies. That gentleman kept talking and talking, until he finally succeeded in engaging me in conversation, with the student joining in also. The gentleman to my left asked me what I

29. *On the Eve* (1860), novel by Turgenev in which the hero is Insarov, a Bulgarian.
30. Probably a reference to Peter Petrovich Pekarsky, a Polish emigrant and historian of literature.
31. Probably a Bulgarian emigrant.

was reading, and, having learned that it was history, recommended several books to me. One of these books the student offered to give me. After dinner I immediately got up as usual, and went into the garden. Walking past Robescourt, I had to stop, as he accosted me. I had barely reached the garden when the student and his lady came down, and he gave me the books. The lady also tried to participate in all this; at dinner she kept turning toward me in a nervous way. This lady is somehow currying my favor: she has her gentleman friend pass me dishes at table, and so on. I respond to it politely. The Englishwoman refuses to eat with us on the grounds that this would mean her having to sit at the same table with a *prostitute*. That's too much. The relationship between the student and the lady is a touching one. At table, she lets him have the choice morsels; when she pours herself some wine, she always lets him have some first. In part, she functions as his servant: she sweeps and cleans his room.

21 September

My landlady is driving me to distraction: I have asked her a thousand times to have my room tidied up, but she won't do it, though she keeps promising. She simply won't pay any attention, promising as though it were a joke only. I gave the maid some money, but even that won't help.

Marie once took my shoes to clean, and then I had to go out. I looked and looked for her and those shoes; the lackey helped me find her, yelling that she should get Suslova's shoes, then finally she responded from somewhere upstairs, saying rudely that she hadn't any time. So I had to go out with my shoes uncleaned, which put me in a bad mood. On the next day, taking my shoes, she said facetiously that she wouldn't do what she had done the day before, and it was I who had to blush. Another time she forgot to give me breakfast, and the next day she was again the first to mention it, while I was apologetic about it.

A few days ago my physician was here. He told me about the governess who had asked him for a cure for her gray hair. I told him that I had some gray hairs, too.

"From unhappiness!" he said.

This upset me very much.

"I haven't been unhappy," I tried to say, able to control myself for a moment, but then the tears came to my eyes, and the muscles of my face began to tremble even more.

"It happens to everybody," he said, apparently moved.

I was trying to say something, but could not control myself.

"You can be helped; at your age this is possible," he began.

"Do you really think that this is what makes me unhappy?" I said with feigned melancholy, and still looking the other way.

"No, I just said it so as to say something," he said excitedly, also looking away, and not at me.

24 September

Yesterday my physician was here, and he and I worked on our French together. I was in a cheerful mood, as a result of which I somehow did not behave decorously. It was simply a case of my nerves being upset. He remarked that I was distracted: "You are probably thinking of Valakh"[32] (I had said something about Valakh just before). I was angry with myself, and I had nothing to say to him, but next time I shall try to behave more decorously. He noticed that there were some young people walking in our garden and asked if this was always so. I told him that whenever I was in the garden nobody walked there, and even if they walked past me, they always approach me sideways, being afraid of me, which was all to the good: it was necessary that they fear somebody.

Today I went to see Mme M[arkovich] and along my way met *him*. As I was riding past the hospital in a cab, I saw several young people outside the gate. He immediately came

32. Apparently a code name for an unnamed Russian—"Rumanian" or "Moldavian."

to my mind, and there, indeed, he was. He came running to
the gate, without his hat, disheveled, his face flabby, unattractive. He immediately recognized me, even though I was
wearing a veil (I was all in black, except for my hat), and,
embarrassed, turned toward his companion (I did not bat
an eye). This is beginning to interest me. And then, after a
thing like this, I am upset all day. I was angry with myself
for the agitation that I felt. Am I never going to forget him?
And I was getting desperate. But why become desperate;
wouldn't it be better if I were to forget him? But, really, did
I feel any better during the winter, when I did not see him?
Did I feel any better even during *our time together?* I remember those nights when I would suddenly wake up and remember with horror what had happened during the day,
then run up and down my room, crying. Was that any better?
Perhaps it was when for the first time I heard the words of
love from him, or the first time he embraced me. Why was
this so good? Because it was new, unexpected. And can one
really wish that all this had never happened? Then, there
would be emptiness, or some other mistake, perhaps a more
colorless one. And how could it have been better with him?
Would it have been good, if he and I had stayed together
until now, even if I had become his wife? He is such a prosaic
gentleman. And what is it I want of him now? That he should
confess his guilt, be remorseful, that is, that he be a F[yodor]
M[ikhailovich]. What would happen then? Meanwhile, now
I have moments of such triumph, aware of my own strength.

I hear about F[yodor] M[ikhailovich]. I simply hate him.
He made me suffer so much, when it was possible not to
suffer.

Now I feel and see clearly that I cannot love, that I cannot
find happiness in the enjoyment of love, because the caresses
of men will remind me of my humiliations and my sufferings.
Something new might interest me, but even that only to a
certain extent.

A few days ago, after dinner, I went out into the garden,
and was followed (for the first time) by Valakh, who started
telling me how pleased he was to see me. I remarked that it

couldn't be too much of a pleasure, since he had not come to Versailles. He explained that he had had an examination. We talked for a long time, and when I went home he firmly pressed my hand. He is a simple, naïve man; that's a novelty.

As we were talking, other young men walked by, not talking so much to their girls. The ladies cast curious glances at us. On the following day I did not go to the garden.

29 September

Sick. Valakh comes exactly every other day. My physican every day. The main cause of my illness is, it would seem, my encounter with the planter.

I told my physican that I was upset by an encounter. He attached great importance to this, and was sad. I also was sad and upset often, and he often was agitated when leaving me. Every time he would press my hand several times, offering his services. When leaving, he would turn back at the door, just to get another look at me. Once he told me that Mme Markovich would be coming on a certain day, and she came, just as my physician and I were studying French together. She stayed a few minutes, behaving somewhat strangely. She spoke very little, saying that she was expected at the Pantheon. Mme Yakobi had mentioned that her son was learning Russian, and she said that she was not worried about his knowing the fine nuances of Russian expressions. I would never have expected such obtuseness on her part. Though it may be true that cultivating a nationality is only a fad, still one must be able to grasp meanings. As she prepared to leave, she asked what street she ought to take. My physician offered to escort her. She declined, saying that she had walked alone to quite different places, but he said that he was finished with me, and they left together.

Today we really talked a lot, though he was sad at first. I said that apparently Mme M[arkovich] was displeased with me. He hastened to dissuade me from thinking so. I said that Mme Yakobi was, it seemed, a phrase-monger. He agreed

with that. I asked: where were his friends from, America or
Spain? He replied that they were all from America and told
me some things about their character, very wittily, saying
that they were very popular with the French ladies. I asked
why. He answered: by their appearance, that they were
young and well-dressed, with eyes as large as this glass, such
white teeth, fresh gloves, and fine shoes.

"Oh, how wicked you are!" I said.

He said that I still did not know him.

He asked why I wanted to know these things, and whether
I wanted to make their acquaintance? I said: "No." "Didn't
I want to take lessons?" I said that I knew an American lady.
Just to say something, I said that he should ask what books
they had in Spain, novels, and added that they probably
wouldn't know. "No, this they know," he said, "when it
comes to a drawing-room education, they've got that." We
had become much more cheerful; I took notice of it, and he
agreed, adding that he had come in a very upset and angry
mood. I asked him the reason. He said that there had been
a clash involving his sense of duty, pointing out that sometimes one did one's duty from cowardice, and sometimes on
account of the fact that we haven't got a right to hurt the
feelings of others. Valakh and I discussed Proudhon,[33] and
Herzen, whom I had been reading.

Then he told me about Moldavia. There, as in Russia,
French fashions are imitated in society, and French is spoken.
He promised to get me Racine.

1 October

Yesterday Mlle Jullette came to see me. She was sad, for some
reason, and I made a remark to her about it. She agreed.
While she was there, Valakh came and sat for a while. He
was cooler than usual as he took his leave, even though I was

33. Pierre Joseph Proudhon (1809–65), one of the founders of French
socialist thought and first friend and then opponent of Karl Marx's brand
of socialism.

cordial enough at parting, and invited him to come again. For some reason it appeared to me that he might be the cause of Jullette's sadness. He asked me about my doctor. As I told him some things, I got carried away and pointed out how much that young man knew. Valakh said, in a sort of serious way, that it was no wonder he knew a lot: when you read a lot, you are bound to find out something.

Later, the Englishwoman came by, offered to have tea with me, and ordered some. She is a worthless woman and a gossip. She has got all the bad (English) qualities, the English ones with a few human ones added, yet she lacks any of the English virtues. Yesterday I had mentioned, in some connection, that I was going to get a sofa, as one of the tenants was moving out. She perked up. "Who is going to leave? When?" I was unable to satisfy her curiosity. Then she suddenly told me, with horror, that Mlle Stward [sic] had a lover (that is Mlle Stward's business, not ours, I should say). "But she isn't spending her nights at home!" the Englishwoman continued, horrified. So what? She and I won't have to christen her children. If Mlle S[tward] were my sister, perhaps I should have had a word with her about this thing. But Mlle S[tward] is not a child, she probably knows what she is doing, she is no concern of ours, and it is in fact unnecessary and improper for us to be aware of her conduct. She wants to move to another house, where only old men and women live—there, morality must reign supreme. There shouldn't be any lovers or mistresses [there], but why put so much blame on poor Mlle Stward? I think that she, just as everyone else, is not going to have a lover when she grows old. The Englishwoman is still undecided about moving away, because the other house is filthy and overcrowded. And so, she must make her choice between morality and comfort. Then she told me about the moral[ity] of the young girl who lives far back in the garden and whom nobody ever sees. "How can you know who lives in that house?" But in England they have homes occupied by only one family. This Englishwoman's husband is a very funny man; all he does is run about Paris; something like five times a day he will run and come back with a bottle

or two under his arm. Wherever I go, I almost invariably
catch up with him, or run into him. He always runs along
the middle of the street, all bent and contorted as though
some outside force were driving him. From time to time he
will dash to the right or to the left, stick his nose into a shop,
then bounce back and rush on. Sometimes he takes a walk
with his wife; I have never seen them together, though. But
in the yard he walks without his usual dash; rather, he drags
behind his *bretonne,* slowly and even more bent than usual.
It would seem that he shows a considerable interest in
women's gossip.

Friday, 6 October

As I was walking to my lesson, I met the Pole who, God only
knows why, visited me twice. The first time he asked for a
lady, and I answered him very angrily, standing in the door;
the other time he came to tell me that he had received a
letter with its seal broken, and asked me whether I had
broken the seal. I asked him to come in, listened to what he
had to say, and when he had finished about the letter, I asked
him, getting up, if this was all he had to say. He was embarrassed, got up, and took his leave. Today, as I was walking
past l'École de Médecine [*sic*], I heard a voice behind me
saying: "My compliments." I did not turn around, but kept
walking. Then, "my compliments" was repeated another
time, and the Pole appeared before me, saying that I had
smiled as I walked by him, that most probably I had laughed,
and was still laughing, at him. I replied that I had not taken
any notice of him. "But I noticed you," he said, "because I am
interested." I answered nothing to this banality. Then he
asked whether I was angry with him for coming to my room
twice. I replied that, no, since I thought that he had come for
a serious reason. He started telling me about the deftness
with which I had sent him about his business, so that he had
found nothing to say, even though he had wanted to stay and
talk some more. He was still keeping up this rather empty

conversation when I reached the house where Mme B. lives.

I said, "Good-bye," and crossed over to the other side. He stayed on his side, but soon came running over to me, saying: "Again you are getting rid of me with the same deftness." I said that I had to go to that house, which I promptly did.

Yesterday before dinner I met Valakh in our garden and got to talking with him. I told him that I had bought some tea, that I was drinking tea from boredom, that it was my substitute for everything: pleasure, friends. He remarked that, apparently, it was not a very good substitute. I agreed. Then he asked me what nationality I loved most and said: "You must love your neighbors, the Romanians." I answered that I did not know them, that they had done nothing to impress the world; "we Russians, though we are no good, at least we make ourselves felt."

Tuesday, 9 October

Yesterday, as I was walking to my lesson (Span.) I met the planter in the Rue Médecins [sic]. He was walking on the other side of the street, with that same friend with whom he had been talking in front of the hospital. He was walking along, talking and chuckling, and bending forward so low, that I barely recognized him; probably he saw me before I noticed him.

A few days ago I wrote a very intimate letter to my physician after he had missed me at home. He responded with a letter which was cold to the point of rudeness, and in which he said that he did not have sufficient time to keep seeing me at home (he had missed me twice). He offered to come once [a week] for lessons and consultation, asking that I myself fix the day and hour, under the condition that it not be at night, because at night he wanted to rest. At the same time he named the day and his fee for the lessons. On the set day he showed up with an air [illegible word] and started by asking me about my health. I answered and reached for my copybook, telling him what I had been studying. He suddenly said that he could not give me my lesson and got ready to leave. I still refused to believe that he was such a fool and asked him if he was angry with me. He made a surprised face and asked where I got that idea. "Apparently the struggle with his sense of duty has come to an end, with virtue victorious," I thought. This tone of his made an unpleasant impression on me; unable to restrain my sadness, I answered that, perhaps, I was wrong, and then added, with a sad smile: "Go then, go." Thereafter, having come on the set day, he immediately started asking me about my health, with a grave air, then suddenly broke off the conversation in a casual manner and suggested that we have our lesson. When he sat down, he pointed at his watch. I looked at him with astonishment and with curiosity, but then suddenly my heart was gripped by some sort of a sad feeling. I felt humiliated, like a fool, and I could hardly restrain my indignation. Some ideas in the book we were reading enhanced my agitation. So in the end I had to leave the room in order to conceal it. When he had left, I cried. Poor heart! It won't stand being touched so rudely. This incident gave me some serious thoughts. Naturally, I shall act resolutely and come out with honor, for I am hiding nothing and I am not equivocating.

But how much strength must I waste on defending myself against such petty attacks!

Mme Robescourt is ill, she had a nervous fit yesterday. The whole house was upside down; all night they kept running to get doctors and medicine. I wanted to go to see her, but I don't know how to go about it, and whether it would be agreeable to her. He had breakfast with us; he came toward the end and happened to sit next to me. He asked me about my health, then everybody began asking him about his lady, and he answered calmly that she was better. I also thought of asking him about her, but didn't; it was too embarrassing.

19 October

My physician and I almost made up. Later, I told him that I could not remember all his calls, that I had not been counting them, and that it was his own fault, his inconsistency; I reminded him that at one time he had actually refused taking money from me, but that now, after the comedy was finished, one might as well be accurate. He acted perplexed and said that there hadn't been any comedy at all on his part, trying to justify himself, but I begged him to postpone it at least until next time: I was too upset. At our next meeting I was cheerful, and after we had conversed for a while, he started like this:

"You are now in a good mood, and so we may take up our previous conversation again."

"Why?" said I. "You told me that there was no comedy, fine; this means, of course, that I must believe you. I admit that I really had no right to say what I said to you, and that I said it only because I had talked to you so much before."

"But tell me, for heaven's sake, freely: do you think that I wanted to annoy you?"

"You didn't even have any way of knowing what might annoy me."

"And do you know what annoys me?"

"You want to tell me that you were sincere with me."

"I am not going to say this, because it would be too transparent an untruth. I will tell you only that I had my reasons, with which you are not familiar. You don't know the tenth part of what is . . ."

He spoke with fervor, and I felt sorry for him. He asked me if it wasn't disagreeable to me that he kept coming, and said that he could leave me alone.

"No," I said, "why? . . . And why are you asking me about this, as if you didn't know that I appreciate your visits," I added, as calmly as I could.

"Yes, but it might become annoying."

I told him that a Russian acquaintance of mine, Utin,[34] had arrived, that he had no one else here, and that, consequently, he would be seeing me frequently.

"Why 'consequently'?" he asked, seriously.

34. Evegenii Isakovich Utin (1843–94). His brother Nikolay (1840–83) was a revolutionary and member of the ruling circles of the secret society called Zemlia i volia (Land and Will) .

I did not understand him, and naïvely asked him to repeat his question.

When he repeated it just as seriously, I guessed what he meant and blushed crimson.

When Utin heard his name from me, he told me that his brother was a bad man. This startled me and made many of his actions clear to me.

Thursday, 19 October

Today at breakfast a Frenchman told me that before I got there they were having a discussion about the advantages of city and country life, and that Monsieur R. was for the city, while he was for the provinces. I said that I was surprised at Monsieur Robescourt, that I did not like big cities, where no friendship or anything was possible. He said that he was afraid of going stale in the provinces, where there was no learning, nothing. (As thought it were impossible to read books.) And I thought that life in a big city is life in a herd, not the life of an individual, and that man must be a man first and foremost, then a citizen, and only then a craftsman or scholar. That this petty life in the city, subordinated to petty interests, is bad for the development of a personality.

Friday, 20 October

Yesterday, all of a sudden, young S[alias] showed up, bringing a note from his mother, in which she told me that she was coming to see me that day. I invited him in. We talked nonsense. Still, I did not like S[alias], though I had not expected that I would like him a great deal; but still, I expected something better: he is somehow flaccid. Certainly, the Georgian is taciturn, too, but that's different. At the same time he tries to create a good impression of himself: it isn't exactly that he is trying to show himself as something he is not, but he tries to show that he understands such-and-such; yet he may look rather simple. He told me that while he was looking me up, he met an old woman who in her day had loyally served her master, but now had saved up enough money and was living out her life enjoying herself.

Utin is a thousand times better: a lively, bold, clever boy. The Georgian is the best of them all.

In the evening Ev[genia] T[ur] and her son came, also U[tin] and the Georgian; the latter arrived first. Not expecting to meet so many people and seeing Ev[genia] T[ur] and her son, he said quietly to me: "I'd like to bolt." "No, it's too late now, you can't," I said, humorously. He stayed. Ev[genia] T[ur], needless to say, spoke more than anybody else, and I met her glance, which seemed to ask, almost outright: "What kind of an impression did V[adim] make?"

Today, in order to meet the C[ountess], I went to see her cousin, and met everybody there who had been at my place the day before (excluding the Georgian); we talked nonsense. They have really become great friends during this time. Cons[equently] I have done them a favor, by introducing them.

To V[adim], I said a few words about language, and I became animated.

Utin asked me about Alkhazov. When I went home, U[tin] and V[adim] walked with me. The latter spoke about Spain. "That is the past," he said. "But it can be turned into the present," U[tin] said, correctly.

"No, that wouldn't be it, that's like marrying a second time, loving the second time, you can love only once."

"This is very sad," said U[tin]; "you think this way because you are young."

"This is most unfair," I thought. I mentioned Luc[rezia] Floriani,[35] who had loved many times, but who always felt as though she loved for the first and last time. V[adim] said that this was still a thing of the future for him, and very distant. "Be ready to die any minute," U[tin] remarked. But the other stubbornly refused to agree with him. "You are a

35. *Lucrezia Floriani* novel by George Sand (1804–76) in which she recounts her relations with Chopin. Its social significance consists of its bold views on marriage and family.

good Christian," Utin said to him; "you're not afraid of death."

What a crude and sensuous notion this is.

They escorted me home. At the gate, I wanted to say good-bye, but V[adim] offered to accompany me further. "Do you want to pay a visit to me?" I asked. They declined. When I stretched out my hand to U[tin], he pressed it firmly and refused to let go. I looked at him in surprise. I invited him to come to my house, saying that I was at home every night. Then I turned to V[adim] and said that I hoped to be seeing him frequently. In the yard, Valakh overtook us. He looked sad to me.

I am looking out of the window right now, the one that faces the garden, and I see Julie with one of the Romanians, the most unattractive of them. They were walking with their backs to me, and it seemed to me that Julie was crying. I took a closer look. Julie screamed and fell down, face up. The Romanian took a look at her, then calmly stepped over her feet, and called the landlady. She entered the garden, took a look from a distance, and said, annoyed, "Comme c'est inutile." She then called the maid. A lackey and a maid dragged the unconscious Julie into the drawing room and apparently left her there alone, for soon after I heard the landlady conversing with the same Romanian quite cheerfully. The words spoken by the Romanian, which I heard, were "mauvais sujet."[36] "Will you come to dinner?" asked the landlady. "I don't know," he answered; "what do you have for dinner?" She began to list the courses. The sick girl was alone. That's not the way it was the first time. A repeat performance is always a failure.

That same night.

Ever since Rob[escourt] told me that he was leaving, I've been getting ready to ask him up to this day for his picture, but somehow I never got around to it. I hoped that he would

36. "Ne-er-do-well."

come to say bood-bye. He was supposed to be leaving today, and he came to my room. I said that I was sorry he was leaving and asked him for his picture. He said that he did not have any, but that he would send me one, and asked me for mine. I wanted to give him his book, but he asked me to keep it for a souvenir. At that moment the Englishwoman entered. Upon seeing that I had a visitor she tried to withdraw, saying, "Pardon," but I asked her to come in. She did and sat there for a while. We chatted a bit. I told them about U[tin]. The Englishwoman left soon. Then Robescourt told me, as we were alone again, that he would be coming back in April and would try to look me up. Then he asked me to write him once in a while, and if I should come to Nancy, to see him there. He left me his address. Then, as he was about to leave, he pressed my hand and kissed it. At this point I began to say something, and my voice trembled. He again kissed both my hands. I looked at him, and threw my arm around his neck, our lips met . . . Then there began an incoherent conversation, interrupted by kisses. He was trembling all over, and he had such a happy, smiling face. I was also feeling happy, but kept breaking off our ardent embraces with my pleas to be left alone. I kept pushing him away, then again passionately stretched out my arms to him. He asked me if I preferred that he not go to Nancy, and asked when he could come to see me. I said, tomorrow night. Several times over we said good-bye to one another. I was trying to make him go, but he kept asking for still one more kiss. Finally I got his hat for him and opened the door myself. After he had left, I recovered my composure a bit, then, with my cheeks still burning from his kisses, I went to see the Englishwoman. As I was returning from her room to mine, I heard the voice of Mme Rob[escourt] on the stairs. I went to the window and saw her walking across the yard, together with him, and accompanied by servants carrying their bags. He came back and discussed something with the landlady. My head is going around; I don't know what will come of all this. It seems to me that he loves me, I even was convinced of it two hours earlier, before I had heard the voice of

Mme R[obescourt]. His face was so genuinely happy. And so were his trembling, and the tremor in his voice.

23 October

Valakh is not here, ror have I any letters from him.

Yesterday my physician was here. I told him that the handsome Spaniard was trash. He replied that this was too categoric a statement. I said: "Of course, but he is still a bad one. And I've been told by people that he is handsome —not at all so." "But his eyebrows, his eyebrows, aren't they something, as wide as my whole forehead." Then I told him that I had done a favor to three people by introducing them to one another. "That is, you have contributed to the spreading of civilization," he said.

About Pechorin he said that he was as much of fool as Grush[nitsky].[37] This juxtaposition struck me, as I had thought exactly the same thing myself.

Utin defended V[adim], saying that he had had a long talk with him, and that he was all right. He was startled by my opinion, which was not harsh at all.

Today the Englishwoman was here and indignantly told me that Mme Caubrigneau sews lace on caps for the poor, and that in Paris it is quite impossible to determine a person's class by her dress.

2 November

Usov and Utin were here. Utin said, in some connection, that the English nation is narrow-minded. Usov stood up for the English. Utin said that their political influence has decreased, since they were defeated both in the Danish and in the Polish question.

"But this does not mean a thing. Foreign affairs are no longer so important. They are sticking to the principle of

---

37. Heroes from Lermontov's novel *A Hero of Our Time.*

nonintervention. Now even Louis Napoleon is taking his troops out of Rome."

"Yes, your principle of nonintervention, to be sure— today he withdraws them, yet only yesterday they were fighting in Mexico; just see, tomorrow they may be fighting again somewhere."

"That is so, but still, this principle of nonintervention shows the trend in British public opinion. In England, freedom is so universal it could hardly be outdone anywhere."

"Yes, everything is in the hands of industrialists."

"The workers are free also."

"Yes, they prosper, without the power of capital, without money."

"Look, even without capital, they have a tremendous amount of money; they live better than our government officials."

"They do? What are you talking about! Why then does Taine[38] mention poverty on every page? And whence the hunger?"

"Why, it is because there is one minor hitch, namely, that not everybody can be a worker."

"Well, there you are, so we still get the same thing."

"No, it is not the same. This situation is improving. Now every worker can himself be a proprietor."

"But isn't this a very small percentage?"

"What can the government do about that? The government cannot interfere. It is good that it doesn't interfere."

"We can see how good this is. Why, then, does it help the bourgeoisie? No, this is too uneven a struggle, with one side having everything on its side, and the other nothing, and you shall see this at the next upheaval, which is bound to happen, for it is being prepared."

"I cannot deny that it might happen. Everything may happen. But I am not a worshiper of the revolution. It seems

---

38. Hippolyte Taine (1828–93). This is probably a reference to Taine's *History of English Literature,* which appeared in 1863. He attempted to explain literary and historical events by the influence of race, environment, and weather.

to me that one should have abandoned this idea a long time ago, the idea that a revolution is the only way to achieve one's ends. Of course, in Russia, where sixty million people are totally ignorant, and if there is one among them who happens to be educated, they shut him up immediately— here any means will have to do; but in a country where conditions are in any way favorable, it is inexcusable. You will see what comes of these modest beginnings in due course, what with the tremendous successes scored even in so short a time. We do not notice them, because we are used to spectacular effects. We need a revolution. (I am not looking forward to the revolution, rather, I look upon it as a sad necessity.)"

16 November

Lately, I have been at the Co[untess's] every night. Bak [unin?][39] was there. I liked him.

Nothing can be accomplished without faith, he said once, but sometimes faith will kill. That which is credited to heaven, is taken away from earth.[40]

A few days ago it happened that my physician asked me for some money. Apparently it wasn't easy for him. I immediately gave him some, in the nicest way possible. He was happy. We talked a great deal. Toward the end, as he was already about to leave, he started to say this: "Talleyrand said that the word was given to man so that he could conceal his thoughts, and Heine said that it was there so that we could say nice things to one another. Which of them is right? Now there is this question: is it necessary to speak at all?" I did not understand him . . . Soon after he left, I

39. Mikhail Aleksandrovich Bakunin (1814–76), influential anarchist and revolutionary, friend of Herzen. He was perhaps Marx's most formidable antagonist, especially in the struggle over control of the International.

40. It is possible that this is an oblique reference to Feuerbach's and subsequently Marx's view that man alienated the best part of himself in religion, that is, by crediting it to heaven.

got the idea only after he had left. Yesterday he was very nice to me. He is a simple and nice man. One could not fall madly in love with him, but one could become passionately enamored of him.

Yesterday, when we had finished the lesson, he wanted to sit closer to the fire and suggested that I move closer to the fireplace. I said no, because I had a headache. "All right, so I'll stay here also," he said, but then again, some time later, suggested that we move.

"Why don't you sit there by yourself," I said; "isn't it all the same? What whims! We can talk very well also that way."

"Yes, it's a whim, exactly, but that's all right, a whim is a good thing."

I wonder how he got up so much courage?

I moved to the fireplace, but he put his chair rather far from me. Seeing some bread, he asked permission to have some. I said yes, and began to eat with him. I offered him some tea, but he declined, saying that this would be too much trouble, and that he wanted to talk with me, and besides he had to go to a lecture.

"You don't have to go," I said.

"You are right," he said cheerfully, but quickly recovered, and added sadly; "I must."

I did not insist. He said nothing special, but as he was saying good-bye, he thanked me so simply and naïvely.

Once, speaking of a handsome Greek, I said that during my first youth I paid no attention to beauty, and that my first love was a man of 40.

"You were probably 16 then?" he said.

"No, twenty three."

19 November

Today Vadim was here. We talked about love.

"What a delicate conversation we are having," I said, "however, it is most decorous."

"No, it's indecorous."

"How then would you talk to a woman about love, about flowers, about poetry?"

"Poetry and flowers are nonsense, but love is a serious thing, it has existed since the beginning of the world, and he who has never felt it is unworthy of being called a man."

"Flowers and poetry have also existed for a long time, and who does not feel their beauty is not a man."

Wednesday, 30 November

On Sunday I attended a gala concert with Carrive. We returned on foot, and talked. I asked him about his native country, where he plans to return soon, but he told me nothing definite.

He told me that he will follow in his father's footsteps, that he will work the land, raise a family, but perhaps he also might get a job somewhere in the city.

Prior to that I had an incident happen to me: a Russian doctor, who arrived here recently, behaved toward me in a way which forced me to forbid him the house. Carrive had seen him at my place on Saturday, and asked about him. I told him that I had been forced to show him the door, and that I considered him a fool. He said that this was precisely what he had thought of him. He was glad that I had told him about it: "I'll know how to conduct myself with him." (They meet at the hospital.) I answered him that I was not asking him for anything.

"I am not going to challenge him to a duel," he said, "but still, it is better that I know what sort of a person he is."

He suggested that we take a trip to St. Germain together, and I gladly accepted.

Yesterday, as I was taking my French lesson, Vadim and U[tin] came to see me. The yentered somehow with a lot of noise, then, seeing that it was a bad time to come, seemingly got embarrassed, but asked permission to stay five minutes, and we talked a bit. When I asked Vadim to tell his mother that I could not go to Châtle that evening, Utin looked at me with such a smile that I felt like going to the Countess's that night just to show that I had no particular interest in staying at home. But still I didn't go. As he was leaving, I said to B., for some reason:

"Don't go away; we might have a good laugh."

He said that he had so much to do, and I knew that he was telling the truth.

"Look, I would very much like to stay. It's good to be here with you, but I must go to my classes, and then to the hospital. At least you might feel sorry for me," he said, already standing at the door.

"Why won't you feel sorry for yourself?"

"Oh, don't think I am so proud that I wouldn't like to be pitied."

"I must pity myself, because there is no one to pity me."

He rapidly stepped up to me and pressed my hand.

"Or should I postpone it until *la transformation* has taken place," he said, remembering the book we had been reading, then answered himself, "Or it will be late . . ."

"Good-bye."

He told me that he would try to see me before Saturday. Then he remarked that the young men had failed to close the door, and that I should give them a scolding for that.

Today the Countess was here. As I was returning her son's story to her, I said to her that if I were a censor, I would forbid it. That was a clever trick . . . flattering and sincere.

Saturday, December 1864

A few days ago I fell ill, and besides there was this silly thing with that money, on account of which I had to go to the bank. I asked the Co[untess] to come and give me some advice about what to do. She came at once, but was cool, advising me to let Beni [*sic*] handle it. I told her that he was busy and that he and I were not on friendly terms. She doubted that he was busy. She suggested that I turn to Alkhazov. This was more out of the question than anything else. Then she suggested

Utin. I said nothing, and when I had to speak up, I said that I would ask the landlady.

On the next day I sent Utin a letter, asking him to come as soon as possible, saying that I was ill. I was told that he would be right over, but he came 4 hours later, with Salias. He had already been at their house and knew my whole problem. I was excited by what I had been reading, and then because of their appearance together I was rude to them, and especially to Salias. When he said, "Should we come to see you?" I answered, "Why?"

Utin came on the following day, and I told him that I remembered having been rude to Salias. He admitted that this was true and that he had really been surprised by it. He also said that the day before Salias had taken offense at something that was not legitimate at all.

I told Utin that I had seen Carrive and that he had asked me for permission to introduce a friend of his to me. "When are they coming?" he asked.

I answered, "I don't know."

There, his vanity is already wounded; they're glad they can come, while I can very well do without them.

"Do you feel bored?" Utin asked.

"No, it's all right," I answered; "you see, I am not very ill and I can study, and what difference is there between my life right now and the life I lead ordinarily?"

"I asked because you sighed."

As he was leaving, he told me that I need not be afraid with him, that he would always understand my words right.

When I fell ill I wrote a note to Benni in the evening. He came early in the morning of the following day, when I was in bed. As I opened the door for him, I told him to wait until I got back in bed. He entered. He was greatly worried, and when he left he pressed my hand so very hard. I held on slightly to his hand. But he left. He came back later that night, and on the next day, and on the following day. On the second day he sat with me for a long time, lounging around in the opposite corner, and talked a lot, and well, yet he was completely calm. He said it was too bad that people would not respect the freedom of others who were their friends, or just their acquaintances: "Well, he is my friend," he said; "what business is it of his that I'm going to steal some money tomorrow? Let everyone answer for himself."

Today I took a lesson from him. I got too warm sitting next to the fireplace; I moved away from it, and finally walked away. He said that I was very far away. "So why won't you come here?" But he didn't. I told him that I needed some money exchanged, and he offered to change it for me himself. I gave it to him, so I could see him once more. He came, but that time Carrive was with me. It looked as though he lost his spirits when he saw him, and he left soon, saying that he would come back on Tuesday, i.e., whenever he was needed, because I was almost healthy now. A proud boy!

Monday

I am now thinking about my return to Russia. Where shall I go, to whom? To my brother, to my father? I will never be as free as I would like to, and to what end should I suffer this dependency? What have I in common with these people? Carry out my ideas! Stupid. Why, besides, no one is going to give me his children. It seems to me that things in Russia are not nearly so bad as some people say they are. Really, the purpose of it all is, properly speaking, that the people should be well off, i.e., that they eat well; and the people today eat better than ever before, and with this, they will go far. And as to the universities being closed—what does it matter?

Once my physician said that he had no fatherland. But what does it mean, "to have a fatherland?"

14 December

On Sunday Alkhazov was here. He told about the repressions back home. He is desperate about not being able to do anything about it, and wants to go to Turkey: there's more freedom there. There you have it, the condition of contemporary man! Looking for freedom in Turkey! I liked this thought.

"At least, there you won't have to wear a dress coat and gloves," he said. Then he said that at one time he wanted to write home that his little brother should join him here— schools are bad over there—but then had thought better of it, having seen the way of life here. Of course, I could look after him, he said, but the many things that I could do for him here, wouldn't replace those things that he would miss: I couldn't replace his mother or his brothers, or nature, or all the things of which those impressions are composed which form one's character—and that's the main thing. An education can be added later, whereas a character cannot be acquired. I really had a heart-to-heart talk with him.

Today I visited with the Co[untess]. She had just returned from a journey, having accompanied Mme O[garev].[41] She told me some terrible things: Mme O[garev], this woman, of whom people of all parties and opinions think so badly, is leaving her husband and has gained control over H[erzen]. In her presence, H[erzen] came to her, drunk, and he had hardly entered when she offered him some wine, under the pretext that she had no place to pour it. It is said that this was also the way she attracted her husband, making him drunk. As Mme O[garev] was parting with [Countess] S[alias], Mme O[garev] gave her a note. "For O[garev?]" the latter asked. "Oh, no, for H[erzen]. Tell him that he must accompany O[garev] and come to me quickly. He is a strong person, but I cannot vouch for myself." Speaking of her children, she compared her relationship to them with the relationship of the Holy Virgin to Her Son.

On Saturday, when I told my physician that I was leaving for P., I noticed a certain agitation in his expression. As he was about to leave, I said rather simply:

41. Wife of Nikolay Platonovich Ogarev (1813–72), childhood friend of Herzen, poet, political thinker, and activist. Collaborator with Herzen in publishing *The Bell*.

"Could you do me a favor and find an address for me?"

"Whose?"

"C."

My voice changed when I pronounced that name . . .

He promised to do it. I asked him not to think that there was any hurry about it. Today he brought the address. I was very much surprised to see him at a time other than we had agreed on.

"Let me have some paper," he said, having greeted me.

I gave him some paper and expressed my surprise at seeing him. He avoided mentioning C.'s name, or the reason why he had come.

I went to get some coal, and as I was dragging it from the closet, I asked:

"You haven't brought me the address which I asked you to get for me, have you?"

Then I asked him to stay a while. He stayed a short while and was very sad.

I feel that I'm becoming petty, that I am sinking into some kind of "unclean mire," without feeling that enthusiasm which used to free me from it, none of that saving indignation.

I have been thinking a lot, and I feel better now. I have many prejudices. If I hadn't loved before, if my physician were not my doctor, our relationship would be quite different. Where has my courage gone? As I remember what happened two years ago, I begin to hate D[ostoevsky]. He was the first to kill my faith. But I want to shake off this sadness.

20 December

My physician said about the Countess (after I had told him that she does not like him, which he admitted; it was embarrassing to him), that she is incapable of loving anybody. How true this is!

Montagnard said that he prefers the character of André

Chénier's[42] poetry to that of the poetry of Alfred de Musset.[43] About the latter he said that he sees evil, finds nothing lofty, and all because he is personally unhappy; that he is too much preoccupied with himself, that he is an ogoist.

21 December

My physician was here. He said that in love there is action and reaction, in the life of individuals as well as in the life of nations; there are periods during which a man loves, and there are periods when he tells himself: enough, let others love me, if they want, but no, enough is enough.

31 December

Today I got a letter from my sister to which I am replying as follows. [The letter is not given.]

14 January

The number of people in whose minds a man's easy triumph over a woman destroys that woman's dignity may be much greater than I had assumed.

15 January

At last I see the effect of propaganda. The landlady complained to me about my not having told her that I pay Léonie. "You should be on the masters' side, not on that of the servants," she told me. "Mme, I can't talk either side,

42. André Chénier (1762–94), French poet who opposed the Terror of the Revolution and was guillotined.
43. Alfred de Musset (1810–57) , renowned French romantic poet.

neither that of the masters, nor that of the servants," I said; "I just stick to what's right; however, if you want me to, I'll give you the money which you lost on my account," and I left. She later asked the maid what I had said, and she said, "Nothing." A few hours later Mme Ruit came to apologize to me. However, the matter did not pass quite without some quixotry. Léonie, in order to get some money from the land-lady, had said that I had not given her anything, that there was a lot to do and a great mess in my room, and that I was the most troublesome and pampered person.

Today U[tin] was here, and we had a great discussion about love, in connection with A. K. The conversation started as he saw her portrait at my place. I argued with him, stood up fervently for V., proving that there may have been some valid reasons for why he was separated from her. I said that it was unfair to demand of a young man that he answer for himself as well as for others. He denied this, saying that he ought to have married her and then, perhaps, get separated immediately after, once he no longer loved her, or he should have provided for her. I like this! In the first case, it means that a young man should, on account of this, renounce hap-piness and love forever, for you cannot marry for a second time. And provide for her?—this would mean that a poor man must not love.

I am leaving Paris for some little French town. I am tired of social lies, I want to be entirely alone—I'll see the truth; this way I am alone, yet at times it seems as if I weren't alone, as if I were involuntarily waiting for something, and hoping, and worrying.

I would like to be closer to Nature. She rewards everybody alike, refusing her gifts to no one. I would like to settle down on the seashore, that would be more grandiose.

Montagnard was somewhat perplexed by my decision. U[tin], too, a little bit. My physician took it with complete indifference, but after I had twice referred to my departure in positive terms, he asked, "Are you really going to leave?" What a question! As if I were making riddles for him. Alkhazov said he was glad for me, my . . .

21 January

Yesterday I had dinner at the Hotel fleures [*sic*]. They talked about a woman who had hanged herself, mentioning details about how the cord was pulled tight. "Who was it who pulled it so tight? her husband, most likely," Mme Verncille [?] remarked.

Today I underwent a medical ordeal. I sought the advice of my physician regarding a good place to go and mentioned Spain, Valencia. "Go ahead to Valencia," he said; "I am also thinking of going there. All you'll have to do is write me." I was puzzled. "That's a luxury," I said, just to say something. Then, not paying much attention to his offer to join me, I changed the subject, suggesting that he become my physician "from his beautiful remoteness."[44] He agreed and offered to give me a letter of introduction to a doctor.

He suggested that we have our lesson in a few hours, but when he came he suggested that we postpone it, finding me rather weak.

After he had left, [I thought] of my grandiose promenade to Spain . . .

26 January

Yesterday my physician was here and gave me my lesson. We chatted as usual. As I was showing him Katenka's picture, I said: "There's a beautiful girl for you." But he did not like her very well, saying that his ideal of feminine beauty was the Venus de Milo. I said that the latter expresses sensuality. He does not find that this is so, saying that she is so proud.

The day before yesterday, as I was returning from dinner in the evening, I got to thinking about the planter and wondered if he was living where I had been told he was living. I turned into the rue Racine as I was passing the Odéon.

44. A quotation from Gogol's *Dead Soul*.—Translator

Getting to the rue Cornel I ran into him, walking with a lady.
It was quite dark there, and I wondered if it was really he. I
turned around several times, and so did he. When I turned
around for the last time, he was standing there with the lady.
My heart pounded like mad; I crossed the street and walked
up the steps of the Odéon. Under the arches, where they
usually sell books, it was dark. I stole closer to him, like a
thief, so I could stand across from him and watch him. By
that time he and the lady had crossed the street and were
walking under the arches on the side where they sell newspapers and where it was lighted. I followed him involuntarily, watching him in the crowd at a distance. He kept
walking and walking along the rue Vaugirar, and I kept
following him. I was still in doubt whether it was really he.
I caught up with him near the Luxembourg and was now
walking in step with him. I wanted to see the face of the
lady, but I didn't succeed. I only noticed that she was a
blonde. He was saying very little to her. There was another
gentleman walking with them, on the planter's side. I could
hear nothing of their conversation. As they got to the rue M.,
the planter turned around. Here I could see him well. He
must have noticed me, but I don't know whether he recognized me; I don't think he did. He had turned around without any visible reason (the power of magnetism, I suppose?).
I fell behind a little. I was seized by shame and grief. I did
not know whether I ought to keep walking, or turn back. I
stopped, some kind of power kept pulling me forward, and
I went on. But where, and why? I stopped again, seeing that
passersby in this thoroughfare were looking at me. "Mme,
what are you looking for?" some man asked me. "Go away,
leave me alone," I answered sharply.

I turned into the dark rue M. and then returned home. My
first thought was to go to the Hôtel du Méd[ecin] and find
out for sure if he lived there. But somehow I could not bring
myself to go there all by myself, and therefore I went to the
Countess's, hoping to find Utin there, or simply to ask Salias
himself to accompany me.

I was terribly excited, talked a kind of silly nonsense, and

finally said that I was going home. Usov offered to walk with
me if I would wait a little, but I said that I had to go right
away. The Co[untess] asked Usov to stay, saying that I could
walk home by myself, since it was only 9 o'clock, but I said
that I was particularly anxious to have someone accompany
me a short distance, and that he could then return. Now
Utin more insistently volunteered to come with me. I tried
to be as calm as I could. "Why do you want to be escorted
a short distance?" he asked. "Because I have to drop in at a
certain place. I have to find out the address of one gentleman," I answered casually, and began to talk about his story
and about my trip.

He started asking me who the gentleman was. I answered
evasively, and he soon began telling me that I was about to
do something foolish, etc. However, we went into that house.
He did not want to ask, so I had to do it myself.

"There is no such name known here," the landlord
answered me rather rudely.

"Well, how did you make out?" U[tin] asked me.

"Oh, nothing, I'll know tomorrow," I answered. Then he
scolded me some more; I made excuses, talking some terrible
nonsense in a very lively fashion.

"You are terribly excited," he told me.

"Yes," I answered and suddenly broke off our conversation, released his arm, and walked away.

And yesterday, as I was saying good-bye to my physician,
I told him that the address of C. which he had got for me
was wrong. He offered to find out, since he was seeing him
every day. And today, as I was on my way to the Countess's,
I suddenly met him in the rue de Médecine. I did not expect
it. Somehow I became embarrassed and lost my composure;
I even blushed all over. I did not look at him, but he seemed
somehow bolder, more self-confident. Poor heart! . . .

It seems that he has grown more handsome. His upper lip
is now covered by golden down, which gives a stamp of
manliness to his unusual, energetic face. What a good face
it is! There is some youthful power in it that is unaware of
itself.

28 January

Yesterday at dinner Usov suggested that we go to the théâtre Babineau, and the four of us went there: I, he, our landlord, and Nikalopoulo. That theater presents some awful filth! Dirty things are said on stage and the actresses make gestures which one is embarrassed to look at. It is a mixture of filth, stupidity, and a soldier's insolence. The public, consisting of working women, for the most part laughed heartily. What is so infectious here is not so much the filth itself, as its boldness and success. If I had seen such a picture in [illegible word], it would have been understandable, but in public, in a theater! A crowd of students got into our box, in which Usov and I sat in the front row. They behaved with extreme familiarity: they stamped mercilessly, shouted, made loud remarks to the actors. Usov assured me that they would be ejected, but all that happened was that the usher gave them a warning. During the intermission U[sov] suggested that we go to a café. What scenes there! A terrible dissoluteness and familiarity appear in everything and everybody. Next to us sat two young men, both looking consumptive. They were playing cards. At the side of one of them a lady was sitting, absent mindedly drinking something from a cup. From time to time she turned toward her neighbor, putting her hand on his shoulder. He, as though half-awake, would then turn around and pat her cheek. On the other side another lady, this one wearing a hat, sat surrounded by men and reading *Petit journal*. The gentleman who sat across from her, with whom she seemed to be on more familiar terms, kept turning toward her and kissing her hand. These ladies are so ugly and so dull. The proprietress came running to our table with extraordinary familiarity. Putting her hand on mine and bending down to us, she said that she would serve our beer right away. And in the theater I noticed how one young man made the acquaintance of a lady who was sitting next to him. During the intermission he was talking with her, looking her in the face, and adjusting her shawl.

Lucrace is zealously courting Mme Verneille, but how stupid and insolent this courtship is. He strikes a picturesque pose at one side, where the others can't see him, and keeps his lovesick eyes fastened on her; or he sits in the dark room next to the dining room when dinner is about over, and fastens his eyes on her from there.

Today my physician gave me my lesson. My nerves were upset, and several times during the reading I nearly started crying. It seemed to me that he was moved, but probably he was unable to determine the cause of my agitation. At first I was sitting on the sofa, and he by the fireplace, but when somebody began to play the piano at the neighbors', he moved up rather close to me, leaning his elbows on the sofa, so that when somebody knocked (it was the landlady's niece), he moved back a bit. But I was not looking at him, and therefore I could see neither his pose, nor the expression of his face. When we had finished, he asked when he should come back. I suggested Tuesday, but he promised to come on Monday, to find out about my health.

I started to say something about my trip to Spain. He said that, to go there, I did not need a visa at all. I asserted that this was not true. "You know everything that has to do with Spain," he remarked (no, I knew very little; if I had known enough, things would be different). However, he did not give me the planter's address. I'll ask him next time. He said, speaking of my trip, that it was a good thing to do, that he would like to visit those parts himself.

I will tell him that the landlady's niece is not greatly taken with him, but that I told her that he is a nice man, only given to womanish whims.

Saturday, 4 February

The other day I got off the bus near the Palais Royal. A little girl approached asking me to buy some buttons from her. I gave her some money and refused to take any buttons, but she insisted that I take them. I took the buttons and gave her some more money, but she again started forcing her buttons on me, which I again refused.

"Enough, she doesn't need any more buttons, leave her alone," the conductor, who was standing nearby, intervened. Then, turning to me, he explained that this girl never accepts money for nothing, giving her credit for it.

Today my physician was here. He had come to say good-bye and to give me his last lesson, but it turned out that we were going to see each other again. He was downcast, and left without having finished the lesson, saying that he was ill.

"I can see that," I answered; "what's wrong with you?"

"I don't know myself."

"Have you caught a cold, or didn't you sleep well?"

"I couldn't sleep, I slept badly. Any time I can't sleep there is some reason for it, but this time there wasn't any."

I said nothing, and we parted as usual.

"You'll surely come on Monday?" I asked him. "Oh yes, I still must get that address for you." (Just for that?) He was speaking of Cor.'s address, but I pretended that I thought he was referring to the address of that doctor in Montpellier.

Earlier, when he was here, I had told him that now, the next time we met, he would have to take second place, as my doctor, while my sister would take first place.

"I will be jealous," he said; "I have a right to that, at least."

Utin was just here. He spoke very sincerely. I told him that one could become infatuated with him, but that one could not love him. He became very interested in this and kept pestering me for an explanation why this was so.

"How is that to be explained? . . ."

"You are a strange man," I said, and stopped.

He again insisted that I explain it to him.

"I was just talking nonsense."

"Well, never mind, a fuss about nothing!"

"I wanted to ask why you don't come to see me more often. It is very simple: you have things to do, and finally, there's the honeymoon with Salias."

"Don't you want to find a more profound reason?" he asked.

I started making fun of that, and he said that what he had said with silly.

"No, I know why you don't see me more often."

"Well, then, is there a reason deeper than those you have mentioned?"

"Yes . . . maybe."

He insisted that I tell him.

"The reason is that not much attention has been paid to us [you]."

He protested against that.

"This is very understandable," I said. "Why go to see a woman? There isn't much interesting about me, is there? If you are looking for intellect and erudition, you won't come here to find them."

He said, in a facetious vein, that he was interested in the Spanish woman. "Didn't you see me talking to her by the fireplace?" I said that I had seen it, but that I hadn't been in society much, so I didn't know the difference between a courtship, being in love, and just being polite. He asked me why I had left so early. I explained it very simply, saying that it was not early for me, and that I wasn't feeling well.

Then he asked whether I was in correspondence with D[ostoevsky], and why I wasn't going to marry him, that I really should take him in hand, and his *Epoch,* too.[45]

"Because I don't want to," I answered.

"Why not?"

"Well, very simply, if I wanted to, I would be there, instead of going to Montpellier."

"Well, maybe it is he who won't marry you," he said, facetiously.

"Maybe," I answered.

To take in hand his *Epoch!* As if I were some Iphigenia!

Montpellier, 8 March

People here are very kind, but they have the most terrible

---

45. *Epoch* was a journal edited by Dostoevsky and his brother Michael It ran from March 1864 to June 1865.

prejudices. When I was sick, the landlady kept sitting at my bedside and offered her services for all kinds of things; the maid kept running herself off her feet doing my errands, which she imposed on herself, and inquired, at every opportunity, whether there wasn't something else she could run and get for me. I like the plain, uneducated people here better than the educated. It is here as everywhere: the uneducated people are ready to accept everything: the reprehensible as well as the good. They respect courage, though they want no part of it themselves, while the educated think that they already know everything, that they have reached everything, and are surprised by nothing. The provincials hate the Parisians, and this hatred reaches comic extremes, something like the hatred of the French for the English. Yesterday Gaut[46] told me that all great minds and talents have come from the provinces, that Parisians are fools; he could prove to a Parisian that a book was not a book but a tree, and the Parisian would agree with it. There is something spiteful, and at the same time fearful, about my teacher's hatred. He and Monsieur Chancel love and respect me; they speak of freedom and justice: all this is to the good, but what do they then say? "Believe me, all this isn't as terrible as it would seem to you."

"Yes, yes, one must be a philosopher," they say.

"A little," I answer.

"No, a lot."

They like to see others act freely, but they won't do it themselves. They love freedom platonically.

Mme O[garev] is a very strange woman. One time she wants women to live apart from men, so as not to let all the petty troubles of a household interfere with family life, and permit them to meet only during their hours of leisure (isn't that like a seraglio?); then again she will say that women should not get married at all, and, in particular, that passions should not exist; another time she wants to emigrate from Europe and form a brotherhood, but there's nobody to

46. Jean Baptist Gaut (1819–91), French poet. Principal work is *Sounet, Souneto et Sounaio* (1874).

go with yet. She keeps trying to convince H[erzen] that he
ought to get naturalized and write brochures for the French.
Today, at last, it seems that we managed to put some sense
into our conversation. I said that one ought to be useful in
some way, even if it was no more than teaching one muzhik
how to read. She tried to prove that there was no use in that,
because so far the muzhik had nothing to read, so he would
forget how to read, since there were no books available to
him. Turgenev was of no use to him, being incomprehensible
to him. Kol'tsov[47] was the only one he would understand,
but you couldn't get very far on Kol'tsov.

"So this means that the people must write their own
books."

"No, not that. What is necessary is that civilized [illegible
word] create a model society, in which people would not get
married in church, nor have their children christened; they
ought to write books for the Russian people (those who have
not forgotten the Russian language)."

"But how will you create such a society? I'm afraid nobody
will ever join it."

"But what about Luginin and Usov?"

I asked to be considered a candidate. But what am I going
to do, if Luginin and Usov happen to be there, too?

Then she asked me to get some poison for her through my
doctor. I, being the unprejudiced, humane, and educated
person that I am, promised her that I would do it, but I did
not know how to approach my doctor with that kind of request; it was too embarrassing. She got it through her doctor,
ahead of me, her doctor being a fool who did not understand
a thing.

Today a funny thing happened to me.

As I was out with Mme O[garev], to rent a flat, I met a Pole,
no longer a young man, who, hearing us speak Russian,
accosted us. And the day I moved, he came in to see me, with
no reason whatsover, as my door was open. I received him
coolly, and did not see him for about two weeks.

47. Alexey Vasilievich Kol'tsov (1808–42), Russian poet who drew on
the literary tradition of folk songs.

Today I ran into him on the stairs and greeted him, I think, first. He responded happily to my greeting and asked if he could introduce me to his wife.

I met an elderly lady in a small room.

As he was introducing me, I felt ill at ease right away.

"Mme," I began, "though I am a Russian . . ."

"But . . . a liberal," said the Pole.

"I do not share the opinions . . ." I continued.

"Of Mur[aviev],"[48] said the lady for me; "yours is not a Russian soul."

"Excuse me," I said, "always Russian." And here I sensed the whole absurdity of this acquaintanceship, and hurriedly changed the subject.

Montpellier, 24 April

The other day Hault [*sic*] and I had a rather nice conversation. He said that Russian women were more pleasant and better than Russian men, the same being true of Italian women also. He said that every Italian political leader has a woman sitting somewhere without fail, she being his inspiration. "I am in correspondence with many Russian women," he said, "but why is it that even the flightiest and most frivolous among them are still sad inside?"

He says that the Russian nation does not promise at all the kind of development Herzen and others expect of it. That Russia, too, had her own civilization and is, in this regard, equal to the other countries of the West, that in the French people also, there is a lot of untapped power.

Then he laughed at contemporary Fr[ench] youth, their reasonableness, and spoke of his own generation, how they had so much élan and enthusiasm in their day.

Yesterday he talked about Italian and Spanish women being so free that a young woman, at an evening party in

48. Mikhail Nikolaevich Muraviev (1796–1866), a government official who was responsible for the pacification of Poland during the uprising of 1863.

her house, would spend most of the time with a man she
liked. All this would be noticed and found natural. Everybody would go home, and he would stay. She would undress
in his presence, even go to bed. And all this is done quite
freely, frankly, and without any abuses.

Yesterday I was at the fair, which has just started here. It's
just marvellous. All kinds of show booths, swings. Some
evening Mme Chancel's niece and I will also go swinging.
And those show booths! *Théâtre de pation, Chiens et singe
savants,*[49] etc. [*sic*] And the clowns! There is one most interesting girl who danced on a platform. She danced with grace
and animation. Later she handed out tickets, showing her
rare good nature. All kinds of sinewy hands were stretched
out toward her from the crowd. With what friendliness she
smiled and nodded to those whom she knew! With what
liveliness she grabbed a huge, ugly dog, kissing its muzzle.
There was another, younger girl standing next to her, resembling her and wearing the same costume (she was more
serious and looked more like a boy).

Montpellier, 6 May

The other day I had an operation, which upset and frightened me, especially since the doctor did not warn me before.
Feeling that I was being cut, I got frightened, and, thinking
that he was going to cut me some more, I begged the doctor
to stop it, but as he refused to stop, I felt sure that he was
going to do some more cutting. The pain, the fear, and the
hurt at his having performed the operation without telling
me, upset me in the extreme. I cried and sobbed. This greatly
embarrassed and moved the doctor. He consoled me and
nearly kissed my hands, and I embraced him, I think. I soon
recovered my composure, and when I was lying on a sofa a
few minutes later, tired and chagrined, resigned, and silent,
he took my hands, seeking to console me, and came so close
to my face that I felt embarrassed and turned away.

49. "Dogs and clever monkeys."

(He told me, with satisfaction, that he wouldn't cut or burn me anymore. This announcement made me feel very glad and grateful.)

He said, as he was putting away his instruments, that after this operation I could have children if I got married. I said that I found no comfort in this. "Why so?" he asked; "all women want to have children." "Because I don't know how to bring them up," I said. The thoughts which occurred to me in connection with this conversation made me sad and caused me to shed tears, which I did not hold back.

On the following day I met him calmly and submitted to his directions with my usual confidence; but when he started torturing me again, I thought for some reason, that he was going to cut me again. Despite his assertions that nothing was going to happen to me, I continued to beg him anxiously that he should leave me alone. My Aesculapian took umbrage at this and said: "You are refusing to accept a medical man's word of honor." There was something in his tone which reminded me of my physician, when he once responded to my remark that if we were to lock ourselves in together, we might "suffer for the sake of justice," that this would, indeed, mean "to suffer for the sake of justice."[50] "Because all people are not Machiavellians," I answered my Aesculapian, and we made up right there.

Yesterday Gaut was here and I had a sentimental discussion with him: on love, marriage, etc. Gaut gave me a lot of equivocal talk; it seemed to me that he was trying to sound me out, inquiring how many times I had been in love and whether I was cured of my last love. I answered him that not quite, yet. Then he asked, in a roundabout way, how I intended to arrange my future life, and advised me to get married, although only the other day he had spoken out against marriage. Throughout this entire conversation he mixed in all kinds of stories and witticisms, and in conclusion suggested that I rely on him, if I should need any advice, etc.

He told me some time ago that though marriage was a

50. A quotation from Gogol's *Dead Souls,* ironic of course.—Translator

useful institution, it was no good for some people, especially those who had known the taste of freedom; that marriage was good for a man who owned property and was engaged in agriculture, but that a man who supported himself by mental work, who wanted to see and learn a lot, should not be tied down. "And love," he said, "passion, what are they? Just a needless scandal. Engage yourself in literature, surround yourself with sensible people, that's all."

I agreed with him. And then, on the next day, my teacher, who adores his young wife and their child, told me that happiness could be found in love only. They are all contradicting each other. Whom should I listen to? Yesterday Gaut told me that I ought to get married, only not for passion; that I ought to select a man with mental, moral, and physical qualities, and with a position in society.

Perhaps he is right, perhaps, if I got married in this fashion, I would not be too far removed from his program for an intellectual life; but be this as it may, and no matter what the meaning of his words might be, I shall not surrender cheaply.

Tuesday, 17 May

"Life is a most amusing joke, once you have tried it. You look, and you see that it's bad. But then you think, no, that isn't it, I've been too rash, too quick, and the next time a man will no longer be either rash or quick," says Gaut. "And you, like everybody else, you'll deceive others, and will be deceived by them."

27 [May]

Today Gaut explained to me why the houses on Espelani are so low. It is because they are across from the citadel built during the reign of Louis XIII.

Zurich 29 June

Today I watched a kind of national festival, a meeting of riflemen. The first to tell me about it was the old man who works in the circulation department of the library, as I was leaving there. Then, when I went down, I met Verigo,[51] who explained it to me and offered to watch it with me. This gentleman has been somehow especially attentive toward me for a long time, ever since I arrived here. Once, at tea, when I ordered wine and was served water instead, I did not want to embarrass the waitress but to show her that it was exactly what I had wanted, but I did not know what to do with the water, since I did not feel like drinking it at all. Then, he boldly poured himself a full glass, gave me an expressive look, and drank it off at one draft. Fortunately, no one saw it. Today, having had our fill of watching the riflemen and then the mountains, we went for a cup of tea together. As we were leaving the dining room after tea, I suggested to [Miss] Kniazhnin that we take a walk. She joined me and said that V. would be coming with [us], but that he needed to drop in at his laboratory first; we went together. In the laboratory, he showed me all kinds of things, some very beautiful substance, and then he produced some artificial lighting. I kept begging him not to do anything dangerous, saying that I was a coward. He said that there was nothing dangerous about it. I believed him and stayed next to him, whereas [Miss] K[niazhnin], a chemist, ran away, and when there was a bang, I grabbed his hand and drew back quickly.

Zurich, 27 June

One day we were all at the riflemen's festival. At a station along the way, some children who had missed their train were crying. I watched them with some anxiety. A young

51. Aleksandr Andreevich Verigo (1835–1905), a chemist and professor at Odessa University.

man who was sitting across from me said, to reassure me, that he would soon move to a different carriage. I have constant arguments with the girls; when we were in Geneva it was the same way . . .

Yesterday, as I was telling them about some Americans who travel all over Europe on foot, they said that this was stupid, that it was unnecessary to know a country, or to see its sights. After that, I wanted to leave, but it did not work out, and why, really? . . . The wife of my neighbor, the doctor, keeps talking about the natural sciences, but tolerates only inferior painting. She says that there is nothing in historical painting, and that no one can understand it. Who, then, can understand a person who does not understand grief [illegible] of whom my Spanish friend made a drawing?

"How do you mean that, you can't study a country?"

"Of course, without the natural sciences you can do nothing."

Zurich, 30 June

Yesterday Lidenka and I went for a walk. She keeps talking about her nonsense; I regret that I argued against it. She asked me to stop and look at some pictures. I pointed the Venus de Milo out to her, and she turned away disdainfully, meaning that this was art, which must be rejected, whereas views of Switzerland on penny postcards—there you have your famous nineteenth-century women. "Hey, you, son-of-a-bitch, kamarinsky muzhik."[52] *Rien n'est sacré pour un tapeur.*[53]

Spa, 17 September 1865

I arrived here only yesterday, coming from Paris, which I left for good, having stayed there en route for three weeks.

52. The first line of a popular Russian song, proverbial for its vulgarity.—Translator
53. "Nothing is sacred for a chronic borrower."

I won't say that it was easy for me. Usov offered to escort me to the railway station, and I accepted his offer very gladly: I was afraid of being alone during those last minutes. And so, I have left Paris, I have torn it from my heart by the roots, and I think that I have acted honestly toward myself, and with resolution. In the evening of the day before yesterday I cried desperately, and I had not thought that I would have the courage for those tears. Yesterday I arrived here, very tired, flung myself on my bed and for the first time after the three weeks in Par[is] slept soundly and peacefully. As I woke up, I saw a clear sky, and greenery, with joy . . .

Along the way I thought of my future and decided that I should live in a prov[incial] to[wn], have my own circle, organize a private school on the model of antiquity, but not in Petersburg, for it is better to be important in the country, etc., not [just to exist] in the country and die of boredom. In this way, the wolves will eat, while the sheep stay healthy.[54] That's decided, then. Stand still at this point and stick to this line.

I'll tell what happened in Paris. Having arrived, with my sister, I called for my physician, without any particular end in mind, moved simply by my desire to see him. He came immediately. I was on the balcony when he came in. My sister was in our room. Hearing somebody come, I turned around and at first failed to recognize him. Having recognized him, I quickly walked up to him and cordially stretched out [my hand to him]. We spoke of all and sundry. I told him about Gaut, told him that I was going to live with my cats and plant potatoes myself, inasmuch as flowers won't grow in Russia. Then he came another time and disappeared for a week. Finally, he showed up, saying that he had been ill. We talked about important people and about art; however, my sister and I did most of the talking. He sided with me rather than with her. I felt so sick and tired of these conversations that I ran out, letting them finish the talk. During all these visits he kept looking for an opportunity

54. A Russian proverb suggesting a happy compromise.—Translator

to speak to me alone, but I did not want to and my sister never left us alone. Once in the evening he asked what kind of a balcony we had and went out to take a look, but I did not follow him. Then he came on the following day. I told him a bit of news, my eyes red with weeping. When he came the next time, I was very sad; I had decided to leave and was writing him a letter asking him to come to say good-bye. He noticed that I was upset; I said that I was not quite myself and for a long time could not tell him the reason. He kept pestering me, asking if he couldn't help in any way, saying that he was ready to do anything for me, but I refused; finally I said that I was leaving. He [asked] when, etc.

"Since I am not going to see you, and you won't let me hear from you . . . " he started. I sat down by the window, sad and resigned.

"Strange thing," he said. "Sometimes people are like children, now looking for each other, now hiding again, as in some fairy tale. There he is, looking, while she is hiding; there, again, it is she who is looking—and so they never find each other."

Then he walked up to me, agitated, and stretched out his hands. I gave him mine. A familiar fire ran through my veins, but I was holding his hands firmly and did not let him come near me. He was all excited and was devouring me with his eyes.

"Sit down," I said to him, in a gentle and sad voice.

"No," he answered abruptly, pressing my hands convulsively.

"Sit down," I repeated.

"I'll sit down, if you'll sit down," he said.

We sat down on the sofa, our eyes met, and we embraced. We sat like that for about two hours. His arms were around my waist, and I pressed his head to my breast. I stroked his hair and kissed his forehead. We talked all kinds of light-hearted nonsense, no worries or doubts of any sort entered my mind. Then I drove over to the Co[untess's]. He accompanied me. As we were sitting in the carriage hand in hand, I felt that his love was not a good one, if this can be called love. We got up. We parted in the park. Having walked a considerable distance I turned around and saw him standing there, following me with his eyes, but it was a farce, and an awkward one, in fact. He came the next night. There was no limit to his rapture and passion, and I surrendered to these moments without any anxiety or doubt.

He wanted more than that, but I wouldn't let it happen, and he saw his mistake. I said that I was leaving. My departure was postponed only until the following day, a Thursday. He came on the next day, that is, Wednesday, showed himself remorseful and apologized for what had happened. He said that he is incapable of love, that he was not created for it, that he wouldn't want any circumstances or feelings to govern his life, etc., etc.

I postponed my departure for another day, until Friday; on Thursday I expected the Countess, who had promised to see me to the station. I was at her place on the morning of that day. For a farewell, she gave me some friendly, motherly advice. Tired of strange people, who were all trying to take advantage of me, each in his own interest, I was deeply moved. "Don't forget God, Polinka," she said, "that will give you strength; without that, you'll be in a bad way. You see where people get to without it . . . " I could not restrain myself, but dropped on my knees before her and began to sob aloud. She was frightened and wanted to get me a glass of water. "No, no," I said, "forget it; I feel good this way." And I was sobbing on her breast and kissing her hands.

"I am too unhappy," I told her.

"Polinka," she answered, "who isn't unhappy? just ask if there is a single happy woman among those who have loved."

On Thursday she came to my place, and we had another farewell scene, which upset me so much that I fell ill and was forced to postpone my departure another day.

He came in the evening, on Thursday. Usov was there, at my place. Usov wouldn't leave, and he had to go away without seeing me alone.

"I am not saying good-bye to you yet," he said as he left, "I hope to see you tomorrow."

"I don't know whether you will find me still here," I said to him, rather coolly.

"Well, I shall try to see you somehow," he said rather insistently.

He came in the evening of the following day. I was glad, nor did I conceal it. I greeted him cheerfully and asked him to sit down, thinking that he would sit down not on a chair, but next to me. I was sitting on the edge of the sofa, with its other half blocked by the table. He asked me to move a bit on the sofa, so there would be some space for him near me. I did that. He took my hands, I said that I still did not know if I was going to leave on the next day, since I still felt ill. He suggested that I stay. I said that I would be staying at Spa, waiting for some money. He asked why not in Paris. Tea was served. Casually, I offered him some. He was almost going to accept. "All right, let's play the role of cool heroes," he said.

"Why keep wringing your hands?" I retorted.

He was stung to the quick by my reticence. I drank up my cup alone. He began to say something.

"Listen," I began, "why did you, at the time when I was sad, express your readiness to help and to do anything to straighten out the thing, if ever possible?"

"I was ready to do anything."

"Well, what did you do?"

"I thought that I would help you with my sympathy, my understanding."

"I never begged for your charity!"

"My God, what terrible words you're saying!"

"Why did you go this far, if you don't love me?"

"I went as far as my love and my feeling for you told me to go, but I was quite wrong. I thought that I was going to help you, and I made it worse. I thought that I would be loved, without anything being demanded of me, that I would be loved the way I wanted: today I want it this way, so it will be this way, tomorrow I'll want it different, and that's what it is going to be. It is always that way in love. There's one who loves, and there are others who are loved.

"But what egoists all people are! Everybody loves only for his own sake. I had thought that you had some feeling for me, but I was wrong."

I was struck by his words. He wanted to take my hands, but I would not let him.

"Leave me alone," I said; "sit further away, go away."

"What does this mean?" he said; "why is this, you loved me before, didn't you? I haven't changed a bit."

"You are saying terrible things."

"What is it, then, I told you?"

"To approach a woman like this, without loving her."

"Oh, my God, but aren't these all merely conventional phrases? How often another man, in my place, would have said that he loved you? I like you very much in many respects, and we shouldn't hate the people who love us."

"Go away, go away," I said.

"Why? What's so terrible about what I said?" And he kept pestering me with these questions, but I was unable to say anything. I turned away, moved over to the side, while he was trying to justify himself. My heart was heavy, I wanted to justify him in my own eyes.

"My God, what is this?" I said; "either I am sick, or I want to deceive myself." I impetuously took his hands and burst into tears. "Embrace me as firmly as you can," I told him, "and then go." I wanted to forget myself for one minute, to think that he loved me.

"Shall I come to see you tomorrow?" he asked.

"No, don't," I answered, bathed in tears, "I'm leaving tomorrow."

I pushed him away, then drew him to me again, crying bitterly.

"Kiss me," he said.

"No, no."

"I'll come tomorrow."

"Don't."

"Let me kiss your hand."

"No, no."

And we parted. I kept on crying for a long time, and I felt worse than before, but I decided to leave, and I left.

At that time of grief and despair I thought a lot about Gaut, and perhaps this thought, the certitude of his friendship, sympathy, and understanding, saved me. Sure of it, I felt as though I stood outside this wretched life and was capable of rising above it. Only here I came to appreciate the true value of the friendship and respect of people who go beyond common standards, and in the security of this friendship I found courage and self-respect. Will my pride ever desert me? No, this couldn't be. I'd rather die. Better die of grief, but free, independent of things external, true to one's convictions, and return one's soul to God as pure as it was, rather than make concessions, even for a moment allow oneself to be touched by base and unworthy things, but I find life so coarse and so sad that I bear it with difficulty. My God, is it always going to be this way! Was it worth while to have been born!

Petersburg, 2 November

Today F[yodor] M[ikhailovich] was here and we argued and contradicted each other all the time. For a long time now he has been offering me his hand and his heart, and he only makes me angry doing so. Speaking of my character, he said: "If you were to get married, you'd begin to hate your husband three days later, and leave him." Remembering Gaut, I said that he was the only man I knew who did not try to get somewhere with me. He said, in his usual manner: "This Gaut may have been trying it, too." Then he added: "Some day I am going to tell you something." I began pestering him to tell me what. "You can't forgive me that you gave yourself to me, and so you are avenging yourself; that's a feminine trait." This upset me very much. While A. Osip. was present, he asked me to come to the theater with them. I said: "I'm not going to the theater with you, since I've never been there with you before; you can ascribe this whim to the reason which you pointed out to me earlier." "Are you agreeing?" he said. "What do I care? I am neither agreeing nor disagreeing with anything, but you with your subtle reasoning will of course find it necessary to think so."

Yesterday I visited with Piotr Ivanovich. He was extraordinarily kind to me.

6 November

F[yodor] M[ikhailovich] was here. The three of us, he, A. O., and I, talked for a long time. I said that I was going to become a holy woman, that I would walk through the Kremlin gardens in Moscow in my bare feet, telling people that I was having conversations with angels, etc. I talked a lot. And this O., who believes that oil flowed from the icon of the Holy Virgin and who won't eat meat on Wednesdays, said in the end: "That's exactly what Filipp Demidov said, but he later admitted that he had been talking through his hat." This struck me. The idea occurred to me how quickly and how easily one can become a source of annoyance to these people. The idea occurred to me to write a story on this theme.

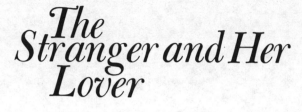

The Stranger and Her Lover

Polina Suslova

*T*he Moscow-Petersburg train flew along rapidly, new stations quickly appeared, as did new passengers, and yet Losnitsky had the feeling that the train was making only very slow progress. He was tired of the road, and understandably so, for he had been traveling for five weeks without ever taking a rest, by stagecoach, by steamship, and now, finally, by train. Losnitsky did not want to stop anywhere along the way. He raced along seeking to escape, as though it were a band of pursuers, the black depression which pursued and drove him along on his journey. He had planned on staying in Moscow for a week, but he was overcome by a terrible heartache as he saw his native city, those streets and houses which he had frequented years ago, when he had been a free and passionate youth, full of bold plans and expectations. He took a cab straight to his hotel, which he did not leave until the very hour when he could catch the first train for Petersburg. As he was driven from one end of town to the other, he looked through the window of his carriage morosely and yet timidly, while his heart ached sorely and feelings of doubt and discontent filled his soul.

Now there remained only a few more stations to Petersburg. Losnitsky turned away from his fellow travelers, who were discussing the convenience of railway travel, and looked out the window. Various thoughts were rapidly going through his mind, and there was one that came back repeatedly: "How is she going to receive me? Does she still love me? And what if she no longer loves me?" They had not seen each other for seven months. Many a change might have taken place in her during those seven months, what with her imagination, and new faces, new impressions. Could one count on the constancy of the love of a twenty-two-year-old woman, passionate and energetic as she was? What if she had fallen in love with another man? What then? Why, she would follow the other man and go away somewhere; she could go, too, for she was free. But who was he? What did he have to capture her heart? She doesn't yield it easily. He would have to be very bright, bold, young . . . And how she could love! And once she loved, she would never waver for a moment . . .

But there was the last station; the end of the journey was near; there was Petersburg. His heart was pounding, slow and hard. "A few more hours, and I shall embrace her. Right now, at this moment, I couldn't see her, it is early, and, besides, I need some rest . . ." He arrived at the hotel, placed his suitcase and traveling bag in the middle of the room, and flung his topcoat and hat on the sofa. Losnitsky paced his room with rapid steps. "I ought to get some rest, I absolutely should, I've got a headache, my nerves are in bad shape." Losnitsky lay down on the sofa, but he could not sleep; his mind wandered. "What's that noise in the corridor? Where does that squeaky female voice come from, that slamming of doors? How early they get up! And why? Who are my neighbors? The sounds of a conversation, the crying of a child, and the clatter of tea things come from their room. Should I have some tea? No, better wait, I don't want any now . . . She has probably changed. One can see from her letters that she has become more serious. That last letter was strange. She must have been under the influence of some special impression. She writes that she had been thinking of the past and had been depressed . . . Depressed about what? About there having been none, or about what had been? . . . Again people running down the corridor and the slamming of doors. Must be that somebody is leaving. But how unpleasant, how noisy it is in a hotel. And how noisy it is in the streets here. When I used to live in Moscow, on Nikitskaia Street, it was almost the same thing, yet at the same time, somehow, one did not notice it. One would get absorbed in one's books, and everything would disappear before one's eyes, with the mind alone working. And what thoughts I had then! What boldness! What ardor! Now it is no longer the same thing . . . And yet, that was not very long ago." Losnitsky tried to focus his attention upon his neighbors, who were now producing twice as much clatter with their tea things, but in vain—his mood was becoming more troubled and depressed than before. He gave free rein to the stream of his thoughts. That familiar depression had seized him with greater force. Losnitsky did not try to dispel it, either; on the contrary, in a certain irritable way, and with a kind of morbid pleasure, he was intoxicated by it. A feeling of regret about the past, a fear of losing that which was still left him, an awareness of a certain debility gripped his soul.

Time went by; it struck twelve. Losnitsky was still lying on his sofa, staring at the ceiling. Another hour went by. Losnitsky finally got up and began to get dressed. His thoughts were now concentrated on a single subject; the knowledge that the things which until now he had dreamed about so often were soon going to become reality caused his former impatience and restlessness to return. It was about two o'clock when Losnitsky found himself standing at the entrance of a rather small house in one of the remote parts of the city, ringing the bell impatiently. An old maidservant opened the door and measured him with a suspicious and displeased glance.

"Is Anna Pavlovna at home?" Losnitsky asked her.

"Yes, she is," she answered laconically and conducted him through a small antechamber into an empty drawing room. Losnitsky took a seat in an armchair by a round table and anxiously looked at the closed door leading into the interior rooms. His anxiety was rising with every moment. But this was not the excitement of a youth in whom the transition from hope to doubt will find such vivid expression, whose sufferings are so lively as to evoke sympathy; there was something strange about the excitement of a man tried by toil and suffering; in him, even an expression of joy would be somehow morbid, while doubt and sorrow, instead of giving rise to tempestuous grief would find their expression in suppressed and gloomy suffering.

Some ten minutes passed while Losnitsky sat there in complete silence. Those ten minutes seemed terribly long to him, beads of cold perspiration stood out on his forehead, his face assumed that somber, tense expression so unpleasant to look at.

But then the rustle of a woman's dress was heard in the next room, and the sound of steps; the door was quickly opened, and a young, beautiful woman entered. Her face was very pale. Anxiety and mental suffering were written on it, and there was a touch of embarrassment and shyness about her every move, but unconquerable strength and passion were also apparent in her gentle and kind features. A deep, though not always visible impression of the fateful fanaticism which distinguishes the faces of madonnas and Christian martyrs lay upon that face. For a moment all doubts and suppositions that were in Losnitsky's mind were scattered by a feeling of joy at seeing her.

He stepped forward to meet her and extended his hands to her. Carried away by a feeling of gratitude and joy, she made a move to give him hers, but then drew them back and covered her face with them.

"Anna, what is the matter with you?" he exclaimed, startled by this move.

"Why have you come?" she said, with anguish.

"Why?! What are you saying?"

He was all eyes as he looked at her, seeking to make out the meaning of her words, while a realization of that meaning was already affecting his heart with insufferable pain. She took his hand and led him to the sofa, on which they sat down next to each other. For a while they remained silent.

"Didn't you receive my letter, the one in which I wrote

you that you shouldn't come?" she began, without looking at him, but holding his hand firmly.

"I shouldn't come? . . . Why?"

"Because it is too late," she uttered, abruptly.

"Too late!" Losnitsky repeated mechanically, as everything went dark before his eyes. He did not say a word for some time.

"Anna," he began, after a long and heavy silence, "I must know everything, tell me everything, if you don't want to kill me."

"Yes, yes, you are right," she said, struck by his grief and by a certain inner bewilderment; "you and I must talk everything over, and as soon as possible, but not here, because my aunt may come in at any moment. Shall we go to your place, where are you staying?"

And, without waiting for his reply, she left the room and returned a few minutes later, wearing her hat and mantilla. They left the house. The carriage which had brought Losnitsky was waiting at the entrance. They got in and drove away. It was a rather long way, along the main thoroughfares. Losnitsky and Anna remained silent the whole time. The young woman sat motionless, looking out of the window and without once releasing his hand. Her face was pale, yet calm and serious. Leaning back in the corner of the carriage, Losnitsky sat there looking crushed, but from time to time he quivered and pressed Anna's hand convulsively. Half an hour passed in this fashion. Finally they arrived. Losnitsky stepped from the carriage, offered his arm to his companion, and escorted her into the hotel. A servant whom they met in the corridor started to grin at the sight of the pretty young woman, but when he saw their faces, quickly turned away and slipped into his corner. Losnitsky and Anna entered the hotel room. Anna wanted to say something, but Losnitsky interrupted her.

"I have lost you!" he exclaimed and, falling to her feet, burst into tears.

The young woman comforted him gently and sadly, but

for a long time his painful sobs shattered her soft words, breaking the hearts of both.

"Well, now tell me," he said, having overcome the first fits of grief, as he sat next to her on the sofa and looked at her sad and severe face with an expression of infinite, almost fatherly tenderness.

"There's nothing to tell," she said quietly; "I love another man, that's all." He broke into convulsive laughter.

"And I, fool that I am, imagine, my dear, I was in such a hurry, thinking that I would spend the Christmas holidays with you, that I would have a good time here—that's right. But that's Fate for you, isn't it." Again he began to laugh, but a moment later his sense of grief returned to him with full force. Losnitsky sighed and released Anna's hand.

"Has it been long?" he asked after a brief silence.

"Just recently . . . unexpectedly, we have known each other ever since I arrived here, but I did not think . . . I was still waiting for you," she said quickly, turning toward him, and an expression of melancholy irony flashed across her face. "It is only since he told me that he loved me that I lost my head."

"Who is he? Is he the one you've been telling me about in your letters?"

"My singing teacher."

"That Italian?"

"Yes."

"Well, what about him—is he young, brilliant, handsome?"

"Why must you ask these questions?" said the young woman, as her cheeks flushed crimson.

"Why, indeed," he said with a smile. A few moments passed in silence. Losnitsky looked at Anna with a kind of naive, almost childlike curiosity, trying to detect any marks of the past in her. She was still the same, even her hair and her dress were the same. The only new thing he noticed was a ring she was wearing, and his attention turned to it involuntarily. "His gift to her," Losnitsky thought, and, without asking a question, merely gave her a look. She understood what he was thinking, and blushed.

"Do you love him very much, Anna?" he asked.

"Yes," she said pensively.

"I knew it, it couldn't have been otherwise, I was just asking . . . Have you given yourself to him, Anna? Does he see you every day?"

The young woman quickly raised her head. Red spots broke out on her cheeks, her eyes flashed under a frown, her whole figure changed, suddenly and sharply, transformed by anger.

"Not a word more," she whispered abruptly.

"Anna," he said fervently, clutching her hand, "you cannot suspect me of a vile thought, for I have loved you with a pure and infinite love; you know that, besides my passion for you, I also cherish you as a dear friend, as a daughter, and that your happiness is foremost in my mind."

He was sincere when he said this; she knew it and pressed his hand warmly.

"You are happy, aren't you, Anna?"

She did not answer, as though she had not heard his question, but the muscles of her face twitched slightly.

"Can it be that you are not? Oh, Anna, can that be possible? Tell me, for heaven's sake, I must know."

"I don't know," she said, barely able to suppress her agitation; "it seems to me that he does not love me very much."

"He does not love you!" Losnitsky exclaimed indignantly. "He does not love you, yet he has been seeking your love!" He clutched his head in desperation and began to run up and down the room.

"Listen, Anna," he said, almost beside himself with excitement, "why, aren't you as free as ever, even with him; you don't love him as though you were his slave, do you? No, that's impossible, I shouldn't be asking that. And how could you become so hopelessly infatuated? He must be a very good talker. Is he proud and bold?"

Anna gave a strange smile.

"He is very young," she said, "he is not fancy in his speech. When I met him for the first time, I said to myself that this man could not tell a lie, and this is true."

"What is he doing here?"

"He is still a student, and later he will go abroad."

"And you will go with him? Oh, of course, you'll follow him anywhere, to the end of the world."

"I'll join my uncle in the country," said Anna, bursting into tears.

"Oh, Anna, why are you so unhappy!"

They sat together for some time after that, talking about irrelevant matters. Anna told him about life in Petersburg, about the people she had met, asked him about former friends, and listened with great interest, although he did not go into any details. Her own opinions were somewhat harsh, for she was no model of moderation either in praise or in censure.

"You are still the same," said Losnitsky, listening to her. "You will have a hard time living with people, you get carried away too easily, you are too trustful. You will have to suffer a lot, Anna!"

"Let it be," she said; "let me be wrong again and again, I still won't stop having faith in people. There must be good and kind people somewhere."

"They are all kind, Anna! Have you ever seen any evil people? But what help is all that kindness?"

Anna raised her head and looked at him with astonished, almost frightened eyes. Then she fell to thinking and remained silent the rest of the time.

When she had left and Losnitsky was alone again, he flung himself on the sofa and lay there all evening, as if he were dead. His consciousness, having wandered about that infinite empty space which his future presented to him, finally lost itself. Black night spread out before his eyes and took possession of everything. Losnitsky was not trying to fight oblivion; on the contrary, he wanted it to last as long as possible, so that dawn would not creep up on him and strike him with the sight of that desert.

On the following day Losnitsky stayed home all day, expecting Anna, who had promised to come in the morning, but failed to come. The next morning he received a note from her, in which she invited him to her house, telling him that she was slightly ill. Losnitsky immediately went to see her. Anna received him in her room. The young woman looked a little pale and perturbed, but appeared to be in good health otherwise. When Losnitsky inquired about her health, she gave him a casual answer and quickly changed the subject. But Losnitsky was in no mood to speak of irrelevant matters and even seemed irritated.

"Better tell me about yourself," he said, "we won't be together for long."

"Why, are you leaving already?"

"What am I to do here? I came here only for your sake."

The young woman could not suppress a sigh.

"You will be writing me, Anna, just as before, won't you? We are still friends, aren't we?"

"Oh, yes," she said, stretching out her hand to him. "Why are you so gloomy?" she asked; "are you angry with me? I can't help it, can I?"

"I know, I know everything, but that is not the point. I hurt, Anna; it isn't easy for me to get rid of a feeling. I am no longer a young man, at my age one does not play with one's affections. You have meant a lot to me. Your love descended upon me like a gift from God, against all hope and expectation, when I was weary and desperate. This young life at my side promised me so much and has already given me so much. It has resurrected my faith and what remained of my former strength.

"You've really put it to good use," thought Anna, but she said nothing.

He continued:

"I had nothing left from my earlier, tempestuous life, and in you I found everything. I saw your deep devotion and thought that I was not going to outlive it. I believed in it, devoutly, unalterably, and never thought that half a year of separation might destroy everything . . . However, it is my own fault," he continued after a moment's reflection, "I got carried away too much, I forgot myself, now it is all clear to me: you never loved me. Don't give me that severe look, Anna, I'm telling you the truth. I saw your sufferings, your transports, but it wasn't I whom you loved, but someone else within me. I told you even then that I was not worthy of you. The time had come for you to love, there was nobody around, I happened to be available, and you believed that you had found what you needed. I was unable to grasp this in time, I was too blinded, too happy . . . Well, then," he continued, after a few moments of thought and as though talking to himself, "I am still ahead; I've had a year of happiness, and what happiness!"

"I must ask you for something, Anna," he continued, after thinking for a long while; "you see, my dear, my life is finished; I haven't lived it well. I never could manage myself, but now it is too late for these reflections, it's no good, there is nothing else for me to expect. You know, Anna, you are the only person I've got in the whole world. I would like to give you what is left of my life. Listen, perhaps some day I may be of some service to you, one never knows what can happen. You are only just beginning your life. Not when you are happy, but when doubt and sorrow come your way, when there is no one else close to you, will you come to me, as to a friend, as to a brother? . . ."

"Yes, yes," said the young woman, with an animation which suggested that she really considered him her friend, and perhaps her only friend. Losnitsky was moved by this. For a long time he looked at this beautiful woman, grief-stricken, yet at the same time full of a certain faith in the future and in all that she felt was beautiful and just. A deep sadness took possession of his heart.

"There is something wrong with you," he said after a long silence; "you are grieving or wondering at something."

"It's nothing," she said softly, without looking at him.

He gave her an intent look.

"Did you see him yesterday?"

"No."

"Why not?"

She gave no answer, struggling with her agitation.

"He isn't here . . . He left," she finally said, in desperation, and the tears gushed from her eyes.

"What! He left! Without saying good-bye?"

Anna quickly raised her head at this exclamation, and the tears stopped in her eyes. She gave Losnitsky a calm and cool look.

"Why should you cry, then?" Losnitsky said drily, offended by her proud gesture. "Surely he will return."

"Oh, naturally," she said with fervor, "Only I cannot understand what business he has to take care of. He was in such a hurry, he wrote me barely a few words, which make no sense to me."

"A man may have all kinds of business."

Losnitsky got up and began pacing up and down the room. Apparently he felt troubled.

"It looks strange to me, Anna," he said, finally, stopping in front of her, "very strange. In such a short time, as you say . . . And there, suddenly, he has left, for an unknown destination and period of time."

"He is very young," she said, "and besides he does not know how much I love him."

Losnitsky sighed and again started walking up and down the room.

"Good-bye, Anna!" he said suddenly, stopping before her.

"Why, are you leaving already?"

"Yes, it's time for me to go . . . I've got some business to take care of; I must write a few letters."

"Well, good-bye. Will you come tomorrow?"

"Yes."

They parted. Losnitsky returned to his hotel. His room seemed insufferably boring and repulsive to him. Unable to get down to work, or to concentrate on any thought, he just kept pacing up and down his room, then took his hat, went out and roamed the streets of the city quite aimlessly, without stopping or looking at anything. In the evening he returned, tired and downcast, lay down on his sofa and stayed that way all evening, staring at the ceiling and giving a deep sigh now and then.

On the following day Losnitsky did not want to go to Anna, but then could not restrain himself and paid her a visit in the afternoon. He found her at home and alone. She seemed sadder than usual but was trying to appear calm. Losnitsky observed her and began to feel sorry for her. It was the first time that he experienced this feeling toward her, and it annoyed him. In order to divert Anna somehow, Losnitsky suggested that they go to the opera. She immediately agreed. The music left a deep impression on Anna. The young woman became animated and reminded Losnitsky of herself as he had known her before. And once again he felt himself defeated and worshiped her.

Several days went by.

One morning Losnitsky had just awakened and was still lying in bed, when somebody knocked on his door.

"Who is there?" he shouted, without getting up.

"It is I," a soft voice answered.

Losnitsky's heart stood still.

"Anna!" he exclaimed, refusing to believe his own ears.

"Yes . . . open up quickly."

Losnitsky quickly jumped out of bed, dressed hurriedly, and opened the door. Anna entered. She removed her veil, and Losnitsky shuddered at the sight of her face. It was deathly pale and severe, the lips pressed together, the eyes looking straight ahead, but with an expression of horror and madness.

"What is the matter with you, Anna?" Losnitsky exclaimed.

"Nothing," she answered slowly, in a slightly breaking voice. "I must speak to you; you must come to my place, however, for I cannot stay here. Good-bye. Come then."

"I'll come, I'll come."

She turned around and left the room. Her sudden appearance left Losnitsky thunderstruck. For some time he stood there, rooted to the spot, racking his brains in an effort to explain it all; then he began to dress hurriedly. His hands and feet were trembling and his heart was pounding hard, when he stepped from his cab in front of the house where Anna lived. He had a foreboding of evil, but everything was peaceful and quiet in the house as before. He did not have to wait long for Anna. She entered fully dressed, though it was still very early, and seemed calm, even cheerful.

"I did not expect you to come so soon," she began.

"I rushed here because, frankly, you frightened me. I am glad that I find you so calm . . . However, who can figure you out," he added; "you are always like that."

"I've just had my breakfast," she said, feeling that her composure was beginning to desert her, and attempting to retain it. "But would you like me to get some tea for you?"

"No, thank you, don't bother."

"As you wish."

She got up and began to pace up and down the room. The muscles of her face were beginning to twitch, and a deep blush appeared upon her cheeks.

"I want to talk to you," she said, stopping in front of him and dropping her eyes; her eyebrows moved and her face began to twitch more perceptibly and frequently. She turned around and again began to pace up and down. Little by little she regained her composure, stepped up to him once more, and sat down facing him.

"A terrible thing has happened to me," she began slowly, almost solemnly . . . "I want you to explain to me what has happened. I am going to tell you everything. You know me, I want you to be my judge. You remember when we first met in that remote corner of our country, where you were stranded against your will and where I was perishing with an unloved husband, among people I could not stand. Our situation, our thoughts drew us together, each of us helped the other to become aware of himself, and, having come to ourselves, we were frightened by the condition we were in and flew into each other's embrace, for fear of being lost again. But it wasn't just despair that inspired me when I surrendered to you, and not in vain you spoke of your regeneration. I thought that I would find in it salvation, a goal, a haven, and found nothing but shame and sorrow . . ."

Here she stopped, unable to continue, overwhelmed by a flood of melancholy memories, and buried her face in her hands. The cruel bitterness of her words hurt Losnitsky deeply. He remained silent and only gazed at her intently. She continued:

"The conditions under which our relationship developed owing to the circumstances were unbearable to me because of their ambiguity, yet I could not renounce you either. I was hoping for *something* all the time; but when, with my heart outraged and my mind deeply troubled, my very health was beginning to fail, I decided to leave. I thought that a new life, new faces, would dispel my anguish, but I found everything here quite different from what I had expected it to be. I was feeling lonely, when I met *him*. This lively face was so new to me, and so full of interest, after all the conventional gestures and commonplaces I had received from the people whom I had met until then. He did not strike me either with his intelligence or with this erudition, yet everything he did and said was his own; in him I found everything that I had not found before in others: passion, boldness, simplicity. He came to see me frequently, and realizing that I appreciated his company, he came more and more often. We read together, took walks, attended the theater. I felt good with him, free and at ease. When he began to talk about love, I was very much surprised and delighted, then, surprised and frightened about my being delighted. Then I saw that I would have either to reciprocate his love or immediately part ways with him. I did not have the strength to do the latter . . . I did not demand any assurance or proof of his love, for every word, every gesture of his told me of a happiness without any mixture of anxiety or doubt. I was not expecting anything more. All I needed was that his love be sincere.

Here she stopped. Memories of the past overwhelmed her. She forgot about her surroundings, about what she had been saying. Losnitsky was observing her closely.

"Well, and then?" he said, finally.

She started, and her cheeks flushed.

"He is getting married," [she said] firmly, looking Losnitsky straight in the eye.

"Who told you?"

"I know for sure."

But Losnitsky was not surprised by this bit of news. On the contrary, he received it with perfect calm, as though he had actually expected it and was glad about such a dénouement.

"But who is going to pay for my suffering and [one illegible word] for all my sleepless nights?"

Losnitsky tried to show her how much futility and vanity there was in such a demand. His arguments had an effect on Anna, and her pride was aroused.[1]

On the following day Losnitsky found her perfectly calm. She met him with a book in her hand. She had been reading. Losnitsky was somehow disappointed this time. His reasoning was profound and resolute, yet at the same time indefinite. Neither he nor Anna touched upon things that were near their hearts. Though they were both sad, it was as though the painful sufferings of yesterday had never been. However, this was not really so. Unfortunately, Anna did not belong to that happy group of people upon whose hearts joy as well as sorrow leaves a deep impression yet also passes without a trace. No, once a thing had entered her heart, it left an indelible mark. So it was also this time: a black thought had descended upon her heart, and was burning it slowly, but surely.

Six months had passed. In a poor French village not far from some . . .[2] in a bright, clean room of a small house, buried in greenery and flowers, a young woman was lying on a sofa. Looking at that woman's face, illuminated by the unsteady glow of the setting sun, or judging by her position, it was difficult to tell whether she was asleep or dead or just

1. The following sentence is crossed out in the original text: "That same evening she wrote to the young man, whom she had met by accident the day before, returning him the ring from her hand."

2. Corrected from "A small town in southern Germany."

lost in thought. Her eyelashes were closed, her arms were firmly crossed upon her breast, her black hair covered her pillow in long tangled strands. Her face bore a strange expression: it was an expression of that calm which is acquired at the price of long suffering; there was something infinite about it—was it a resigned acceptance of her fate, or a certitude of a near future wished for [so in the original], or ultimate peace? The young woman made a move and opened her eyes; she cast a quiet glance about the room and closed her eyes again with an expression of pain and anguish. There was a light noise behind the door, and a tall, pale, lean man entered the room, stopping at the door; she raised herself slightly, and, her elbows resting on the head of the bed, gave him a tender, pensive look.

"Have you had a good rest?" he asked.

"Yes," she answered mechanically, with that same pensive expression, looking through the open balcony door into the garden, where a light breeze rocked beautiful garlands of vines between the olive trees and spread the fragrance of a southern spring, pouring forth sweetness and bliss, lulling the heart to sleep, making it forget temporarily the evil and the sorrow of life. Losnitsky approached Anna and sat down on a chair near her sofa. And while she was following the thought about what curse it might be that prevents men from taking advantage of all the gifts of this Earth, he was looking at her beautiful face and thinking of something else. Losnitsky did not take his eyes off that face, and little by little another feeling, a feeling of secret hope and joy, sweet to the point of being painful, a feeling which he didn't dare admit to himself, agitated his soul. While he was persuading her to take this trip and while he accompanied her on it, he had thought only of soothing and diverting her. But now another thought appeared which, against his will, took precedence over all others. This thought was: she is here, with me, now it is up to me to make her return to me.

"What are you thinking of?" he asked her, just to rid himself of that annoying thought.

"Thinking of what?" she repeated mechanically, still looking at the balcony door, and answered, after remaining lost in thought briefly: "I was remembering the first time I went to Petersburg, the hopes I had then, and what has come of them. I was comparing the feelings with which I arrived in Petersburg with the feelings with which I left there . . . Oh, how hard it was for me to leave Petersburg, how hard! I feel as though the graves of my loved ones were there.

"Why must you have these thoughts?" Losnitsky began with fervor; "you have your youth ahead of you, and the realization of your cherished idea; this is no trifle."

She made a move with her head, gave him no answer, and again fixed an intent gaze at the balcony door.

"The realization of your cherished idea!" This thought vaguely flashed through Anna's head, touching all the strings of her sensitive being, causing a strange movement within it; but this movement gradually died down, leading her to a clearer, conscious thought: "And so, I am free once more! There is no longer any slavish anxiety of expectation and fear, there is nothing to be feared, there is nothing to lose. My dream of happiness, which is no more than the gibberish of idle fantasy, the wretched refuge of cowards and fainthearted men, has vanished, and reality, naked reality, stands there alone, arid, hungry. Your future is open. Choose your own way."

For a long while Anna remained under the influence of these thoughts, without paying any attention to Losnitsky, as though she didn't notice that he was present.

A feeling of vexation flared up in him. Unable to control himself, he quickly got up and left the room.

"Where are you going?" asked Anna, raising her head from the pillow.

"Me? . . . ." he said, trying to conceal the emotions which were troubling him, "I thought that, perhaps, I was bothering you. Perhaps you would rather be alone."

"No, I feel better with you," she said simply, and without noticing what was going on inside him.

At these words, he quickly turned around, but then suddenly stopped and slowly walked to a chair which was standing rather far from her. She asked him to come and sit closer to her. Anna began to talk, saying what an egoist she had been until that time, how during their four months of traveling together she had been preoccupied with herself alone, and how she had actually failed to notice, so it might have seemed, his concern for her. She hastened to assure him that she knew and appreciated all that he had done for her, and that he had done much more for her than he might think. She said that their departure and the presence of a close friend, who had given her encouragement with his invigorating words, which had always held sway over her, had saved her from a terrible desperation. She added that she had wanted to tell him this for a long time, but that, somehow, she could not make herself say it.

"I didn't dare say this to you," she said, "because earlier I was often unfair to you. Once, before our departure from Petersburg, I told you that your love had brought me nothing but suffering. This was said unfairly. I was happy!" she said, with melancholy emotion.

These warm words, the very ring of emotion in her voice which, while remaining soft, would occasionally rise and sound solemn and prophetic, while she lay there with her arms crossed on her breast and with her eyelids closed, and then fall off again, expressing a deep and resolute submission to that which could not be changed, filled his heart with delight and adoration. She had long since stopped talking and was still lying there in the same attitude with her eyes closed, but he was still looking at her face, which was animated by her feeling of kindness. He meanwhile continued to be under the influence of emotions aroused in him by her words and did not have the strength either to express them or to rid himself of them.

"You know how to say a kind word, Anna," he said finally. Anna said nothing and fell back into her earlier pensive mood, while he was thinking of her alone. He was interpreting her very silence, her pensiveness, in his own favor, as an expression of something which she had failed to say in words. She made a move with her head, turning it toward the light. He jumped from his chair and lurched forward, but then suddenly stopped, embarrassed and undecided.

"What is the matter with you?" she asked calmly, looking at the ceiling.

"I wanted to move the table,[3] it isn't in the right place," he muttered.

"So go ahead and move it."

"No, it isn't necessary," he said a moment later, returning to his former place.

She said nothing.

"You don't know what just happened to me," he began a minute later, with a ring of excitement in his voice.

"What?" she asked anxiously, raising her head and fixing him with frightened eyes.

"You won't be angry?"

"What is it?"

"I just wanted to come and kiss your foot, but I stumbled over this rug, and thought better of it."

A blush of modesty appeared on Anna's noble, chaste brow, giving her face a purely maidenly expression.

"Why that?" she uttered in a leading voice and instinctively covered the end of her narrow shoe with the hem of her gay-colored frock.

"You must forgive me, Anna," said the embarrassed Losnitsky.

"Oh, yes! just don't speak about it anymore."

But Losnitsky did not find such generosity overly flattering to himself. He quickly started a conversation, of the most trivial variety, but it did not go very well; Losnitsky's glances were fixed on Anna with great persistence and passion, and he kept forgetting what he had been talking about. Anna noticed this and it made her feel uneasy. Anna got up from

3. First written "to close the window" as in the diary entry, then changed to "adjust the lamp" and finally to "move the table."

her bed, stepped to her writing desk, quickly rang and asked the servant to light a lamp, then sat down by the open window.[4]

"Will you be leaving soon?" she asked him.

"Why?"

"Just so . . . I am sleepy."

"So early"

"Yes, I feel tired for some reason."

Losnitsky approached her in silence, kissed both of her hands, and walked out resolutely.[5] Anna locked the door behind him and, without getting undressed, flung herself on her bed. She lay there for a long time, involuntarily giving thought to her situation, and troubled by certain unpleasant feelings. She finally fell asleep with them, without undressing, or even blowing out the lamp.

On the following day Anna got up very late. Losnitsky waited for her a long time in the adjoining room which divided their two rooms and served as a living room and dining room. Breakfast had been on the table for a long time, but Losnitsky did not even think of touching it. He kept walking up and down in the room, stopping from time to time to listen for any stir coming from Anna's room or simply to look out of the window. Finally Anna appeared. She was calm, as always, and majestic in a melancholy way. They sat down to breakfast, but he thought he noticed in her attitude something particularly proud and derisive. He met her with a certain embarrassment. They sat down to breakfast. All morning a certain awkwardness showed itself in Losnitsky's behavior toward Anna. Somehow he could not settle down, but Anna's simplicity and sincerity and her kind

4. The following appears in the margins: "meanwhile night had fallen and covered everything with impenetrable blackness, but the light of the moon was stealing in through the high windows, cutting through the darkness with its bright rays and in some strange and fantastic fashion mingling with it, filling it with enchantment and mystery."

5. The first version, crossed out, went this way: "I feel tired for some reason"; this was followed by: "But he did not make a move until several minutes later, when she reminded him that he should leave. 'I don't feel like leaving you,' he said with a sigh, but got up, kissed her good-bye on both hands . . . "

and trustful words put him back on the right track; and Losnitsky, though not without some sadness, yet with noble resolution, extended his hand to her.

"Anna," he said, "yesterday I was stupid and base, I am guilty before you, will you forgive me?" And Anna gladly accepted this expression of remorse and promised to forget what had happened last night, realizing how difficult it was. He assured her that he had left on this trip with her without any ulterior motive, even though he had had certain indefinite hopes; but when he had suddenly found himself alone with her, and in a totally strange place, among unknown people . . . his mind had suddenly gone blank. He promised that in the future he would be her friend, her protector, whatever she wanted him to be, and this in spite of the fact that her passion for another man and the new relationship which had developed between them as a result of the latter, had made her twice as attractive as before.

Anna believed his promise, exactly as he believed it himself, and boldly placed her hopes in the future. They spent the whole day together, taking walks and talking. Losnitsky embarked upon various abstract reflections. He let himself be carried away by this mood, particularly since it appeared to amuse Anna; he had the habit of forgetting himself in such reasoning. But this happy mood did not last long, no more than a single day, and it would be followed by boredom, vexation, and melancholy, which would alternately take possession of him.

Little by little Anna was regaining her peace of mind, as the corrosive, destructive torments of her heart turned to quiet melancholy, as she gradually returned to her former pursuits and habits. Her favorite books again appeared on her table and her favorite melodies, in her own voice, began to be heard in their quiet abode, expressing one and the same irremediable grief in different variations. Meanwhile he turned somber, irritable, or would not leave his room for entire days. Often, when he sat motionless in a corner or paced up and down the room in silence for hours, the young woman would steal a glance at him from behind her book, and her heart would be wrung with apprehension. She realized that all his love, all his efforts and cares were remaining unrewarded, and it was beginning to weigh on her mind. Once, when he was sitting in his room, his elbows propped on the table and his head bent, a tired and sad expression on his face, Anna walked by several times and looked at him through the open door. He took no notice of her, or pretended that he had not noticed her. Suddenly she entered his room and went down on her knees, so she could look him straight in the face.

"Forgive me," she said, taking his hands and fixing him with a sad gaze which penetrated into his very soul. He looked at her with feigned absentmindedness and smiled.

"Forgive me," she repeated, continuing to look at him with that same deep, gentle and loving, sadly pleading glance, through which she wanted, so it would seem, to pour forth all her soul. "I know this glance," said Losnitsky, deeply moved, and gently stroking her hair; "it is a long time since I met it last."

"Why are you so somber? Why won't you be cheerful?" she said pensively, groping for the right expression.

"Come now, what are you saying? Why am I not cheerful? Just because."

"You don't want to talk to me! You are angry with me."

"What nonsense!" said Losnitsky and sighed involuntarily.

"I am bored," he began, seriously and sadly; "everything around here is foreign, everything is hateful. I took the trip to divert you, to calm you down, to entertain you, to give your mind something to work on, and here we are, traveling for four months already, and you are still sad, and, it seems, this is all you want to do."

"Don't you know me? I've always been that way."

"You were that way, that's right, but now that you are free to go where you want, do what you want—tell me, what is it you need?"

"What? I have lost everything. I have nothing. My youth has passed without joy. I have exhausted myself in a day-to-day struggle with people and with circumstances. My strength has failed me, and people have branded me with mockery and contempt; my family has turned away from me. Where shall I go? Who needs me? What shall I do?"

"Can't you create a field of activity for yourself, and make people love and respect you? No, this is not it. There is another, more substantial reason, something that outrages me and that I cannot explain to myself. You might as well tell me that you love . . ." And he gave her an intent look.

Anna's pale cheeks flushed momentarily, but turned even paler a minute later.

"You are not saying anything . . . You do not want to refute what I just said! . . ."

Anna had in fact remained silent.

She sat there, lost in thought, either engrossed by dreams of the future, or reminiscing about the past; anyway, her thoughts were far, very far away.

"You love, so you still have hope."

"I have nothing to hope," she said.

"This is what reason tells you, but the heart has its own logic." He expected an objection on her part, but it did not follow; on the contrary, Anna got up and left. She went to her room and closed the door behind her.

Several days passed. It was a clear and quiet evening. Losnitsky and Anna were walking along a road through the fields, not far from their house. They were taking a walk. Anna was in a calm, contemplative mood; she remained silent all the way. Losnitsky also appeared to be lost in thought, but from time to time he looked at Anna's face, that wonderful face which was the image of her soul, mirroring every one of its movements. At this moment, Anna had wholly surrendered to the impact of the scene that surrounded her. Before her there stood the town, its dark gray, rather dirty coloring sharply outlined against a bright sky; the pointed domes of its churches extended high into the air and vanished imperceptibly in the shimmering expanses of space. Between them there was a huge building, half in ruins. It towered above all that stood around it, like the rapacious body of a beheaded giant, presenting its grandiose dynamic form to the wonderment of centuries. A leafy growth adorned its top and covered its disfigured limbs, reaching far out with its supple, creeping branches and trying to lock it [the building] into a delicate embrace. On the other side there stood out high, elegant in their snow caps, tinted by the delicately colored rays of the sun, the Cévennes. The pure, transparent air of the south, embracing everything around with trustful love, made their outlines appear in sharp relief; it would not hide, in a mysterious mist, from the enamored glances of men even the most remote objects.

Fatigued by the enjoyment of this sight, Anna stopped. She sat down on the ground at the edge of a hillock sharply cut in half by the road, and her whole soul flowed into her eyes . . . Her heart was filled with a marvelous calm.

"What are you thinking about?" Losnitsky, who was standing next to her, asked her suddenly.

"Oh, nothing."

"Meanwhile, I can't stop looking at you. Sometimes your face is strange, when you get lost in thought; this time, too, it changed so rapidly and so sharply . . . What a pity that you can't see your face at these moments! You haven't any idea what it is like. It is so beautiful! I now recall people's talking about your beauty. But what they say about your beauty is nothing compared to what I alone know."

"Please, don't speak about my face," Anna interrupted him.

"I knew that you would get angry, and I still said it."

"Well, enough, let us go," said Anna, getting up.

"It would seem that you even dislike my admiring you; I understand you," said Losnitsky, with bitterness.

"What an idea, yet, stop it!"

"Very well. Let's go. But where shall we go?"

"Wherever you want," said Anna, and Losnitsky detected a familiar ring in her voice: it was one of sadness, or of apathy, or both. Forgetting about himself, he took Anna's hand with particular tenderness and escorted the young woman home. She followed him almost mechanically, but the movement of his heart did not go unnoticed by her, and

Anna's heart, in turn, was filled with a melancholy tenderness. Memories of her first love, memories of her youth passed through her mind, changing to a quiet, tender melancholy. "Where has all this disappeared?" she thought. And, instead of any answer, another question came to her mind: "Could it really be true that all is finished?" And then, a whole series of further questions followed.

In the meantime they had reached home. Perhaps for the first time, Anna found it pleasant and comforting to be in her room, where owing to his care everything was arranged and adjusted to her taste and her habits. She sat down in her wide, low armchair, and he took a seat near her. She was beginning to feel free and comfortable; she turned cheerful; a stream of witty jokes, laughter, and conversation flowed from her lips, but soon she fell silent again. Losnitsky tried to support her cheerful mood. Whether it was with this in mind, or simply because he got carried away by this unexpected surge of mutual good cheer, he started telling her various anecdotes and stories from his own life. These tales might have been, perhaps, of some interest to other people, but Anna saw little wit, and even less refinement, about them. She listened seriously and in silence, but when he narrated adventures which occurred during Anna's last absence involving a certain gay lady of the city of B. and various escapades of that frivolous woman, and of a man no less frivolous in his attitude toward her, all told in a casual, cynical tone, Anna could not stand it any longer and asked him not to continue his narrative. She was struck by his tone of bravado, a tone which a certain type of men like to display, but which she had not expected from him.

Anna knew Losnitsky very little; in their earlier relations there had been so much that was serious and desperately bitter that the everyday aspect of his character, which is so very important in an intimate relationship, had gone unnoticed.

"I find your displeasure strange," said Losnitsky; "however, this is one of your perfectly feminine traits. Relations between men and women, such as I have just been telling you about, are most natural and excusable; they are even necessary. Not only do they not interfere with a true and exalted love for another woman, but they actually enhance and support it. Unfortunately, no woman is capable of understanding this . . ."

Anna was more and more astonished: "I did not expect this, I absolutely did not expect this," she said. And, straightening her slender, majestic figure, she began to pace up and down the room.

"This may seem sordid to you," said Losnitsky, "but, believe me, my heart is capable of loving and understanding beauty."

Anna, quite naturally, answered nothing to this.

Seeing such a reaction on her part, Losnitsky began to take his leave, and though it was quite early, Anna made no effort to stop him.

Within a short period of time Anna could not help discovering a number of traits in Losnitsky's opinions and views which she disliked a great deal. Their way of life, isolated and monotonous as it was, and lacking in any major interests which would allow a man to reveal his full personality, made the petty sides of his character appear even more strongly, leading to unpleasant clashes caused by the latter. Anna would stand up harshly against anything that she considered a fault or a weakness, and no qualities of the intellect or of the heart could make her forget these things. She reacted to them with ever so much more hostility, since this man had at one time appeared to her a paragon of perfection. In her severe judgments, Losnitsky saw merely attacks, nagging, directed against a man whom she had suddenly stopped loving, attempts to motivate somehow her unprovoked cooling toward him. It is clear that, their mood being such, their life together went extremely badly. Even those brotherly, trustful feelings, on which they had been able to count as friends, now disappeared. Their relations turned more than cold and strained. They were unbearably hard on both of them. Losnitsky saw how difficult and how dangerous his position was; he saw that by staying with her he might risk losing his last asset, her respect, and he could not make up his mind to do anything at all . . . Meanwhile, the life which they were leading, the absence of any work to do, or of a circle of friends, under conditions of mutual discord, all this was becoming unbearable to him. He suggested to Anna that they return to Russia together, without giving any thought to the question whether this would be good for her. Anna agreed, without making any objection, without giving the matter any thought, without even asking when and how. It seemed as though she did not care where she was living, or with whom; she cared little for her reputation, since there was nobody and nothing for whose sake she might have valued it. But Losnitsky did not hurry her to leave. He was waiting for something.

Meanwhile, there had been a change in Anna for some time. A strange, feverish excitement would seize her whole being from time to time. She avoided all company, went away to remote, lonely places on her daily walks, and there, walking back and forth among the hills, seemed to be pondering something. Or, she would take up her books and spent day and night over them, prepare thick notebooks and write or make notes in them very hurriedly. But then she quickly abandoned the books too, as though she had not found in them what she was looking for, and from here on she read nothing at all, falling into a sort of moral torpor. The color which had recently appeared in her face, disappeared again, her transparent skin turned a deep yellow, and rings appeared under her eyes, making her large eyes look even larger and more expressive.

Quietly and majestically, the young woman roamed about the hills nearby, watched pensively every evening how a bright, triumphant day would burn down, met each new day without joy, and kept thinking, thinking all the time . . . Or, she would sit on the bank of a small river and gaze at its small, monotonous waves. Lazily and drowsily they rolled before her eyes, driven from above by some invisible power, at times dashing against the bank, leaping back quickly, colliding, turning, dividing into small ripples, then returning to the former shap, and continuing to run with their former abandon, without ever hurrying or stopping anywhere, with a steady constancy, yielding their place to other waves that were following them. Watching one and the same sight all the time did not seem to bore Anna but, on the contrary, she observed the regular change from night to day, and from day to night, from life to death, with sympathy, finding in these sights something that was a part of human life also. She lost her former interest in books: they solved nothing but merely obscured and complicated the countless questions which were forming in her mind.

Losnitsky watched her with apprehension, begged her to consult a physician, to get some treatment, but she stubbornly refused. Losnitsky did not know what to do, whether they should stay there or travel somewhere else. However, an event which took place soon solved his dilemma.

One day Anna went for a walk early in the morning, as usual, and failed to return all day. Losnitsky was not worried at first, since it was not the first time she had been gone for such a long time, but when night fell and it got dark and she still had not returned, his heart quivered fearfully, and he rushed from the house in the direction where Anna would most often take her walks. He knocked at the doors of cottages, stopped passersby, asking people, with growing apprehension, if they had not seen such-and-such a lady. The more or less unsatisfactory answers which the peasants gave him merely enhanced his confusion and his fear. They had seen the young woman in the morning, by the river, others had seen her three days ago; she had asked for some water to drink and had asked where she could cross the river, and how deep it was.

Utterly exhausted from anxiety, Losnitsky decided to go home, thinking that he would perhaps find her there. Everybody was sound asleep when he got back to town. The lights were all out. Losnitsky had to knock hard to get into his own flat. When he asked if Anna was in, the old servant gave him a puzzled look. One could see that he either did now know, or that he had forgotten about the absence of the young woman. A feeling of outrage flared up in Losnitsky's heart, but it died down fast and changed to helpless anguish and gloomy dejection. He went through the empty rooms in silence, and sat down by the window, not knowing what to do, or what decision to make. A foreboding of evil took possession of him at this point. He just kept sitting there, leaning his head on his hand and expecting something to happen, until he fell into a heavy, troubled sleep which made him forget everything, even his grief.

When he woke up, the sun was high in the sky, covering the town with its rich sparkle, giving everything a joyous appearance. Everybody was busy with their daily activities. People were working, buying, selling, and talking, talking especially about the young woman whose body had been found in the river a short time earlier. It was assumed that she had fallen into the water as she was crossing the river using a narrow footbridge, since the body was found not far from the bridge, and in the very middle of the stream, where it flowed faster. She must have become dizzy when looking into the rapidly flowing waters, though the Lord, who sees the intentions as well as the deeds of men, knows better. But we, on our part, shall neither reject nor affirm such supposition.

Selected Letters

1. DOSTOEVSKY TO V. D. KONSTANT

Paris, 1 September (new calendar) [1863]

[. . .] Varvara Dmitrievna, during those four days I took a close look at the gamblers there. There were several hundred people playing there and, believe me, I saw only two who knew how to play the game. Everybody loses his last penny, because none of them know how to play. There was a Frenchwoman there, and a British lord—those two knew how to play, nor did they lose, but on the contrary, it was the bank that was almost ready to crack. Please do not think that I am bragging for joy that I did not lose when I say that I know the secret how not to lose, but to win. It is true that I know this secret; it is very silly and simple, and amounts to keeping control over oneself at any given moment, regardless of the phase of the game, and to never getting excited. This is all there is to it, and it is simply impossible to lose that way, and most probably you'll win. But this is not what matters, but rather, whether a man who has mastered this secret is abled to take advantage of it. You may be a Solomon and possess iron will power, and still lose your patience. Even our philosopher Strakhov[1] would lose his patience. And there-

1. Nikolay Nikolaevich Strakhov (1828–96), collaborator on Dostoevsky's *Time* and *Epoch*. Antagonist of Chernyshevsky, Pisarev, and Russian radical materialists. Confidant of Dostoevsky and Tolstoy.

337

fore, blessed are those who won't gamble but view a roulette table with loathing and consider playing the game the greatest stupidity. But on to business. By dear Varvara Dmitrievna, I won 5,000 francs, i.e., I originally won 10,400 francs, brought them home, and locked them in my traveling bag, having decided to leave Wiesbaden the following day, without ever going back to the casino. But I broke down and lost half of what I had won. Thus, I was left with only 5,000 francs. I decided to keep a part of my winnings, just in case, and to send another part to Petersburg, as follows: a part to my brother, so he would save the money for me when I get back, and a part to you, so you could hand it, or send it, to Maria Dmitrievna.

2. DOSTOEVSKY TO V. D. KONSTANT

Baden-Baden, 8 September 1863

My dear friend and sister, Varvara Dmitrievna, I am writing you only a few lines, to inform you and ask you for a favor. I am leaving today, in an hour, or maybe even sooner, and therefore I haven't a moment's time. The whole thing is that here in Baden I just lost everything I had on me at roulette, everything to the last penny. I lost over 3,000 francs. I've got only 250 francs left in my pocket right now. I had left Paris with the intention of going to Rome. I cannot go to Rome on the money I have now, and therefore I shall stop over at the junction in Turin to wait for some money to arrive from Petersburg. I am writing my brother, asking him to send me some, but since that won't be enough, I have written to Maria Dmitrievna, asking her to send me 100 rubles of the money which I had sent her. Just 100 rubles, no more. Why, she is so very, very kind, she might want to send me everything that I sent her from Paris.

[· · ·]

3. DOSTOEVSKY TO
M. M. DOSTOEVSKY[2]

Turin, 8/20 September 1863

[. . .]

I will tell you orally about the details of my trip in general. There were adventures galore, but still it was awfully boring, in spite of A.P.[3] In a situation like this, one can even be too happy, because one is separated from all those whom one loves and of whom one thinks so often with nostalgia. To seek happiness after having abandoned everything, even that [occupation] in which one could have been some use, is egotistic, and this thought is now poisoning my happiness (if indeed this is happiness).

You write: how could one lose everything to the last penny, while traveling with the one whom one loves? My dear Misha: in Wiesbaden I came up with a system of play, applied it in practice, and immediately won 10,000 francs. The following morning I abandoned my system, having got excited, and immediately lost. In the evening I returned to my system, applying it rigorously, and without any trouble again won 3,000 francs. Now tell me: after such events, how was I not to allow myself to be carried away, how was I not to believe that so long as I was following my system, luck was in my hands? And I do need money, for myself, for you, for my wife, to write my novel. Here, people win tens of thousands with ease. Yes, I went there with the idea to save all of you, and to get out of my difficulties myself. And then there's that faith in my system. And moreover, having arrived in Baden-Baden, I walked up to the roulette table and won 600 francs within *a quarter of an hour*. That whetted my appetite. Suddenly I started losing, was no longer able to hold myself back, and lost everything to the last penny. After I sent you

2. Dostoevsky's brother Michael, who collaborated with him in editing and publishing *Time* and *Epoch*.
3. Initials for Polina Suslova.

that letter from Baden, I took my *last* money and went gambling; having started with 4 napoleons d'or, I won 35 napoleons in half an hour. I let myself be carried away by this unusual luck, took a chance on those 35, and lost all 35. After paying our landlady, we were left with 6 napoleons d'or for the road. In Geneva I pawned my watch.

[. . .]

4. DOSTOEVSKY TO N. N. STRAKHOV

Rome, 18/30 September [*1863*]

[. . .]

Right now I have nothing ready. But there has occurred to me a rather promising (in my own judgment) plan for a story. For the most part I've got it down on scraps of paper. I actually tried to start writing it, but it's impossible here. It is hot, and (2), one has come to a place like Rome *for a week;* can one really write during that one week, *having Rome before one's eyes?* Besides, I get very tired from walking around. The subject of the story is the following: a type of Russian abroad. Note this: last summer there was, in our journals, a great deal of talk about Russians abroad. All of that is reflected in my story. And in general, it will reflect (as far as this is possible, of course) the present moment of our inner life. I am writing of a character with a spontaneous nature, yet a man who is developed in many ways, though unfinished in every respect, one who has lost his faith, yet *doesn't dare not to believe,* who rebels against authority, yet is afraid of it. He soothes himself by asserting that he has *nothing to do* in Russia, and hence criticizes severely those people who call upon our expatriates to come back to Russia. But I couldn't possibly tell you all of it. This is a living character (it is as if I saw him standing before me) and he will be worth reading when finished. But the main thing about it is that all his vital juices, strength, aggressiveness, boldness, all go into *roulette*. He is a gambler, and not a plain gambler, just as Pushkin's covetous knight[4] is not a plain miser. (I do not say this to compare myself to Pushkin. I mention it only for the sake of clarity.) After his own fashion, he is a poet, but the thing is that he is himself ashamed of this poetry, for he very deeply feels its baseness, even though the element of risk involved [in gambling] ennobles him in his own eyes. The whole story is a story about how he goes into his third year of playing roulette at various gambling houses.

If *The House of the Dead* drew the public's attention as a depiction of convicts, whom no one before *The House of the Dead*[5] had described *graphically*, this story will certainly draw attention as a *graphic* and most detailed depiction of roulette. In addition to the fact that such articles are read in Russia with extraordinary interest, gambling at the various watering places has a certain (and perhaps not so unimportant a) role particularly in regards to Russians abroad.

5. DOSTOEVSKY TO N. P. SUSLOVA

Petersburg, 19 April 1865

My dear and esteemed Nadezhda Prokofievna,

I am attaching to this letter to you, a letter of mine addressed to Apollinaria, or more exactly, a copy of my letter to Apollinaria, which I have addressed to her in Montpellier by the same mail. Since you write me that she may be joining you in Zurich very soon, it may well happen that the letter I sent to Montpellier will arrive when she is no longer there. And since I feel it to be absolutely necessary for me that she get this letter of mine, I am asking you to hand her this copy when you see her. I am also asking you to read the letter yourself. In it, you will find a clear answer to all the questions

4. One of Pushkin's little tragedies, "The Covetous Knight" (1836).
5. Dostoevsky's account of his experience in Siberia, published in 1860.

which you ask me in your letter, i.e., "whether I like to feast on the sufferings and tears of others, etc." And also an explanation regarding cynicism and filth.

I would like to add, expressly for you, that this is, so it would seem, not the first year of our acquaintanceship, that I have come to see you, to find relief for my soul, at every trying juncture, and that of late you have been the only one I have seen every time my heart has been just too heavy. You have seen me in my most sincere moments, and therefore you can judge for yourself: do I like to feast on the sufferings of others, am I crude (inside), am I cruel?

Apollinaria is a great egotist. Her egotism and self-esteem are colossal. She demands *everything* of people, perfection in every respect, she won't forgive a single imperfection in deference to a person's other, good traits, whereas she herself refuses to show people even the slightest consideration. To this day she keeps reproaching me, saying that I was unworthy of her love, complaining to me, and upbraiding me incessantly, but then she herself, in Paris in 1863, welcomed me with this phrase: "You've arrived a little late," i.e., she had fallen in love with another man, while only two weeks earlier she had been writing me ardent letters, saying that she loved me. I am not reproaching her for having fallen in love with another man, but for those four lines which she sent to my hotel, with that rude phrase: "You've arrived a little late."

I could write a great deal about Rome, about our life together in Turin, in Naples, but why should I? To what purpose? Besides I have told you a lot in our conversations.

I love her still, I love her very much, but by now I wish I did not love her. She is *not worthy* of such love.

I feel sorry for her, because I can foresee that she will always be unhappy. Nowhere will she find either friend or happiness. Whoever demands everything from others, while not feeling any obligation on his part, will never find happiness.

It may be that my letter to her, about which she complains, is written in an irritable tone. But it is not rude. What she considers to be rude about it is the fact that I dared to contradict her, that I dared to speak out about my hurt. She has always treated me with disdain. She took offense at my desire, finally, to speak up, to complain, to contradict her. She refuses to admit the notion of equality in our relations. There is no human feeling whatsoever in her attitude toward me. Why, doesn't she know that I still love her? Why then is she tormenting me? Don't love, but then don't torment a man, either. Also, a lot in that letter was said facetiously. Things that were said facetiously she, in her anger, takes for serious, and then they may sound rude.

But enough of this. Don't you, at least, blame me. I have high regard for you; you are a rare human being among all whom I have met in my life, and I do not want to lose your affection. I have high regard for your opinion of me, and for your remembrance of me. I am writing you *with such frankness* about these things, because, as you well know, I do not solicit anything from you, nor do I hope to obtain anything from you, so that you cannot ascribe my words either to flattery or to my trying to ingratiate myself with you, but will simply take them for a sincere expression of my soul.

Your sister writes that you will stay in Zurich for a long time. Listen (if you can and if you want): wherever you are, drop me at least an occasional line about yourself, let me know. I am not asking you to exert yourself, or to write often. I would only like you to remember me occasionally. It will always be most interesting for me to hear about you.

Let me once again repeat my perennial advice and good wishes to you: Don't get bottled up in your isolation, abandon yourself to nature, abandon yourself to the outside world and to things external, just a little bit. External, real *life* develops human nature to an extraordinary extent, serving as material for it. Don't laugh too much about me, though.

My situation is horrifying. How I am going to settle it, I don't know. You will learn a thing or two from my letter to Apollinaria. My address continues to be the same. If you write me soon, I shall answer you and get myself a *more permanent* address, which you could use permanently.

Au revoir, some day? Good-bye. Be happy all your life. Let me press your hand heartily. I would like very much to see you some day. What are we going to be like then? I shall always remember you very well.

All yours,

F. Dostoevsky

P.S. You are now in the spring of life, you have youth, your life just begins—what happiness! Don't lose your life, take good care of your soul, believe in truth. But *keep looking for it intently* all your life, or else it is awfully easy to go astray. But you have a heart, you won't go astray. But I am finishing out my life, I feel that. It doesn't matter—you are dear to me, as you stand for what's young, and new, besides that I love you as one would love one's favorite sister.

6. DOSTOEVSKY TO I. S. TURGENEV

Wiesbaden, 3/5 August [1865]

My dearest and most esteemed Ivan Sergeyevich, when I met you in Petersburg a month ago, I was selling my works for whatever price I could get, since I was about to be put in debtor's prison for those journal debts which I foolishly allowed to be transferred to my personal account. Stellovsky bought my works (the right to publish them in book form) for three thousand, part of it in promissory notes. I used these three thousand to satisfy my creditors, just barely and for the time being, giving the rest to various parties to whom I was obligated, and then went abroad, in order to restore my health even to the smallest extent and to write something. Of those three thousand, I left myself no more than 175 silver rubles for my trip abroad, this being all I could afford.

But two years ago, in Wiesbaden, I had won nearly 12,000 francs in an hour's time. Even though I had not thought of mending my finances by gambling, I did feel like winning 1,000 francs or so, enough to cover my living expenses for these three months. Now it is my fifth day in Wiesbaden, and

I have lost everything, to the last penny, even my watch, and I also owe some money at my hotel.

I feel very bad, and ashamed, having to bother you with my personal affairs. But there is absolutely nobody here to whom I could turn at the present moment, and besides, you are much more clever than the others, as a result of which I find it incomparably easier to turn to you. Here is the situation: I am addressing you man to man, asking you to lend me 100 (one hundred) thalers. I am also expecting some money from Russia, from one of the journals (the *Reading Library*), from which I was promised a small amount of money at my departure, and from a certain gentleman who is *obliged* to help me. It stands to reason that I might not be able to return the money to you for *three weeks*. However, perhaps I will return it even earlier. At any rate, one month. I feel rotten (I had thought it would be even worse) and, what's more, ashamed to have to bother you; but what can a drowning man do?

My address:

Wiesbaden, Hotel Victoria, à M. Théodor Dostoiewsky.

Now what if you are not in Baden-Baden?

All yours,

F. Dostoevsky

7. DOSTOEVSKY TO SUSLOVA

[Wiesbaden] Tuesday, [22/10 August 1865]

Dear Polia, to begin with, I can't understand how you made it there. Added to my very nasty anxiety about myself, there is now my anxiety about you.

Well, what if you hadn't enough money in Cologne even for a third class ticket? So you are now in Cologne, all by yourself, and don't know what to do! That's terrible. In Cologne, the hotel, cab fare, living expenses on the road— even if you had enough money for your railway fare, you still must have been hungry. All of this keeps going around in my head and takes away my peace of mind.

It is Tuesday already, two o'clock in the afternoon, and
no word from H[erze]n though it is about time. At any rate,
I shall wait until the morning of the day after tomorrow; by
then I will have lost my last hope. At any rate, one thing is
clear to me: if there isn't any word from H[erze]n, this will
mean that he is not in Geneva, i.e., he may have gone away
somewhere. I will come to this conclusion for sure, because
I am on very good terms with H[erze]n, so it would be quite
impossible for him not to give me an answer one way or
another, even if he did not want to, or could not send me
any money. He is very civil, and he and I are on friendly
terms. And consequently, if there isn't *any* word at all, he
is not in Geneva at this moment.

Meanwhile, my condition has deteriorated to an unbelievable extent. As soon as you left, early in the morning of
the following day, I was told at the hotel that their staff had
instructions not to serve me either dinner or tea or coffee. I
went to clear this up, and the fat German who owns the hotel
declared that I did not "deserve" dinner, and that he was
going to send me only tea. And so I haven't had any dinner
since yesterday and live on tea only. The tea they serve is also
very bad, made without a samovar. They won't clean my
clothes or polish my shoes, they won't come when I call, and
all the servants treat me with an inexpressible, and most
German contempt. There is no greater crime in the eyes of a
German than to have no money, or not to pay one's bills on
time. The whole thing would be funny, but it is nevertheless
most inconvenient, too. And therefore, if H[erze]n does not
send me any money, I anticipate great unpleasantness here,
namely, they may seize my things and throw me out, or something worse yet. An abominable situation.

If you have arrived in Paris and could manage to get anything at all from your friends and acquaintances, send me a
maximum of 150 gulden, and a *minimum* of whatever you
want. If you could make it 150 gulden, I could settle with
these pigs and move to a different hotel to wait for the money
to arrive. For it is quite impossible that I will not receive it
very soon, and at any rate I shall return it to you long before
you leave France. First, from Petersburg (from the *Reading*

Library), they will *definitely* send [some money] in *10* days
or so, at the very latest, addressed to your sister in Zurich,
second, even if H——n should not be in Geneva; in any
case, if he has left Geneva for a longer period of time, they
will forward any letters addressed to him in Geneva, and if
he is gone for a short time only, he will of course answer
immediately, as soon as he comes back, so, consequently, I
will have an answer from him soon in any case. In short, if
you can do anything for me, without inconveniencing yourself too much, do it. My address here is the same, Viesbaden
[*sic*], Hotel Victoria.

Au revoir, my dear, I can't believe that I did not see you
before your departure. As for myself, I don't even want to
think of it; I sit here reading all the time, so as not to give
myself an appetite by moving about. I embrace you heartily.

For God's sake, don't show my letter to anybody, or tell
anybody. It's a nasty business. All yours, F. D.

Describe your trip in detail for me, if there was any unpleasantness. Regards to your sister.

But if Herzen sends me [money] before your letter arrives,
then, in any case, I shall make arrangements, before leaving
Wiesbaden, that your letter be forwarded to me in Paris,
because that's where I am immediately heading.

8. DOSTOEVSKY TO SUSLOVA

[Wiesbaden] Thursday, 24/12 August [1865]

I keep bombarding you with letters (and all "postage
due"). Has my letter of the day before yesterday (Tuesday)
reached you? Have you arrived in Paris safely? I am still
hoping to get word from you today.

My situation is vile to the point of *ne plus ultra,* one can't
go any further. What will follow from here on must be another streak of misfortunes and dirty tricks of which I have
no conception as yet. I have received nothing from Herzen
so far, no answer or response. Today is exactly a week since
I wrote him. Today, too, is the deadline for my money to

arrive, as I told the owner of my hotel on Monday. What's going to happen—I don't know. It is only one o'clock in the morning right now.

It couldn't be that Herz. does not want to answer! Could it really be that he does not want to answer? That couldn't be. Why? Our relations are of the most excellent, as even you have witnessed. Could it be that somebody has denounced me to him behind my back? But even in that case (rather, even more so) it would be impossible for him to answer *nothing* to my letter. And therefore I am still convinced, at this point, that either my letter to him got lost (of which there is little likelihood), or that my luck was bad enough to find him absent from Geneva at this time. The latter is the most probable. In that case, here's the situation: (1) He is gone for a short time only, and in that case I can still hope to receive an answer from him one of these days (as soon as he is back); or, (2) he is gone for a long period of time, and in that case my letter will most probably be forwarded to him, wherever he might be, because he must certainly have made arrangements to have letters addressed to him forwarded to his new address. And consequently, in that case, too, I can hope to get a reply from him.

I will keep hoping for a reply all week, until Sunday— nothing but hope, of course. Meanwhile my situation is such that hope alone just won't do.

But all this is nothing, if compared to my anguish. I am tormented by my inactivity, by the indefiniteness of a situation where I have to wait without a firm hope, the loss of time, and this accursed Wiesbaden, which makes me so sick I can't even look at it. Meanwhile you are in Paris and I am not going to see you! Herz. also torments me. If he got my letter and *does not want* to answer—what humiliation, and what behavior! Have I really earned this, and how? By my irregularities? I admit that I have been guilty of irregularity, but what bourgeois morality! Then answer me at least, or don't I "deserve" help (as I don't "deserve" dinner with the owner of my hotel)? But it just could not be that he wouldn't answer; it must be that he is away from Geneva.

I asked you to help me out by borrowing some money for

me from somebody. I am almost without hope, Polia. But if you can, do it for me! You must agree that it is hard to find a situation which is more troublesome and more difficult than the one I am in right now.

This will be my last letter until I get some kind of news from you. I keep imagining that my letters either won't be delivered promptly or may be lost altogether at the Hotel Fleurus, when you are not there yourself. I am sending them without postage, because I haven't got a kopeck. I continue to go without dinner, subsisting on my morning and evening tea for the third day now, and strangely enough, I am not very hungry at all. What's bad is that they keep me down by sometimes refusing me a candle in the evening, if even the tiniest candle end is left from the preceding day. However, I leave the hotel at three o'clock every day, returning at six, so as not to let them know that I am not having any dinner at all. Tricks worthy of a Khlestakov![6]

It is true, there is one remote hope: In a week, or in ten days at the latest, there will be something coming from Russia (via Zurich). But I cannot survive without help until that time.

I don't want to believe it, though, that I won't be in Paris before your departure. It just couldn't be. But inactivity makes one's imagination run high. And when it comes to inactivity, I've really got it.

Good-bye, my dear. If nothing particularly new happens, I won't write you anymore. Au revoir. All yours, Dos.

P.S. I embrace you once more, very heartily. Has Nad. Prok.[7] arrived, and when? Give her my regards.

4 o'clock.

My dear Polia, I have just received an answer from Herzen. He had been to the mountains, and that's why his letter came late. He sends me no money, saying that my letter caught him at a moment of extreme impecuniousness, that he couldn't give me 400 florins, but might have 100 or 150 gulden; if I could manage on that little, he could send

6. The main character in Gogol's *The Inspector General*.
7. Polina's sister.

me that amount. Then he asks me not to be angry, etc. Strange thing, though: Why, then, didn't he at least send 150 gulden, if he says himself that he could send this much? If he had just sent 150 and told me that this was all he could afford. That's how things are done. But it is obviously this: either he is in a tight spot himself, i.e., he hasn't got it, or he just won't part with his money. Yet he could have no doubt about my returning the money: why, he's got my letter. I am no outcast of society, am I? Must be that he is in a tight spot himself.

To send him another letter, begging him for help, is in my opinion impossible! What, then, am I to do now? Polia, my dear, help me out of this, save me! Get me 150 gulden somewhere, that's all I need. In 10 days, [some money] will *surely* come from Voskoboinikov,[8] addressed to your sister in Zurich (and maybe it will come even earlier). Though it won't be much, it will still be more than 150 gulden, and I shall return them to you. I don't want to place *you* into a bad situation. I could not. Talk it over with your sister. In any case, answer me as soon as you can.

All yours,

F. Dostoevsky

Now I definitely don't know what is going to happen to me.

9. DOSTOEVSKY TO
A. V. KORVIN-KRUKOVSKAIA[9]

Moscow, 17 June 1866

Esteemed Anna Vasilievna,

Don't be angry with me for not having answered you for so long—all this time I have been undecided about the

8. Nikolay Nikolaevich Voskoboinikov, journalist and engineer. Contributor and later on editorial staff of Katkov's the *Russian Herald*.

9. Anna Vasilievna Korvin-Krukovskaia (1847–87), revolutionary and novelist. Took part in the Paris commune. Dostoevsky published two of her stories in *Epoch* and paid court to her for about three months and proposed to her, a proposal she rejected.

future and did not know myself what I would be doing in the summer. If I did not respond to your letter immediately, it was because I thought that I would be seeing you soon in person, on my way abroad. But now, though I have received permission to go, things have turned out so that I no longer can go, at least not at present. I must first complete a bit of business in Moscow. In short, I was unable to write you anything definitive or precise, which is why I did not reply to your letter. I have been in Moscow only for four days or so, and I have absolutely no idea as to when I will be free. The main thing is that, in addition to having to complete my novel (of which I am sick and tired), I have so much work that I simply can't see how I shall take care of all my business. And this is important business, as my future depends on it. Imagine what happened to me, among other things (a most amusing and very characteristic case). Last year I was in such financial straits that I was forced to sell the publication rights on all my previously written works at once, to a speculator, a certain Stellovsky, who is a pretty bad man and understands nothing of the publishing business. But there was a clause in our contract, according to which I promised to write a novel of no less than 192 pages for his edition, and if I did not deliver it by 1 November 1866 (the final deadline), then he, Stellovsky, acquired the right to publish gratis, and at his own discretion, over a period of nine years, everything that I might have written, without reimbursing me in any way. In short, this clause of the contract is exactly like those clauses of Petersburg leases where the landlord demands that if fire should break out in his house, the tenant is to cover all losses caused by that fire, and, if necessary, rebuild the whole house. Everybody signs these leases, even though people laugh as they do it, and so I signed my contract, too. The first of November is in four months. I thought that I could pay off Stellovsky in money, by offering to pay a forfeit, but he does not want it. I asked him to grant me a three-month extension—he turned me down and told me *outright:* since he was convinced that by now I simply *did not have the time* to write a 192-page novel, especially since I had written only half of my novel for the *Russian Herald*,[10] it was much to his advantage not to agree to any extension or forfeit, because then everything that I might write hereafter would be his. I want to do an unheard-of and eccentric thing: write 480[11] pages in 4 months, working on two novels simultaneously and writing one of them in the morning and the other at night, and finish both on time. You know what, my dear Anna Vasilievna, I still relish such eccentric and extraordinary things, I actually do. I am just not fit to be counted among people of solid habits. Forgive me: I've been bragging! But then, what else is left for me but to brag, all the rest being anything but attractive. But what kind of literature is this, after all this? I am convinced that not a single one of our writers, past or still living, has ever worked under such conditions as those I write under *all the time*. Turgenev would die at the very thought of. But if you knew to what extent it depresses you to spoil an idea which was born within you, which used to awaken your enthusiasm, which you know yourself to be a good one—and to be forced to spoil it, and consciously at that!

You want to come to Pavlovsk. Write me when exactly this will be. I would like very, very much to visit you at Polibino. But could I work there the way I must? That's a question as far as I am concerned. Besides, it would be impolite on my part to come there and then work all day long. Write me about everything. Please do not forget me. My greetings to all your family. Au revoir.

Your sincerely devoted
Fyodor Dostoevsky

If you answer me *immediately,* here is my address: Moscow, c/o Aleksandr Pavlovich Ivanov, Konstantinovsky Surveying Institute, Staraia Basmannaia Street, by St. Nikita the Martyr's, for Fyodor Mikh. Dostoevsky.

10. An important journal of a conservative cast edited by Mikhail Nikiforovich Katov (1818–89). Dostoevsky published most of his major novels in this journal. Here he refers to *Crime and Punishment.*
11. Dostoevsky gives his numbers in printer's "signatures" of sixteen pages, which I have converted into regular book pages.—Translator

Forgive the untidy corrections in my letter and don't interpret them as a mark of negligence.

10. DOSTOEVSKY TO SUSLOVA

Dresden, 23 April/5 May 1867

My dear, your letter was delivered to me at Bazunov's very late, just before I left Russia, and since I was in an awful hurry, I did not manage to answer you. I left Petersburg on Good Friday (14 April, I think), traveled rather slowly, with stops, and therefore only now have I finally got around to having a chat with you.

So, my dear, you know nothing about me, at least you knew nothing when you mailed your letter to me. I got married in February of this year. I was obligated by contract to deliver to Stellovsky by 1 November of last year a new novel of no less than 160 pages of ordinary print, if not, I would have been subject to a terrible forfeit. Meanwhile I was writing my novel for the *Russian Herald,* I had written 384 pages, and had another 192 to go. And there were still those 160 pages for Stellovsky. It was 4 October, and I had not even started. Miliukov[12] suggested that I hire a stenographer to whom I could dictate the novel, which would allow me to work four times as fast. Olkhin, a professor of stenography, sent me his best student, who agreed to work for me. We started to work on that very day, 4 October. My stenographer, Anna Grigorievna Snitkina, was a young and rather attractive young girl of 20, of a good family, graduated from secondary school with honors, and of extraordinarily kind and serene disposition. Our work progressed excellently. On 28 November, my novel *The Gambler* (it has appeared in print by now) was ready, having taken 24 days. As the novel was reaching its conclusion I noticed that my stenographer was sincerely in love with me, even though she never

12. Aleksandr Petrovich Miliukov (1817–97), writer, historian of literature, and close friend of Dostoevsky. He has left reminiscences of Dostoevsky.

said a word about it, while I was getting to like her better all the time. Inasmuch as I have found my life to be terribly boring and depressing ever since my brother's death, I asked her to marry me. She accepted, and here we are, married. The difference in our ages is awful (20 and 44), but I am more and more convinced that she will be happy. She has heart, and she can love. Now about my situation in general. You are familiar, in part, with the fact that after my brother's death I completely ruined my health messing about with the journal, but finally abandoned it, my strength sapped by a futile struggle with the indifference of the public, etc., etc. Moreover, those 3,000 [rubles] (which I received when I sold that work of mine to Stellovsky) I spent on a journal which did not belong to me, on my brother's family, and on satisfying his creditors, without hope of ever getting that money back. It ended up by my getting deeper in debt on account of the journal, which, together with my brother's unpaid debts, for which I had to assume responsibility, amounted to over 15,000 [rubles] of extra indebtedness. Such was the condition of my affairs when I went abroad in 1865, with a capital of 40 napoleons d'or in all at my departure. While abroad, I decided that I could return these 15,000 only if I set my hopes entirely on myself. Besides, with the death of my brother, who meant everything to me, life became very miserable for me. I was still hoping to find a heart that would respond to mine, but failed in this effort. Then I threw myself completely into my work and began to write a novel. Katkov paid me more than anyone else, and so I gave it to Katkov. But 592 pages of that novel, plus 160 pages for Stellovsky overtaxed my strength, though I completed both.

My epilepsy has grown monstrously worse, but on the other hand I managed to divert myself and, besides, saved myself from prison. My novel (along with its second edition) brought me nearly 14,000, on which I lived and, besides, repaid 12 of the fifteen thousand which I owed. Now I still owe 3,000 in all. But these three thousand are the most wicked. The more money you return, the more impatient and more stupid your creditors get. You must not that if I had not assumed responsibility for those debts, the creditors would not have got a kopeck. And they know it themselves, why, they were asking me a favor when they begged me to transfer those debts to my account, promising, as they did, not to bother me. The return of 12,000 merely awakened the covetousness of those who had not yet received payment on the notes they were holding. Now I won't have any money before next year, and that only if I complete the new work, on which I am working at present. But how can I complete it, with all these people giving me no peace? This is why I (and my wife) went abroad. Besides, I expect some relief from my epilepsy abroad; in Petersburg of late, it became almost impossible for me to work.

I can no longer sit up at night, I have a fit immediately. And this is why I want to improve my health here and finish my work. I took an advance from Katkov. They were glad to let me have it. They pay extremely well. I told Katkov from the very beginning that I was a Slavophile[13] and that I disagreed with some of his opinions. This made for better relations between us, facilitating them greatly. As a private person, though, he is the most decent man on earth. I did not know him at all before. His boundless self-esteem does him a great deal of harm. But who hasn't got boundless self-esteem?

During the last days of my stay in Petersburg I met Brylkina (Globina),[14] and visited with her. We spoke a great deal about you. She loves you. She told me that she was very sad that I was happy with another woman. I shall be in correspondence with her. I like her.

Your letter left a melancholy impression on me. You write that you are very sad. I am not familiar with your life during

13. Slavophilism was a movement which believed in the sanctity of purely Russian roots and was inimical to Western influences, especially to those instituted by Peter the Great. The important theorists of these views were Alexey Stepanovich Khomyakov (1804–60) and the brothers Kireyevsky, Ivan (1806–56) and Peter (1808–56).

14. Apparently a friend of Polina and her sister.

this past year, or what has been in your heart, but judging by everything that I know about you, it must be difficult for you to be happy.

Oh, my dear, I am not inviting you to any cheap *routine* happiness. I respect you (and have always respected you) for your exactingness, but don't I know that your heart cannot help demanding to live, while you take people to be either shining [examples], or outright scoundrels and vulgar nonentities. I am judging by the facts. Make your own conclusions.

Au revoir, my good friend forever! I am afraid that this letter may not reach you in Moscow. You can be sure at any rate that I will be here in Dresden until 8 May, our calendar (that's *minimum,* maybe I shall stay even longer), and therefore, if you want to answer me, then answer immediately after receiving this letter. Allemagne (Saxe), Dresden, Dostoiewsky poste restante. I shall be sending you my further addresses. Good-bye, my dear, I press and kiss your hand.

Yours,
F. Dostoevsky

11. DOSTOEVSKY TO A. G. DOSTOEVSKY

Homburg, Sunday, 19 May [1867]
10 o'clock in the morning

How are you, my dear, my beloved angel? I am writing you a few, daily lines. First of all, about business:

I had a most wretched day yesterday. I lost too significant an amount (relatively speaking). What is there to do: with my nerves, my angel, I shouldn't be gambling. I played some ten hours, and wound up with a loss. During the day, there were times when it was very bad, and a few times I won, too, when luck turned my way—I'll tell you everything when I get back. Now, as to what is left me (very little, just a pittance), I want to give it a last try today. Everything depends on today, i.e., whether I leave tomorrow to join you, or stay longer. In any case I'll let you know tomorrow. I would not like to pawn my watch. It's really a tight spot I'm in. What will be, will be. I'll give it a last try. You see: my efforts are successful every time, so long as I retain my sangfroid and calculatingly follow my system. But the moment I start winning, I immediately begin to take chances. I can't control myself. Let's see then what today's last test will show. The sooner the better.

My angel, yesterday I went to the post office to mail my second letter to you, and the postmaster handed me the letter from you. Thank you, my dearest. I read it right there at the post office, and how I liked it to be written in pencil (my stenographer). It reminded me of all those things in the past. Don't be sad, my dear, don't be sad, my angel! You moved me almost to tears, as you described your day to me. What a queer situation we are in! Would it enter the head of any of our family in Petersburg that we are separated from one another at this moment, and to what end! A queer situation, most definitely. Oh, if only this would all come to an end, and if there only were some kind of a decision. Would you believe it, my angel, that I am beginning to feel terribly bored here, i.e., the game as such is boring me? That is, it isn't exactly that it bores me to play, but my nerves are terribly tired, I have become more impatient, I am trying to get results quicker, I hurry myself, I take chances, and that's why I have been losing.

My health, in spite of it all, is very good. My nerves are upset and I get tired (while sitting in one place, too), but nevertheless I am *actually* in *very* good condition. It is an excited condition, full of anxiety—but my nature sometimes demands it. What a delightful day it was yesterday. I did take a short walk in the park. One must admit that this is a charming locality. The park is magnificent, also the casino, the music is marvellous, better than in Dresden. It would be a fine place to live for a while, but for that accursed roulette.

Good-bye, my angel, my gentle, my dear, my kind angel, do love me. Right now I am thinking to myself that, if I could see you for just one minute, there would be so many things we would discuss together; I have accumulated so many new impressions. You couldn't write it all in a letter, and I have told you before, quite often, that I don't know how to write letters, that I have no capacity for letter-writing, but now as I have put down these few short words to you, I feel a little better. In Christ's name, watch your health, try to distract yourself in any possible way. Remember my pleas: If anything at all should happen, immediately send for the doctor, and let me know. Good-bye now, my joy. I kiss you a thousand times. Remember me. Wish me luck, today will decide everything. I wish it would be soon, but don't become upset, and don't worry too much. I embrace you,

All and always yours,

Your husband Fyod Dostoev

P.S. I am not giving any details about how much I won, and how much I lost. I'll tell you everything when we see each other again. In short, it's bad as of right now.

12. DOSTOEVSKY TO A. G. DOSTOEVSKY

Homburg, Monday 20 May [1867]
10 o'clock in the morning

[. . .]
And yesterday was definitely a nasty and miserable day. The main thing is that all this is silly, stupid, and base. And still I can't tear myself away from this idea of mine, i.e., leave everything as it is, and join you. And besides, it is, at this point, impossible, too, at this moment, that is. Let's see what tomorrow will bring. Would you believe it: Yesterday I lost everything, to the last kopeck, to the last gulden, and so I had already decided to write you right away, so that you could send me some money for my train fare. But then I remembered about my *watch* and went to a watchmaker's to sell or pawn it. This is terribly common here, this being a gambling town. There are whole shops of gold and silver things whose whole business consists of this. Imagine how

mean these Germans are: he bought my watch, with the chain (it cost me 125 rubles, at least), and gave me only 65 gulen, i.e., 43 thalers, i.e., almost 2½ times less. But I sold it to him with the condition that he would give me a week's time to redeem it, and that if I should return within week, he would return it to me, charging interest, of course. And imagine, with that money I did recover my losses and today I shall presently go and redeem my watch. I shall be left with 160 gulden after that. I won them back yesterday by restraining myself and by simply not allowing myself to get carried away. This gives me some hope. But I'm afraid, I'm very much afraid. Today will surely tell me something. In short, tomorrow I'll let you know *for sure,* one way or the other.

And so, will you ever forgive me all this? Oh, Ania! Let us suffer through this period and perhaps it will be better later on. Don't be too anxious about me, don't worry. The main thing for you is not to worry, and *to be healthy:* why, I'll be back *very soon* in any case. And after that we will be together forever. This momentary separation may even help toward our greater happiness. It has made me aware of many, many things. Write me more details about yourself, don't leave out anything. If you don't feel well, don't conceal it, but write me about it. I am in perfectly good health here. Yesterday the weather was marvellous; today it does not look very bad either. Yesterday was a Sunday, and all these Homburg Germans, with their wives, came to the casino after dinner. Usually on weekdays it is mostly foreigners playing, and there is no crush. But here now [on Sunday], it's quite a crush, the air is stuffy, it's crowded, people get rude. Oh, how mean these Germans are. Good-bye, Ania, good-bye, my joy, be cheerful and happy. Do love me. Until tomorrow. I embrace you, heartily, very heartily. I love you boundlessly.

All yours, to the last drop,
F. Dostoevsky

I shall write you tomorrow for sure.
P.S. For God's sake, Ania, *don't send me* any letters here.

Nothing can be so very important [to write about], particularly from Moscow. Let it wait. Besides, I may be leaving
here any day now, and so might miss the letter.

13. DOSTOEVSKY TO A. G. DOSTOEVSKY

Homburg, Wednesday, 22 May [18]67
10 o'clock in the morning

[. . .]
Forgive me, my angel, for going into some details concerning my enterprise, concerning this game, so it will be clear to
you what this is all about. Already some twenty times or so I
have gone to the gaming tables and had the experience that
if I play with sangfroid, *calmly,* and calculatingly, there is
absolutely no chance of losing! I swear it to you, there is no
such chance! There's blind chance, while I have a calculation
on my side, consequently, the odds favor me. But what has
usually happened? I have usually started play with *forty
gulden,* took them from my pocket, sat down, and placed
them, one or two gulden at a time. In a quarter of an hour,
I have usually (*always*) won double. That would be the time
to stop and go away, at least until the evening, so as to give
my excited nerves a chance to calm down (besides, I have
made the observation—most certainly correct—that I can be
calm and composed for *no longer than half an hour at a
time,* when I am gambling). But I would walk away just to
smoke a cigarette, and then return to the gaming table immediately. Why did I do that, knowing almost for certain
that I would not contain myself, i.e., go on to lose? That's
because every day, upon getting up in the morning, I told
myself that this would be my last day in Homburg, that I
would be leaving the next day, so that, consequently, I could
not play a waiting game at roulette. I tried hurriedly, with
all my strength, to win as much as possible, right, away, that
very day (for I was to leave on the following day) lost my

sangfroid, my nerves got excited, I started taking chances, I got angry, proceeded to place my bets without any calculation, having lost the thread of it, and eventually lost (because anybody who plays without calculating, helter-skelter, is a madman). My whole mistake was to have parted with you, rather than taking you with me. Yes, yes, this is so. And here we are, I am yearning to see you, and you, nearly dying without me. My angel, I repeat, I am not reproaching you for that, and I love you even more for your yearning to see me. But judge for yourself, my dear, what happened to me yesterday, for instance: Having sent you the letters asking you to send me some money, I went to the gambling casino. I had altogether *twenty* gulden left in my pocket (just in case), and I took a chance on *ten* gulden. I used almost supernatural efforts to remain calm and calculating *for a whole hour,* and wound up winning 300 gulden. I was so overjoyed, and had such a terrible, almost *mad* desire to finish off everything right there, *that very day,* to win perhaps twice that amount and then leave immediately, that I threw myself at the roulette table, without having given myself a chance to rest up and collect myself, took to betting gold pieces, and lost *everything, everything,* to the last kopeck, i.e., all I had left were *two* gulden for tobacco. Ania, my dear, my joy! You must understand that I have debts to pay, that I'll be called a scoundrel unless I pay them. You must understand that I will have to write Katkov, and stay in Dresden. I had to win. *Absolutely!* I am not playing for my amusement. Why, this was my only way out—and there, everything is lost on account of my miscalculation. I am not reproaching you, but cursing myself: why didn't I take you with me? Playing at a slow place, every day, *there isn't a chance* not to win, that's true, quite true, I have tried it out twenty times, and here now, knowing this for sure, I am leaving Homburg with a loss. I also know that if I could give myself only four more days, I would surely win back everything. But, needless to say, I shall not play anymore!

[. . .]

14. DOSTOEVSKY TO A. G. DOSTOEVSKY

Homburg, 24 May 1867

Ania dear, my dearest, my wife, forgive me, don't call me a scoundrel! I am guilty of a criminal act, I lost everything that you sent me, everything, everything to the last kreutzer, I received it yesterday, and lost it yesterday. Ania, how am I going to face you now, what are you going to say about me after this! One *and only one* thing horrifies me: what will *you* say, what are you going to think of me? It is your judgment alone that I fear! Can you, will you respect me now! And what is love, even, without respect! Why, this has shaken the very foundation of our marriage. Oh, my dear, don't condemn me altogether! I hate gambling, not only now, but even yesterday, the day before yesterday, even then I was cursing it. Having received the money yesterday, and having cashed the note, I went there with the idea of winning back at least a little something, to increase our funds by even the tiniest little bit. I so firmly believed in winning in a small way. In the beginning I lost a little, but as I started losing, the desire came to win it back, and then, as I lost even more, I nevertheless went on playing, in order to get back at least the money needed for my train fare—and lost it all. Ania, I am not imploring you to take pity on me, better, be dispassionate, though I am terribly afraid of your judgment. I am not afraid for myself. On the contrary, now, now after this lesson, I have suddenly become quite calm about my future. From now on it will be work and toil, work and toil, and I shall prove yet that I am capable of accomplishing! I do not know what the next development will be like, but for the time being, Katkov won't turn me down. And everything thereafter will, I think, depend on the quality of my work. If it is good, there will be money, too. Oh, if only the matter rested with me alone, I wouldn't even be giving it much thought, I would laugh it off, and leave. But how could you fail to express your judgment of my action—and this is what embarrasses and torments me. Ania, I am worried about losing your love. With our circumstances being bad as they are, I spent over 1,000 francs, that is nearly 350 rubles, on this trip to Homburg and my gambling losses!

But I did not spend the money because I was flighty, or greedy, it wasn't for myself, oh no! I had other aims! But what's the use of trying to justify oneself now. Now I must hurry back to you. *Send me as soon as possible, this very moment, some money for my train fare—even if it is the last you've got.* I can't stay here anymore, I do not want to keep sitting here. Back to you, back to you as soon as possible, to embrace you. Why, you will embrace me, you will give me a kiss, won't you? Oh, if it hadn't been for that nasty, cold, and damp weather, at least I would have moved to Frankfort yesterday! And nothing would have happened, I would not have played! But the weather was such that, with my teeth, and with my cough, there wasn't *a chance* to make a move, traveling the whole night in a light overcoat. It was simply impossible, it would have meant risking an illness. But now I shan't stop even for that. Immediately after receiving this letter send me 10 imperials (i.e., exactly the same as that note to Robert Thode, and here I actually don't need to have it in imperials, but it may be simply an *Anveisung* [sic],[15] just as last time). Ten imperials, i.e., a little over 90 guldens, so that I can pay my bills and my train fare. It is Friday now, I'll get it on Sunday, and *on that same day I will be in Frankfort,* where I will take a *Schnellzug,* so that I will be with you on Monday.

My angel, don't think that perhaps I might lose this money, too. Please, don't offend me to such great extent! Don't have so low an opinion of me. I am human, too, you know! There is something human in me, after all, you know. Don't get the idea, somehow, of *traveling here yourself* to meet me because you don't trust me. Such lack of trust in my coming would kill me. I give *you my word of honor* that I shall leave immediately, regardless of whatever may be, even rain or cold. I embrace and kiss you. I wonder what

15. "Anweisung," check or bill of exchange.

you may think of me now. Oh, if I only could see you at the moment when you read this letter!

Yours,
F. D.

P.S. My angel, don't worry about me! I repeat, if I were all by myself, I'd just laugh and forget about it. *You, your* judgment, that's the one thing that is torturing me! That's what pains me, and nothing else. Meanwhile I have tortured you to death! Au revoir.

Oh, if only I could be with you sooner, if only we could be together, we would come up with something for sure, wouldn't we?

15. SUSLOVA TO DOSTOEVSKY

rough copy of a letter

You [are angry]¹⁶ ask me not to write you that I am ashamed of my love for you. Not only will I not write this, I can [even] assure you that I have never written such thing, or thought of writing it, [because] I was never ashamed of my love for you: it was beautiful even grandiose. I might have written you that I blushed on account of our earlier relations. But there can be nothing new to you in this, for I have never concealed them, and how many times I wanted to break them off before I left abroad.

[I admit that it is useless to talk about this, but you already I have nothing against the fact that you may have considered them proper].

It is clear to me now that you could never understand this: they were proper from your point of view [as]. You behaved like a serious, busy man, [who] understood his obligations after his own fashion] but would not miss his pleasures either, on the contrary, perhaps even found it necessary to have some pleasure, [because] on the grounds that some great

16. Brackets in this letter stand for words or phrases crossed out by Suslova.

doctor or philosopher once said that it was necessary to get drunk once every month.

[You must not get angry if I sometimes], that it is useless to talk about this, [I] it is true that I express myself with some facility, but also true that I don't adhere to form and ceremony too much.

16. SUSLOVA TO DOSTOEVSKY

Versailles, 1864, Monday [early June]

A few days ago I received your letter *of 2 June,* and I hasten to reply to it. I can see that you are quite at your wit's end: I wrote you from Versailles and sent you my address, yet you are wondering how to address your letter to me: to Paris or to Versailles.

I shall be going to Spa in exactly two weeks. Today I settled things with the doctor once and for all. You may come and see me in Spa, it is very near to Aix-la-Chapelle, consequently en route for you. I did not want to see you in Spa,—I'll probably be having a bad fit of melancholy there, but otherwise the chances are that we won't see each other for a long time, since you don't intend to stay in Paris very long, and I am not going back to Russia very soon. I don't know how long I shall stay at Spa; I intended to go there for three weeks, but now it turns out that it may be more, or less, meaning that I'd be going to a different watering place after Spa. If the cure is successful, I'll spend the winter in Paris, if not, I'll go to Spain, Valencia, or the Island of Madeira.

What sort of a scandalous story are you writing? We are going to read it. Ev. Tur has been getting the *Epoch* on occasion. But I don't like you to write cynical things. Somehow, it is not in keeping with you; at least not as I imagined you to be earlier.

I am wondering why you no longer like my character [you write this in your last letter]. I can recall how you used actually to indulge in panegyrics about my character, panegyrics that made me blush, and sometimes made me angry: I was right. But this was so long ago that you did not know my character then, seeing only its good sides and not suspecting that it might take a turn to the worse.

You sing the praises of Spa in vain; it must be quite nasty there. I hate the country there for its smell of coal. You console me by telling me that the Viskovatovs are in Brussels, but they left for Petersburg a long time ago.

Good-bye. I'd like to take a look at you, see what you are like after a year and find out what you people back there are thinking these days. You once wrote me and tried to persuade me to return to Petersburg, because there was so much good there now, such a wonderful change in people's opinions, etc. I see quite different results, or my taste is different from yours. It goes without saying that my return to Russia has nothing at all to do with whether people back there think well or not—this is not the point.

I thank you for your care about my health, and for your advice to take care of it. This advice is having so much effect that you could blame me for excessive care of myself, rather than for neglect and causing my own illness. These accusations are entirely groundless, and I can explain them only by your politeness.